Dare to _____

"I highly recommend this wonderful contemporary romance that steams the pages. Be prepared to savor *Dare to Be Dirty* and enjoy the sizzling romance between the sexy cowboy and the modern woman who wins his love."   —*Romance Reviews Today*

"A refreshingly fun and entertaining read. In fact, the series, Dirty Girls Book Club, has proven to be wickedly delightful so far."
                                                        —*Romance Junkies*

"A wonderful story of a hero's and a heroine's journey, which shows the cultural differences of Asian versus Canadian, which figure so prominently in Vancouver. Great story, great writing."   —*Manic Readers*

"Emotionally realistic plus overflowing with steamy sex. *Dare to Be Dirty* is a romance about intense desire, and how this temptation affects your whole being."   —*Sensual Reads*

"The story line is strong, unique, and stresses the importance of compromise in a relationship. Though we all want and crave a happy ending, in books and in real life, readers will appreciate the author making this novel unpredictable."   —*RT Book Reviews*

The Dirty Girls Book Club

"Filled with emotion and hot sensuality.... Pick up *The Dirty Girls Book Club* for a sizzling read that will leave you with a smile on your face."   —*Romance Reviews Today*

continued . . .

Bound to Be Dirty

SAVANNA FOX

HEAT | NEW YORK

THE BERKLEY PUBLISHING GROUP
Published by the Penguin Group
Penguin Group (USA) LLC
375 Hudson Street, New York, New York 10014

USA • Canada • UK • Ireland • Australia • New Zealand • India • South Africa • China

penguin.com

A Penguin Random House Company

This book is an original publication of The Berkley Publishing Group.

Library of Congress Cataloging-in-Publication Data

Fox, Savanna.
Bound to be Dirty / Savanna Fox.—Berkley trade paperback edition.
pages cm.—(Dirty Girls Book Club)
ISBN 978-0-425-26875-9
1. Book clubs (Discussion groups)—Fiction.   2. Erotic fiction.   I. Title.
PS3606.O95653B68 2014
813'.6—dc23
2013028715

PUBLISHING HISTORY
Heat trade paperback edition / February 2014

PRINTED IN THE UNITED STATES OF AMERICA

10 9 8 7 6 5 4 3 2 1

Cover art: Blue scarf © Sarah Frost / ImageBrief; blue fabric © Ruzanna / Shutterstock.
Cover design by Danielle Abbiate.
Text design by Laura K. Corless.

AUTHOR'S NOTE

When I conceived of the Dirty Girls Book Club, I hoped that each member would have a chance to enjoy her own sexy literary inspiration and her own erotic romance. In *The Dirty Girls Book Club*, when the club read historical erotica, marketing executive Georgia Malone found her unlikely soul mate in hockey star Woody Hanrahan. In *Dare to Be Dirty*, artist and confirmed city girl Kim Chang discovered that the words "cowboy" and "erotic" went together very nicely when she met sexy rodeo star Ty Ronan.

Now the club has decided to research the popularity of BDSM. Will their selection, *Bound by Desire*, be the catalyst that puts the spark—and the love—back in Dr. Lily Nyland's faltering ten-year marriage to helicopter bush pilot Dax Xavier?

Thanks to my editors at Berkley, Katherine Pelz and Wendy McCurdy, and to my agent, Emily Sylvan Kim of Prospect Agency, for their support of the Dirty Girls Book Club series.

Thank you to Laura Langston and Nazima Ali for critiquing a draft of this book. Thanks to Lacy Danes and Jodie Esch for research assistance. And my very special thanks to bush helicopter pilots Rob Foers and Steve McKinnon for answering my many questions. All factual errors are mine, not theirs!

Bound by Desire, the book the club is reading, is purely my creation.

If you enjoy *Bound to Be Dirty*, I hope you'll check out my other titles at savannafox.com, where you'll find excerpts, behind-the-scenes notes, recipes, a monthly contest, my newsletter, and other goodies.

I love hearing from readers. You can contact me through my website.

One

sn't it time we tried a little bondage?" Marielle asked.

Lily Nyland frowned across the table at her. "You're not serious." The four members of their book club occupied a corner of the Gerard Lounge in Vancouver's elegant Sutton Place Hotel. Lily had chosen this week's meeting place, and the fireplace and cozy shut-away-from-the-world ambiance were perfect on a chill December day. The topic of conversation, not so much. Lily caught the eye of the waitress and gestured that she'd like a second martini.

Marielle flicked her dark, wavy hair back from the scoop neckline of her coral sweater. "We need to try BDSM. You know, dominance and submission, bondage, spanking, all that stuff." Her slight Caribbean lilt gave the words a sultry nuance that, to Lily's mind, the subject did *not* warrant.

"Could you say that any louder?" Kim, seated on Marielle's left, asked dryly. Her spiky black hair was streaked in shades of green and blue, complementing the pattern on her hand-painted denim jacket. In the windowless lounge with its décor of brown leather and glowing wood, accented by red Christmas poinsettias and pine boughs, the petite Chinese woman resembled an exotic bird perched in the middle of an English gentlemen's club.

Fortunately, the lounge was only half-full and no one sat beside them. Still, Lily found it surreal to be discussing BDSM here, at five o'clock on a Monday afternoon. She'd agreed to read—and even, surprisingly, enjoyed—the historical erotica and the sexy cowboy novel the other women had chosen earlier this year, but to her mind, BDSM bordered on abuse. Only this morning a patient had come in with a broken arm, bruises, and cuts, saying she'd tripped on the basement stairs. Twice previously, she'd come in with serious injuries she attributed to her own clumsiness, and her body bore testament to other wounds.

"All that *stuff*," Lily stated firmly, "is demeaning to women, and can be dangerous." For the third time, Lily had given her patient a brochure about domestic abuse, information about women's shelters, and a referral to a counselor. "I see patients who've been abused by the men in their lives. Believe me, there's nothing sexy about it."

"Of course not," Marielle said, "but BDSM is different from—"

Leaning forward, elbows on the table, Lily interrupted. "The idea of a man dominating a woman, tying her up, and hitting her sounds awfully close to abuse to me."

George, seated to Lily's right, put down her glass of red wine. "I agree, and that's not something I want to read about." A striking redhead, her real name was Georgia but only her fiancé called her that. In her sage green wool suit, yellow blouse, and patterned scarf, she fit the classy bar perfectly.

George Malone, a marketing executive, always came across as professional and feminine. Marielle Clarke, with her ever-changing jobs, was more casual and chose vivid colors that complemented her Jamaican coloring. Kim Chang, an artist and budding entrepreneur, created her own distinct style. The three women were very different, and all beautiful.

Once upon a time, Lily, with her short wheat-blond hair and light blue eyes, had felt attractive. Now, the oldest of the group at thirty-two, perpetually tired and stressed, she knew she looked older than her years. Her taupe pantsuit and tailored white shirt were classic, yet today they made her feel drab.

Marielle, never quick to take "no" for an answer, said, "I haven't read any BDSM, but it's such a hot—pun intended—trend. I've heard successful career women rave about these books. I can't believe the authors promote anything that's abusive or demeaning. Women don't fantasize about abuse."

"I don't really know what BDSM is," Kim confessed cheerfully. "Ty and I might be doing it, and I wouldn't even know."

"I've done it," Marielle announced.

"Of course you have," Lily said, torn between amusement and dismay. Vibrant Marielle believed variety was the spice of life, and liked her own life highly seasoned—in terms of drinks, jobs, and men.

"What did you do, Marielle?" Kim demanded, her near-black eyes dancing.

"I met this superhot cop. He strip-searched me, handcuffed me to the bed, and made me give him a blow job."

"That's sex play," George said. Then, questioningly, "It *was* sex play, right?"

"Yeah, a really fun game."

Lily and her husband had never done anything like that. It was ridiculous. And yet . . . the thought of Dax strip-searching her triggered pulses of arousal between her thighs. She'd always found his bad-boy side extremely sexy. Not that she'd seen it in a long time.

He'd be home for the holidays on Thursday, after two months at a mining camp. A bush helicopter pilot, he'd been away more and more over the past couple of years. Clearly, he'd rather fly in the remote wilderness than be with her. Even when he was home, they barely spoke, and not about anything important. That distance made her worry that he was cheating on her, but she'd been afraid to ask. Afraid their marriage might be over. Now it was time to face that fear. She had to know the truth.

Life without Dax . . . A pang of soul-deep sorrow stabbed through her. When the waitress approached with her second martini, Lily reached gratefully for it. "Thanks." She took a long swallow. *I won't think about Dax right now.*

She refocused on Marielle, who was expanding on the strip-search scenario. "George is right," Lily said. "That's sex play. BDSM is no game."

"Oh, you've read those books?" Marielle's chocolate eyes twinkled.

"Of course not. But as a doctor I'm aware of a range of sexual behavior. At least from the physiological standpoint." And just how stuffy could she sound?

"But sex is about more than physiology," George said. "It can be—should be—about emotion."

Once upon a time, making love with Dax was the most blissful, erotic, loving act Lily could imagine. They'd become lovers when she was seventeen, a virgin. Her sexy bad boy had initiated her, taught her to experience passion. In the past couple of years, though, it was like he was phoning it in. They both were: going through the motions, climaxing, yet never truly connecting. With so many doubts and fears on her mind, how could she surrender to intimacy?

Roughness under her right index finger made Lily realize she was twisting her wedding ring, the band of small diamonds Dax had put on her finger a decade ago.

George was still talking. "Is BDSM just a different kind of sex between two people who care about one another, or is it abuse?"

"Look how pathetic we are," Kim said. "It's this hot trend and we're not even sure what it is."

"If you want to know, research it online," Lily said.

Kim reached for her glass of designer beer. "Fiction's more fun. We're a book club and this is a popular trend. We should read it and discuss it."

"Thank you," Marielle said. "So you're in. George?"

The redhead's topaz and diamond engagement ring sparkled as

she lifted her wineglass. "I see Kim's point." She sipped then said, "Yes, I think we should read it. We'll have interesting discussions."

Lily made a sound in the back of her throat.

"She snorted," Marielle said.

"Sounded more like a growl to me." Kim grinned, then sobered. "Lily, do you really hate the idea? You chose the last book."

Marielle nodded. "It was good, but man, it was dense. I had to concentrate on every word, and re-read whole pages."

Lily pressed her lips together. She'd enjoyed the prizewinning literary novel for exactly that reason. Reading it absorbed her totally; she couldn't stress over her failing marriage or worry about her crazy-busy medical clinic.

The waitress arrived with the platters of appetizers the women had ordered. When she'd gone, Marielle raised her fruity cocktail like she was proposing a toast. "Come on, Doc Lily. Open your mind."

"It'll give us so much to discuss," Kim chimed in.

"If I can give it a try," George said, "maybe you could too?"

In the ten months since the four of them, strangers with an interest in books, had formed the club, the others had figured out her triggers. Yes, she believed in keeping an open mind, being flexible, and trying new things—even if she sometimes had to be reminded. But the few minutes she stole from her busy schedule to read gave her the only pleasure and relaxation in her life. And while it was true that the two erotic novels the club had read this year had given her most of the orgasms she'd experienced recently, she'd rather read anything other than BDSM. Oh well, it was only one book. If she hated it, she'd skim. "Fine. Pick a book."

Savory aromas drifted from the appetizer platters. Starving—no, a diet of yogurt for breakfast and coffee for lunch was *not* something she'd recommend to a patient—Lily spread hummus on a piece of grilled flatbread and took a big bite. Mmm, garlic and spice.

"We should read that book everyone's been talking about," Kim said.

George, who was lifting a ring of calamari to her mouth, stopped her fork. "That's a series. Don't you need to read all three to get the full story arc?"

"Oh yeah," Kim said. "That's a bit much."

"It certainly is." Lily shook her head. "No way do I want that much BDSM."

Kim gave a quick splutter of laughter and tilted her head toward the neighboring table.

Lily realized that, as they'd been talking, the lounge had filled up and the four of them had automatically raised their voices. At the table beside them, a couple of tailored guys with big black cases— lawyer bags, in all likelihood, as the courthouse was a block away— shot surreptitious glances in their direction. Her cheeks heated.

"One book," Marielle agreed, spearing a buffalo-style hot wing. "After we eat, I'll pull out my iPad and we'll choose. By the way, are we meeting next Monday? It's Boxing Day."

Because the club members led such busy lives, they'd discovered they could never agree on one full evening a month. Instead, they met every Monday for an hour after work. For Lily, who ran a busy family practice clinic, it had the benefit of getting her out of the place early for once. They'd also found that weekly meetings let them discuss their impressions as they read the books.

"I like sticking to our routine," Lily said, and the others agreed.

In the first months, all their chat had been about books, but over time it had become more personal. Now she turned to Kim. "Did your parents arrive safely?" They were flying in from Hong Kong for Christmas.

Kim nodded, her color-streaked hair flicking like a tropical bird's wing flutter. "Yes. They've been in Vancouver the last few days, and

I'm driving them out to the ranch tonight. And guess what? Umbrella-Wings is official now. The name and logo are trademarked, the company's incorporated, and the board of directors is Ty, me, Mom, and Dad." Kim, who had degrees in business administration and fine arts, was launching a company. UmbrellaWings would make umbrellas and parasols with distinctive shapes and patterns modeled after the wings of butterflies, birds, and other flying creatures.

"But it's your company, right?" Marielle said. "You won't let your parents tell you what to do."

"They can suggest," Kim said. "After all, they've built a successful business. But no, they can't tell me what to do. I think they're getting the message."

Lily swallowed a mouthful of tender calamari. "Good for you." She wished her own parents—who always thought they knew what was best for Lily and her younger brother—would do the same.

"It was tough for them to accept that I'm not moving back to Hong Kong," Kim said.

"And not marrying a nice Hong Kong boy," George said, "but living in sin with a sexy rodeo star."

Kim grinned. "We downplay the rodeo part. To my folks, Ty's the responsible owner of a successful family ranch. This week my parents will see how impressive the ranch is. We're going to try to get them up on horses." Kim, who'd never ridden before meeting Ty, now owned a rescue horse named Distant Drummer that she'd helped Ty heal and train.

"I hope everyone gets along," Lily said. Her parents didn't approve of Dax, which created strain at family gatherings. She wasn't looking forward to Christmas dinner on Sunday.

"Are your parents staying with you and Ty?" George asked Kim.

"No way. That'd put a cramp in our sex life. They'll stay with Ty's parents." After Ty had bought Ronan Ranch with rodeo earnings, his parents had come from Alberta to help run it. They lived in the old ranch house, and he'd built another house down the road from them.

"Are your parents hinting that you should get married?" Lily asked.

"Hinting?" Kim rolled her eyes. "Does a steamroller hint? Ty and I ignore them. We're enjoying being truly, madly, deeply in love, for the first time in our lives." A bright smile split her face. "Isn't that cool, that it's a first for both of us?"

"It's pretty cool when it's the second time, too," George said. The redhead was a widow and hadn't believed she'd ever find another soul mate—until Canada's Mr. Hockey, Woody Hanrahan, entered her life earlier this year and turned it topsy-turvy.

"Chee-sy." Drawing out the word, Marielle rolled her eyes. "The hearts and flowers and throbbing violin strings are making me nauseous."

They all laughed, and then Lily said, "George and Kim, love looks very good on both of you. And Marielle, variety suits you." She reached for her martini glass again, finding it almost empty. No one said that ten years of marriage looked good on her. If they had, it would be a lie.

Once, she'd been positive Dax Xavier was the love of her life. Over the years she'd met loads of men: cultured, intelligent ones; sexy athletes; physicians who volunteered in third-world countries. Amazing, appealing men. She'd been attracted to a few, but never with the same magnetic force as she was to Dax. But did she still love him? She was too confused and conflicted to be sure. If he was cheating on her, if he no longer loved her . . . then she had to protect her heart.

Last year, when she'd first suspected he might be having an affair, she had protected her body. She'd lied and told him she'd gone off the pill for health reasons so he had to wear a condom.

How bitterly ironic, to be using both condoms and the pill when the thing she most wanted in the world was children. Since she was a little girl, she'd known she wanted to be a mom. Now that want had become a soul-deep craving. Every time she held her baby niece, her biological clock ticked faster.

Though she and Dax hadn't discussed having kids in years, she'd assumed they'd have a family when the time was right. His genes should make wonderful babies; he was smart, courageous, strong, fit, and handsome. What he wasn't was *there* for her. She had to find out how he felt, how she felt, what they were going to do about their faltering marriage.

Stop thinking about Dax!

She'd been listening with half an ear as Marielle talked about family plans and holiday parties. Now Marielle said, "How about you, George? It's your first Christmas with Woody. He'll be in town, right?" The redhead's fiancé was captain of the Beavers, the Vancouver hockey team.

"Yes, thank heavens, what with home games and days off. We're hosting Christmas at our place." George had moved into Woody's penthouse condo in Yaletown this fall.

"Is his mom coming?" Lily asked. Woody's mother had almost died of cancer, but was now in remission. He'd bought her a house in Florida and paid for a live-in caregiver companion.

"No, her health is still too fragile for a trip north, but we'll Skype with her. My mom and her guy Fabio will come over. We're being hopelessly old-fashioned—the girls cooking dinner; the boys watching football. A few of Woody's teammates will be there. And a couple of special guests from Manitoba. Sam was Woody's best friend and hockey buddy as kids, and his father, Martin, was Woody's mentor and coach. They had some issues for a while, but they've reconciled."

"Nice," Kim said. "That's the Christmas spirit."

George turned to Lily. "How about you? Do you and your husband have any Christmas traditions?"

Arguing over whether they really had to go to her parents' house, which they always ended up doing, which spoiled Christmas Day. "My parents have a family dinner at noon." It was formal and more filled with parental fault-finding than with Christmas spirit. But she hated to say no to her parents. Bad enough that she, the daughter of a neurosurgeon mom and a cardiologist dad, had chosen the less prestigious field of family medicine and had married a guy from the wrong side of the tracks. She tried not to disappoint them in any other ways.

The waitress came by to offer more drinks. Longingly, Lily twisted the stem of her empty martini glass. She wasn't driving, but two drinks were her limit. When the others all said, "No, thanks," she echoed them.

Marielle pulled out her iPad and checked online for books. Kim, beside her, looked on. The two of them pointed, debated, and then agreed on one. Marielle turned her tablet to face Lily and George.

"*Bound by Desire?*" George said. "Okay, sure."

Lily scanned the blurb.

International businesswoman Cassandra Knightley is at the top of her game, respected and even feared by colleagues and competitors. When it comes to her sex life, she picks, chooses, and discards men as frequently as she chooses the latest pair of designer shoes—because, ultimately, none satisfies her.

Billionaire Neville Winter guesses a secret that even Cassandra isn't aware of. A man used to dominating in every area of life, including the bedroom, he initiates her into a new world of sexual pleasure. Though initially she's intrigued by the notion of spicing up her sex life, it isn't until she submits fully and puts her pleasure—and her pain—in Neville's hands that she learns her true sexual nature. When she is bound by desire, can Cassandra find the true satisfaction that has always escaped her?

Lily barely managed to hold back one of those snort-growl sounds. "Whatever you want."

"I'll text you the deets," Marielle said. "I need to get going. One of my friends has a staff party and invited me as his date."

The staff party for Lily's Well Family Clinic had been last week. She'd reserved a private room at a nice restaurant and arranged a sumptuous buffet. One of the receptionists, Jennifer, had organized a Secret Santa draw, which had livened things up. Lily had drawn Jennifer's name and given her a gift certificate for her favorite cupcake bakery. She was very curious which of the doctors or staff had drawn her name and why they'd chosen a desktop Zen garden: miniature tray, sand, rocks, and teeny rake.

"I'm wrapping presents tonight," George said. "Woody's going to love the tee you made, Kim." The redhead had asked Kim, who designed clothing as a hobby, if she'd create something unique for Woody.

Not having a clue what to give Dax for Christmas, Lily had seconded the request. The charcoal tee with its dramatic abstract design of a hawk would look perfect on her rugged husband. "And Dax will love the hawk one. Thanks so much for doing that, Kim. I know how much you have on your plate these days."

"I thrive on it," Kim said. "Life's good. Speaking of which, let's do gifts!"

They'd agreed to exchange gifts, but only small ones. Lily had found purse-sized notebooks with lovely Japanese-designed flower covers. Marielle gave lip gloss with fruity flavors, then Kim handed them each a roll of paper tied with a red ribbon. She'd done watercolor drawings of each of them, accurate but also flattering.

Lily gazed at the portrait of a short-haired blonde with delicate yet striking features and wide blue eyes. "Wow, Kim, this is what I looked like ten years ago."

"It's what you look like now," Kim said, "when you're relaxed and having fun."

George reached into her tote and handed them all packages, which turned out to be tank tops: hot pink for Marielle, vivid purple for Kim, and powder blue, the color of her eyes, for Lily. The cotton was soft and fine, the quality excellent.

"You went way over the five-dollar limit, girlfriend," Marielle said.

"I didn't spend a dime," George replied. "They're samples from my client, VitalSport. Part of the new spring line."

"Great gifts!" Kim said. "Thanks, everyone. And now I have to run and pick up my parents. Ty's mom is cooking up a feast."

They all rose, and Lily thought about her own evening plans.

No feast to look forward to; she'd heat up canned soup to accompany a handful of rice crackers and a slice of Edam. No gift-wrapping; instead, an hour's run along the icy cold seawall, a necessity if she hoped to sleep tonight. No party either. She needed to analyze the Well Family Clinic's schedule. Her clinic's priority—and her own true calling—was patient care, but the workload was expanding and she had to figure out a solution. Thanks to the book club's new selection, she didn't even have a good book to look forward to.

Also on the list of "not looking forward to," there was Dax's return home on Thursday, and the talk they needed to have. Maybe by the time Christmas dinner at her parents' house rolled around, she'd be going alone. Alone, to be unfavorably compared to her perfect younger brother, the oncologist, with his perfect lawyer wife and the adorable baby girl who tugged at Lily's childless heartstrings.

No, there wasn't a single thing in life she was looking forward to.

Two

Dwayne Arthur Xavier—who'd gone by Dax since he was old enough to understand how geeky his given names were—stepped into the lobby of the condo building in Leg-in-Boot Square, just off Vancouver's False Creek. An artificial Christmas tree decorated with silver balls stood in one corner. Dax shook his head, scattering raindrops. If you were going to have a tree, it should be a live one, its needles green and pliant under your fingers, its fresh scent bringing the wilderness into the room.

A six-pack of Granville Island lager in one hand, he hiked his duffel bag higher on his shoulder and strode to the elevator. Would Lily be there? Likely not. Though it was the day before Christmas, it was also a Saturday. On Saturdays she volunteered at a health clinic in the Downtown Eastside. Besides, he was two days late. He'd swapped schedules with another pilot who'd had a family emergency. After all, it wasn't like Dax had a lot to come home to.

He stepped into the elevator and pressed the button for the fourth floor of the six-story building.

Home. Though he'd pumped a lot of his income—which was considerable, in his line of work—into paying off the mortgage, the two-bedroom condo didn't feel like home. But then, when in his life had any place felt like home? Not the numerous rental apartments where he and his self-absorbed, drug-using parents had lived. Nor his mom's parents' house in ritzy Southlands, where she and Dax had gone for a few months after his dad was thrown in jail for killing a guy in a drug deal gone bad.

His grandparents had shunned his mom when she ran away to marry a bad boy whose parents hadn't even set foot on the social ladder. But when, broke and desperate, she showed up on their doorstep with seventeen-year-old Dax, they took them in. That was how he ended up attending twelfth grade at the same school as Lily Nyland.

He unlocked the door to the condo, feeling, as usual, almost like an intruder. "Lily?" Nope, no answer. Hanging his battered leather bomber jacket in the hall closet, he made sure the damp fabric didn't touch Lily's coats.

Just like back in school, when their paths never crossed. The lovely, classy, brilliant blonde was busy with her studies, clubs, and equally wealthy, brilliant friends. Dax blew off school, drank too much, got in trouble, and hustled girls. Following in his dad's badboy footsteps, as his grandparents said contemptuously. It had been the next summer, at Camp Skookumchuck, when he and Lily had connected and his life had turned around. And now look where they were. Virtual strangers.

In the kitchen, he put his beer in a fridge that contained yogurt, skim milk, cheese, fruit, and a few condiments.

He walked into the living room. The only sign of Christmas was a pink-and-white poinsettia on the coffee table. The place was, as usual, immaculate. When Dax moved through the world of nature, he tried to never leave a trace. That was how Lily lived at home. She didn't leave clothes, dirty dishes, or magazines lying around. When he first saw her family home, he understood where she'd learned to be so neat and unobtrusive.

When they took possession of this condo, he'd been heading off to fly for a logging company and had left the décor to Lily. Six weeks later, he'd come back to nutmeg-colored furniture, rugs with geometric designs, abstract art. It was comfortable, functional, and tasteful. Lily said she'd taken a decorator's advice. He'd have chosen wilderness paintings and put a few pieces of First Nations art on the mantel, but what did he know about decorating? His parents had used thrift store junk, macramé, and ivy.

In this room, he saw no traces of the old Lily, the girl who'd gone a little crazy that summer at camp, away from her parents' eagle eye. The one who'd snuck out from Heron cabin, where her young charges slept, to go canoeing at midnight or skinny-dipping. Who'd made love on the beach with a boy her parents wouldn't give the time of day to—a guy who worked with the construction crew that was building new cabins. The son of a killer.

Dax went into the home office, where he took his netbook from his duffel and put it on the bare surface of his desk. Lily's desk held her notebook computer, her monitor, keyboard, and mouse, plus stacks of papers, all very neat and organized.

Over the years, she'd grown up and stopped playing. He'd forced himself to grow up too, to become responsible, to deserve the amazing woman he loved. He missed the kids they'd once been. The kids who'd fallen so head over heels for each other. Who'd made love with wild abandon, and spun dreams on moonlit summer nights.

He moved on to the bedroom, and into the walk-in closet where he unpacked, slotting the few clothes he'd brought with him into their allotted space. Her half dozen tailored suits and shirts, three or four good dresses, and few casual clothes looked almost interchangeable in the browns, grays, creams, and white that she favored. The only touch of vibrancy was that one rose-colored sweater he'd once given her. No, wait, what was this?

Cautious of his rough fingers against delicate fabric, he separated Lily's shirts to reveal one he'd never seen before. It was pale yellow, the style soft and kind of floaty. Butterflies covered it, painted in beautiful shades of blue and green, with gold outlining them. It was a work of art, feminine and sensual.

Sensual? He slammed the hangers back in place. Who the hell did she wear it for? And what would he do if he found out, for sure, that she'd cheated on him?

He stripped off his clothes, chucked them in the laundry hamper, and went into the master bathroom, where he turned the shower on full force. He stepped under the spray.

Infidelity . . . He had no proof, but over the past year or two his wife had changed. Her light blue eyes didn't warm for him and she didn't reach for his hand. When they had sex, she climaxed but didn't show passion, much less joy. She'd told him he needed to wear a condom because she'd gone off the pill. Initially, he'd accepted it without question, but now doubts drove him crazy. There were other forms of birth control that didn't require condoms.

And then there were the books she read. Earlier this year, on one of his increasingly rare visits to Vancouver, he'd mistakenly picked up her Kindle rather than his own. When he clicked it on, he found a detailed, vivid, highly explicit sex scene. His wife had always read highbrow books. This book, *The Sexual Education of Lady Emma Whitehead*, was labeled an "erotic novel." It seemed like soft porn to him, but what did he know about great literature? The next time he was back in town, he checked her reading material and found *Ride Her, Cowboy*, another "erotic novel."

His wife was reading erotica—and she sure wasn't bringing any of that erotic passion into their bed. Was she sharing it with someone else?

The pounding spray of the shower beat against his tense shoulder muscles but did nothing to relax them.

Dax was a take-charge guy. Always had been, until now. No one who knew him—not in the army where he'd earned a Medal for Military Valour for rescuing injured soldiers pinned under Taliban fire and air-lifting them to safety, nor out in the bush where he'd fought forest fires and rescued fishermen in the middle of a storm—would ever call him a coward. But that's what he was when it came to his marriage.

"Fuck." Roughly, he scrubbed his body with soap that smelled of lemon and eucalyptus.

He and Lily had always been a mismatch. In the beginning, lust and love overcame the barriers, but now their marriage seemed to be nothing but barriers. Did some other man—a man better suited to her, a man her damned parents would approve of—have her passion? Her love?

It sure wasn't like she needed Dax. She might look like a princess—fair, elegant, and delicate—yet she was smart, capable, and had an iron will. He admired her independence, couldn't imagine being with a clingy, dependent woman, and yet . . .

His parents had been so absorbed in themselves and each other, they'd barely noticed him. Lily had a full life without him. He was a self-sufficient guy—a loner, some folks said—and it wasn't like he needed to come first with Lily. It had been enough that she loved him, that they got together whenever they could and had a great time together. Now it seemed they'd lost even that. Or that she was giving it to some other guy.

He fisted his hand in anger and frustration and thumped it against the tiled wall of the shower, wishing he could punch whoever the hell Lily might be fucking.

Women came onto Dax, but he believed that if you said marriage vows, you stuck to them. Or else you split.

He turned his face into the shower's needle-fine spray.

Was it that time? He'd hung in there over the past year, hoping they were just going through a rough patch, but he couldn't take it any longer. He had to find out what the hell was going on. With her, and with them. As for him . . . Did he still love Lily? He'd never met another woman who made him feel the way she had in the early days, when he'd been crazy enough to hope that with her he might find the things he'd always secretly dreamed of: love and safety, a home and family. Over the years, growing up, he'd abandoned some of those dreams. He wasn't cut out to be a dad; Lily's clinic had become her "baby" and she put it ahead of everything else; neither of them was the type for a conventional home life. Still, he'd believed in their love, and it sustained him when they were apart. It got him through Afghanistan.

The thought of losing Lily was gut-wrenching. But maybe he already had.

When she got home, he'd put the questions out on the table, hear her answers, and fucking deal with them like a man. Resolved, he turned off the shower, reached for a towel, and dried off.

He ran a comb through his hair. Lily would think it needed cutting and so would her uptight parents, but that was their problem. Nor would he shave off the beard he'd grown. Chances were, this marriage was going to blow up. "Shit." Love, marriage, dreams. Should have known all along he wasn't that kind of guy.

His muscles as taut as when he'd climbed into the shower, he strode jerkily to the closet and pulled on jeans and a tee. He checked his smartphone and found a text from Lily.

Working late. If you're back, have dinner without me.

He hurled the phone onto the bed. Working late, or with a lover, or just avoiding him? She didn't want to talk to him or she'd have phoned. But he wanted to talk to her. Damn it, he had to know the truth. He wanted to settle things tonight.

Her Kindle sat on her bedside table. He flicked it on. This time, she wasn't in the middle of a book; the device opened to show several covers. One book, with a choker-style necklace on the cover, was titled *Bound by Desire*. More erotica? He opened it, skimmed the review quotes at the beginning, and his eyes widened. BDSM? Lily had chosen to read BDSM? Was she, maybe, into this kind of sex?

No, he couldn't imagine it. She was no submissive; hell, she always had to be in control.

Well, not in the bedroom. There, in the beginning, he'd been the teacher. Once she'd caught up, he'd always thought they were equals. Had she fantasized about being dominated? About dominating? Did she get off on tying a man up? On spanking him? Had she found a man who satisfied those needs?

Dax grimaced. "Oh, fuck it."

He ripped off the clothes he'd just put on, donned waterproof running gear, and headed out to try to release some tension. Though in some ways he preferred the pristine whiteness of the snowy north, he had to admit there was a lot to be said for being able to run outside rather than on a treadmill in a gym.

The rain still pounded down, dusk was falling, rush-hour traffic was at its peak. Lights from cars, streetlights, and buildings slashed in jagged patterns through sheets of rain. Dax's shoes thumped the pavement, splashing water. He headed across the Cambie Street Bridge, noticing the construction cranes with multicolored Christmas lights. Festive. The opposite of his mood.

He ran through Yaletown and into the West End, on Robson Street. Strings of sparkly white lights looped through the boulevard trees, clothing store windows showed party wear, and pedestrians chattered excitedly as they headed to restaurants and parties. He turned right on Denman, crossed West Georgia, and ran into Stanley Park.

The thousand-acre park, much of it undeveloped, was a frequent destination for him when he was in the city. A paved, six-mile seawall ran along the outside. This Christmas Eve, the seawall and the road beside it were quiet.

Normally, running outside made him feel free, powerful, and connected to nature. Tonight, nothing was going to make him feel good. He tried not to think, only to mindlessly push forward. He returned over the Burrard Street Bridge, then along the seawall on the south side of False Creek. By the time he got home, he'd run roughly ten miles.

He opened the condo door, dripping with rain and sweat. Doubting Lily would be home yet, he still called, "Hello?" No response.

Again, he headed for the shower, and again he dried off and dressed. He still felt like crap, but at least he'd worn off some nervous energy and filled an hour. He'd also worked up a bear of an appetite.

He rummaged through the delivery menus in the kitchen drawer, and phoned in an order for butter chicken and lamb vindaloo. Food at the mining camp was plentiful and decent, but basic. Then he took a beer and Lily's Kindle, and settled at the table in the dining nook, facing the view over False Creek. It was night now, but Vancouver never got truly dark, not with all those streetlights, apartment lights, vehicle lights. He missed the midnight black of nights in the bush, broken on clear nights by crystal stars and a glowing moon, sometimes even by the rippling, dancing sheets of colored northern lights.

When he and Lily had gone house shopping after he left the army four years ago, his pick was a place with a yard, close to a park. The house was old, rundown, but he'd liked the natural setting. Lily had pointed out that his new career as a bush pilot meant he wouldn't be home much. She didn't have the time or interest to deal with a fixer-upper house and a yard, nor did she want a long commute to work. They'd settled on this condo: easy care, a ten-minute walk to her Well Family Clinic, and within nice running distance from Stanley Park and from Pacific Spirit Park up by the university.

Turning away from the cityscape, he started to read Lily's book. Normally, he chose outdoor stories or thrillers, either real life or fiction. *Bound by Desire* didn't exactly hook him. A woman who was tired after a stressful business trip checked into a ritzy hotel, went to the bar for a drink, and flirted with a stranger, then accepted his invitation for dinner. She found him commanding and charismatic. Dax thought he was a bit of an asshole.

The building-door buzzer sounded and Dax took delivery of his dinner, put the takeout containers on the table, and found a fork. For a few minutes, he just ate, enjoying the taste of savory spices. Then he turned back to the book.

The couple ate dinner and put away two bottles of wine, flirting all the time. For dessert, he ordered a rich chocolate cake, and they shared it.

The cake was sinfully delicious, yet after only two bites, Cassandra found herself sliding the plate over to Neville. "You finish it."

Watching the pleasure on his face as he ate it was even more enjoyable than tasting it herself. But after only a few more bites, he shoved it aside. "Come to my room."

She gazed into his piercing black eyes. Truly, he was the most compelling, sexy, utterly masculine man she'd ever met. Decisive, powerful, charismatic. She'd always been drawn to strong men who weren't threatened by a confident, successful woman. But never had she been as attracted as she was to the man seated across from her. Her body craved him so badly her panties were soaked. And her judgment, which almost always proved reliable, told her she could trust him. "I might be persuaded," she responded, hoping her coy comment might win one of his dazzling smiles.

Instead, his black brows rose. "Persuaded? That's not my strong point."

She frowned. "What do you mean?"

"Cassandra, I'm a dom."

"A what? You mean, uh, sexually? Like with BDSM?" She'd never been with a dom. The idea—okay, it titillated her, especially with a man as sexy as Neville—but it also horrified her.

"Exactly. And you're a submissive."

She jerked back in her seat. "I certainly am not!" At work she was known as a ball-breaker; no way would she ever submit to a man.

"You're in denial." He nodded. "Yes, I thought so. It will make tonight even more interesting."

Glaring, she said, "If you think I'm going to let you, uh, let you . . ." What did doms do? Tie women up? Beat them?

"Let me? No, you'll beg me to."

Damn. So much for having great sex tonight. "You're wasting your time. I'm not into that kind of thing."

A slight smile edged his lips. "You say one thing but I can read you, Cassandra. You don't enjoy vanilla sex."

"Well, no. I mean, it's nice, but . . ." Though she'd had sex with a dozen men in the past year, each experience had been too damned bland.

"Something's missing, that you want very badly. There's no spice, no fire, no passion. You feel like you're standing outside your body, watching. You never truly connect intimately with your own body or with your partner. There's no intensity. You climax, but it's like a sneeze, a ripple. It doesn't wrench you apart and make you scream."

She squeezed her legs together, barely able to stop herself from squirming with arousal. Yes, that was what she wanted. Intensity. "All right." Her voice sounded husky. "I wouldn't mind spicing up my sex life. Playing a few kinky games. I thought you might be into that."

"Playing games. That's really not my thing." He leaned forward, and she was unable to look away from his dark gaze. "Being a dom is not a game, it's who I am. My true nature. As, I believe, being a sub-missive is your true nature."

"No." It was perverted, that kind of sex. She was a liberated woman.

"Let me show you."

That deep voice, his compelling gaze . . . She found herself shifting her weight, as if to rise and go with him. He drew her, the way no one else ever had; something about him made her want to obey him, to please him. Struggling against an almost overwhelming urge, she said, "I can't. It's not me."

"Then we're done here." He took the napkin from his lap and tossed it on the table. "A pity. We'd be good together. Imagining it has kept me hard since we first sat down."

Hard. His cock would be as strong, as powerful as the rest of him. God, how she wanted him inside her. She wanted amazing orgasms—for him as well as herself. But he was rejecting her. How could she let him walk away? "You said you would show me. I don't think that will happen. But maybe we could, uh, try one or two things? Nothing too, uh . . ."

"The relationship between a dominant and his submissive begins with a negotiation."

That was encouraging. Sort of. At least he believed in negotiating, rather than just dictating terms. "But I'm not your submissive. Can't we negotiate something else? Some non-vanilla sex, for tonight?"

He studied her, face impassive and eyes glinting with some emotion she couldn't read. Was it annoyance? Humor? Desire? "You want to dip your toe in the deep waters of my world."

"I guess I do. Without being in danger."

"A sub never faces danger. Safe, sane, and consensual is the fundamental rule. And the sub has a safe word. If she speaks it, the dom stops immediately, without question."

"Hmm. That's reassuring, but it's still way too much for me. Can't we just have some kinky sex?"

After long, silent moments of staring at her, he finally said, "What is it about you, Cassandra?"

"How do you mean?"

"With any other woman, I would have walked away. But in you, I see so much. I see things you don't let yourself acknowledge and I want to help you find your true self, your deepest pleasure. I'm drawn to you."

Did he really mean it? "I'm drawn to you, too." In ways she understood, for his charismatic personality and pure male sexiness, and in ways she didn't understand, like a desire to please him and win his smile.

And now that smile flashed, so dazzling that it made her catch her breath. "Then you will come to my room and dip your toe, perhaps your entire foot. And once you've done that, I believe you will want to dive from the highest diving board."

His meal finished, Dax rinsed the takeout containers and put them in the recycling. Noticing that the kitchen faucet had a persistent drip, he got the tool kit from the back of the hall closet and replaced the washer. Then, with another beer in hand, he took Lily's Kindle to the living room and flicked on the gas fire.

His wife was a strong, independent woman like Cassandra. Had she too met a man who made her want to dip her toe in a taboo world of dominant-submissive sex? Or was it the connectedness and intensity that appealed to her? How had he and Lily lost that?

He settled in the recliner and began to read again.

When Cassandra stepped out of the bathroom, she was dressed as Neville had instructed, wearing only her thigh-high black stockings and four-inch-heel shoes. Proud of her toned, voluptuous body, the idea of flaunting it in front of him sent tingles of heat racing through her, as did the idea of a night of kinky sex games with this man.

He stood beside the king-sized bed in the bedroom of his luxurious hotel suite, watching her with a gleam in his dark eyes. He'd taken off his tie and suit jacket, undone a few buttons at the neck of his white dress shirt, and rolled the cuffs up his forearms. His powerful body was supremely masculine, his style casually elegant. His voice, when he said, "Come here, Cassandra," was anything but casual, though. It was deep and commanding.

That tone of command sent quivers of arousal racing through her blood.

Just slowly enough to make a point, she strolled toward him.

He frowned. "I'm not sure you really want this. Perhaps you should go."

After stripping off her clothes for him? Not likely. She wanted sex, kink, orgasms. "I do want it. Honestly, Neville."

He shook his head. "Here, you call me master."

"M-Master?" Her voice squeaked in disbelief.

"I agreed that tonight we only play games. But we'll play them by my rules."

How badly did she want a night's walk on the wild side, sex that made her cry out with the intensity of her release? If he could give her that, she'd call him whatever he wanted. Besides, she still felt that inexplicable desire to please him and win his approval. "I'm sorry, master."

"That's better. Now my pet, I have jewelry for you. Let's see how you like it."

From a black case, he took a wide collar, black leather studded with what had to be rhinestones. It was sleek, sexy. Oddly, though, it had a ring in the center. "It's lovely, but what's the ring for?"

He studied her, his lips pressed together, then said, "There are a few things we need to get clear, and—"

"I'm sorry," she said, tongue in cheek. "I forgot to call you master."

"Cassandra." He said it icily. "If you want to dip your toe in my world, you will respect me."

"I do. And I respect that you're a dom. But this is hard for me to relate to, because I'm not a submissive."

"Forget the labels, and forget your fears. Put yourself in my hands. I and only I know your deepest needs and desires, and will fulfill them. Put your pleasure in my hands." His deep voice caressed the word "pleasure" in a lingering way that made her skin quiver with need.

"I can do that." There was something about Neville that made her suspect he knew how to bring a woman to screaming climax.

"Realize, though, that in order to achieve the deepest, purest pleasure, you will also experience pain. You can handle it, can't you, my pet?"

Another thrill of excitement rippled through her. Spanking? Maybe nipple clamps? Tonight, she wanted to push the bounds a little. "Yes, master." Somehow, the term came more easily each time she said it.

"Good. Now here are two simple rules. You will not question me, or even speak unless I give you permission. And you will obey my commands. Disobedience will bring punishment."

"Punishment?" The word flew out of her mouth, and she quickly said, "I'm sorry, master. I shouldn't have spoken."

"Indeed." He reached into his bag and drew out a black leather object with a handle and a flat, heart-shaped head. Perhaps he read the question in her eyes because he said, "This, pet, is a paddle. One that will set the sweet cheeks of your fine ass on fire."

She'd anticipated spanking, but with his bare hand. Flesh on flesh seemed sexy, but leather . . . Not that he'd use the paddle on her, if she never disobeyed him. All the same, the sight of that heart-shaped leather head sent a tingle across her skin, a forbidden thrill racing through her blood. Maybe just the tiniest hint of disobedience, to get a taste of what the slap of leather might feel like on her tender flesh . . . One quick flick would hurt, but surely not too much. Just enough to break her through to a new level of sensual awareness and excitement.

"Now," he said. "One final thing. Choose your safe word."

"Uh . . ." She glanced around the room for inspiration. A cream-colored orchid plant sat on the dresser. "Orchid."

"So be it." His face lightened and he smiled at her, the same sexy, charismatic smile that had compelled her when he first spoke to her downstairs. "Now, pet, let us begin."

She nodded, body quivering with anticipation, then lowered her head to let him slip the collar around her neck. His fingers caressed her flesh as he lifted her hair out of the way and fastened the clasp. The cool, smooth leather settled against her skin, feeling oddly right there.

From the black case, he next took a coiled strip of black leather. A belt? Did he plan to hit her with a belt?

"This," he said, "is your leash, my lovely pet. Down on your hands and knees, so I can attach it to your collar."

Her mouth fell open. He was going to treat her like a dog? That sounded more humiliating than arousing. And yet, some instinct made her want to obey, to please him. After all, he had promised her pleasure beyond what she'd ever experienced before . . .

Dax broke off, shaking his head. Putting a woman on a leash like a dog? Sounded sick to him, and he'd had enough of this book for now. Shouldn't Lily be home by now?

He reset her Kindle to the beginning of the book so she couldn't tell he'd been reading, and returned the device to where he'd found it. Then, back in the living room, he turned out the light and paced restlessly, his path lit only by the subdued flicker of artificial flames. What did it say about his wife that she read this stuff?

She'd been a virgin when he met her, shy but eager to learn. He'd taught her a lot but didn't figure she'd be into the really raunchy stuff. Yet she'd chosen a book about BDSM, after reading other erotic novels. An idea occurred to him. Fiction could be insightful and make you think, but it could also let you explore fantasy worlds.

Maybe Lily wasn't unfaithful, but bored with the sex that used to excite her. Cassandra wanted to kick her sex life up a notch; perhaps Lily craved that, too. His body, which hadn't responded to *Bound by Desire*, tightened at that thought.

When they were teens, she, like lots of other girls, had been attracted to his bad-boy persona. He'd done his best to grow up, to deserve her. But maybe she missed his rougher side. He couldn't imagine her wanting to be collared and leashed, but did she want him to be more macho with her?

He walked over to the window and gazed out. The rain had eased off. When would she get home? What would he say to her?

Why did women have to be so damned complicated? No wonder he spent most of his life in the bush. Weather and geography were challenging, but the challenges were straightforward.

Thinking of challenges and that first summer, he remembered the challenge he'd set himself then. She was on one path—to become a doctor—and he was on another, as a construction worker. She and her friends took college for granted but he'd never thought of going, and with his crappy marks and troublemaker record he wouldn't get in. He might well turn out to be the same kind of loser as his dad. Drink, drugs, no impulse control. Maybe one day he and dear old dad would share a jail cell.

Lily deserved more, and Dax wanted to be that *more*. When she asked him what he'd choose if he could do anything in the world, the answer was, of course, to fly in the wilderness, but he also added going to college because he knew that'd be important to her. Both seemed like impossible dreams—until she did some research and told him about the ROTP, the subsidized Regular Officer Training Plan with the Canadian Forces. He could go to college, learn to fly, serve his country—and, down the road, become a bush pilot.

It was a lot to contemplate for a messed-up kid like him. But he figured he'd either straighten up or he'd fail, and if he failed, he didn't deserve Lily.

On the day he graduated from the Royal Military College with top marks and Lily told him how proud she was, he proposed to her. Despite her parents' disapproval, she married him.

Now he had another tough decision to make. Did he scrap his marriage or fight for it? A few hours ago, he'd almost reconciled himself to the idea that their marriage was over. And yet, they'd been together fifteen years. Their entire adult lives. That was a hell of a lot to just scrap.

Was it possible that he and Lily could recapture the passion and love they'd once shared? Did that book of hers hold the clues for doing it?

Dax paced again, slowly this time. No way was he putting a collar and leash on Lily, but what else might he learn from the book? Neville had looked past Cassandra's words and read the way she responded to him. He'd told her to put her pleasure in his hands.

Once, Dax had been pretty good at figuring out what Lily wanted and making her happy, in bed and out. But now she was so reserved, so controlled. He stood as good a chance of getting his face slapped as of seducing her.

But hell, this was a challenge. Energy surged through him, filling him with resolve. With hope. "Hurry up and get home, woman."

Three

Lily, normally a brisk walker, trudged slowly from the Olympic Village SkyTrain station toward the condo in False Creek. Christmas Eve, and she felt the opposite of festive.

Her body ached from head to toe after more than twelve hours at the Downtown Eastside clinic. Not that she'd had to stay after her day shift, but cold weather and the holiday had brought a lot of patients. She enjoyed helping the destitute, the down on their luck, the addicts and street people. Healing was her passion, and it was nice to concentrate on it, rather than worry about administrative issues like Dr. Mark Brown's announcement that he had to move to half-time at the Well Family Clinic.

She'd also been too busy today to worry about Dax being home. All right, maybe she'd volunteered for that extra shift in part to put off facing him.

Once upon a time, she'd have been so excited about seeing Dax when they'd been apart. She'd bathe and perfume herself, do her hair, anticipate hours and hours of lovemaking. Their lives had always been so separate that seeing each other was a wonderful treat. She'd done undergrad, med school, and residency while he'd attended military college then gone through military training and served with the army, including two tours in Afghanistan. She'd been building her practice when he got out of the army and went to work as a bush helicopter pilot.

The temperature was a few degrees above freezing. Though it wasn't raining, chill dampness brushed her face. In her boots, winter coat, and scarf, she was comfortably warm and that cool caress felt fresh and cleansing after the clinic's distinctive funk of antiseptic and unwashed bodies.

She'd grabbed a quick cheese sandwich and apple during the day and now had no appetite. All she wanted was a long, hot bath, a potent martini, and bed.

Instead, there'd be Dax. They had to talk.

She rubbed glove-clad fingers across her brow, trying to ease her headache. How did you say, "Is it time to end this marriage?" Or should she start with, "Are you sleeping with someone else?"

"Damn." They should have had this conversation two days ago, when he was supposed to come home. Instead, his job had, as always, taken priority over her. Or perhaps that was a lie, and he'd spent those extra days with a lover.

The misty damp air condensed into drops of rain and she pulled out her umbrella. An UmbrellaWings prototype, it was made of overlapping "wings." Done mostly in shades of brown, the design was accented by dramatic stylized eyes of blue, black, and yellow. Kim had based it on the polyphemus moth.

Tomorrow, Lily's parents expected her and Dax for the noon Christmas dinner. Maybe she should defer the conversation until after that. Avoid anything but the most superficial topics with her husband.

"Defer and avoid," she muttered. That seemed to be her current strategy for everything in her life. She hadn't resolved workload issues at the clinic and she hadn't even started the book club novel. *What's wrong with me?* She'd always been focused and organized; she made plans and executed them. Though she'd never be as perfect as her younger brother, Anthony, she usually came close. And now she was a mess.

Tomorrow, she couldn't let her parents or Anthony see any signs of that mess. So, yes, she'd defer the conversation with Dax, but the moment they got home from Christmas dinner she'd tackle her husband and they'd determine the fate of their marriage.

Tonight, she'd tell Dax she had a headache and needed to be alone. And it would be the truth. The heel-click of her boots speeded up as she neared the condo building.

Inside, she stepped into the elevator. Once, absence had made the heart grow fonder. Each time she saw Dax again, she'd feel a "this is right" click of emotional intimacy and physical desire. Now absence only reinforced all the ways they didn't need each other, didn't connect. And yet, now her heart did a hop, skip, and a jump that wasn't just anxiety; it was a thrill of anticipation.

When she unlocked the apartment door and called, "Dax?" her voice was breathy.

"In here." His voice came from the living room. Dax had a deep voice with a slightly rough edge, a voice that suited him perfectly.

Trying to calm her racing heart, she put her umbrella in the stand, took off her coat and hung it up, then bent to pull up a pant leg and unzip her boot.

His bare feet, strong and well-shaped beneath frayed jean hems, moved into her field of vision. He walked so quietly, she hadn't heard him approach. Why did he have to catch her like this—limp hair hanging over her forehead, chilled fingers fumbling with her boot zipper?

"Stop." One word, said with a tone of command she might never have heard from him before.

It did make her stop, and straighten up to stare at him.

Oh God. Dax. The heat of sexual awareness rippled through her, and she surrendered hope of steadying her heartbeat. How unfair that, as she turned drab and middle-aged, he got even better looking. His six-foot-three frame, strong and rangy, was displayed to perfection in well-washed jeans and a faded black T-shirt. Hair blacker than the tee, glossy as a raven's wings, fell past his ears, long and a little unkempt, but oh so sexy. His features were craggy and utterly masculine, and a short, dark beard accented his stubborn jaw. His striking eyes, the storm-cloud irises ringed with slate gray, studied her with a strange expression. Almost as if he'd never seen her before and wondered who she was.

"You made it home," she said inanely.

A muscle twitched at the corner of his mouth. "So did you."

She braced herself, waiting for a frown and the comment that she looked tired and stressed, the same greeting he'd given her the last time he came home. Maybe he was concerned, but it came across more as a reminder that a guy like him could come home to someone younger, prettier, sexier. He had that *thing* that drew women. He'd had it at seventeen; he had it at thirty-three; the damned man would have it in his eighties.

But Dax didn't speak again. He squatted with the powerful grace she'd always found so attractive. He lifted the bottom of one of her pant legs and unzipped her boot.

Her mouth opened in wonder. He'd never done anything like this.

A warm hand curved around the lower part of her calf, holding her gently but firmly, and as her stocking-clad skin tingled with awareness, he eased off her boot. Then he repeated the process with her other boot, and straightened.

Was this foreplay? Much as her body might tremble with the craving for his touch, she really didn't want to have sex. Not with the clinic odors clinging to her skin, her head pounding with tiredness and stress, her mind and heart so tormented. Besides, the last times they'd had sex, her body might have spasmed in release, but she felt detached. Empty. Alone. She didn't need her husband for a meaningless orgasm; her vibrator and an erotic novel worked fine. "Dax, it's been a long day and I have a headache."

Now that big, masculine hand reached toward her face.

Quivering with nerves, she held still, wondering what he intended.

He scooped her wispy bangs back from her forehead then ran his fingers firmly across her brow, finding the tension knots. "Run a bath. I'll make you a martini."

She cocked her head. This too was different. Oh, he'd said similar things before, but more like, "Bet you could use a bath. Want me to make you a martini?" Now those same thoughts came out as . . . well, almost as orders, spoken in a deep, rough-edged voice that didn't brook argument.

Lily Nyland did not take orders. Only from her parents, though she preferred to think of that as daughterly respect. Still, there was something compelling about Dax right now that was strangely appealing. "A bath sounds good. So does a martini. Thank you."

Without another word, he turned and walked toward the kitchen.

Puzzled, she stared at his retreating back: the sleek black hair, powerful shoulders, narrow hips, taut butt, long legs. What was he doing? Being nice to her, yet ordering her around. Was he leading up to something? To sex, or to saying he was ending their marriage? It could be either, or anything in between.

She was exhausted and achy and she did want that bath, so she headed for the bathroom. After turning on the taps, she went to the adjoining walk-in closet to strip and dump her clothes in the hamper. Dax's voice came from the bathroom—"Martini's on the counter"—making her grab her terrycloth robe and bundle herself into it. He didn't come into the closet, though, and she heard the bathroom door close.

When she stepped cautiously into the steamy room, she was alone. A martini glass sat on the vanity, its surface damp with condensation. She took a sip. It was perfect, right down to the twist of lemon. No surprise. When Dax chose to do something, he did it extremely well.

She swallowed a heavy-duty headache pill, took out her contact lenses and gold stud earrings, and tossed lavender-scented Epsom salts into the bath. Breathing in the fragrant air, it was impossible not to relax a little. Whatever Dax wanted, she'd find a way to defer it.

Martini glass in hand, she stepped into the bath and settled back, her head on a bath pillow. Sipping, she tried to clear her mind. Occasionally, she took a course on the latest relaxation technique, but she was always a dismal failure. She'd aced self-defense, but failed meditation. The only time she felt truly relaxed was when her life was in perfect control. Which—hah!—hadn't been the case for a long time.

Setting the martini glass in easy reach on the tiled surround of the tub, she closed her eyes. The warm water soothed her tired body. The even warmer burn of alcohol radiated through her, its potency reminding her that lunch had been a lot of hours ago.

She breathed in. Slowly, deeply.

The lavender took her back to Camp Skookumchuck. Mr. and Mrs. Broadbent, a childless couple, had turned their oceanfront Gulf Islands property into a camp for kids and teens. Mrs. B was not only a great cook, but an avid gardener. She grew vegetables and herbs behind a deer fence. The flower beds around the house featured lavender, yarrow, and other plants that were deer-resistant.

The scent of lavender was tied to those wonderful summers when Lily had been free of her parents' rules and expectations. Free too of the pressure of competing with her two-years-younger brother Anthony, who'd attended a different camp. At Camp Skookumchuck, Lily was a kid like any other kid, able to explore, play, learn, even make mistakes. She attended from the time she was ten until she was seventeen, the last two years as a counselor.

It was that last summer that she and Dax had gotten together.

Lily sipped her martini and, behind her closed lids, pictured her

first night at camp. When her eight ten-year-old charges had finally
fallen asleep in the four pairs of bunk beds in Heron cabin, she'd
slipped silently out the door. In her wrinkled camp shorts and tee,
her shoulder-length hair pulled back in a sloppy ponytail—her
mother would be appalled!—she headed for the beach. Growing up
near the ocean, she was used to air with a salty tang, but here, with
no city smells to dilute it, the scent was even fresher and more pun-
gent. She found a smooth log to perch on, gazed out at the ocean and
stars, and savored the idea of two full months away from home.

From behind her, where the dozen rustic cabins nestled among
fir and cedar trees, came the occasional muffled laugh as the camp-
ers settled down for the night. Then, from closer at hand, she heard
a clunk of wood on metal. Startled, she gazed around.

At one side of the small bay where she sat, the camp dock extended
a weathered wooden finger into the ocean. On the scrub-grass bank
by the dock, canoes and kayaks rested in metal racks, their bright colors bleached by the moonlight. But one of the canoes was moving. She
made out the shadowy figure of a person—adult-sized, not a kid. Was
one of the counselors sneaking out for a paddle, or was someone stealing a canoe?

"Hey," she called, rising from the log and hurrying over, her bare
feet tender from a winter in shoes.

"What?" The voice was male, rough and challenging. It didn't
sound like one of the four male counselors', and it sure wasn't mellow-
tempered Mr. B's.

She stopped abruptly. If this was a canoe thief, she should run for
help, not challenge him. But then the guy stepped toward her and
details materialized from the darkness. A lean, muscular body in
frayed cutoffs and a tee with the sleeves ripped off; a face with bold,
striking features; hair blacker than the night sky. Recognition
locked her in place. "You're Dax Xavier." The words came out as

breathy as a puff of wind. He'd been in her twelfth grade class. The hot new bad boy who had every girl dreaming wild and crazy dreams.

His eyes widened in apparent surprise, and his gaze raked her, then a grin tilted that sexy mouth. "You're Lily Nyland."

He'd noticed her at school? Knew her name? Suddenly, she was aware of every wrinkle in the olive-drab shorts and red tee, of the loose hairs straggling from her ponytail, of her total lack of makeup.

"Camp counselor?" he asked.

She nodded.

"Figured you'd spend your summers at chess camp or finishing school." It was a taunt, yet something about the lazy, teasing way he spoke made the comment sound almost seductive.

Warmth crept through her. If she'd been Lily back home, she'd have stiffened her spine and strode up to the Broadbents' house to report him. But she was Lily at camp, and instead she tilted her head and studied him, trying to look casual and confident. "Not that I thought about how you'd spend your summers, but I suppose if I had, stealing canoes would have been right up there."

He gave a quick, low chuckle. "If I was gonna steal something, I'd pick a Ferrari, not a canoe."

"Maybe you're starting small, honing your skills."

Dax took a step closer, so their bodies almost touched. "My skills are plenty honed."

That memory had Lily, in her scented bath, opening her eyes and sitting up. Yes, Dax had proved that point over and over.

She finished the last swallow from her martini glass. Summer camp, attraction of opposites, summer love. If she read that story in a book club novel, she'd call it cliché. Maybe she and Dax should have let it go when September rolled around. And yet . . . Over the following years, they'd had such fun when they got together. She'd loved him with all her heart. And now her heart was so confused.

Did she still love him? Sometimes she was sure she did; other times, she told herself it was only nostalgia, memories, history. But was she telling herself the truth, or trying to build a shell to guard against heartbreak?

And what's wrong with self-protection?

Briskly, she lathered soap onto her bath sponge and washed herself, then climbed out of the tub, dried off, and pulled on her robe. Where was Dax? If only they could be civil until after Christmas dinner, then they would deal with the future.

She took a birth control pill, an act that these days sent a pang of regret through her. She left her glasses in their case, unable to face *Bound by Desire*.

Though her headache had eased, she was a little spacy from the potent meds, the alcohol, the steamy bath, and, maybe, the memories. Sleep, that was what she needed.

What she got, when she stepped into the bedroom, was the sight of Dax lounging on the bed, dark and virile in his jeans and tee, pillows stacked behind him. The lamp on the dresser gave the room a warm, golden light. Even though her vision was far from twenty-twenty, it was good enough that she saw how rugged and masculine he looked, sprawled across the caramel and cream-striped duvet.

A tug of arousal pulsed between Lily's legs. How annoying that, despite her doubts about their marriage and his fidelity, the man still turned her on.

Dax pushed himself off the bed and walked over, to stop a foot away. "Take off your robe."

His words, so unexpected, had the force of a command. She'd unknotted the sash and shrugged off the robe before she even paused to think. But then awareness returned and anxiety twitched her shoulders. She resisted the urge to grab the robe from the carpet and bundle herself in it again. Dax had seen her naked thousands of times. But what did he see now? She was thin, thinner than she'd ever been, but also more taut and muscled. She used exercise—weights, running, self-defense workouts—to counteract stress and tire her enough that she stood a chance of sleeping.

Dax said nothing. Instead, he bent and effortlessly scooped her up in his arms.

She gasped in surprise then her body heated at the strong, possessive clasp of his arms, pulling her tight against his broad chest. So good. But she barely had a moment to enjoy it, to wonder what he was doing.

He took three or four quick strides to the bed, then tossed her—actually tossed her—down.

A shiver of excitement rippled through her as she gaped up at him. On his last visits, Dax's sexual approaches were dispassionate. Tonight, with his commanding manner and unaccustomed beard, with her poor vision and light-headedness, he seemed a different man. "Dax, what are you doing?"

"Don't talk."

Another order. Had he said anything since she arrived home that wasn't an order? She should protest. Except . . . as she'd decided earlier, tonight she didn't want to talk.

She'd also decided she didn't want sex. But now her body urged her to reconsider. Her husband's behavior had an edge that reminded her of the bad-boy vibe of his youth, though now he was definitely a man and this edge was, well, edgier. It was arousing, and a tiny bit scary. But she'd known Dax for fifteen years. He would never hurt her, never harm a woman.

Squinting up at him, she saw a gleam in his gray eyes, but couldn't tell if it was lust or something else. The lines of his face were set, hiding his thoughts and feelings.

"On your stomach," he said.

Doggy-style sex. Disappointment brought a quick rush of moisture to her eyes and she rolled, to hide her face. He wanted sex where they couldn't see each other's faces, where kissing was impossible. Sex with no intimate connection. No, she wouldn't do it. Forcing back the tears, she tensed her body, readying herself to roll back again.

Before she could move, Dax pinned her down, planting his denim-clad knees on either side of her hips and curving his hands firmly around her shoulder caps.

She twisted her head to the side. "Let me go."

"I told you to keep quiet."

"You have no right—"

"Keep quiet." His fingertips dug into her flesh, almost punishingly hard. "I'll look after you." His touch eased and turned into massage, kneading into the tight muscles of her neck and shoulders.

Again, he'd surprised her. It felt so amazingly good, she groaned with pleasure. All this macho stuff, just to give her a massage? She couldn't remember the last time he'd tended to her aches and pains.

"Put this under you." He handed her a pillow and she shoved it under her chest so that her back arched toward him.

With controlled strength, Dax used the heels of his hands, his fingers, his thumbs, even his knuckles to work out knots. Pain made her wince, but she knew his touch was healing. She drew in a deep breath and tried not to tense against those probing fingers, but to let her muscles relax.

And yes, the knots slowly released. Her body warmed, loosened, softened. As the tension eased, she almost purred with relief and pleasure. Dax, touching her this way—what did it mean?

As he moved from her lower back to her butt cheeks, his touch gentled and became more of a caress.

A sensual, sexy caress, or at least that's how it felt to her. Arousal throbbed between her legs and quickened her breath. Her nipples tightened, pressing into the pillow beneath her. She wanted to squirm, to rub her nipples against the crisp cotton, to wriggle her hips in a wordless request that he slide his hand between her legs. But she was unsure what he intended.

When she'd been young, Dax had told her she was the most beautiful woman he'd ever seen. Now did he think her lean, lithe body was attractive? Sexy? Did he mean his touch to be erotic or was her sex-starved body overreacting?

She got her answer when his finger traced the crease between her buttocks, then slid between her legs. He traced her naked flesh slowly, igniting arousal inch by inch and making her quiver as need mounted. When he brushed her labia, spreading the moisture that slid from her body, she pressed against his hand, wanting more. Massage as foreplay. She liked it. Yes, she wanted sex with him, but face-to-face. "That feels so good, Dax."

His hand withdrew and a slap stung her butt cheeks.

"Oh!" She jerked and automatically started to turn over.

He planted both hands at her waist and held her down. "I told you to keep quiet."

What had gotten into him? Dax had never hit her before. She should yell at him, except . . . the slap hadn't been all that hard. It hadn't hurt as much as created a tingly burn that, to her embarrassment, brought a fresh gush of arousal trickling onto her inner thighs.

Dax rubbed the spot where he'd hit her, and the sensual burning sensation spread.

She almost wished he'd slap her again. Which was ridiculous.

"Roll over," he said.

Now he'd let her do it? On his terms, not hers? Though his behavior was baffling and out of character, she knew one thing: she was more turned on than she'd been in a very long time.

Four

Dax stared at his wife's shapely ass, stunned to see the flush of pink his hand had left on her pale skin. He might've had a bad-boy rep as a kid, he might be more comfortable in the bush than in the city, but despite his rough edges, he'd never imagined hitting Lily.

The only thing that shocked him more than his behavior was her response. Or, rather, lack of response. She hadn't yelled at him or leaped off the bed. Did that mean that, at some level, she really was into this dom-sub stuff? Would she obey him and roll over? If she did, what did she want from him?

Did she have another lover who did these things with her?

Fuck, no; he couldn't think that way. Tonight, there was only him and Lily. He'd challenged himself to read his wife's needs, to satisfy them, to see if the two of them could recapture the passion they'd once shared.

His cock strained against the fly of his jeans. He'd been rock hard since he'd worked his way down the slim lines of her back, digging knots out of her muscles. Such a contrast, her delicate, feminine shape and silky skin with those tough, lean muscles. She'd been working out. For herself, or for a lover?

No! Don't go there. Concentrate on her, on the two of us.

The distinctive musky odor of her arousal made his nostrils flare with primal need. Dax wanted nothing more than to drive into her, to claim her. To claim this fiercely independent, controlled woman who was his wife.

She pushed up on one elbow and tugged the pillow out from under her chest.

What could he do next, to play this dominant role without hurting her?

He rose and strode to the closet. Wooden pegs held her scarves, ranging from featherlight silk to soft wool, all in the muted shades she preferred. He grabbed four long, silky ones.

Lily was on her back now, settling the pillow under her head. A rosy blush colored her cheeks and the top of her chest, staining the upper curve of her small, firm breasts. Her feathery brown lashes were lowered so he couldn't see her eyes, but he knew she watched his every move. The room, with the closed curtains and golden lamplight, seemed like an oasis cut off from the busy city. A place where he and Lily could do anything they chose to, and no one need ever know.

He grabbed one of her wrists, lifted it to a bedpost behind her head, and secured it with a scarf. Her arm was stretched out, but not to full extension so that it'd be too uncomfortable.

Her eyes flared open. "What are you doing?"

"I didn't say you could speak." He captured her other wrist, though she struggled to evade him. When he'd tied it to a bedpost on the other side of the bed, he went for an ankle.

She twisted her body and kicked out, landing one bruising blow on his forearm. He won the battle and tied both of her feet. Now she lay spread-eagled on the bed. She tugged against the scarves, testing them.

He stood back and studied her.

She glared up at him, her light blue eyes dazzlingly bright, her cheeks rosy. He read shock, outrage, but also arousal. God, but she was beautiful. Gone now were the lines of tiredness and strain he'd seen when she arrived home.

In the past, when he'd commented that she looked tired and tried to be considerate, she'd snapped his head off. But tonight, his take-charge approach had relaxed her, and turned her on.

"Dax, what's going on?"

He wondered the same thing himself. Instead of answering, he cast his gaze with slow deliberation down her body, to stop at the vee of her spread legs. His cock jerked painfully against the distended fly of his jeans. Seeing her opened wide for him, powerless to close her legs, was amazing. Her swollen folds, a rich, deep pink, gleamed with her juices and her clit was engorged.

He raised his gaze to Lily's face. "Have I done anything you didn't like?"

Her eyes widened, the outrage winning out. "You tied me up, for God's sakes! You hit me!"

"Slapped you once. And it turned you on. Look at you." He leaned over the bed and slowly swiped his finger across her slick folds. Then he held it up and, because he couldn't resist, slid it into his mouth. He loved the taste of her, so musky and earthy compared to the crisp, tailored way she presented herself.

She moaned and now it was pure sexual heat he saw in her eyes.

He was about to ask if she trusted him, but a dom would make it a command. "Trust me."

Her throat rippled as she swallowed.

Did she trust him? He had never hurt her, not physically, but he hadn't contributed a hell of a lot to this marriage. Not that he'd ever sensed that she really wanted him to. Her life was neater and tidier without him. "Trust me with your body," he amended. "With your pleasure."

Slowly, maybe reluctantly, she nodded. "But if—" she started.

If she was into dom-sub stuff, she had to know by now where he was going with this. "One of the rules is, you don't talk. You're in my hands. There's only one word you can say. Your safe word. If you say it, I stop, untie you, leave you alone."

He read the uncertainty on her face. "What word?" she whispered.

"Your choice, Lily."

A pause. Then, softly, "Skookumchuck."

What did it mean that she'd chosen that name of the place where they'd first met, had sex, fallen in love? "Fine. If you say 'Skookumchuck,' I stop. If you say anything else, you'll be punished."

Her mouth opened on a protest or a question, then slowly closed.

Did she, like Cassandra in *Bound by Desire*, find the idea of punishment titillating? The idea that pain might give Lily pleasure—and that in fifteen years he'd never known—disturbed him. It wasn't in him to give her more than a light slap or pinch—and to fuck her with all the pent-up need in his body.

To relieve the pressure against his cock, he stripped off his jeans, and then added his boxer briefs and tee to the pile on the carpet.

Lily stared at him and the tip of her tongue came out to lick her lips.

His cock pulsed and Dax forced back a groan. It had been a couple months since he'd had sex—other than with his own hand—and he longed to bury his aching hard-on either between her pink lips or deep in her hot, wet pussy. But he'd damned well give her a climax first, or maybe even two.

He'd learned Lily's body years ago. Learned her triggers, as she'd learned his. On a bad day, he could make her come in five minutes flat. And today, with her steamy wet already, was definitely not a bad day.

But now . . . His wife lay naked and vulnerable, trusting him with her body. Trusting him to give her the pleasure he'd promised. And, just as when he'd massaged her, he wanted to do it. Not fast and hard, the way his body urged him to, the way she no doubt expected. Not doing the same old stuff he normally did. And not through pain.

So far tonight, he'd surprised her. And she was hot for him. He wanted to keep surprising her, and he wanted to make love through slow, lazy, sensual torture—torture that was pleasure, not pain.

Dax knelt at the foot of the bed and circled his hand around her right ankle where the silk scarf wrapped it. Gripping her firmly, he bent to kiss the top of her foot. Lily's feet were strong and smooth, the nails—like her fingernails—unpainted and clipped short. Neat, elegant feet, just like the rest of her.

He tongued soft flesh that smelled like a summer garden, massaged her sole, and, impulsively, sucked her big toe into his mouth.

She gave a breathy gasp.

He worked that toe the way he liked her to work his cock, giving it his all: sucking hard then easing off, giving firm, swirling swipes with his tongue, scraping the edges of his teeth over sensitive flesh. His penis throbbed and leaked drops of come.

Taking his time, he moved from her foot up her leg, stroking, massaging lightly, kissing and licking. Reading her reaction. She didn't like him lingering on her kneecap, but moaned when he caressed the back of her knee. And, as he moved up her thigh, her muscles quivered.

The sultry odor of arousal mingled with the lavender from her bath as he licked moisture from her inner thigh. He swiped his tongue across her pussy lips, and more drops slipped from her body.

If he licked firmly, pumped three fingers into her, and sucked her clit, she'd come.

So he didn't. He poked his tongue inside her, circled, then withdrew. Laved her with two long swipes then retreated. Flicked her clit lightly, enough to tease but not give her the pressure she needed.

She panted and her hips lifted, pushing her pussy toward his face in a silent request.

He slid two fingers inside her, then a third, pumped rhythmically, but avoided touching her clit.

"Dax," she moaned. "Please. I need to come." Her head thrashed on the pillow.

He pulled his fingers out of her and sat back on his heels. "You spoke." This was easy punishment—not giving her the orgasm her body craved. "I'm in charge. Trust me to give you what you need."

Her eyes flashed pale blue fire. "I need to come."

Like she was the only one? He fought back a grin and played tough. "There's only one word I'll listen to from you. Are you ready to say it?"

She groaned, turned her head to the side, closed her eyes.

"Good." He resumed teasing her with caresses that were almost, but not quite, enough to take her over the edge. Each time her body tensed, telling him she was at the peak and it would only take one more touch for her to climax, he pulled back.

She groaned in frustration, twisted her hips, but didn't speak.

"That's right, Lily. You're obeying the rule and you deserve a reward."

He thrust his fingers deep and hard, pressed her sweet spot. "Come now," he commanded, then sucked her sensitive clit.

Her body spasmed against his fingers and mouth. She cried out, something wordless and wild.

Dax's self-control shattered along with her body. He reached into the drawer in his bedside table, found a condom package, and sheathed himself. Lily was still trembling with the aftershocks of orgasm when he drove into her in one long, forceful thrust.

She cried out again, and tugged against the scarves that restrained her.

"Don't," he grated out. "Stay still."

Her eyes squeezed shut as if to disavow knowledge of what they were doing. Bright pink patches blazed on her chest and cheeks. Her short blond hair, normally so neat and stylish, stuck up every which way as her head thrashed on the pillow.

Normally, she'd wrap her arms and legs around him and cling as their bodies took up a familiar rhythm. It felt strange to have her spread wide and open, unable to touch him, but she wasn't motionless. She lifted her pelvis as far as she could, pressing up against him as he plunged in and out of her.

She gave panting gasps, a counterpoint to Dax's guttural, animal-like sounds.

Fuck, she was hot. Lily hadn't been this hot in . . . he couldn't remember when. Nor had he.

Torturing her and delaying her release had been torture for him too, and he couldn't hold out much longer. His balls were tight; the desperate need to come burned at the base of his spine. Knowing how sensitive her clit would be now, he reached down to press it. Her body convulsed, then release crashed through Dax in a wave of pleasure so extreme it almost hurt. Dimly, he was aware of Lily crying out again, of her body's spasms matching his jerky thrusts.

His heart pounded so frantically it might burst out of his chest as he struggled to draw air into his lungs.

Gradually, his breathing slowed. Clumsily, his legs and arms rubbery, he lifted himself off Lily's body and headed to the bathroom to deal with the condom. The mirror showed a wild man: cheeks with a hectic flush, hair even messier than Lily's, beard glistening with her juices.

When he returned to the bedroom, she slanted him a quick glance through lowered lashes. She didn't say a word, but tugged gently at one of the scarves.

His wife, the strongest, most tough-minded woman he knew,

was tied to the bed. She'd opted in. Dax felt powerful and macho like that wild man in the bathroom mirror, but also, he realized, vulnerable. Being in control meant he was solely responsible for her pleasure. He risked failure if he didn't read her signals correctly.

In the book, Neville thought he understood Cassandra's deepest desires better than she did herself. How the hell did a man do that?

Five

Dax was—almost—a bad-boy stranger again, this sexy, powerful naked man with his disheveled hair and dark beard who stood watching her. Without her contact lenses, his face was slightly out of focus, but she had the sense of a hawk studying its prey. How appropriate that Kim had chosen a stylized hawk for his shirt.

Tonight reminded Lily of that first summer. Dax had been sexually experienced and confident, while she was a nervous, inhibited virgin. The way he'd made her feel, the things she'd learned from him . . . It had been a whole new world. And now, again, he'd taught her things she'd never suspected about herself. She'd always found the idea of dominance and submission repellent, yet this sex play turned her on. A lot.

He'd bossed her around, spanked her, tied her up, teased and toyed with her—and given her mind-blowing orgasms that left her weak and quivering. It had been almost surreal to not be able to move or speak. To put her pleasure in his hands. To know she could stop him with one word, yet to choose not to.

When Dax had asked her to provide a safe word, her memories of their first meeting were so fresh that "Skookumchuck" had leaped to her lips. She'd seen the flash of surprise on his face.

Now, as he stared down at her, she was grateful he'd told her not to speak. What would she say? Though what she most craved from her husband was an intimate connection, she'd opted into something very different. But at least, for once, he was seeing her; all his attention and passion focused on her. Though she had to wonder about this change in him. Had he always craved this kind of sex, or had a new lover show him this side of himself?

If only he'd untie her, she could roll over and feign sleep. She gave a second tug at the silk scarves that bound her wrists. The knots had tightened when she'd wriggled and thrashed. Surely now he'd take the hint and untie her.

"Yeah, I know you're tied up," he told her. "And you'll stay that way."

What? Her eyes flicked open wide and she frowned.

"I'm not done with you yet."

Her breath hitched with anxiety—and, yes, curiosity.

She could say "Skookumchuck" and he'd stop. Despite his out-of-character behavior, she knew he wouldn't force himself on her. Yet he seemed determined to push her out of her comfort zone. And damn it, her body responded. Her mind wasn't convinced, but the ripple of heat pulsing through her was undeniable.

Dax caught her left ankle. His hand was strong and warm, his grip firm, even possessive. Oh God, was he going to inflict the same erotic torture on her left leg too?

Yes, he was. When he sucked her toe and his teeth scraped her skin, her body, which hadn't stopped trembling from that first bone-rattling orgasm, shuddered. Heat flashed up her leg, drenched her pussy anew, had her biting her lip to hold back a moan of pleasure.

And that was just her toe.

She squeezed her eyes shut, not wanting to see the familiar bedroom, longing only to lose herself in this utterly sensual experience. People talked about "out-of-body" experiences. Well, she wanted an "out-of-mind" one. She didn't want to think, to worry, about what this meant.

He worked his slow, tortuous way to her inner thigh, the calluses on his fingers and the curls of his beard making each kiss, lick, and nip even more erotic. Her body twisted with need. When his tongue explored her labia and clit, tightening the coil of arousal yet not pressing firmly enough to offer release, she held back her protest. If she complained or demanded, he'd stop touching her, keep her hovering on the brink even longer.

Although there was something to be said for the hovering. That first orgasm was one of the most powerful she'd ever experienced. Mind you, the second one, coming fast and hard, was spectacular too.

She wasn't sure she could withstand a third. And yet Dax left her no choice as his tongue, lips, and fingers played her skillfully. Shuddering, she exploded against his face.

He moved up her body, trailing kisses across her belly, her ribs. Finally, he reached her breasts. Her nipples were so tight and hard, they ached when his thumbs brushed across them and when he pinched them gently. But it was a good ache, the kind that resonated deep in her sex.

Her skin was hyperalert to every brush of his body: his lightly haired leg against her knee, the hard thrust of his cock—yes, he was erect again—against her thigh. Her sex was swollen, achy, needy. Despite three orgasms, she wanted him inside her.

The boldness of the way he'd commanded her contrasted so dramatically with the subtle way he treated her body. Now, exploring her chest, he didn't just suck on her nipples, one of her most sensitive erogenous zones. He moved on to kiss her collarbone, her exposed armpits, the place where her shoulders met her neck. They weren't the standard erogenous zones, yet he brought them to humming, tingling life.

He returned to her breasts and took a pebble-hard nipple gently between his teeth, and sensation echoed in her vagina. He sucked, licked, then moved to her other breast and did the same thing.

She whimpered, her hips twisting against the rumpled sheet. Her core clenched, shuddered, and a rippling wave of orgasm made her gasp with pleasure. Oh my, she'd never come that way before.

Dax moved quickly down the bed, then his mouth was on her clit, his fingers buried deep inside her, catching the fading spasms of that orgasm and building the tension again. Taking her higher until, whimpering helplessly, she broke again and came hard.

He rose above her, so handsome, so powerful. She squinted to see him more clearly. His glossy black hair was tousled, his strong cheekbones burned with color, his eyes blazed silvery-gray. His cock rose full and hard up against his belly. So swollen, so big.

When he reached for a condom and sheathed himself, she couldn't imagine her exhausted body surviving intercourse. A whimper of protest escaped her lips.

Dax stopped, one hand at the base of his shaft where he'd rolled the ring of the condom down. "Too much? Say the word and I'll stop."

He would. She believed him.

She might be tied to the bed, but she could control this strong, aroused man with a single word. Knowing that, she realized she didn't want to stop him. She wanted her husband inside her.

For the first time tonight she saw, simply, the man she'd fallen in love with and married. Her doubts about their marriage, her fear that he'd been unfaithful, her confusion over his odd behavior and her strange response—they all dropped away. She smiled at him.

His intense expression lightened and warmed. "Lily."

To her surprise, he untied the knots securing her feet to the bedposts, and then did the same with her hands. As she shook out her legs and arms, easing the strain from being bound, he turned off the lamp on the dresser and the room went dark.

A moment later, he was on the bed again, between her legs. Enjoying her newfound freedom of movement, she bent her knees, the insides of her legs brushing the outsides of his.

He slid a pillow under her, relieving a slight ache in her lower back, and then his fingers stroked between her legs. The head of his cock nudged her, but this time, rather than plunge inside, he eased in slowly.

Slick and sensitive, she clung to him and pulsed around him, welcoming him, wanting all he could give her.

Once he was fully seated, he leaned forward, his firm chest brushing her taut nipples. Resting one arm on the bed beside her shoulder to take his weight, he touched her face gently, smoothing damp, messy hair back from her flushed skin. His fingers bore the musky scent of sex.

After being restrained, it felt odd to lift her arms and curl them around his broad shoulders. So familiar, this male body. So wonderful. If only she knew the man inside half as well.

Was she allowed to speak now? It didn't matter. She had no idea what to say. Words would only complicate things.

He didn't speak either. His cock was embedded deep in her channel, but he didn't thrust. Instead, his lips brushed hers.

She'd always loved kissing Dax. Now she kissed him back lazily, too worn out to be energetic. He'd never had a beard before, and she enjoyed the brush of springy curls against her chin.

His lips caressed hers, his tongue teased their fullness, and then, after long minutes, he dipped inside.

Her tongue met his, and only then did his hips pump. He thrust in and out in the tiniest movements. His penis was so swollen that it filled her completely, and each thrust created a delicious warm burn.

Normally, she'd have wrapped her legs around him, taking him even deeper and speeding things up, but her leg muscles trembled and she couldn't even keep her knees raised. Slowly, her legs collapsed down on the bed.

Dax tugged the pillow out. His thrusts quickened, lengthened.

Even though Lily was no longer tied up, the exhaustion in her muscles kept her from moving much.

But she didn't need to. Dax slowly, gently, but relentlessly drove her toward climax. A tight, trembling coil of arousal built, deep in her core.

His back was so hot, rigid with tensile strength under her hands. How familiar it was to hold him like this as their bodies moved together. It was like the old days, when their love had been strong and sure.

He'd stopped kissing her and his breath came in rasping pants. He reached down between their bodies, as he always did when he was close to climax and wanted to ensure she came with him.

Her clit was so sensitive that, at the first brush of his fingers, she gave a soft gasp of pain.

With a barely there touch, he spread the moisture of her arousal on her clit, circling that achy bud, making her whimper with pleasure.

He pumped faster, his caution and control vanishing as he thrust vigorously, driving into her core.

And now, exhausted or not, she had to move, to cling and meet his thrusts.

He yelled, "Fuck, Lily," and exploded in a series of violent jerks that shattered the tension inside her.

Crying out, she broke in waves of orgasm so intense they were both pleasure and pain.

Their bodies shuddered together, and he slowly collapsed on top of her. They lay together, damp and heaving. Neither said a word.

After a few minutes, Dax rose and went to the bathroom.

Lily didn't have the strength to sit up and reach for the covers. She curled onto her side in her normal sleeping position. It was the only normal thing about this night.

While they'd been having sex, she'd let herself be caught in the sensations and tried to turn off her mind. Now she was too exhausted to think straight. What did all of this mean? He'd massaged her, sucked her toes, given her incredible orgasms. He'd spanked her and tied her up; he'd untied her, kissed her, and it had felt like they were truly making love. Was tonight a step toward rediscovering intimacy? Or was it a sex game, maybe something Dax had learned from another woman?

The bed shifted under his weight. He raised the covers, tucked them around her, lay down on his side of the bed.

She lay still in the darkness in a warm nest of covers. Did he think she was asleep? She almost was, her body heavy and limp, her breathing slow, her mind craving oblivion.

He shifted onto his side and moved closer. She smelled his familiar scent, a fresh, outdoorsy one that now mingled with her lavender and their sweaty, earthy sex.

They always used to drift off to sleep spooned together.

Without her consciously intending to do it, she inched back toward him.

He moved forward until his front curved around her back. His arm came around her waist.

Like the old days. The good days. Drifting to sleep like this had made her feel so secure. So loved.

Now she didn't know how she felt about Dax, or how he felt about her. Was this the last night they'd fall asleep like this? She had told herself she was prepared for their marriage to break up, but that was before he'd come home. Before he'd kissed her and made love to her as if he meant it. Now she was more confused than ever.

Dax's hand brushed hers.

She didn't move. Except for the tears that tracked silently down her cheeks.

* * *

ily struggled slowly from sleep. She felt almost as if she'd been drugged, and every single muscle ached, like she'd—

Lying on her side, she tensed, remembering, and bit her lip. What had she been thinking? What had they been doing? What did it mean for their marriage?

From behind her came a rustle as Dax shifted position. Was he awake? Hardly breathing, she held still.

It was Christmas morning. The alarm clock on her bedside table read seven o'clock, an hour and a half later than she usually got up. She and Dax were expected at her parents' house at one.

They needed to talk. But not until they got through Christmas dinner.

He hadn't moved again, so with any luck he was still asleep, as exhausted as she was. If only he'd stay asleep until it was time to shower and leave. But Dax was normally an early riser too.

Defer and avoid. She'd choose that strategy for a few more hours. Cautiously, she inched out of bed, and he didn't stir. Though she desperately craved a shower, best to do it at the clinic. The place would be deserted today. She could work, think. Maybe go for a run first.

In the walk-in closet, she slipped into her running clothes and packed a change of clothes in her gym bag, then she tiptoed through the silent bedroom. She made a quick stop in the kitchen to write a note.

Gone to the clinic. Back by twelve.

She paused, gripping the pen tightly. Dax would go to her parents' with her, wouldn't he, rather than force her to make some awkward explanation? He hated those formal meals with her folks grilling both of them, but they always went. This year was different, though. Their marriage might be ending. Last night's sex only emphasized that things weren't the same between them. After deliberation, she added:

We'll need to leave for my parents' at 12:30.

Six

A sound woke Dax. He came to alertness quickly, as always, and took inventory. He was at the condo, alone in bed. It was Christmas morning. And Christmas Eve had been pretty damned wild.

It had turned him on, being with Lily like that—less for the physical acts like slapping her ass and tying her up as for the fact that she'd given herself over to him. She'd let him take charge of her pleasure, and he'd brought her to climax again and again. The last time, with her untied, it had felt like real lovemaking, not just sex. They'd fallen asleep spooned together the way they used to.

He crossed his arms over his chest and grinned smugly. His strategy was working. No, he wasn't dumb enough to think that one night had solved their problems, but it was a step forward.

Where was his sexy wife? Making coffee? He sure could use a cup. Then he intended to pull her back into bed. Whistling, he got up, put on a pair of boxer briefs, and headed for the kitchen.

No Lily. No coffee. A note.

His whistle died. "Crap." Christmas morning, after great sex, and she'd blown him off for work? And still expected him to endure the torture of turkey dinner with her family? What the fuck was that all about?

Had she ditched him to be with a lover on Christmas morning? Suspicion churned in his gut and he no longer craved coffee.

Outside the window, the sky was gray and cloudy—rain clouds, not snow. Too bad for all the kids who hoped for snowmen and snowball fights on Christmas Day.

He and Lily'd done that, one Christmas in Moose Jaw and another one in Vancouver when the city had, for once, delivered a white Christmas. Used to be, on Christmas morning, they'd make love, have a leisurely breakfast, exchange gifts. Go for a walk until their cheeks and noses were rosy, then come home and warm up in bed before they headed off for the stressful meal.

What would he do with this long, gray morning?

If they'd bought a house with a big yard, the way he'd wanted, he'd have plenty to keep him busy. As it was, when he was in Vancouver he had shit-all to do. Other guys who worked in the bush talked about coming home to long "honey do" lists, but the condo didn't generate much of that stuff, and Lily handled it herself. So, because she was always at work these days, he tried to pick up day work flying. This trip, with the mining camp shut down until January second, Dax would be flying with a company that offered scenic helicopter flights out of Vancouver Harbor, but the job didn't start until tomorrow.

He drummed his fingers on the windowsill and wondered what Lily was doing. And with whom.

"Oh, hell." He went to get his smartphone, and dialed her number. If she was with some other guy, she wouldn't answer.

"Dax?"

"Where are you?"

"At the clinic, dumping my stuff. I'm heading out for a run, then I'll do some work." She sounded a little stiff.

Was running a euphemism for hooking up with some guy? Maybe not; he'd seen how toned she'd become. "You've taken up running?"

"I've been running for over a year."

She knew he ran, but had never suggested they do it together. Not even on Christmas morning. Still, he was beginning to believe she really did plan to run and work, not hook up with some other guy. "You never told me."

"You never—" She broke off. "Why are you calling? Please don't say you don't want to go to Christmas dinner."

He snorted. "Want? I never want to go. You know that."

"It's only a couple of hours." She paused, and her voice softened. "I know it's a drag, but it would mean a lot to me if you went."

It would've meant a lot to him if he'd found her beside him in bed when he woke up. But guys didn't say shit like that. "I'll go," he agreed grudgingly.

"Thank you, Dax."

He gripped the phone, wishing things were the way they used to be. "Merry Christmas, Lily," he said slowly.

She didn't respond for a moment, then said, "Merry Christmas, Dax." Was that regret he heard?

He ended the call and stood there, holding the phone. Regret. Yeah, he felt that. So much regret for so many things. Then resolve stiffened his spine and he tossed the phone onto the unmade bed. Last night had given him hope. He wouldn't let go of that.

After they survived the afternoon meal, he and Lily'd be alone again. This time, he wouldn't let her escape to the clinic; he'd take her back to bed and give her another reminder of how good the two of them could be together.

After a light breakfast, a long run, a workout, and a shower, Dax dressed in the kind of clothes he hadn't worn in months. He'd long ago settled the suit issue—as in, no fucking way was he wearing a suit and tie except to a wedding or funeral—so instead he wore black dress pants, polished black shoes, and one of the handful of fancy shirts Lily had given him over the years. This one was silvery gray.

He retrieved a small, gift-wrapped box from a pocket of his duffel: Lily's present, ordered online from a First Nations arts and crafts store. The stylized hummingbird pendant, hung from a gold chain, was made of silver and gold. It matched, best as he could tell, earrings he'd given her last year. They'd never been extravagant about gifts; neither of them was extravagant by nature. When they'd been students, they said that being together was gift enough. He shoved the box in his pants pocket. Was there any hope they'd ever feel that way again?

She should be home soon. Looking out the living room window, he saw that the clouds had indeed delivered rain, a hard, driving one. A bone-thin male jogger sloshed past; an elderly couple shared a large umbrella as they walked a white terrier in a plaid jacket; a woman in a camel-colored coat turned onto the street and walked toward him.

Though her umbrella was angled toward the rain, hiding her head, he recognized Lily's coat and her determined stride. The umbrella, though, was a surprise. It made him think of an owl: subtle camouflage colors and bold, startling eyes. Fanciful, like that beautiful shirt in her closet. Definitely not her usual tailored, understated style. More in keeping with the young Lily—or the uninhibited woman he'd made love with last night. Remembering her wildly tousled hair and flushed cheeks, the way her body had twisted against him then shattered in release, his cock swelled.

She didn't look up as she stepped into the entryway of the building. A few minutes later, the front door opened. He went to meet her.

"Hi, Dax." Her striking blue eyes searched his face, but before he could kiss her, she was in brisk motion. She dumped her gym bag on the floor, stuffed her umbrella in the stand, took off her coat, and crossed her arms over her chest. "Good, you're already dressed. I'll go get changed."

"You look great." Perfect, to his mind, in jeans and a tan sweater. Perfect for some lazy cuddling in front of the fire, then some shedding of clothes in a trail all the way to the bedroom.

She frowned. "I can't wear jeans to Christmas dinner."

"I didn't mean that. Only that you look good."

"Oh. Well, thanks." Her surprised tone made him wonder when he'd last told her that.

Again he started to reach for her, but she'd bent to heft her gym bag. It knocked against the umbrella stand, toppling it and spilling the wet umbrella.

He put things to rights. "I saw your umbrella from the window. Nice. It looks like an owl's eyes."

"It's based on the polyphemus moth. When the moth's wings are closed you don't see them, but when it spreads its wings, the false owl eyes scare off predators."

"Huh. Interesting. I didn't know you were into moths." Or fanciful designs.

She gave a quick head shake, her short hair, the pale gold of wheat at harvest time, flicking. "A friend is starting an umbrella-making company. Each design is based on a butterfly, bird, or some other winged creature. She includes a tag with a picture of the bird or insect, and a bit about it."

"Smart idea."

"Yes. And, speaking of Kim . . ." She gazed up at him, looking uncertain, then swallowed. "I have a small Christmas present for you."

"I have one for you."

"Oh. Really? I wasn't sure, but—" She shook her head. "We'll talk later. Let's exchange gifts before we go to my parents'."

Talk later? What did that mean? Talk about last night's sex? Or about the state of their marriage? It had been a long time since they'd talked about anything significant.

At camp that first summer, Lily was the first person he'd ever really talked to. She'd said the same about him. Yes, there'd been lots of sex, but they'd also drifted in a canoe on the moonlit ocean and stared into the red and yellow flames of a beach fire, opening their hearts to each other. But for her, he'd have ended up in jail like his dad or, at best, been a beer-bellied laborer who spent his free time hanging out with his buddies at a bar watching sports on a big-screen TV. Instead, he flew helicopters in some of the most spectacular, challenging country in the world.

Career-wise, he'd done great. When it came to their marriage, though . . . Yeah, they needed to talk.

Lily was walking toward the office, so he followed. From a desk drawer, she took a flattish rectangular box wrapped in silver and gold paper. Another shirt, he guessed. He'd swap the silver one for the new one.

He reached into his pocket for the small box. "Here's yours."

They swapped gifts and then he said, "Merry Christmas, Lily."

Her pale eyes softened and for a moment he saw the old Lily, the love they had shared. "You too, Dax."

Not about to lose this moment, he put the parcel down, took her fine-boned face between his hands, and tilted it up as he leaned down. His lips touched hers, still cool from being outside. For a long moment, she didn't respond as he kissed her, but then her lips softened and moved against his. Though his cock stirred again, he didn't attempt to slip his tongue into her mouth, just kept things gentle. Last night, he'd reminded her of the lust and passion they could share. This, now, was about something more tender. Love, maybe. If they might still share that.

Her eyes, normally so clear and incisive, went misty. Or was he imagining things? She blinked and was sharp-eyed again. Easing away, she said briskly, "Let's open the presents. We don't want to be late."

He held back the retort that he didn't want to go at all. "You go first." At least she'd returned his kiss. It was another step forward.

She carefully untied the ribbon and removed the wrapping paper. "Jewelry?" When she opened the box, a smile lit her face. "Oh, Dax, it's lovely. It matches the earrings you gave me." Holding the box in one hand, she put the other hand on his shoulder and stretched up to press a quick kiss on his cheek. "I love it."

"Good." How easy for her, to say she loved a pendant. When was the last time she'd said she loved him? When was the last time he'd told her that? How had things become so damned complicated?

As he mused, he unwrapped the gift she'd given him. A shirt box, as he'd expected. He lifted the top off and— "Wow!" His eyes widened and he removed the garment. Not a shirt, but a soft cotton tee. Charcoal gray with a painted design done mostly in black. The abstract design made him think of hawks, of the wild, free spirit of nature. "This is great, Lily."

She smiled. "Thank Kim, the artist. The umbrella woman does clothing as a hobby, and for friends. I told her a few things about you, and this is what she came up with."

"You mean it's not, uh, off the shelf? It's unique?"

"As unique as you are." A shadow flickered in her eyes and she turned away. "I need to hurry. I'll be ready in fifteen minutes."

As she walked out of the office, he joked, "Guess you won't let me wear the tee to your folks' place."

One word came back over her shoulder. "Hah."

Boring tailored suits and ties fit her parents' world; abstract art that touched the soul didn't. He draped the tee over the back of his office chair, looking forward to changing into it later.

With a little time to kill, he powered up his netbook and checked e-mail. He answered holiday greetings from a few guys he'd worked with, a fisherman he'd airlifted from a life raft in a storm, and a family he'd evacuated when a forest fire changed course and headed for their cabin.

"Dax? I'm ready?" she said from the doorway.

He turned to see his wife in a cream-colored dress and tan pumps. He'd always liked that dress. The simple lines and lightweight wool showed off her slim curves. She was wearing the hummingbird pendant and earrings, which brightened the outfit and drew attention to her pretty face. "You look nice, Lily." He might wish she'd sometimes wear brighter colors and more sexy clothes, but she did always look great. Elegant. Way too good for a guy like him.

"Oh Dax, you've seen this dress before."

"And you always look good in it." She wasn't big on shopping, saying she'd rather buy a few classic items she could wear for years. It was kind of odd, considering she'd inherited a fortune from her grandmother as a teen, but Lily'd never been big on spending that money. She hadn't been big on telling him about it either, he remembered bitterly. She'd kept it a secret until after they were married, making him feel like she didn't trust him.

Stifling that old resentment, he shut down his netbook and went to join her.

"You look good too." Her gaze scanned him, she nodded, and then she picked up a zipped leather tote.

"Aldonza's port?" Aldonza, a wonderful woman from Portugal, was the Nylands' longtime housekeeper. She lived in an apartment on the third—top—floor and ran the place, with the assistance of a maid and gardener who came in regularly. She also did the grocery shopping and often cooked dinner. She'd been widowed at a young age, had no children, and had never remarried, though she did have a number of friends in Vancouver. Aldonza enjoyed port, and each year Dax and Lily gave her an expensive bottle of it.

He took the bag from Lily, surprised at its weight. "There's more than port in here."

"Presents."

"Huh?" Her parents had never done a gift exchange. Instead, they encouraged everyone to donate to a charitable organization, preferably health-related. He respected that, and it sure made things easier.

"For Sophia." Humor lit Lily's eyes. "A baby doesn't understand about materialism, conspicuous consumption, and the shallowness of Christmas gift-giving."

He grinned. "Yeah, your parents' beliefs may work for grown-ups, but not for kids. How old is Sophia now? Four or five months?" He'd been home once since Lily's niece was born, but hadn't seen her yet.

"Almost five. And utterly adorable."

"You see much of her?" he asked as they headed toward the front door. Lily and her brother Anthony had an iffy relationship, more competitive than supportive.

"I do some babysitting." She took her coat from the front closet, and handed him his jacket.

"You always did like kids." Once, she'd said she and Dax should have at least two, but she'd clearly changed her mind over the years. She hadn't mentioned kids since . . . he couldn't even remember, and she was so diligent about birth control. He'd seen how her medical clinic had become the focus of her energy and emotion, the way she'd once thought kids would. Yeah, people changed. What had he been think-ing, as a teen, that he might be dad material? Crazy. With his family background and the lifestyle he chose, he wasn't cut out for parenting.

She straightened from zipping her boots and shot him a rather strange look. "I love kids." She tucked her pumps into a plastic bag, then into the tote.

"Yeah, kids are cool." And they deserved excellent, committed parents, not dysfunctional ones like his or overbearing ones like hers.

On the way out the door, he collected the moth umbrella. They rode the elevator to the basement parking garage. Their silver Lexus had been purchased secondhand and chosen for its reliability. Lily only drove it once or twice a month. As always when they were together, Dax climbed into the driver's seat. It was an old joke, that he always had to be the pilot.

The radio was set to CBC. The announcer was giving the local news as Dax pulled out of the underground parking and headed toward Broadway, windshield wipers working hard. Lily's parents had a ritzy house in Dunbar-Southlands, the same upscale area where his mother's parents—who he hadn't seen since they booted him out in the spring of twelfth grade—lived. It was a ten to fifteen minute drive.

As he turned left on Arbutus, he remembered he owed Lily an in-person apology. "I'm sorry I didn't get home on Thursday."

She glanced at him. "You said something came up at work?" There was an odd edge to her voice.

"I swapped schedules with someone."

"What do you mean? Why?"

He clicked off the radio. "I was supposed to fly some of the crew out on Wednesday and Thursday, finishing up here myself after the last flight. Another pilot, Billy, was going to bring the rest out on Friday and Saturday. But his sister was in a serious accident, and he wanted to be with her."

"Really? That's too bad. How's she doing?"

He shrugged. "Haven't heard. Hope she's okay."

"Right." Her voice still sounded strange.

"I'm sorry if you're pissed off. I figured you'd be working anyhow, so it wasn't a big deal."

"It's not a big deal if you swap shifts with someone who has a family emergency. But it seems a little odd that you didn't find out how Billy's sister is doing. What's her name anyhow?"

"Uh, I don't know. Mary? Marion? Something like that." He glanced over. "Why?"

She shook her head.

Was he supposed to read her mind? "What is it?"

"So you spent the last two days flying people from the mining camp home for the holidays?"

"Isn't that what I just said?"

"Is it?"

Exasperated, he said, "What's your problem?"

"There's no problem, if that's what you really were doing," she snapped.

"What else would I be doing?"

"Hanging out somewhere else?" Then she slapped her hand over her mouth. "No, forget I said that. We'll talk later."

Talk about what? "Wait a minute. What are you saying?"

"This isn't the time."

"What do you mean about hanging out somewhere else? Where else would I be?"

"Okay, fine!" She stared at him, eyes huge, looking nervous but determined. "Is there another woman?"

His mouth fell open. "Of course not!" Anger and hurt flooded through him, clenching his gut. He yanked the car into a parking spot along the curb, shut off the engine, and glared at her. "Shit, Lily, you think I'd cheat on you?"

"I wondered." Her lips trembled. "You really haven't?"

"Never. I wouldn't. If we're together, we're faithful." Then, thinking of his suspicions about her, he said, "Right?"

She nodded.

That wasn't good enough. He needed words. "Tell me you've never cheated on me."

"Dax! I wouldn't. Never." The shock on her face attested to the truth of her words. Then her eyes narrowed. "Why did you need to ask?"

"You made me wear condoms. You said you had to go off the pill, but there's other kinds of birth control. People wear condoms for protection." And then it hit him. "You were protecting yourself because you thought I was screwing someone else."

She nodded. "I never went off the pill."

"You lied to me." He dragged a hand across his bearded jaw as it sank in. "Jeez, Lily, I never thought you'd lie to me."

"I'm sorry. I just . . . I don't know. I didn't have the guts to ask. If you were, I wasn't ready to know about it."

"Fuck." He thumped the side of his hand against the steering wheel.

"You never asked me either."

He shook his head. "Same reason, I guess. Didn't know how I'd deal with it. Crap, we're messed up."

Huge, sad eyes studied him. "Is there any trust left between us, Dax?"

He swallowed. "I don't know. Guess we'll have to figure that out."

"I didn't mean to have this talk now."

"We have to talk about this shit, Lily. It's killing our marriage, keeping secrets."

"I know that," she snapped. "I meant to do it later. After Christmas dinner. I didn't want all"—she waved her hand in jerky circles—"*this* hanging in the air. And speaking of dinner, we need to get going."

He slammed his hand down on the steering wheel.

"Dax?"

"Whatever." He started the car again. He ought to be used to finishing a distant second. His parents had been wrapped up in themselves, each other, and their druggy little world. With Lily, her work came first. Her parents came first. Where the hell did he fit? Did he even want to fit anymore?

They drove in silence for a few minutes. Then she touched his thigh, running her hand over the black wool of his pants. "Dax? We've started to talk. To be honest. That's a good thing. When we get back home this afternoon, we'll talk some more. We'll ... figure things out."

Her touch, her words sent a glimmer of light to pierce his black mood. This morning when he woke, he'd thought there was hope for them. Now he knew she'd been faithful. And yes, they were talking. These were positive steps. "Okay." He dropped his hand to cover hers, and squeezed. "Okay, Lily. But we have to be honest. No more lies."

"Agreed."

Her small hand felt so good, sandwiched between his palm and his thigh. But he had to let go. The tall hedge and giant, leafless maple trees marked her parents' property. He turned through the open gate, wishing he and Lily were anywhere other than here.

The house loomed ahead: black Tudor-style half-timbering against cream walls, heavy chimneys, and leaded-glass windows. Attractive enough, but he preferred houses that blended into the environment. A holly wreath hung on the door. Inside, he knew there'd be a beautiful tree in the sitting room, decorated by Aldonza.

He got out and unfurled the umbrella for Lily, then retrieved the tote bag. She tucked her hand through the crook of his elbow as they walked to the door. She knocked twice then opened it.

Aldonza, in a plain gray dress and a white apron, came bustling to greet them.

"Merry Christmas, Aldonza," he said, kissing her cheek as she took their coats and umbrella. He liked the housekeeper; she was by far the nicest person who lived in this house.

Lily echoed the greeting, giving the other woman a hug. She took the bottle bag from the tote and handed it over, then bent to remove her boots and put her pumps on.

"Thank you so much. And Merry Christmas to you, too, Miss Lily and Mr. Dax." She gestured down the hall. "Everyone is in the sitting room." She hurried away with their coats and Lily's boots.

Aldonza always prepared the mid-day Christmas dinner for the Nyland family, then dealt with the dishes before getting together with friends for her own Christmas meal. Her cooking was the only good part of these painful get-togethers. "Let the fun begin," he muttered, reaching for Lily's hand.

Seven

An hour later, Lily cut a slice of Aldonza's perfectly cooked turkey and listened as Anthony talked about a rare form of brain
cancer he'd been treating in a nine-year-old. How tragic, but how
lucky the boy and his family were to have Anthony as their doctor.
He might be an annoyingly perfect younger brother, but he was an
excellent doctor.

Anthony, in a charcoal suit and gray-and-white striped tie, his
hair the same wheat blond as Lily's, sat across from her. His wife,
Regina, an intellectual property lawyer, was beside him, her strawberry blond hair lying in sleek waves against the shoulders of a lovely
green dress. Dax sat beside Lily. Her silver-haired father, in his suit
and tie, was at one end of the table. Her mother presided at the other
end, wearing a tailored taupe dress and jacket, her neatly styled
blond hair's color attributable to dye these days. Aldonza was in the
kitchen and so was baby Sophia, in her bassinet.

So far, most of the conversation had consisted of her parents and
brother discussing challenging cases. Lily listened, interested, but
didn't mention her own patients. As a family practice doctor, she
ordered tests and diagnosed, then referred the most complicated
cases to specialists.

Beside her, Dax ate in silence.

Her attention drifted from the medical conversation to the
talk—the almost fight—they'd had in the car. He hadn't cheated on

her. That was the good news, and it was huge. But also huge was the lack of trust between them. Could they rebuild it? And what about love? Had they lost that too? She was too confused to know her own heart. And then there was last night's wild sex. Just thinking of it heated her body. She squirmed against the sudden throb of arousal between her legs.

Dax leaned toward her and murmured, "Eat, or your mother will ask if you're sick."

The brush of his shoulder against hers felt good, and so did the fact that he was looking out for her.

She smiled her thanks and picked up her fork again. Whether or not she loved Dax the way she used to, he still turned her on, and she still cared for him. He cared too; she was sure of it. But was that enough to build a future—and a family—on? Later this afternoon, they'd talk. Anxiety sent a shiver across her shoulders and stilled the pulse between her legs. She took a sip of French chardonnay.

Her parents, who tended to grill their children rather than converse, were now asking Anthony about the clinical trial he was leading, testing the effect of a new treatment for prostate cancer. Lily had referred a Well Family Clinic patient to the trial, so was particularly interested in how it was going.

Aldonza entered the room quietly and passed around the serving dishes, offering seconds to everyone. She topped off the wineglasses then slipped away.

The discussion of the clinical trial wound up with Anthony winning a nod of approval from their father.

"Yes, it's valuable work, Anthony," their mother said. She turned to Lily. "Speaking of work, how are things at your clinic?"

Of course her turn had to come. "Good. I think we've reached the optimum size, though it's inevitable there will always be some growth through referrals and so on." Now if only she could figure out the workload issues. Niggling pain at her temples warned that a stress headache was starting up.

"Then you should now have time for something more challenging and worthwhile," her mother said.

"Indeed," her father chimed in. "A research project, or a clinical trial like Anthony's."

They had finally accepted, grudgingly, that they weren't going to convince her to switch from general practice to a specialty, and now they were pushing her toward other areas they considered more worthwhile, not to mention prestigious, than her clinic.

Dax spoke for the first time in ages. "Lily busts her butt at the Well Family Clinic." His voice held an edge, and she wasn't sure if it was directed at her parents or at her. More than once he'd told her she let the clinic take over her life.

Her mom frowned. "Lily, if you've reached optimum size, surely it shouldn't take that much work to maintain things."

Maybe it shouldn't. Her parents always made her feel like a failure. She wished Dax hadn't said anything.

"And she does do other work," Dax said, his voice cool. "She volunteers Saturdays at the Downtown Eastside clinic."

Lily winced. She hadn't told her parents about her volunteer work. Perhaps Dax meant to be supportive, but she wished he'd kept quiet.

Her mom frowned. "You're working in the Downtown Eastside?"

Her dad said, "Treating drug addicts, prostitutes, and street people? You consider that a good use of your talent?"

On the bright side, he'd implied she had talent. "Yes, I do. The poor and disadvantaged are just as deserving of health care."

"They squander it," her mother snapped. "You can't tell me you don't see the same people, over and over again."

"And Anthony treats people with lung cancer who've smoked all their lives despite the warnings. We don't make judgment calls on our patients." She reached for her wineglass, only to find it was almost empty again. The headache was rapping on her skull with small, dull hammers.

"True," her brother said. "But still, Lily, if you worked on a research project or clinical trial, you might help find solutions rather than put Band-Aids on problems."

Lily frowned at him. Yes, he was entitled to his opinion, but did he always have to side with their parents? She and Anthony had always been competitive, but she'd thought that, since Sophia's birth, things between them were improving.

"Exactly," her dad said.

"But that's—" Dax started.

Lily interrupted, clamping her hand on his thigh. "I'll certainly consider that." And she would, for a nanosecond. Her parents and brother had a valid point—but her calling was to treat people who were hurting, not to do research.

Dax made a sound low in his throat that hopefully only she could hear. She squeezed his thigh more gently, in silent apology, then lifted her hand and picked up her fork again, though the conversation and her headache had destroyed her appetite.

"And you're still doing the same thing, Dax?" her father asked, a hint of censure in his voice.

"Yup."

Lily frowned at his abbreviated response. Her parents might never truly approve of him, but couldn't he make more of an effort? "He's working for a mining camp in northern B.C.," she explained.

"Way out in the bush?" her mom said.

"Way out," Dax said. "Temperatures below zero. Living in modular housing. At least the bears are hibernating now."

Was he *trying* to annoy her parents?

"I can't understand why a man would want to live that way," her mother said.

"I'm sure you can't," Dax replied.

"At some point a man needs to grow up and settle down," her father said stiffly. "Most men do it in their twenties."

Lily shot Dax a warning glance, hoping he wouldn't rise to the bait.

He gave a slight shrug, then said, "Great dinner, as always."

"Thank you," her mother said.

"Aldonza sure is a good cook," Dax added.

Lily closed her eyes briefly. Yes, he was right that credit went to Aldonza, but couldn't he just thank her privately? Lily had learned long, long ago that, with her parents, making nice worked far better than making waves.

"On the subject of settling down," her mother said, "Lily, you should learn from Anthony's example. He's two years younger yet he's establishing a brilliant career, he's married to a bright young woman who's on the partnership track, and they've produced a lovely little girl. You're thirty-two, Lily."

Implying that it was a ripe old age and she'd yet to achieve anything of significance. And hitting her in her vulnerable spot, her desire to have children. Doubly wounded, she fought to keep her voice even as she said, "Not everyone wants the same thing, Mom."

"On the subject of that lovely little girl . . ." It was Regina, speaking for the first time in a while. "I should check on her."

"Nonsense," Lily's mom said. "She'll be fine with Aldonza."

"If I'm not mistaken," Regina said, "Aldonza will need to clear the table and bring in dessert."

"Ah yes, I suppose it is that time." Her mother clapped her hands together and called, "Aldonza?"

Regina rose. "I'll tell her." She headed for the kitchen.

A moment later, Aldonza bustled in and started gathering plates. Dax pushed back from the table and rose. "Delicious dinner, Aldonza. Thanks." He lifted the platter with the remains of a large turkey. "This is heavy. I'll carry it out."

"Thank you, Mr. Dax."

As the woman cleared the table, Lily sought a neutral topic of conversation. She asked her brother, "Is Sophia still waking you and Regina up every night?"

He gave a fond grin. "She'll go five hours now, on a good night. It sure makes a difference."

"I still say you should hire a live-in nanny," their mom said

"We're keeping that option open," Anthony said.

Lily's lips twitched. She knew, from times she'd babysat, that neither he nor Regina had any intention of having a nanny. Day care worked for them, and when they were home they wanted to care for their baby themselves. When Lily and Anthony were children, they'd spent far more time with nannies, housekeepers, and tutors than with their parents. Neither of them, nor Regina, thought that was a good model for child-rearing.

Aldonza had made several trips back and forth to the kitchen, yet Dax hadn't returned. He wouldn't skip out, would he? The way things were between them, she wasn't absolutely sure.

"I'm going to see if Regina needs help with Sophia," she murmured, and headed for the kitchen.

She stepped through the door then held it for Aldonza, who was heading out with a pie server in each hand, one displaying a latticed mince pie that smelled spicy and rich, the other with Lily's dad's favorite, pumpkin pie. Inside the kitchen, the sight that greeted Lily held her immobile.

Regina stood at the sink, holding a baby bottle under running water. "I can't believe I forgot the electric bottle warmer," she said over her shoulder. "Before Sophia, I never forgot anything."

Dax sat at the kitchen table with the baby, wrapped in a pink-rosebud-figured blanket, cradled securely in his arms. He smiled down at her as he said to Regina, "Cut yourself a break, woman." With his carved features and dramatic black hair and beard, Dax was a striking man and his face could look almost harsh. Now, though, the smile softened it, as did the long black lashes on his downcast eyes.

"In this house?" Regina gave a wry chuckle and shook the bottle gently, then tested the liquid against the inside of her wrist. Turning away from the sink, she spotted Lily. "Oh, hi, Lily. Are they waiting for us?"

Dax glanced up too.

"I'm sure Dad's eager to have his pumpkin pie," Lily said absent-mindedly. Never had she seen Dax with a baby, and he and tiny Sophia looked surprisingly comfortable as he held her against his big chest. Was there any hope that one day he would cradle their own child? She swallowed and regained her train of thought. "But Sophia's lunch should come first."

"She does cry when she gets hungry." Regina scooped the baby out of Dax's arms. "Thanks, Uncle Dax. I can take it from here."

Uncle Dax? Well, of course he was. She was Aunt Lily.

If the two of them somehow worked things out, they might be Mom and Dad one day. *Please.* The wish was so vivid in her mind, for a moment she was afraid she'd spoken it aloud.

Normally, she'd have given Sophia a kiss, but her legs had gone weak and she instead sank into the closest chair.

"You okay?" Dax asked.

"Just needed a breather."

"I know the feeling," Regina said. She kissed her daughter's head as the baby sucked up milk. "And you give me excuses, don't you, my darling?"

The kitchen door swung open again and Aldonza came in. "They are asking for you." A sympathetic smile lit her plump brown face. "Better to go."

Another person who'd learned that survival depended on not making waves. As the housekeeper started setting up the coffee tray, Lily stood, kissed the nursing baby, then headed toward the door. The pounding in her head had eased a little. "Come on, Dax. Regina, I'll tell them you'll be there in a minute."

The other woman nodded. "It's my turn to be grilled. I know there's no escape."

"You always come through beautifully," Lily reassured her with a twinge of envy. When Lily had first met Regina, when she was Anthony's girlfriend, she liked her and respected her, but found her too perfect to really warm to. Sophia had softened Regina and Lily felt closer to her sister-in-law—and sometimes even to her own brother.

Dax rose with lazy grace. "Why not bring the kid? She'd provide a distraction."

"No children at the dinner table," Regina said. "That's been made quite clear."

"Quite clear," Aldonza echoed.

"You agree with that?" he asked Regina.

She shrugged. "Their house; their rules."

He glanced around, from her to Aldonza to Lily. "You all just knuckle under to them."

Aldonza, a gentle but proud woman who adored Dax, stared him straight in the eye. "They pay me well, Mr. Dax. I live in this beautiful house, have much free time, and rarely see them."

He went to her and kissed her cheek. "I'm sorry."

Regina lifted her chin. "And I don't want to cause trouble for Anthony with his parents."

Lily was tempted to suggest that her husband be as considerate, but kept her mouth shut.

Regina put a burp cloth over the shoulder of her green dress, hiked the baby up, and gently patted her back. "At our house, Anthony and I do things our way. We're raising Sophia according to our ideas of good parenting. You've seen that, Lily." She glanced over to Lily, standing near the kitchen door.

Lily nodded. "You're wonderful parents. You're patient, encouraging. You focus on the positives, not the negatives."

"It's not that we don't believe in rules and discipline, at least when Sophia's older. I think my mom and dad are—no insult intended to yours, Lily—terrific parents. They care about who each of their children is, our strengths and weaknesses, our dreams and goals. They motivate by example, encouragement, praise for achievements, not by criticism. They accept and love us for who we are, rather than trying to mold us into their idea of perfect kids."

"They don't make you—" Lily broke off.

Dax gave her a curious look. "What?"

She shook her head, aware that the three other people in the room were all staring at her. "Nothing."

"Say it," he told her. "No one is going to tattle to your parents."

He was right. Anthony might have, but Regina, Aldonza, and Dax never would. And she wanted to say it aloud, just one time. "They don't make you feel like you have to agree with them to be loved," she said slowly.

Regina's greenish-gray eyes softened with sympathy. "No. And we'll never do that to Sophia."

"I don't think my parents intend to be that way." She wanted to believe that. "It's how they were raised."

Regina bit her lip. "I should shut up. But instead I'll point out that Anthony was raised by your parents. That doesn't mean he has to repeat the pattern."

"If my Filipe and I had been blessed with children," Aldonza said softly, "I would treasure them. I would bring them up the way Miss Regina says."

"So would I," Lily said.

"Hmm," Regina said teasingly, rising to place Sophia back in her bassinet, "does that mean you have news for us?"

"No! No, of course not." She cast a quick glance at Dax, who studied her quizzically. Though she so badly wanted to have a baby, this was the worst time to do it, with the future so uncertain. "Just speaking hypothetically."

Eight

Dax closed the passenger door after Lily settled inside. Before walking around to the driver's side, he rotated his shoulders to loosen the knots and took a few deep breaths of rain-soaked air. When he climbed into the car, Lily had reclined her seat and closed her eyes.

"Your parents take the merry out of Christmas."

"Let's not do a postmortem." She touched his arm, then, as if her hand was too heavy to hold up, let it flop back into her lap. "I have a headache. I know we need to talk, but right now I just want to go home and lie down."

He started the engine. "Radio on or off?"

"Off, please."

He waved good-bye to Anthony and Regina, who were heading over to Regina's parents' house for another turkey dinner.

It occurred to him, as he pulled through the open gate, that if he and Lily broke up, he'd never see her parents again. That was a definite plus. They irked him, and he wasn't all that crazy about who she turned into around them. Still, as he glanced at her pale, strained face, he knew that he'd gladly—well, maybe not gladly—suffer through social occasions with her parents if he and she could recapture the feelings they'd once shared.

* * *

Three hours later, Dax, in the recliner by the gas fire with a half-empty bottle of Granville Island lager beside him, shut down Lily's Kindle. While she'd slept off her headache, he'd changed into jeans and the hawk tee and finished reading *Bound by Desire*. A few scenes were titillating, but others he found bizarre and degrading. He didn't like Neville. Seemed to him, the guy used his "I'm a dom" thing to legitimize disrespecting women and inflicting pain. But on the other hand, the relationship was consensual. Cassandra didn't use her safe word and Neville gave her what she seemed to want. So, Dax supposed, the two of them were well-matched.

People were different. That was what it came down to. As for Dax, while he could definitely get into some games and toys, he was no dom. If Lily had discovered that she was a true sexual submissive, he couldn't give her what she needed.

When the bathroom door closed and water ran, he went to the kitchen to mix her a martini. A few minutes later, she joined him there.

"Hey there." He handed her the drink. "How are you feeling?" She looked fresh and lovely in a long, slim, silver-gray sweater and black yoga pants that clung to her legs. She wore the First Nations pendant and earrings.

"My headache's gone." She took a long drink from the martini glass. "Thanks, this is perfect." She studied him and smiled. "The T-shirt looks good on you."

"I like it. Great gift."

"I guess we need to think about dinner."

"No thinking required. Aldonza has provided. She forgave me for that stupid comment."

Humor sparkled in her eyes. "She'd forgive you anything. The woman's crazy about you. What did she give us?"

"Piri piri chicken and fried potatoes to microwave, green bean salad, and Portuguese buns. Leftover mince pie and, of course, bolo rei." She made the traditional Portuguese Christmas dessert for her friends.

"A feast." Then the light in her eyes faded. "We need to talk first."

He read determination in her face, plus a trace of doubt or vulnerability. He could identify. "Yeah."

When she turned and headed for the living room, he followed. He hadn't closed the blinds and Lily walked over to the window. With her back to him, she lifted her glass and took a drink.

Figuring this wasn't a side-by-side-on-the-couch conversation, he sat back down in the recliner and picked up his beer bottle.

Lily seated herself in an upholstered chair, setting her martini glass on a coaster on the table beside the chair.

"Where do we start?" he asked. Knowing Lily, she'd have her thoughts organized to present. As for him, all he knew was, he wanted their old life back, the way they'd been together when they first got married.

She crossed her legs, sitting neat and prim. "You said you thought I might be cheating because I asked you to use condoms. That's an awfully big leap."

That wasn't what he'd expected her to say, but he responded. "There were other things. You seem different. You're never around. Always at work or—"

"The clinic is busy," she said defensively.

"Yeah, I know, it's your baby. But even when you're here, you're not. You're distant."

She folded her arms across her chest. "So are you. And talk about never being around. You've hardly been home in the past couple of years."

He took a long swallow of beer. "Haven't felt like there's much here for me," he said gruffly. "Or that you want me here. It's your home, not mine."

Her mouth opened, then closed, and she glanced around the room. "If you were here more, you'd make it your home."

"It's not so much the place, it's you. It doesn't feel like you want me in Vancouver."

"I do, Dax. But yes, I have a life. I can't sit at home and wait for you to show up every now and then." She sounded indignant.

He shook his head. "Jeez, Lily, I know that." But couldn't she, once in a while, make time for him? Didn't she ever want to be together, the way they used to be? "What made you think I was cheating?" he asked quietly.

She glanced down at her folded arms, then up again. "You being away so much. Being distant when you were here, even when we . . ." Color stained her pale cheeks. Had sex, she was thinking, and she was right. "And then, last night, you were . . . It was so unlike you."

Heat pulsed through his body at the memory. Testing, he said, "I thought you might like it."

"Why on earth would you think that?"

"Are you saying you didn't?"

Her cheeks went a brighter pink, a sexy flush that made his groin tighten. "It was, uh, different." She firmed her jaw. "And, obviously, I climaxed multiple times."

She sure did, her body coming apart hard and hot and wet on his lips and around his cock. He shifted and crossed his legs, trying to control his arousal.

"But I feel strange about it," she went on. "And you didn't answer my question. Why did you think I'd like it?"

"That book on your Kindle."

"Oh," she said on a note of revelation. "You picked up my Kindle instead of yours and found *Bound by Desire*."

No need to admit he'd checked deliberately, after finding erotic novels before. "I thought if that's what you like reading, maybe it's what you want in bed."

She pressed her hands to her flushed cheeks. Above her fingertips, her blue eyes danced with amusement. "Dax, I didn't choose that book. I haven't even started it. It's a book club selection."

Likely, so were the previous ones. "You belong to a book club? What kind of club picks that kind of book?"

"Mine, apparently." She reached for her martini glass. "When I joined the club, I was expecting literary fiction. But the other members have their own ideas about what we should read, so I've gone along. I did protest against *Bound by Desire*, but they, uh, made persuasive arguments."

Not many people other than her parents could best Lily. Dax was really curious about the other members of this book club. "Persuasive arguments about BDSM?"

"About keeping an open mind and discovering why so many women are reading this kind of book."

Yeah, Lily was big on research and analysis.

She gazed at him over the rim of her glass. "So last night was about what, exactly? You thought I got off on BDSM, so you decided to spank me and tie me up?"

"I didn't spank you. I gave you one light slap on your ass." His hand tingled, remembering.

"It stung." She probably meant it as a protest, but the breathiness in her voice told him she too was turned on.

He studied his wife. Legs neatly crossed; simple, tasteful clothes; hair cut short in a style that was attractive and practical; a touch of eye makeup but no lipstick, no nail polish. Beautiful, but so refined and controlled. Except for the flush on her cheeks. Wanting to rattle her a bit more, he said in a low, suggestive voice, "It made you wet."

She drank the last mouthful of her martini in an undignified gulp.

"Why does that embarrass you?"

"I don't know." She sounded annoyed, though he wasn't sure whether it was at him or at herself. "I'm a doctor, I spend a good part of my day examining naked genitals, female and male. I discuss sex with my patients. But this is . . . personal." She took a deep breath. "Okay, yes, it was arousing. But not the pain so much as the, uh, unexpectedness. The fact that you were, well, definitely *not* being distant. You took charge. You *saw* me, from suggesting a bath, to massaging me, to the passionate sex. You were more like the way we used to be, back when—"

"When what?" Did she feel the same way, that things had been perfect when they first got together? Could they find their way back?

Nine

Back when we loved each other. That was what Lily'd been thinking. So far, they'd beaten around the bush and avoided the fundamental questions.

She summoned courage and pushed herself to her feet, curling her bare toes into the short nap of the area rug with its nutmeg, taupe, and cream geometric pattern. Facing her husband from six feet away, she said, "Dax, do you still want to be married to me? Do you still l-love me?" Her voice quavered and pain lanced her heart. What if he said no? Yet their marriage had foundered so badly, perhaps the only sensible thing to do was cut their losses.

His storm-cloud eyes darkened and for what seemed like forever, he didn't say anything. Finally, voice grating, he said, "I don't know."

Lily realized she'd been holding her breath. Now she released it. He didn't know if he loved her. It hurt, yet she also felt relief. He wasn't calling it quits. Indecision meant there might be hope for them.

"Do you?" It sounded like he forced the words out.

She studied his face, the face she had loved for so long. "I don't know either, Dax. You're the only man I've ever loved, but I'm so confused. I do know I don't want the kind of relationship we've had for the last year or two."

"Agreed." He gazed at her solemnly for long, silent moments.

Then he rose and held out his hand. "Let's have dinner, drink some wine, and talk."

She gazed at him, not taking his hand. "Just a minute. We need to agree on what we're trying to achieve."

"Achieve?" He drew his hand back.

"I don't mean just now, at dinner. You're home until New Year's. What's our goal for that time period? I don't think it's to save our marriage, because neither of us is sure we want that." Her heart gave a painful throb, but she forced herself to go on. "So is our goal to find out how we feel about each other, and about our marriage?" Would they mark the new year by deciding to get a divorce? It was a horrible thought, but nothing could be worse than the past months.

"That sounds right." He swallowed. "We're in this together, Lily." Again, he held out his hand.

"Together." There was a mountain in front of them, but they'd taken the first steps and were at long last moving forward. She grasped his hand. Holding Dax's hand had always been one of her favorite things in the world, her small, slim, often cool fingers linking with his big, strong, always warm ones. It made her feel as if she belonged somewhere, with someone.

Hand in hand, they went to the kitchen and worked quietly, bumping into each other in the small space. Lily heated up the spicy chicken and potatoes while Dax dished out bean salad and opened a bottle of malbec. When she rinsed her hands, she said, "The tap's stopped dripping."

"Needed a new washer."

"I know." Did he think she was a ditz? "I would have done it, but I hadn't had a chance."

"Lily, you don't have to do everything yourself. I saw the problem; I fixed it."

Had she sounded defensive? "Thank you, Dax."

She set the small dining table and he poured wine. How rare this had become, having dinner together. If only it could be a relaxed, even romantic evening, but that wasn't in the cards. They both tasted the food. The spicy flavors burst on Lily's tongue, a pleasant contrast to this cold winter day.

"Aldonza's a great cook," Dax said.

"She is. And a generous woman."

They ate in silence for a few minutes. Anxiety fluttered through Lily, making it hard to breathe, much less eat. She put down her fork and toyed with her wineglass. "Why is this so hard? After fifteen years, we should be able to talk about something that's so important."

His lips kinked up ruefully. "It's easier to talk about things that don't matter."

She nodded at the wisdom of that. "Where do we start?"

He broke open a Portuguese bun and buttered it, but didn't lift it to his mouth. "This probably isn't the right place, but I'm curious. Why did you pick Skookumchuck for your safe word?"

"In the bath, the scent of lavender brought back memories. Remember Mrs. B's garden?"

A smile flashed. "Deer-resistant plants."

She smiled back. "Such a gentle, kind woman, but it was all-out war when it came to the deer." For a moment, she enjoyed the simple pleasure of smiling with her husband over a shared memory. "Anyhow, I was thinking about camp, and the evening we met."

"When I saw you, I barely recognized you. The flawless princess from high school, in rumpled shorts and a stained camp T-shirt, hair pulled back in a messy ponytail."

"Hardly flawless."

"Seemed that way to me." He dragged a chunk of bun through the sauce from the chicken.

"Maybe compared to you," she teased. "The guy who got suspended for corrupting two cheerleaders with beer, pot, and sex under the bleachers." More relaxed now, she began to eat again, enjoying the bite of peppers in the piri piri, the subtle yeastiness of the bun, the tanginess of the green beans.

"Those girls weren't exactly innocent."

"No, and I'm sure they were dying to get it on with the school bad boy, just like every other girl."

"Except you, who never gave me a second glance."

"Like you ever glanced at me either."

"Why waste time gazing in the store window at something you'll never be able to afford?"

"Or gazing across the fence at the sexy bad boy surrounded by a crowd of far prettier, sexier girls?"

He shook his head. "Not prettier or sexier. Never, Lily."

The unexpected compliment brought a quick rush of moisture to her eyes. To hide her reaction, she dipped her head and busied herself buttering a crusty bun until she'd regained control. "It was a real attraction of opposites. And yet, it *was* real. Wasn't it, Dax?"

"Seemed that way to me."

"You made me feel..." She trailed off, remembering skinny-dipping at midnight, making love in a starlit meadow filled with daisies. "Alive and uninhibited. Sexy, even though I was so inexperienced." Long talks as they held hands beside a beach fire. "Grown up, like I could plan my own future and follow through. Listened to, like my opinions and my desires mattered."

He swallowed. "You made me feel like *I* mattered. You made me want to be a better person, a person who deserved to be with you."

"Deserved to be with me?" Was he serious? "Like I was such a prize." She hated to think about the prissy girl she'd been before meeting Dax. "That summer sure changed me." It gave her more confidence, more of a sense of who she was, or might become, as a woman. "Talk about the cliché uptight virgin."

"You were a little naïve." A sparkle danced in his gray eyes.

"Inhibited, insecure. I was a science student, planning on being a doctor, so I knew the anatomical and physiological facts, but the real thing's very different." Her lips curved. "Good thing I had an excellent teacher."

"Oh hell, Lily, I wasn't that great. Yeah, I was far from a virgin, but I was an eighteen-year-old boy. Finesse wasn't my strong suit."

No, bad boys weren't supposed to have finesse. "Passion, though . . ."

"Oh, yeah. There was passion. But in the beginning, you didn't even climax half the time."

She shook her head. "Lots of women don't, especially when they're still learning about their sexuality. Even when I didn't, it felt wonderful to be naked with you, to explore each other's bodies. You helped me learn what worked for me." And for years it had worked beautifully.

If there was any hope for the two of them, she had to be honest. "The past year or two, I climax but it feels like"—she bit her lip— "we're going through the motions."

"The passion is gone." He stated it as a fact, with no inflection.

Tears threatened to surface, but she forced them back. "The passion, the trust. We've lost so much. The love . . ." She had to swallow before she could go on. "We had it all, Dax. I loved how we were together."

"Me too. If we could get that back . . ."

Yes, if they could get that back, then surely they'd find a route forward, one that included children. "Things need to change, but I'm not sure how we do that."

Dax refilled their wineglasses. "Last night was a change."

Her sex throbbed at the memory. "That's for sure."

"Neither of us was going through the motions."

A laugh spluttered out. "No. It was . . . new, almost like that first summer."

"There was passion, Lily."

"Yes. Somehow, last night, you made me stop thinking, stop

worrying, and just . . . experience. Though I'm embarrassed about being turned on by some of the things you did."

"We've always been pretty, uh, conservative in bed. I thought, well . . ."

"What?"

"That you wouldn't be into kinky stuff."

"Dax, I'm really not a prissy princess."

"Sorry, I didn't mean, uh . . ."

"Did you want to try other things? Were you bored with our sex life?" Why hadn't it occurred to her that a guy like Dax wouldn't be satisfied with a conventional sex life?

"I thought our sex life was great, until we lost the passion." He picked up his wineglass, took a sip, and then said, with a wicked grin, "As for kinky stuff, hell, I'm a guy. Sure, I think about that stuff."

"What kind of things appeal to you?" she asked, curious but almost afraid what he might say.

"I dunno."

"Of course you do." She narrowed her eyes. "May I remind you, I'm a doctor and I volunteer in the Downtown Eastside? I doubt you'll come up with anything I've never heard of."

"Aw hell, I'm gonna disappoint you, my ideas are so tame." Another sexy grin.

"Try me."

"Okay, tying you up and seeing you spread out like that, just for me, was pretty cool. A blindfold might be fun. Games, role play. Going out with you to some nice restaurant, you wearing a dress and no panties, and me playing with you under the tablecloth and making you come."

Imagining that scenario, her eyes widened and the heat of arousal thrummed in her blood and pulsed between her legs. She took a hurried gulp of wine.

"Some toys," he went on. "Not the heavy BDSM stuff like spreader bars and ball gags and butt plugs, but—"

"You know about those things?" she broke in. She was only aware of them because of her job. To think that her husband spent time thinking about ball gags and butt plugs . . . That definitely did *not* turn her on.

"I'm a guy," he said again. "Plus, that book of yours is enlightening."

"You're not making me want to read it. But I need to get through the first part before tomorrow's book club." Everyone had to read a third of the book, no more than that, before each Monday meeting, so they could have a meaningful discussion.

"Those things don't turn you on?"

She shook her head vigorously.

"Any of the other stuff I mentioned?"

Knowing her cheeks were pink, she said, "Maybe."

"Cool."

The very male comment made her chuckle. "You're saying I shouldn't be embarrassed, I should embrace my, uh . . ."

"Down-and-dirty side?" he filled in. "Wouldn't hear me object. Hell, Lily, there shouldn't be anything wrong or embarrassing in sex if it's what both partners want."

"And consent to, with full information and from equal positions of power."

"Yeah, of course."

She knew he meant it. Dax didn't have a sexist bone in his body. She'd been pleasantly surprised, that first summer, when she discovered that fact about her bad-boy lover. "We learned a lot about each other at Camp Skookumchuck."

"Camp's for learning and exploring," he joked. Then he said reflectively, "Hmm. That summer was about exploring, discovery, passion. Right?"

"And falling in love."

He nodded. "Last night, we explored different things and that rekindled our passion."

"True."

"So maybe we could do more of it. See where it takes us."

Lily liked having a clear, logical course of action. But there was no formula for finding out if two people wanted to save their marriage. Counseling worked for some couples, but she was a private person, and she couldn't imagine tough-guy Dax spilling intimate secrets to a stranger.

She stared across the table at her husband. Did she still love him? Sometimes she thought yes, but then wondered if it was just history, habit, maybe insecurity. Other times she thought no, and then questioned whether she was only erecting defenses to guard against a broken heart.

If they did love each other, could they change their marriage into one that they were both happy to recommit to? Was the mountain in front of them climbable, or impassable? To find out, they had to pick a path to start down. He'd just proposed one.

Their jobs and lifestyles were a huge issue, but she couldn't see an easy solution. Fifteen years ago, passion had developed into a deep emotional connection, a commitment to share their lives. Perhaps there was a strange logic, now, to choosing their sex life as the path to follow in rebuilding their love. If that worked, surely they'd have the motivation to figure out the rest of their lives.

"All right," she said slowly. "Let's explore. Where do we start?" The question made her nervous, so she rose abruptly. "Let's deal with the leftovers and the dishes and then . . ." And then, what?

Dax cocked an eyebrow. After a long moment, he said, "Get one of the scarves I tied you up with and wait for me in the living room." His voice had the same commanding tone as last night.

Would he tie her up again? But with only a single scarf? Excitement pulsed through her, along with nerves. "What are you going to do?"

He stood and came around the table. His big, strong fingers stroked short hair away from one cheek, traced the rim of her ear, gently tugged on her earring. Then he gripped her chin firmly. "That's for me to know. The moment you want me to stop, you know the word to say."

It was too soon. They should discuss what games they were both okay with. He shouldn't just take charge this way.

Except, wasn't that what had excited her last night? Trusting Dax to control what they did, to control her pleasure? Giving up the need to always think, plan, be responsible for every damn thing?

"Do you accept my rules?" he asked.

"Yes."

"Yes, *master.*"

Seriously? And yet, she supposed this was what she'd opted in to. "Yes, master."

"Very good. Now get that scarf and bring it to the living room."

Ten

Dax used the ice dispenser on the fridge and put a bowl of cubes in the freezer, then tidied up the dinner leftovers and put the dishes in the dishwasher.

Maybe there was hope for him and Lily. If that hope began with sex games, he had a fantasy or ten he'd be happy to play out with her. Maybe she'd confess to some fantasies of her own that he could indulge. He wasn't fool enough to think the only problem with their marriage was sex, but it might be the easiest to fix. If they could bring the spark back to their love life, maybe the rest would follow.

"Dax?" she called from the living room. And then, "I mean, master?"

Master. No, it didn't sound right. It reminded him of Neville. He strode to the other room to join her. She had her back to him and was reaching out to pull the blinds.

"Don't."

"I was just—"

"Don't." He moved the leather recliner back from the window, facing it. "Sit here."

She obeyed, and he took the scarf. "Don't call me master, call me Falcon." It was a nickname he'd become known by among his colleagues.

Her eyebrows lifted. "Yes, Falcon. If I may say, the name suits

you." She put her hands on the arms of the chair, likely waiting for
him to bind one of them.

"I'm going to blindfold you."

Her eyes flared with surprise, then a touch of panic. "You could
just pull the blinds and turn out the light."

"I want the light on. I'll be able to see and you won't."

"But the window. If you don't pull the blinds, then—"

"We face the ocean. It's not likely anyone can see in." They'd
have to be on the other side of False Creek with a powerful telescope. The possibility of a distant voyeur added an edge that heated
his blood.

He ran the scarf through his hands, from one end to the other.
"You don't question me. I'm in charge. You obey without question.
You don't speak unless I ask you a question or give you permission. Or
unless you want to say your safe word and stop me."

Slowly, she dipped her head in a nod. Then her gaze met his. Her
light blue irises often looked cool, but now they glittered with curiosity and excitement.

He folded the long scarf in half lengthwise and looped it around
her head, three turns, secure but not bindingly tight. He tied a knot.
"How do you feel?"

"Strange, Falcon. Off balance, even though I'm sitting still."

"Off balance is good. It means you'll pay attention to—" He
brushed her forehead with three fingers, just one darting touch.

She started and twisted her head, obviously trying to anticipate
his next touch.

He ran his fingers down her nose, traced the upper bow of her
mouth. Pale pink lips. She rarely wore lipstick, only a neutral lip
gloss. "Take off your shirt and bra, then put your hands on the arms
of the chair and don't move them. Rather than tie you up, I'm going
to trust you."

He walked away, moving more heavily than usual so she'd hear his retreating footsteps. In the kitchen, he got the bowl of ice cubes. When he returned, he walked silently.

Lily had stripped to the waist, leaving her jewelry on. She sat neatly, her feet on the floor and her forearms on the arms of the chair. Her skin looked pale and delicate against the brown leather. The gold chain and dangling hummingbird drew attention to her naked breasts. With the gas fireplace lit, the room wasn't cold, but her nipples, the same soft pink as her lips, had budded.

Dax was aroused too: at the sight of her; at the idea of playing this game with her; at the possibility that someone watched through a telescope. He'd have stripped off his clothes and freed his erection, but she'd have heard him doing it and he wanted to take her by surprise. Quietly, he kneeled in front of her chair, took a cube from the bowl, and ran it around one of her areolas.

She gasped and involuntarily pulled back, settling deeper into the chair. "What is— I'm sorry, Falcon, I shouldn't have spoken."

"Do it again and you'll be punished."

The cube melted as he swirled it over her flesh, water dripping a trail down her breast and onto the top of her rib cage. He applied his tongue to the bottom of the trail, swiping up the cool drips, brushing her warm skin with his chilled tongue. Purposefully, he licked his way up until his tongue circled her areola, then flicked up and around her nipple like he was swirling his tongue around the top of an ice-cream cone, gathering it to a point.

She shivered, but the flush on her chest said it was from arousal, not cold. The same arousal that tightened his groin and thickened his cock.

He swirled a cube around her other areola, but this time didn't lick up the drips. "Open your mouth."

She obeyed, likely having figured out he was using ice cubes and expecting one. Instead, he slipped two cold fingers between her lips, darting them in and out to mimic sex. She began to close her lips, to capture his fingers, and he drew them quickly away.

He bent to lick the drips of water from her ribs and breast. "Open your mouth." This time, when she opened, it was his cold tongue he dipped inside. Hers met it and they kissed hungrily, but before the kiss could get too intense he pulled away.

Now he did unzip his jeans, knowing she'd hear the rasp of metal. He shucked off all his clothing, breathing a sigh of relief as his hard-on escaped confinement. Then he tugged her stretchy black pants over her hips. She lifted her lower body, allowing him to pull them off.

Her panties were simple beige ones a few shades darker than her skin. Her mound and pubic hair pressed against the thin fabric. At her crotch, the fabric was dark with moisture.

His cock pulsed at the sight of her wearing only arousal-dampened panties and the jewelry he'd given her. He wrapped a hand around his shaft, which jerked with need. He could pump himself to climax, and if he kept quiet, she'd never know. But he didn't want his orgasm to come from his own hands, so he released his grip.

Kneeling in front of her, he reclined the chair, tilting her backward. He hooked his hands into the top band of her panties and in one quick move ripped them off and down her legs.

"Oh!" she gasped.

He spread her thighs and admired her swollen pink pussy, glistening with dampness. Her flesh would be hot, almost burning. He gathered two ice cubes and pressed them against her, making her jerk, then moan.

Dax wanted to moan too as he bent between her spread legs and inhaled her distinctive scent. Alternating strokes, he swiped the melting ice then his firm tongue against her labia. He took a fresh cube and pressed it inside her, then licked up the drops that trickled from her.

She writhed against his face, panting with need.

Damn, but he wanted to plunge his aching hard-on deep inside her. "Don't come. Not until I tell you to."

Her body froze, like she was holding her breath.

With forceful swipes, he licked her labia, up and down, faster and faster. Now, rather than wriggle against him, she tried to evade his touch, hands clamping down tightly on the arms of the chair as she pulled away. He gripped her hips and held her steady as he continued to lick relentlessly. This was torture for him too, fueling a painful ache in his balls.

When she groaned, he eased off, dropped light kisses on her inner thigh, let both of them cool down. Then he returned, to tease her budded clit.

She panted, whimpered, tensed so her body was taut with self-control.

His was too. If he touched his hand to his cock, it'd take all of two strokes to make him shoot.

When he sensed Lily was at the point where heightened pleasure would tip into pain, he said, "Come now," and stroked his tongue firmly along her labia then her clit.

She broke, crying, "Oh God, Dax." Violating the rule of silence, and the other rule about calling him Falcon. He guessed she wasn't aware of it. It felt good to hear his name on her lips when she came.

Before she'd finished spasming, he applied the last melting ice cube to her heated crotch. She gasped in shock, then he licked her, eating her as she pressed against his face, came apart again, and kept climaxing under his demanding tongue.

When she tried to pull away, to resist his touch, he knew she'd had all she could take. He let go of her hips and sat back on his heels. His cock leaked pre-come and it took every ounce of willpower he possessed to not just blindly fuck her, or fuck his own hand.

He knew what he wanted: the feel of her lips on his aching flesh. But right now, even the slightest touch would make him blow. He had to cool off, but how could he— Wait a minute.

"Don't move," he ordered, then went to the kitchen.

Activity helped ease the pressure in his body; so did opening the fridge door and letting the cool air wash over him. He deliberated between mince pie and bolo rei. The traditional Portuguese sweet-bread studded with fruit and nuts would make a great breakfast, so he instead chose pie. He put a slice on a plate, couldn't resist taking a couple of bites, then returned silently to Lily.

She slumped in the recliner, boneless as a sleeping cat in the warm light from the lamp and the gas fire. The window was a black square of night studded with distant lights from other apartment windows.

Dax said, "I'm going to put the chair up."

She jerked to alertness as he activated the recliner switch until she was sitting upright again.

"Open your mouth," he ordered. "Open wide, Lily."

Slowly, she opened her mouth.

He slid a forkful of pie inside.

She slipped it off the fork and ate it with an expression of pleasure.

Dax put the plate aside and placed his feet on either side of hers, not touching them. He leaned forward to rest one hand on the sturdy back of the chair, and with the other hand grasped his erection. "Open wide again."

When she did, he guided his cock to her lips and between them, stretching them wider.

She gave a startled, smothered, "Mmph" sound, and then her tongue stroked his shaft. Her lips sucked against his burning flesh and he knew he wasn't going to last.

He put his other hand on the back of the chair, bracing himself.

Lily reached her hand toward his cock.

"No. Stop. I didn't tell you to move your hands." Though he loved feeling her fingers circle his shaft and caress his balls, right now that wasn't what he wanted. There was something unbearably erotic about the sight of Lily, her naked body flushed from climax, sitting prim and proper in the brown leather chair, blindfolded, as he leaned over her. Their bodies didn't touch except in one place, where his cock thrust into her mouth.

The heat of her mouth, the heat of his organ . . . he felt like he'd burst into flames if not for the dampness she spread across him with her tongue. She laved his shaft, tightened her lips around the sensitive base of his crown, slid up and down, sucked him in.

Sucked him so relentlessly that there was nothing in his world except that sweet, hot pressure and the irresistible need to . . . He let out a hoarse cry as he exploded in her mouth, his whole body jerking with the force of his release.

She took him, swallowed, and he kept coming. She swallowed again and again, until finally he was finished.

Though his legs and arms trembled, he managed to push himself upright, easing his cock from her mouth.

Her pink lips gleamed with his come. She licked first the top lip, then the bottom one, and he didn't know if she was deliberately being seductive or merely cleaning her lips.

Wanting to see her eyes, he untied the knot in the scarf and unwound the silky fabric.

Her lashes fluttered and she blinked as her vision adjusted. Wide-eyed, she gazed at his face, then past him to the unscreened window. She started to raise her arms to cover her breasts then stopped. Without looking at him, she said, "May I move now, Falcon?"

"Yes, Lily. The game's over. How do you feel?"

Head bowed, she said, "Exposed."

"Here." He retrieved his T-shirt from the floor. "Put this on."

As she pulled it over her head, he climbed into his jeans, not bothering with underwear, and lowered the blinds. When he turned back, she'd curled her legs up in the chair and was huddled inside the hawk tee, looking more vulnerable than she had when they'd been playing the sex game.

"Are you okay?" He sat on the rug in front of her and reached for her hand.

She let him take it, but it lay inert in his. She nodded then finally looked into his eyes again. The line of her mouth softened and she squeezed his hand. "It was great. Very sexy. Just different and, uh, a little embarrassing."

"Don't be embarrassed about how we have sex."

"I know." Her lips curved slightly. "Did you eat all the pie?"

"I got distracted." He released her hand, picked up the plate, and took a large bite of mince pie. Man, that was good. Too bad neither he nor Lily was much into cooking.

She uncurled her body and he handed her the plate. For a couple of minutes, they ate in silence, passing the plate back and forth.

"So," she said, "you're in Vancouver until after New Year's, right?"

"Yeah, camp's shut down for the holiday. I picked up some work here, flying sightseeing trips."

"Dax, don't you want time off?"

"There's nothing for me to do in Vancouver."

"Don't be ridiculous. It's a wonderful city."

Her outraged expression made him grin. "Yeah? So what would you do, if you ever took a day off."

"Oh. Well, I'd . . ." She handed the plate, with one last bite, back to him. "Go for long walks, visit the galleries and Science World, go out to the Museum of Anthropology, go to the theater—"

"Stop. You sound like the tourist bureau. When's the last time you did any of those things?"

"Um, well . . . Okay, but I've always been so busy."

"Nothing against all that tourist stuff, but in my downtime, I like hiking, running. In nature, not on city streets. If we'd bought that old house with the big yard, I'd have had garden and house stuff to do, but as it is . . ." He shrugged.

"You're blaming me because we bought the condo? Dax, you're never home. I couldn't look after a house and yard, not with—"

Again, he held up his hand. "I know. I'm only saying there's not much here for me." He cocked his head. "Except you, but you're always at work."

"And now we're back to that." She pushed forward in the chair and stood, carefully avoiding touching him where he sat on the rug in front of her chair.

He gazed up at her, seeing slender, shapely legs and his loose tee concealing the rest of her. "I'm just saying, our lives aren't so compatible."

This time, she scraped both hands through her light blond hair. "No. But I guess the first thing is to figure out whether you and I are compatible. And for some reason, we thought sex might help."

She'd had multiple orgasms and now she was complaining? Trying for some of his old bad-boy spark, he winked. "Can't hurt, can it?"

Humor twitched her lips before she straightened them. "I honestly don't know, Dax. I'm confused and tired. I need time to think."

"Okay." He rose too, unsure where this was going.

"And we need to talk some more, or, uh, whatever."

Play at BDSM? "Okay. We'll take it one day at a time and figure it out as we go."

She nodded. "I'm going to have a shower, and then I really need to read that book." She gathered up her clothes and headed for the door, then glanced over her shoulder. "Dax, last night was nice, the massage and all, but . . ."

"I get it. You need time to think." Last night, they'd gone to sleep wrapped up together, the way they always used to.

In the "one day at a time" thing, was tonight a step forward or back?

Eleven

On the SkyTrain from Olympic Village to downtown Vancouver, Lily pulled out her Kindle to skim the last bit of this week's reading.

Crouched on her hands and knees at Neville's feet, her ass tipped up to him, Cassandra moaned as the leather paddle slapped wickedly against the already burning flesh of her buttocks. Yet, even as she moaned, even as she wondered whether she could stand another moment, the hot honey of her arousal drenched her thighs. How was this possible, that he could hit her, hurt her, and yet she was more turned on than ever before?

A sixth sense told her the paddle was again whipping toward her tender flesh, and she automatically flinched away.

The leather never hit.

Instead, a moment later, Neville's hand descended in a stinging blow that made her gasp. Then he massaged the sore flesh, and a pleasant heat radiated through her whole buttock. "The paddle hurts, doesn't it, pet?"

"Yes, master." She wanted to twist her head to look at him, but the leash he'd tied to the heavy table leg tethered her too tightly. Her hands weren't bound; she could free herself if she wanted to. Yet she obeyed his command to stay still. If she moved, he'd find a punishment worse

than the bite of the paddle. He might abandon her, leave her wet and burning, and not bring her to climax.

"You aren't sure you can take it."

"N-no, master." She wanted the intense arousal, but not the pain. Could she have one without the other?

"You can, pet. I know you can." He pinched the aching flesh of her ass so hard she was sure she'd have a bruise.

She bit her lip. She wanted so badly to please him, but could she stand any more?

"Trust me to know your limits. To take you where you need to go. Breathe deeply, breathe into the pain, let it fill you and heat you until you're ready to burst into flame."

Yes, that was how it felt. How did this man who she'd met mere hours ago know her body better than she did? "Yes, master," she said, and tilted her ass upward in invitation.

Frowning, Lily turned off her Kindle and stood to get off at her stop. She couldn't wait to hear what the others thought about this novel.

For Cassandra, it was all about sex—about what she needed to do to get the kind of sex she wanted. For Neville, it was about his dominant nature, as much as or more than about sex. He needed to control Cassandra, to initiate her into his world. She wanted to please him, he wanted her to trust him, but neither appeared to have feelings for the other.

Lily reflected on the parallels to her and Dax. They were having the best sex they'd had in a long time, yet they weren't sure if they loved each other. Still, they did care; they'd cared about each other for fifteen years. She couldn't imagine being intimate—much less playing dangerous games that required trust—with a stranger. When she'd been seventeen and given her virginity to Dax, she'd been falling in love with him. Now . . . For months, even years, she'd built protective layers around her heart, trying to prevent him from hurting her too badly. If she started to peel back those layers, what would she find? And what would she risk?

Lily walked east on Georgia Street, the flow of pedestrians and traffic light since it was Boxing Day. With the clinic closed to patients, she'd had a quiet breakfast with Dax, enjoying Aldonza's bolo rei and not talking about anything in particular. Then he'd headed off for a day of flying sightseers and she'd gone into the clinic. There, she found that someone had unboxed the mini Zen garden and set it up on her desk. She'd shoved it aside to catch up on some patient files, then forced herself to address scheduling and budget issues—issues that seemed to get more unsolvable the longer she spent on them. Now, as was so often the case these days, she had a niggling headache.

Since she preferred not to take meds, she hoped a martini and an hour of chat with the book club would fix the problem. Dax was picking her up for an early dinner. He'd texted in the afternoon to suggest it, and she'd agreed. They would talk. There was nothing else to do but eat and drink, no possibility of being distracted by kinky sex. Talk was a good thing, even if the idea made her nervous.

Using the GPS on her smartphone, she rechecked the route to Pivo Public House. The club members took turns choosing meeting spots. When it was Lily's, she played it safe with lounges in good hotels. It was always interesting to see what the others came up with.

Pivo, near Rogers Arena and BC Place, was Marielle's choice. When Lily entered, she saw it had the stark style that was trendy, brightened by a string of multicolored Christmas lights draping the bar. Marielle sat on a bench seat at a corner table, and George on a chair across from her. Lily shed her coat and took the seat beside Marielle as they exchanged greetings.

George, who on work days came straight from the office, was dressed casually today in jeans, a beige tee, a cinnamon cardigan, and a pretty copper necklace and earrings, an outfit that looked great with her flaming red hair. She'd ordered her typical winter drink, a glass of red wine. Marielle, in navy jeggings, high boots, and a blue-and-green-patterned sweater that hugged her curves, didn't have the usual cocktail glass in front of her. Instead, she was drinking something tall and slightly amber-colored. "What's that?" Lily asked.

"Gastown lemonade. Jack Daniel's and peach schnapps, lemonade, a hint of rosemary. Want to taste?" The brunette pushed the glass toward her.

"No, but thanks for the offer."

Kim arrived in a rush, and peeled off her jacket to reveal black jeans, a turquoise sweater, and a long, hand-painted scarf in shades of blue with gold accents. Today, the highlights in her spiky black hair were turquoise and gold. Her eyes sparkled and, as she slid into the chair across from Lily, she said, "Wait 'til you hear—"

She broke off as the waitress came to ask what she and Lily would like to drink. Lily ordered a martini and Kim, who usually studied the beer menu intently, said, "Some kind of light beer."

When the waitress started to list the options, Kim said, "The first."

As soon as the waitress left, Kim said, "Guess what? I'm engaged!"

They all squealed, congratulated her, and bombarded her with questions.

"Hold on, hold on." She held up both hands, laughing. "Let me answer. Ty proposed on Christmas Eve, when it was just the two of us. No, I don't have a ring because he's arranged for one of my friends, a jeweler, to make it, and he wants me to have input. And yes, both sets of parents gave us their blessing."

"That'll make things easier," Lily said enviously. Kim's parents had initially been adamant she marry a Chinese man, and Ty's parents had wanted him to marry a country girl. How fortunate that the young couple had managed to win them over. Lily reached over to squeeze Kim's hand. "I'm so happy for you."

Kim filled in more details until the drinks arrived, then the four women ordered appetizers: buttermilk onion and pepper rings, spicy chicken wings, and mojito fries with lime, cilantro, mint, and garlic.

Lily took a long swallow of her martini, willing the alcohol to ease her headache. "Did you get your parents out riding?" she asked Kim.

"Once, but it's not their thing. Actually, they just don't know how to relax. They're happiest on the Internet keeping the company running, and taking breaks to enjoy Ty's mom's cooking. Anyhow, enough about me. George, how was your Christmas, with all the family and friends there?"

"Great. And Woody absolutely loved the tee you made."

"Dax too," Lily broke in. "It was the perfect gift." Then she said to George, "Sorry to interrupt. Go on, tell us more."

George shared a few stories, then Marielle took her turn, then said, "How about you, Lily? Did you have a good one?"

"A midday family meal, then a late dinner at home with Dax. Nothing special." She sure wasn't going to tell them about ice cubes, or mention how seeing Dax cradle baby Sophia had sent a pang of longing through her heart. "We should discuss the book. What does everyone think so far? Marielle, are you glad you suggested it?"

The brunette nibbled an onion ring. "Haven't made up my mind yet."

"I can't relate to Cassandra," George said. "If a man tried to put a collar on me and treat me like a dog, I'd be out the door in a second. The same if he hit me."

Remembering the sting of Dax's slap against her buttock, Lily sipped her martini and kept quiet.

"But she's choosing it, right?" Kim said. "They each have their agendas. Neville's a dom, and he's determined to show her she's a submissive. What Cassandra wants is to experience intense sex. She's using him as much as he's using her."

"Which sure isn't my idea of a relationship," George said. "Mutual using? Yuck."

Marielle said, "Don't we all do that? I mean, we don't choose sex partners as some kind of charity work, right?"

They all chuckled, and Marielle went on. "We pick sex partners and friends because we expect to get something out of the relationship. Pleasure."

"Surely that's not all it comes down to," Lily said. "Get into a relationship for mutual pleasure then, when the pleasure ends or it's outweighed by inconvenience or worry or whatever, you bail?" Was that her and Dax's situation?

"No," George protested. "For most people, it's more than pleasure, it's caring. But as far as I can see, Neville and Cassandra don't have feelings for each other."

Before Lily could agree, Marielle snorted. "And you were madly in love with Woody when he humped you on that boardroom table right after you met."

"Oops." The redhead grinned. "Point taken."

"Yeah, George," Kim teased. "I at least talked to Ty and danced with him. I knew him a couple hours and liked him before we went at it on the hood of his truck in the parking lot."

"You did what?" Marielle exclaimed. "Girlfriend, you told us you hooked up with Ty that first night, but seriously, on a truck in a parking lot?"

Kim shrugged. "What can I say? Book club was reading *Ride Her, Cowboy* and I'd just read that sex scene under the stars. And there was this hot cowboy I'd been lusting after all day, and there were stars in the sky. Not to mention, I'd been slugging back beer and didn't have a single inhibition left."

"Inhibitions should be banished forever," Marielle declared, taking a chicken wing. She glanced at Lily. "Hey Doc Lily, aren't you going to argue that one?"

After letting herself be tied up and blindfolded? "Inhibitions can get in the way, but if you're going to banish them, you need to be sure you're in a safe situation."

"Neville told Cassandra it was, uh . . ." Kim paused. "Safe, sane, consensual, wasn't that it?"

"Which brings us back to the sex with a stranger thing," Marielle said. "If you're going to do it—and Kim, George, and I have—you need to trust you'll be safe. Right, girls?"

The other two nodded, and they all looked at Lily.

"I've never had sex with a stranger." Or anyone other than Dax. "Personally, I think I'd have trouble trusting a stranger enough to be intimate with him. For me, I need some emotional attachment before having sex. George and Kim, you did it the other way around: sex led to deeper emotions." If she and Dax continued to have passionate sex, could that lead to recapturing their true love and commitment?

"And then there's my way," Marielle said. "For me, liking a guy and having fun, not tying myself down to just one, that's what works." She nibbled a mojito fry. "Man, these are good. Somebody else eat some and save me from myself."

Kim took a fry. "You and Lily are saying we're all different, and that's okay. So what Cassandra's doing with Neville is okay." She bit into the fry.

"I have trouble with that," George said. "Even the term 'submissive' makes me cringe."

"Me, too," Lily agreed. "If a woman's submissive to a man, it can be a fine line before that tips over into something degrading and abusive."

"Exactly," George said.

"Who says the woman has to be the sub?" Marielle asked.

"True," Lily said.

Marielle gave her a cheeky grin. "You, I'd figure for a dom."

Kim and George giggled, while Lily rolled her eyes. "Gee, thanks for that, Marielle."

"So you've never had an urge to tie up your hubby and have your way with him?"

Into Lily's mind sprang an image of role-reversing Saturday night—and then Sunday, with the blindfold and ice cubes. "I never had an urge to do that," she forced herself to say, adding a silent amendment: *until now.*

"George, is there anything you like about the book?" Marielle asked.

"No." Then she said grudgingly, "Well, there's one concept I find appealing, at least in theory."

"What's that?" Lily asked. Though she didn't want to spoil her appetite for dinner, she snagged a couple of fries before the others polished them off.

"The idea of a man knowing what his woman needs in order to experience sexual satisfaction, and giving it to her."

"Isn't that what men are for?" Kim said flippantly. Then, "No, seriously, that's what being lovers should be about."

"Hey, you know I love men," Marielle said, occasioning another round of laughter, "and they can definitely come in handy, but a woman has to look out for herself."

"Exactly," George said. "She shouldn't give up control to a man."

"Hear, hear," Lily said.

"Wait," Kim said, "that's a really black-and-white statement.

There are different kinds of control. Like, of course a woman should be in ultimate control of her body. She gets to say no, which in the dom-sub world means saying a safe word. But if the woman does have that ultimate control—and if her man's giving her the best sex of her life—what's so bad about giving up some degree or type of control? Like, putting aside the whole BDSM thing for a minute, just, oh, letting the guy decide where you'll have sex this time and who'll be on top."

Or letting him tie you up or blindfold you . . .

"Sure," Marielle said. "A woman needs to know she can look after herself, but sometimes it's cool to just, like, let the guy handle stuff. In bed and out. Change the flat tire, fix the plumbing, buy the dinner—"

"Have you heard of feminism?" Lily interrupted.

Marielle winked and continued. "Buy you chocolates, give you multiple orgasms."

Lily grinned. "Well, okay, I wouldn't say no to chocolates and multiple orgasms." Yes, the climaxes Dax had given her the past couple of nights had been exceptional.

"We were talking about feminism this weekend," Kim said. "Mom and Betty Ronan are that generation, the real women's libbers. Anyhow, they say being a feminist doesn't mean you have to do everything yourself."

Like when Dax had fixed the kitchen faucet and saved Lily the trouble of doing it.

Kim went on. "It means you know you're equal and you're treated as equal."

"Equal? Oh come on," Marielle said teasingly, "we all know women are superior." She took a battered red-pepper ring and said to Lily, "What do you think of the book?"

"It troubles me. But it seems that's true for all of us. We haven't made up our minds yet."

"If you didn't have to read it for book club," Kim said, "would everyone keep reading? I would, because I want to understand Cassandra and Neville better."

"Same," Marielle jumped in. "Plus, I figure it'll give me some ideas." Her exaggerated wink made it clear what kind of ideas she was talking about.

"I don't like it," George said, "but I'd read on because I'm trying to understand why this kind of book appeals to so many women. Lily?"

Lily tapped her finger against the side of her nearly empty glass. "I'd keep reading."

"To analyze why these books are so popular?" George asked.

"Right." No way would she mention that the book had some weird connection to her and Dax's relationship and that, as Marielle said, it was giving them some sexy ideas.

"Are you okay?" Kim asked.

"Yes, of course." In fact her headache was gone.

"You've hardly eaten anything."

"Dax and I are going for an early dinner. By the way, if we're finished discussing the book . . ." She glanced around, collecting nods. "Can anyone recommend a restaurant? Smallish, not too fancy, but nice ambiance and food."

"What kind of food?" Marielle asked.

"Doesn't matter."

"Book club's been to some good places," George said.

"I feel like going someplace I've never been before." A place that had no memories attached, so it'd be just her and Dax, starting fresh.

"Do you like Greek?" Marielle asked. "There's a cute place on Davie, Takis' Taverna."

Marielle typically liked pubs and clubs where other twentysomethings hung out, so Lily said, "No offense, but it's not too clubby, is it?"

The brunette laughed. "Nope, the opposite. Cozy. Greek photos and stuff. Yummy food. The owner's from, um, I think it's Cyprus. I went there with a Greek guy who knows him."

"I've walked past it," Kim said. "She's right. It looks like a nice neighborhood restaurant."

"Sounds perfect. Thanks."

Kim cocked her head. "I'd have thought you'd prefer something classier."

"Hawksworth is excellent," George put in.

"I've been there." With her family, on her mother's last birthday. "It was great, but that's not the ambiance I'm looking for." Lily had enjoyed Hawksworth but Dax would probably think it was snotty. She wanted a place where she'd be comfortable in jeans and where conversation might flow more easily.

She turned curiously to Kim. "Why did you think I'd want something classy?" Yes, she'd grown up well off and had inherited a small fortune from her grandmother, but she never shared that information and she always tried to be unpretentious.

Kim said, "You always look so, you know . . ."

"Boring and conservative?" Lily asked wryly.

Kim's lips kinked. "Well, I do like artsy. I just meant, you have this upper-class vibe."

Damn. This was why guys like Dax never paid attention to her in high school. She didn't like it and honestly didn't have a clue how to shed it. "My mother taught me all these rules about clothes and appearance, and I don't have any confidence in my own judgment so I follow those rules."

"If you're ever in a rule-breaking mood, give me a call," Kim teased.

"And me," Marielle said promptly. "I'm the expert on breaking rules."

After they all chuckled, George said, "What are you doing these days anyway, Marielle? Are you still working at the liquor store?"

"No, it's holiday season so I'm taking a holiday."

Lily didn't know how much Marielle made at her constantly changing jobs, but she always had enough money to live the way she wanted to.

The waitress cleared the empty plates and they paid their bill.

"I have to go," Lily said, sliding off the bench seat. "Dax is picking me up here."

"Ooh," Marielle said, "we get to see the hubby."

"Gee, Marielle," Kim said, "I was going to surreptitiously sneak out after Lily rather than be so blatant about it."

Suddenly, the other three were rising. The four of them walked over to the door and clustered inside, getting into coats and scarves.

Through the pub window, Lily saw the silver Lexus pull up at the curb. Her husband climbed out of the driver's side. "That's Dax." She felt the usual thrill of excitement. He looked lean, strong, and a little dangerous in jeans and his battered brown leather jacket, worn unzipped over a black sweater. His longish black hair was damp; it wasn't raining out, so she knew he'd just showered.

"Oh, man," Marielle said, staring through the window. "You girls definitely know how to pick them."

"Very hot," Kim said, "though I've never been big on black-haired guys."

"That's lucky for Ty," George commented. Kim's rancher boyfriend had light brown hair with a sun-streaked look. "Lily, you and Dax are the perfect opposites, him so dark and rugged, and you so fair and elegant."

"Oh yes," Lily muttered, "we're opposites all right."

Twelve

A pretty young woman with wavy dark hair and coffee-colored skin came out of the pub and strode toward Dax, her hand extended. "Hi, I'm Lily's friend Marielle."

He shook. "Dax Xavier. Pleased to meet you."

"Hey there," he said to his wife as she and a couple of other women joined him and Marielle.

"Hi, Dax." She reached up to press a kiss on his mouth too quickly for him to respond. Then she introduced Kim, a petite Asian with short, color-streaked hair, and George, a slender redhead.

Each of Lily's friends was attractive in her own way. His wife was the most understated, in her tailored camel-colored coat and jeans, yet with her pale blond hair, fine features, and regal bearing, she drew the eye. Or, at least, she drew his eye, as she always had.

To Kim, he said, "You're the umbrella artist. I like your work."

"Thanks."

"And you're a helicopter bush pilot," Marielle said. "I bet you have some fascinating stories."

"Maybe one or two." He wondered what Lily had told these women about him. Usually, she was reserved about sharing her private life, but then he'd never known her to have close friends before.

"It sounds dangerous," Marielle said.

Nothing like flying in Afghanistan, but yeah, he'd had his close calls. Those were stories he never shared with Lily. She'd worried enough about him when he was in the army. "Not so much," he said.

"He's an excellent pilot," Lily said. Then, "We should head off."

"Nice to meet you all," he said. "Anyone need a ride?"

They all said no then exchanged good-byes. He opened the passenger door for Lily, then went around and climbed in. "I feel eagle eyes watching me." He started the car.

"I haven't said much about you or our marriage." She glanced over. "They think you're hot. No surprise."

Not knowing how to respond to that, he instead said, "Where do you want to go for dinner?"

"Marielle recommended a Greek restaurant on Davie. What do you think?"

His mouth watered. "Greek sounds good."

He drove through the sparse traffic. Rather than park in a two-hour curb slot, he pulled into a flat outdoor parking lot across from Takis' Taverna.

When he and Lily walked inside, he was relieved to see it wasn't the kind of fancy place his in-laws went for. Tables lined each side of the long room, and the décor was simple and attractive: white walls with bright blue accents, blue tablecloths set at an angle over white ones, bench seats and cushions in shades of gold. A white brick archway strung with Christmas lights added a welcoming touch, as did plants, Greek photos and paintings, and old-fashioned lamps. "Looks nice."

"It does."

At ten to six on Boxing Day, the place was almost empty. At a table by the window, a gray-haired couple chatted over an appetizer platter. Farther back, a youngish woman in a Beavers jersey sat alone with a glass of red wine and a tablet device.

Lily murmured, "See the jersey? George's fiancé is captain of the Beavers."

"Oh, yeah?" He caught a hockey game now and then, and had seen the Beavers win the Stanley Cup this year.

A middle-aged blond woman in a blue top came, smiling, to meet them. "Pick your table, folks."

Dax left the choice to Lily, and she selected a table for four near the back. It should be quiet there and give them a bit of privacy. When he'd suggested dinner, he'd remembered the early years, long meals filled with conversation and flirting. Lily'd never been big on public displays of affection, but flirting had been great foreplay. Tonight, he hoped they could recapture some of that relaxed fun.

Lily took the bench seat against the wall, peeling off her coat to reveal a sand-colored cardigan over a matching round-necked sweater. In her ears were the small gold studs she wore for work. She looked great, as always, but not exactly touchable.

Dax slung his bomber jacket on the chair across from her and sat down, shoving the sleeves of his lightweight wool sweater up his forearms.

"What would you like to drink?" the waitress asked.

"Martini for the lady, with a lemon twist. I'll take a bottle of beer. Got something Greek?"

"We have Mythos."

When the waitress had gone, Lily raised an eyebrow. "What if I didn't want a martini?"

"You always like a martini at the end of the day." Or had that changed too? "Don't you?"

"Well, yes, but . . . Am I really that predictable?"

He shrugged.

She frowned. "When was the last time I surprised you?"

That answer was easy. "This weekend. Your reaction to the things I did." His body heated at the memory.

She flushed, and when he tipped her a wink, her color heightened. "Other than that," she said primly.

"The books you've been reading, the umbrella." The pretty shirt in her closet, which he figured Kim must have made. "And they're all due to your book club," he pointed out.

The waitress served their drinks then left them alone with the menus.

"When's the last time you surprised yourself?" Dax asked. "Aside from this weekend."

She toyed with her martini glass. "All right, I get it. Book club's about the only thing that shakes me out of my routine. I try different foods, read books I wouldn't normally buy." A smile flickered across her face. "We went to a rodeo and a country and western bar." Then, seeing his expression, she said, "And that surprised you, didn't it?"

"Totally." Intrigued, he cocked his head. "How did you like the rodeo?"

"It was fun. Quite earthy and raw. Exciting. Those guys are crazy, doing what they do." She sipped her drink. "It was fun hanging out with other women. Kind of like high school, where the girls giggled over what guys were hot. That'd be you, by the way, though at the rodeo it was Ty and Blake."

"Ty and Blake?" Jealousy put an edge in his voice.

"Blake was Marielle's one—no, two-nighter. Ty is now Kim's fiancé, and they live together."

"Wow. Some rodeo."

"And bar, after. But yes, it was a fun day. We just, I don't know, acted like girls."

She was always a beautiful woman, but when her face softened like that, she took his breath away. "It's nice to see you making some friends."

So much for the softness. Stiffly, she said, "I have friends."

She did? He'd never met them, or even heard her mention them. She really did shut him out of her life. "Like who?" Again, his voice had an edge.

So did hers when she said, "No one you've met." Then she sighed. "Why are we like this? I feel like you're criticizing me, and I'm being defensive."

"Not criticizing," he said gruffly. "It's just that you don't include me in your life."

"Oh." The word sat there for a long moment before she said, "There are a few colleagues I have a drink with at medical conferences and events. You're right, I don't really have friends. When I went to premed in Toronto, I lost touch with my girlfriends from school. Since then, I've been too busy to make new ones."

"But now you have book club."

She nodded. "When I saw Marielle's poster in a coffee shop early in the year, it called out to me."

"All work, no play?" She'd always been disciplined and goal-focused, but she used to take time out to play with him, when they managed to be in the same city at the same time.

"Well . . ." She smiled. "I thought it would be highbrow literary conversation, but it really has become an hour of play each week. Discussing books got us talking about our views, values, experiences, and we've come to know and like each other. And I'm reading and thinking about things I wouldn't otherwise."

Like kinky sex. The woman sitting across from him, looking so proper in her sweater set and gold earrings, had let him tie her up, blindfold her, rub ice cubes over her body. Bring her to climax again and again. His cock swelled and he shifted position to try to ease the strain against his fly.

His body language or expression must have given him away. She rolled her eyes. "Other things than that." She picked up her menu and perused it.

Dax did the same, trying to think about food rather than sex. "Want to share a couple of appetizers? Maybe calamari?"

"Sure. And dolmades?"

"Done. Think I'll have the kleftiko for my main course." He closed his menu.

"What? Oh, the roast lamb. Sounds good. I'll have chicken souvlaki."

He glanced toward the waitress, who picked up on the cue and came to take the order. Dax added a request for a basket of pita bread and tzatziki, and they were set.

"It's so nice to have all these food options, after being in the bush," he told Lily.

"See," she teased, "there's something about Vancouver that you like."

"Touché."

They shared a smile then she said, "Did you have many flights today?"

"Yeah, I was busy. It worked out well, me being in town. One of their pilots had wanted to take a holiday, but the company didn't want to turn customers away."

"People really want scenic flights in winter?"

"It's pretty spectacular. Ocean, mountains, snow."

"If you can see anything for the rain."

"The satellite photos give a good idea when visibility will be the best. And if it's raining or foggy, well, that's West Coast ambiance."

She studied him curiously. "You like flying tourists?"

"I like flying. I like the ocean, the mountains. The tourists"—he shrugged—"sometimes they're great, sometimes they're awful, but they're not in my life for long. Same as anyone else I fly, on whatever job I'm doing. Geologists and engineers, fishermen and hunters, loggers and firefighters, doctors, lawyers, and First Nations chiefs."

"There are awful doctors?" she joked.

"Hard to believe, eh?"

"Do you fly doctors on holiday, or are they working?"

"Both. I've flown docs into remote mining or logging camps to do checkups and deal with minor illnesses and injuries, though if there's something urgent I'll fly the patient to a hospital. A few times, I've flown doctors to accident sites to patch up people enough that I can fly them out, if what's needed is beyond the scope of my paramedic training." He and Lily had never talked much about his work. When he'd been in the army, those stories hadn't been for sharing with his worried wife. It had become a habit, he guessed, for him not to tell and her not to ask. Now her interest warmed him.

She nodded thoughtfully. "What kind of accident sites?"

"Plane crashes, skiing or hiking accidents, snowmobile crashes. Often in places that can't be reached by ground transport, or where that'd take too long. A heli doesn't need much space to land. That's the beauty, compared to a small plane."

"I remember you saying that when you were in basic flight training."

Their appetizers arrived on a platter and they served themselves. Dax tasted, and sighed with satisfaction. Lily ate a calamari ring, which for some reason struck him as a sexy act, making his cock throb again.

"It's been four years," she said, "since you started your own business."

Dax swallowed a bite of pita and tzatziki. "Right." When he left the army, he hadn't suffered from PTSD, but his head had been kind of messed up and he hadn't slept much. He hadn't been comfortable around people, even Lily, and she'd eyed him warily—when she wasn't occupied in growing her Well Family Clinic. Feeling unsuited for a regular pilot job, a regular life, Dax had craved the peace and purity of nature, the independence of making his own way in the world.

"You did well right from the beginning."

He shrugged. "I knew some guys. Being ex-Forces didn't hurt. Means you know what you're doing up there, better than someone who's taken a basic flying course and put in his hours on Mickey Mouse flights. More offers come my way than I can handle."

"You could hire other pilots to work for you."

He snorted. "Don't want to be a boss. Want to fly helicopters."

"Nice work if you can get it," she said with a touch of bitterness, and sliced into a stuffed grape leaf.

Now what was up with her? "It is," he said evenly. "You have a problem with it?"

She ate the bite slowly. "There aren't many people who can go off and do whatever job they want, exactly the way they want."

Huh? "You're upset about my job? Lily, you've always encouraged me to be a pilot. You told me about ROTP. And when I was finishing my last tour of duty in Afghanistan, we discussed what I'd do next. I thought you supported the idea of doing bush flying."

"I do, Dax, honestly. You have a job that makes you happy." Her mouth twisted in a slight grimace. "At book club a few months back, we were talking about how some people have a special thing that they feel they were born to do. And how great it is if they can make a living doing it. You're doing that."

"So what's the problem?" Then a light dawned. "You mean because I'm away so much?"

She drained her martini glass. "That's one thing. It makes it hard to have a proper marriage."

Just like her devotion to the clinic did. But he'd long ago realized he and Lily would never have a traditional marriage. He was about to say so, but she was going on.

"The other thing is, it sounds so easy for you. You want to fly helicopters and don't want to be a boss. By which you mean not doing administrative tasks, managing people, and so on. Right?"

"You bet." He was trying to follow her, but wasn't clear what she was getting at.

The waitress came by to ask if Lily would like another martini.

"No, thanks. Could I please get a glass of red wine? Whatever you'd recommend."

"Of course." She turned to Dax. "Sir?"

"The same, please."

When she'd gone, he said to Lily, "Yeah, I don't like admin stuff. I do what I have to, like pay taxes, but that's it. Is that bad?"

"Nice work if you can get it," she said for the second time.

"I don't follow."

She sighed. "My thing, the thing I always believed I was born to do, is heal people."

"Yeah, of course." He'd known that since the night he met her. "To heal normal people who're sick or injured. It's why you chose family practice and stood up to your parents when they wanted you to go into a prestigious specialty."

"Yes, exactly. But now I spend more time on administration than on seeing patients."

"Why?"

"Because it's my clinic. I started it, I grew it. I'm responsible for it. For the patients, the doctors, the staff."

"How many doctors do you have now?" She'd never talked much about her work either. When she did, it was usually to share patient success stories, not the business end of things.

She groaned.

"Did I ask the wrong thing?"

"No, it just reminded me—" She broke off as the waitress brought their wine and cleared the empty appetizer plates.

"I'll be right back with your meals," the woman said.

Dax and Lily both stayed quiet until she'd served dinner and left.

"Reminded you?" he prompted as he cut into his tender meat.

"The Well Family Clinic has five doctors including me, which is barely enough to handle the existing patient load. And we keep getting new patients." She forked up some of the Greek salad that came with their meals.

"Stop taking them."

Her mouth tightened. "Our patients have babies. Or they beg us to take relatives and close friends who've moved to Vancouver, and it's hard to say no. On top of that, the baby-boom patients are getting older and having more health issues that bring them in to see us."

"Hmm. Yeah, I see what you mean. Sorry for being so flip about it."

She smiled briefly. "Thanks, Dax. Anyhow, now one of the doctors has to move to half-time. His wife is seriously ill and of course he wants to be with her. Her prognosis is uncertain. If she becomes terminal, which I sure hope doesn't happen, he'd take a full leave."

Dax's gut clenched at the thought of Lily being sick like that. It was one thing to know that their marriage might end, but the idea of her being seriously ill, maybe even dying . . . Shit. It was unthinkable. "Poor bastard," he said softly.

"I know. I'll give him every support I can, but it sure doesn't help the workload problems."

"Can't you find someone to fill in? A locum?"

"Maybe, though good ones are hard to find. Top priority is being great with patients, and the last locum we hired was. But she asked me so many questions, it would have been quicker to see the patients myself. Anyhow, yes, you're right. I'll have to put out the word, review applications, interview people. I just don't know when I'll have the time."

The answer seemed obvious. "Get one or two of the other doctors to do it."

She frowned. "Dax, it's my clinic. I'm responsible."

And a perfectionist control freak. It was one of the admirable things about Lily, the way she took responsibility and never shirked.

It was also one of the frustrating things, that she wouldn't share the load. He couldn't say any of that without pissing her off, so he settled for, "Tough situation," and took a bite of his delicious lamb.

"I'll handle it." The lines of stress around her eyes belied her words. "But see why I'm envious that you get to do what you enjoy, without the administrative hassle?"

He hated to see her looking so strained and unhappy. "You don't have to run a medical clinic. You could work as a doctor at someone else's clinic."

She shook her head. "You don't understand. I—"

"Ever since you went into practice, you've been making things bigger and better. Trying to impress your parents." And to compete with Anthony, who'd chosen a specialty—and a wife—they approved of.

"What's wrong with wanting my parents' approval?" She stared at him over the rim of her wineglass.

"They'll never give it. You should stop trying."

"That's not fair. To them or to me. They believe in the self-fulfilling prophecy: have high expectations of your children, and they'll meet them."

"*High* expectations?" He snorted. "No, Lily. *Their* expectations. They don't care about what you want. They won't be happy if you turn your clinic into the largest in the city. And they won't be happy as long as you're married to me." He picked up his own glass and took a hearty slug of wine.

"That's—" She bit her lip. "They're still my parents. I can't just ignore them, and—"

"Yes, you can." He put the glass down with a thump.

"No." She shook her head vigorously. "*You* can do that." Her voice rose. "You did it with your parents and grandparents. I'm sure you had your reasons, though I certainly don't know because you always refuse to talk about them. I know your father went to jail, and I can only guess that your mother and her parents did some pretty awful things."

"Whatever." His life up to the time he met Lily had been crappy. He hated thinking about it, so why would he want to talk about it?

"But my mom and dad aren't bad parents."

"That's a matter of opinion."

Blue eyes icy, she glared across the table. "What's that supposed to mean? They gave me everything. A good education, nice clothes, all the technological gizmos any student could possibly want, private lessons in French, Latin, piano, and—"

"They don't respect you," he said roughly. "They don't care about your feelings. They don't want a daughter, they want a puppet."

"You're wrong!"

"Hey, you're the one who said you feel like you have to agree with them to be loved."

"That was . . . I was overreacting. Of course they love me."

He should've known better. Her clinic and her parents were hot buttons. If he dared criticize the way she handled either, she got pissed off and defensive. Still, something drove him to keep trying, to make her see the truth. "They never accepted your choices. When we were dating, they tried to break us up. They never gave a damn that you loved me. They only agreed to the wedding when you told them we'd get married in the registry office. We've been married ten years and they still treat me like shit."

"You don't even try, Dax. Look at Regina, making nice because they're her in-laws. Why don't you do that, rather than provoke them?"

Be a doormat? No fucking way. "They're the ones who provoke me. They have since the day they met me."

"They wanted something different for me."

"Well, maybe they were right all along!"

Thirteen

Did Dax really mean that? His stormy gray eyes and the harsh lines of his face said that he might.

The waitress stepped up to their table and gestured to their nearly full plates. "You're not enjoying your meals?"

"They're very nice, thank you," Lily said quickly. "We were talking." Glancing around, she saw the restaurant was now two-thirds full. The table beside them was still empty, thank heavens.

"More wine?"

They both shook their heads.

When she left, Lily gazed back at Dax. Her husband; the only man she'd ever loved. "I don't know where this marriage is going," she said with sorrow, "but I do know that I loved you. I couldn't have married anyone else. Maybe we won't make it, but it wasn't wrong— at least for me—to marry you."

His grim expression dissolved into a troubled one. "It wasn't wrong for me either. You were the best thing that ever happened to me." Now there was pain in his eyes, which she knew her own mirrored. They were both talking about the past. What did the future hold?

The waitress brought two younger couples to the table beside them. The four promptly started sharing Christmas experiences and showing off gifts.

"I wish it wasn't Christmas," Lily said. "It's a tough time of year

to deal with difficult things, when everyone else seems so . . . cele-
bratory."

He nodded then a smile flickered. "We had some good Christ-
mases."

They'd always spent most of their time apart: Dax in Kingston
at Royal Military College and her at University of Toronto for
undergrad and med school; him in officer and pilot training then at
armed forces bases in Canada or deployed overseas; her doing her
residency at McGill then returning to Vancouver to set up her family practice. But, except for the years he'd been in Afghanistan and
couldn't get leave, they'd always come together at Christmas. Her
parents had hated it when she'd gone to Dax rather than come
"home" for Christmas. But for Lily, being with him, even in some
cold, run-down shack, felt like home to her.

"Remember the year I came to Saskatchewan? You had that
rental cottage near CFB Moose Jaw."

The grin returned and this time stayed. "Sure do. I was almost
finished with basic flying training."

Each time she and Dax got together those first years, she saw
new signs of maturity. His body was firmer and stronger and he had
confidence and presence. But that Christmas . . . She chuckled
softly. "You were so nervous."

"Yeah. Once we finished BFT, they decided on our next training:
rotary wing, fast jet, or multi-wing."

"Rotary wing being helicopters. I remember. You wanted so badly
to fly helicopters." More relaxed now, she returned to her meal.

"You bought me that pin for Christmas. Before I knew their decision."

She'd given him a gold helicopter pin. "You'd done so well, I was
sure you'd get assigned to rotary wing training."

He reached across the table and touched her left hand. "You
believed in me."

His gesture, his words, brought moisture to her eyes. She nodded, because if she'd spoken her voice would have quavered.

"That pin's on my flight jacket. It's my good-luck charm. Even when I had to wear a uniform, I pinned it inside my pocket."

He'd told her that when he went overseas. She'd hugged that thought tight, feeling as if a little piece of her was with him wherever he went, holding him close to her heart and keeping him safe.

He cleared his throat and released her hand. "Yeah, that was a good Christmas." He cut a piece of lamb then glanced at her again. "Even though you never wanted to go outside."

She resumed eating too. "I'd never been so cold in my life."

"Oh, come on, it couldn't have been all that much colder than Toronto."

"In Toronto, the temperature would go above freezing in December. In Moose Jaw, it never got near freezing. On the other hand, it gave us the perfect excuse to stay inside and snuggle by the fire." The tiny cottage had a wood-burning fireplace, and they'd spent much of their time in front of it.

They smiled at each other. "We did have good times, Dax," she said quietly. "We had something special."

"I know." His gaze turned speculative, and she wondered what he was thinking. But when he spoke, it was a change of subject. "When will the clinic be closed for New Year's?"

So he didn't want to keep reminiscing. It did emphasize how much they'd lost. "We're closing at noon on Friday, the thirtieth." She prepared a forkful of rice pilaf and roasted potato, an odd combination that she found particularly tasty. "Reopening on the second." She would use the time off for administrative tasks, including hunting for a locum.

For a few minutes, they ate in silence. When he'd cleaned his plate and she'd eaten all she could, the waitress cleared the table and asked if they'd like coffee. They both said yes.

They sat in silence. Lily was very aware of the lively chatter from the foursome beside them. She tried to think of a safe topic of conversation. Dinner had been more than a little edgy. Some nice memories and a lot of tension.

"So you finished that book," Dax said. "What did the book club think of it?"

Was *Bound by Desire* a safe topic? "We didn't finish it. Our rule is to only read a third each week."

He cocked an eyebrow. "Let me guess. You set that rule."

Amused and a touch exasperated, she asked, "Why do you hate rules so much?"

"Lily, I've told you before, I think rules have their place. Like preflight checks and VFR—visual flight rules." He paused then flashed a wicked grin. "Or rules like you having to obey me."

Her breath caught and a tingling sensation rippled over her skin. Had he introduced the topic of *Bound by Desire* to get them talking about sex? Glancing toward the noisy table beside them, she said in a low voice, "Or you stopping if I say Skookumchuck?"

"See?" The grin widened. "Those rules make sense." Then he sobered. "You can't run your life by rules. Rules and lists and plans."

So much for the sexy buzz. Now he was criticizing her again. "The one-third rule does make sense," she defended herself.

"Because God forbid someone actually get carried away and read all the way to the end?"

"That's right. People form impressions as they read. When they reach the end they've often forgotten what they thought when they began. This way, we can talk about how perceptions grow and change."

"Huh." He studied her. "Okay, I'm sorry. That does make sense."

"Thank you." One thing she'd always liked about Dax was his willingness to admit when he was wrong. She was less good at it herself; she hated admitting to any weakness.

"So, what does everyone think of the first third?"

"Troubled and intrigued. None of us relate to Cassandra and Neville." Her cheeks warmed. In a voice barely above a whisper, she said, "It's different from what you and I did."

"Yeah, it is." His voice was a low rumble. "It's one thing to slap your ass, but I'd never get turned on by causing you real pain. But, hmm, imagining you collared and leashed . . ."

She gave a snort of laughter. "Not going to happen." Then, in a mischievous whisper, "Marielle figures me more as a dom."

He'd been drinking coffee and almost choked as he laughed. "You are a take-charge kind of woman," he teased.

"Uh-huh. By which you really mean bossy."

A suggestive gleam lit his eyes. "Hey Lily, you can boss me around in bed any time you like."

The air between them was charged with an almost palpable fizz of sexual possibility. Her pulse raced. Feeling daring, she said, "Don't think I haven't imagined exactly that."

He sucked in a breath, audibly. Then he leaned forward and said, under his breath, "And now I'm hard. Tell me what you've imagined. And maybe, if you're very, very nice to me, I'll let you do it."

Not knowing where the words came from, she said, "*Let* me do it? No, Dax, you'll beg me."

"Jesus." A flush burned on his cheeks. "Let's get out of here." He glanced around, found the waitress, and gestured for the bill.

Oh God, what had she done? Did she have the guts to follow through on one of the scenarios she'd fantasized about? Even then, she'd only be role-reversing what Dax had done. Surely she had the imagination to come up with something original . . . She slipped her arms into her coat and buttoned it, then gathered her purse and umbrella.

Dax stood, holding his jacket casually in front of his body. To conceal an erection, she thought smugly. His own, very intimate, concealed weapon. That notion triggered a memory of Marielle talking about her cop boyfriend pretending to arrest her and doing a strip search.

Lily had never been good at improvising. Tonight, her mouth had raced ahead of her brain. She could either back down or forge ahead. She'd rely on a tactic she'd perfected in high school: when in doubt, bluff and pretend you know exactly what you're doing.

When they stepped outside, it was raining. She put up her umbrella, he shrugged into his jacket, and they jaywalked across to the parking lot. It was half-full of cars, but they were the only people. He unlocked the passenger door and she tossed her purse and umbrella inside. But she didn't get in. Heart racing with nerves, she turned to Dax.

"What's the—" he started.

"Sir." She deepened her voice and adopted a no-nonsense tone. "I'm a plainclothes police officer, and you're under arrest."

His eyes widened in surprise.

Oh God, what if he laughed? She'd be humiliated. "No sudden moves," she ordered. "Don't reach into your pockets. Keep your hands in sight. Take off your jacket and give it to me." No way could she physically control him, not with his size and strength. He'd have to opt in.

His eyes sharpened with a speculative gleam. "Yes, ma'am." He removed his jacket and handed it over. Under his fly, he was semi-hard.

Saturday and Sunday nights, she'd opted into his rules. Now he was obeying hers. Hopefully, he wouldn't challenge her as to whether they made sense. This wasn't about logic; it was about sex. "Don't call me ma'am, call me officer. Obey my orders. Speak only when spoken to." She tossed his jacket into the Lexus, trying to ignore the rain trickling down her face.

"Yes, Officer." A half smile curved his lips.

"Face the vehicle and bend forward with your hands on the roof. I need to search you." From the street, no one could see them, but anyone could walk into the parking lot. If someone she knew came by, Lily—who'd been raised to be on her best behavior in public—would die of embarrassment.

Dax braced his hands on the roof, arching his body back toward her.

How could she make this arousing rather than humorous? Her self-defense lessons had taught her about leverage and how to catch an opponent off guard. She bent slightly, took a deep breath, then on the exhale, she shoved her shoulder into his lower back, thrusting his body forward against the car.

He let out a surprised "Ooph."

"Spread your legs." When he did it, she said, "Hold that position." She leaned close to his ear. "Unless you can't take it. In which case, you know the word to say. Right?"

He tilted her a curious and, yes, aroused, glance. "I know the word, Officer."

"Good. I'm going to body search you to make sure you aren't carrying a concealed weapon." She took his right wrist between her hands and ran them slowly up his arm, feeling the clingy dampness of his sweater, the heat of his skin despite the chill rain, and the firmness of his muscles. When she reached his upper arm, his biceps flexed under her touch.

She did his left arm then patted down his back, from broad shoulders to narrow waist. Then she reached around to pat down his chest and ribs, forcing herself to stop at his waist. Her heart thudded, more with anxiety than arousal. What if a real police officer came along? What if she and Dax got hauled off to jail? What on earth was she thinking? She should know better than to improvise.

On the other hand, she was no quitter. If she started something, she finished it.

Her hair was slicked to her head now, dripping water onto her face. Definitely not her sexiest look. "Don't move." She bent to pat down the bottom part of his right leg then worked her way up. When she reached the top of his thigh, the roundness of his balls pressed against the crotch of his jeans. His hard-on was firm now, distending his fly. God, what a sexy sight, illuminated by the artificial gleam of the parking lot lights. Heat surged through her veins, making her quiver with the sudden rush of excitement. Her fingers itched to fondle him, but she forced herself to bend and pat down his other leg.

She froze at the sound of male voices, far too close. Glancing up, she saw two young men, holding hands, walking past the line of parked cars. One glanced toward her and Dax, did a double take, and nudged his friend, who also looked.

Dying of embarrassment, Lily stared back. They didn't know her. Bluffing was better than crumpling into a heap of mortification. Should she tell them to move along, that this was police business, or was that going too far? Impersonating an officer was an offense. Fortunately, they both shrugged and carried on. No doubt they'd seen weirder things in the West End.

The little rush of fear ramped up her excitement. Despite the chill rain, her flesh burned and tingled with sexual awareness. She drew in a breath and carried on with her search. This time, when she reached the top of Dax's thigh, she did cup her hand over his balls.

His body jerked.

"I told you not to move." His sac was so firm, so warm through the soft denim.

"Sorry, Officer."

"What's this?" she asked, running a finger up his fly, the firmness of his swollen penis triggering a needy ache deep in her sex. "Sir, are you carrying a concealed weapon?"

"No, Officer. That's all me."

"That's what they all say. I'll need to verify." Casting a glance around, she checked that they really were alone. Using her body to block the view of anyone who might walk by, she boldly unzipped his fly and reached inside his boxer briefs to grasp his naked penis.

"Shit!" It jerked in her hand.

She squeezed the hot, firm shaft. "You spoke. You disobeyed me. I'll have to take you in."

Unless they got arrested for indecent exposure first.

Fourteen

Was this really his wife? Classy, proper Lily fondling his cock in a public parking lot, setting up some crazy cop-criminal sex game?

"I'll come peaceably, Officer." In fact, he was on the verge of *coming* right now. It took all his self control to not pump himself against her hand.

She glanced over her shoulder then released him. "Adjust your clothing, prisoner."

He could barely stuff his swollen organ back into his jeans and zip up. Though his hair and clothes were soaking, he wasn't cold. Lily's coat protected her from the worst of the rain, but wet hair clung to her head in a sexy, fresh-out-of-the-shower way that made him imagine her naked body.

"I should handcuff you, but, uh, I used my handcuffs on the last person I arrested. So you'll drive. Keep your hands in sight at all times and don't make any sudden moves."

He was tempted to ask, "Or what?" but hell, he was enjoying this. They both climbed into the car and he started the engine.

"I'm taking you to a private holding facility," she said, and gave him the address of the condo.

What kind of "private holding" did she have in mind? He was tempted to turn the tables, to have the prisoner overpower the cop and take her hostage, but he'd had two nights of being in charge. It was her turn—and anticipation kept him hard.

When he parked the car underground, they both got out. She'd dried her face and fluffed up her hair so she looked almost normal now. She didn't act that way, though. "Clasp your hands behind your back and walk to the elevator."

He obeyed, finding it disconcerting to not see her, but hear the click of her boot heels on the concrete floor behind him. In the elevator, she had him face the door with his hands clasped at his back, and she stood behind him.

The elevator pinged at the first floor and stopped. "Keep quiet," Lily hissed as the doors opened.

The gray-haired couple with the white terrier stepped in. The woman's eyes widened at the sight of Dax's soaked clothing. "Young man, you really must remember to carry an umbrella in Vancouver."

Lily had told him to keep quiet, but he wasn't about to be rude to an elderly woman. "Yes, ma'am."

The couple got off on the second floor and Lily and Dax carried on to the fourth. She marched him down the hall and unlocked the door to their condo, pulling off her damp coat as they went inside. He automatically took off his shoes.

"Open the closet, prisoner. Hang up my coat then remove my boots."

He obeyed, tempted to caress her feet, but she pulled away and denied him that opportunity.

"Take out the toolbox, open it, and find a bungee cord."

When he did, she took the red-and-yellow cord. "Take your sweater off, turn around, and clasp your hands behind your back again. I'm going to handcuff them together."

He tugged the sweater over his head, glad to be rid of the wet, clingy wool. Naked to the waist, he turned his back, hands clasped, head bowed like a suitably humbled prisoner.

She wrapped the cord around and around his wrists, pulled it tight, and interlocked the two hooks.

Testing, he flexed his arms and tugged lightly, then harder. The cord bit into his skin and didn't give. Maybe if he tried hard enough, he could free himself, but he wasn't positive.

"Down the hall," she said.

He strode toward the bedroom with her following. Having his wrists bound, his freedom restrained—even if just in play—threw him off balance. Emotionally, as well as physically. It was a small taste of what giving up control and trusting someone else was all about—and it didn't come easily. Thank God this was just a game.

When he reached the middle of the bedroom floor, she said, "Stop. Don't move." She closed the blinds, turned on the lamp on the dresser, then went into the walk-in closet and slid the pocket door closed behind her.

Left alone, he chose not to move. What was she doing? This was more disconcerting than sexy. What had it been? Two minutes? Five? His jeans were cold and wet, his erection a thing of the past.

Finally, she emerged, and his body quickly heated again. Lily wore a tailored, slim-fitting white shirt, buttoned to the neck and at the cuffs, and her long legs were bare. The shirt skimmed the top of her thighs, just low enough that he couldn't tell what, if anything, she wore underneath.

"Prisoner." She came to stand in front of him. "I haven't decided whether to charge you. If you're a model prisoner, I might consider leniency."

"Thank you, Officer."

"First, I need to search you more thoroughly. And this . . ." She reached forward, unbuckled his belt, and yanked it through the loops. "Has to go. You could use it to hurt yourself, or as a weapon." She flung it across the room and put her hands at the waist of his jeans. His erection pressed against his fly. She fingered the waist button. "As for your jeans, you could twist the legs into a rope and use it to strangle yourself. Prisoner, do you feel an urge to harm yourself?"

He felt an urge to fuck her, preferably with his hands untied. "No, Officer."

She frowned. "Can I rely on your word?"

Realizing that of course he wanted his jeans off, he said, "Maybe not. I might turn suicidal."

Her eyes twinkled even as she forced her mouth into a firm line. "I appreciate your honesty. The jeans must go." She slid the button through the hole and in a quick swoosh unzipped the fly. Yanking on both sides of the waistband, she tugged his jeans down his hips and legs. They pooled at his ankles and he stepped out of them and kicked them aside.

Lily squatted and pulled off his socks. When she rose, she stared at the front of his black boxer briefs, where his hard-on bulged against soft cotton. "I have a dilemma. Is that still just you, or did you manage to slip a concealed weapon inside your clothing?"

"Best to check, Officer. You know I can't be relied on."

She made a choked sound in her throat and struggled to keep a straight face.

When she peeled down his briefs, he stepped out of them and stood with his feet apart, hands bungeed behind his back. It was, basically, the military "at ease" position—except that his cock thrust upward and slightly in Lily's direction. What now? If he was damned lucky, she'd wrap her mouth around him and give him relief, but he figured she had some kind of sexual torture in mind.

She tilted her head and gazed at him, cheeks flushed. "Prisoner, there's something I need from you. Will you give it to me?"

His cock. Damn right. "If I can."

"I certainly hope you can." She took a deep breath then said in a rush, "I need an orgasm."

Okay! Now she was talking. "Yes, Officer. I can give you an orgasm." Just let him get his hands on that sweet body, peel off the shirt and find out what lay beneath, thrust his fingers, then his cock, deep into her. He turned around so she could unbungee him.

"Oh no," she said in a surprised tone. "I can't take off the handcuffs. After all, you did say I can't rely on you."

What? He turned back, saw a challenging gleam in her blue eyes. She wanted him to bring her to climax without using his hands? As the idea sunk in, his cock thickened even more. He'd always been up for a challenge, and he was especially *up* for this one. But there was a potential problem. If he couldn't get her shirt off and carry her to the bed with his hands, he needed words. "Officer, may I have permission to ask a question?"

"Yes, prisoner."

"I'd be better able to meet your need if I could speak. May I speak?"

She cocked her head and he could see that, while she was pretending to consider his request, she'd already made up her mind. "No. Only to answer if I ask you a question."

Or, he knew, to call the whole thing off by saying "Skookumchuck," but no way would he do that.

He stared at the front of her shirt and tipped his head down then up, raking his gaze from hem to neck.

"No. My uniform stays on."

If she wanted to play dirty, so would he. He could use his body to herd her toward the bed, but instead he sank down on the rug to kneel in front of her. Her legs were close together and she didn't spread them.

He nudged the hem of her shirt upward with his head. No panties. Only pale, naked skin, blond curls, and pink pussy lips tucked shyly between her pressed-together inner thighs. Her scent told him she was aroused and he glimpsed a hint of moisture.

Dax had never realized how automatically he used his hands and arms, and how he relied on them, until he leaned in to lick the vee between her legs. It was hard to balance on his knees with his hands locked at his lower back. But the reward was sweet as he insinuated his tongue between her legs, licking and catching drops of her juice.

She eased her legs apart, and he could lap more freely, exploring her labia, firming his tongue to thrust inside her, flicking it over her clit. With each lick, heat pulsed through his blood to tighten his groin.

Lily gripped his head like she was steadying herself.

He continued to work her, rewarded with a moan of pleasure. Her legs trembled, then she said, "I need to lie down," and stepped away to walk to the bed.

Hiding a grin at getting what he wanted, he rose. Soon she'd be spread wide for him, quivering and whimpering as he drove her higher until she came. Then he'd plunge his aching cock inside her, and she'd climax again as he drove to release.

She sat on the edge of the bed. "I've changed my mind. I want two orgasms."

Exactly what he had in mind. "Yes, Officer." He kneeled and nudged her with his head, urging her to lie back. Her upper body tilted onto the bed, her feet remained on the rug, and her ass was on the edge of the bed. The prim white shirt covered her torso and arms, rode up her flat belly, and left her pink, gleaming sex exposed to him between her bent-kneed legs.

"Oh," she said with pretended casualness, "I did mention the other rule, didn't I? In giving me these orgasms, you can't use your cock."

He was taut with the need to come. How would he hold out? Even as a hormonal teen, he hadn't resorted to techniques like mentally reciting sports statistics—not that he knew many anyhow—to stave off orgasm. He figured it was insulting to his partner; besides, if you were having sex, why would you want to think of anything else?

Now, though, he might have to. In lieu of sports stats, he could recall helicopter technical specs. "Yes, Officer."

He leaned between her legs and used his tongue and lips on her. No slow torture this time; he wanted to work her to climax quickly. Twice. Then surely she'd let him seek his own release. Being the sub in dom-sub sex play was new and strange. Voluntarily giving up control. Trusting that she'd look after his needs—eventually. It disconcerted him, yet also turned him on something fierce.

He knew Lily's body inside and out. When he sucked her clit, her sharp moan told him she was on the edge. Though he couldn't use his fingers, he gave her everything he could: the rasp of his beard against her sensitive flesh, the quick probe of his tongue, the long, flat swipes that made her whimper. And he kept returning to her clit.

She lifted her lower legs, hooked her ankles behind his neck, and pressed herself, writhing, against his face.

Her musk filled his nostrils, her juices were tangy on his tongue, and damn it, he wanted to do her properly. His balls were hard and aching and his cock leaked pre-come.

He remembered his strategy. Helicopter specs. Earlier today, he'd been flying a Bell 429 on sightseeing flights. *Empty weight: 4,245 pounds*, he recited in his head. *Standard internal gross weight: 7000 pounds. External gross weight—*

Lily cried out and shuddered against him in climax.

He licked her, prolonging the sensations until her moans turned to a protest, then he pressed kisses to her tummy, letting her ease off and come down. But not for long. He wanted to give her that second orgasm, and hopefully then get his turn. *Useful load, standard: 2545 pounds.* He returned his attention to her pussy, gentle at first, then more demanding. And speaking of demanding, Christ, he needed to come. *Maximum external load: 3000 pounds.*

Hell, it felt like there were three thousand pounds of load in his balls and cock, ready to shoot free. He tongued her clit carefully, knowing it was more sensitive after she'd climaxed.

Her thigh muscles were taut; her body arched into him. "Oh God," she muttered, "oh God, oh God. Oh, oh!" and then she climaxed again, on a high cry.

He stayed with her until her legs relaxed and she unhooked her ankles from his neck and scooted up the bed. Once she was stretched out flat, she just lay there, the white shirt moving as she sucked in breath.

Dax stood, stretching out his knees. His cock rose straight up his belly, as full as it had ever been, the head purple and shiny with precome. If he could touch himself, he'd come in a stroke or two. But with his hands tied, he couldn't orgasm unless Lily let him. She was extracting sexual revenge for when he'd told her she wasn't allowed to come.

She pulled herself up to a sitting position, crossing her legs and adjusting her shirt so her pussy was again hidden. Her eyes widened slightly when she gazed at him. "Well, I'd say that was good behavior." Her voice was husky, as it often was after good sex. "Perhaps, prisoner, you deserve a reward."

"Thank God, Officer."

She shifted onto her hands and knees and crawled across the bed toward him, then again sat on the edge. With lazy movements, she unbuttoned one of her shirt cuffs, then the other, then undid a couple of buttons at the neck. She pulled the shirt over her head, revealing that she wore nothing under it.

Ah, he'd missed those rosy-tipped breasts. The sight of them made him leak another few drops.

"Come here," she ordered.

Cock leading the way, he obeyed eagerly.

She leaned forward, catching his cock between her soft, full breasts. With one hand she held him there, squeezing her breasts together to hug his organ. He groaned at the sweet, tantalizing contact.

She cupped his balls, rolled them gently. "So hard, everything's so hard and full and—"

"Fuck." That was it, he couldn't hold it any longer. Whatever she'd intended to say or do, it was too late. He pumped between her breasts, the soft friction of her hand and the sides of her breasts caressing his shaft. The orgasm he'd been fighting to control roared through him and he exploded in long, hard jerks, spurting across her chest and the tops of her breasts.

The force of his climax turned his legs to jelly and he barely managed to stay on his feet. Embarrassed by his lack of control, he pulled away. "Sorry. That was just too damned hot."

She touched her chest, dabbing a fingertip in his come, and lifted her hand to her mouth. She sucked her finger then, finally, gazed up at him. "It was. Very hot."

"Could the prisoner be released now?" Deliberately, he didn't add "officer." It seemed to him the sex game was over, but if she had a different idea, she'd let him know.

"I'd say he's earned it."

He turned and she fumbled with the bungee cord. "This is tight. I can't get it unhooked."

"Well, I can't help," he said dryly. "And it'll be embarrassing if we have to ask a neighbor."

"Very true." There was humor in her voice. She struggled harder, the cord digging into his wrists, then suddenly he was free and she said, "Whew."

He shook out his hands, arms, and shoulders gratefully. "You can say that again. Weird enough that those two guys saw us in the parking lot." He sank down beside her. "I can't believe you did that, Lily."

She slanted him a glance. "Not so predictable after all?"

"That's for sure." He eyed the come dripping between her breasts. "Want a shower? Or bath?"

She gave a slow, lazy smile. "I'd rather just go to bed." She spread his fluid over her breasts and chest, smoothing it into her skin. She'd once told him that semen contained protein, which was good for the skin. It had been years since he'd seen her do this, but then it had been years since he'd spilled anywhere other than in her pussy or mouth.

"Contact lenses," she said, and slipped off the bed.

He turned down the duvet and top sheet and climbed in.

A couple of minutes later she slid in to her side, then met him in the middle for a gentle kiss. "Night, Dax." She rolled onto her side away from him, into her normal sleeping position.

"Night." Mischief made him add, "Officer," as he spooned her, wrapping his arm around her waist.

A quiet chuckle shook her, and her hand settled atop his.

Fifteen

Wednesday afternoon, when Lily went to reception to ask Jennifer to book an ultrasound for the patient she'd just examined, the receptionist said, "Dr. Nyland, your sister-in-law's on the phone, holding for you. Line three."

"Thanks." Heart racing, Lily hurried past a handful of waiting patients, including a couple of toddlers playing around the artificial, child-friendly Christmas tree. It wasn't like Regina to call at work. What was wrong? She shoved the Zen garden out of the way—why did someone keep moving it to the center of her desk?—and grabbed up the phone. "Regina? Is something wrong with Sophia?"

"No, no, she's fine. I'm sorry to bother you, and I hate to ask this." Her normally poised voice sounded frazzled. "Our babysitter's come down with the flu and—"

"You want me to babysit tonight?" Lily made quick calculations. She had eight patients to see before the end of the day.

"I wouldn't ask, not with Dax home for Christmas, but my parents just left for the Caribbean and yours have plans. It's a holiday party being thrown by one of my biggest clients, so I can't bail. Anthony could stay home, but—"

"Regina, it's fine. You know I adore Sophia. What time do you need me?"

"Would six thirty work?"

"That's fine. I'll be there."

"I really appreciate this. Lily, bring Dax if you want. Sophia likes him."

"Uh . . ." Would Dax want to babysit an infant? Did she want to try on the roles of mom and dad when their future as husband and wife was still unresolved? "We'll see. How late are you likely to be?"

"Well, it's a dinner dance, so . . ."

"Could be late. No problem. See you at six thirty."

Now running late for her next patient, she called Dax's smart-phone, planning to leave voice mail. But he answered.

"You're not flying this afternoon?"

"Came in from one flight and we're fueling up for another. You got my message?"

"No, I haven't checked my phone since noon."

"This guy I flew with in the army is in town for a couple of days and wants to get together for a drink. I didn't know if you had plans for tonight." The previous night had been quiet. Rather than stay at the clinic, she'd brought her work home, doing online research on treatment options for one of her patients while Dax read.

"Regina just called. Their babysitter cancelled and they're des-perate, so I said I'd help out."

"Oh, sure. So you won't mind if I go out with Hank?"

"No, of course not." She pressed her lips together. Should she invite him to come babysit? No. How often did he get a chance to catch up with an army buddy? "Have fun."

Wow, look at you," Lily said to Regina, who'd answered the door. Her sister-in-law was svelte in a gorgeous black eve-ning dress and four-inch heeled sandals, her strawberry blond hair pulled back from her face with sparkly clips that matched her ear-rings and necklace. "You look fabulous."

Regina glanced down at herself. "I know, right? I barely recognize myself now that I've lost the pregnancy weight." She leaned forward to touch Lily's shoulder and air-kiss her cheek with shiny red lips. "Thank you so much for doing this."

"I'm always happy to spend time with my niece." Even if it made her biological clock tick faster. "Speaking of whom, where is she?"

Regina called, "Anthony? Lily's here." Then she muttered, "Where's my evening purse? I put it down somewhere. I swear, having a baby changes everything. Life was so organized before she came along, and now I'm a disaster."

"You're not a disaster," Lily's brother said, coming down the stairs. He wore a beautifully tailored black suit, a dove gray shirt, and a black-and-silver striped tie. Five-month-old Sophia rode on one arm like the princess she was. "You're perfect, Regina. Not to mention gorgeous." He came over to Lily. "Hi sis. Thanks for helping us out on such short notice."

"Not a problem." Lily pecked him on the cheek then peered more closely at his tie. "Hate to tell you, but you have"—she wrinkled her nose—"something undesirable on your tie."

"Oh, man." He squinted down at it then shook his head at the baby. "What have you done to me now, my girl? Regina, you take her. I'll go change my tie." He made to hand off the baby to his wife.

Lily intercepted the move and scooped Sophia into her arms. "Best not let you near that beautiful dress. And speaking of beautiful . . ." She buried her face in silky blond curls and inhaled the sweet scent of baby shampoo, milk, and Sophia.

Regina slipped into a black evening wrap and eyed them enviously. "I'd rather stay home with her than go to this party."

"Are you sorry you didn't take a longer maternity leave?"

"Yes and no. I love my job and I'm close to making partner. But when I'm with her, I don't want to be anywhere else."

"She does have that effect."

Anthony hurried downstairs again and he and Regina bestowed final kisses on their daughter and headed off.

When the door closed, Lily hugged the baby. "Just us now. How shall we spend our evening, precious?" Sophia was an easy child, happy to eat, play, crawl around exploring.

They did all of that until her niece tired, then Lily tucked her in, noticing that the butterfly mobile she'd given Sophia for Christmas hung above her crib. After checking the baby monitor, Lily went downstairs and settled on the couch. Opening her tote, she deliberated between computer and Kindle. She should work, but instead she decided to take this alone time to read.

Would she relate any better to BDSM now, after playing the cop dom? It had started as a challenge she'd set herself and had morphed into awkwardness, but then she'd felt an exhilarating and, yes, titillating sense of power. *And* a thrill that strong, utterly masculine Dax, had played along.

She picked up *Bound by Desire* where she'd left off, with Cassandra in a collar and leash, getting turned on by being paddled and spanked. Neville played her with his fingers, telling her not to climax. Finally he ordered her to, and her orgasm was instantaneous and powerful. Then, with her still on her hands and knees, leashed to a chair, he fucked her from behind. Again she came, several times, with the intensity she'd longed for.

Cassandra felt like melted wax, soft and warm and boneless. Oh yes, she'd been right about Neville. He'd given her the best sex of her life, better than she'd ever imagined.

When he pulled out and rose, she shuffled forward to ease the tension created by the leash and collar and slumped to the rug. Curled on her side, she was totally blissed out.

"Pet?" His voice was harsh. "I didn't tell you to move."

Sexy as the man was, her body couldn't handle any more orgasms right now. Besides, she had an early meeting and needed to catch two or three hours' sleep. Pretending meekness, she said, "I'm sorry, master. My arms and legs gave out."

"Ah. I see." His tone was more neutral than affectionate, but then their relationship was about sex, not caring. "Would it be correct to assume you'd like me to remove your collar?"

Glad that he got the picture, she said, "Yes, please, Master." Did he still expect her to use that term, or were the rules no longer in effect now that the sex was over?

He stood above her, naked. It was the first time she'd seen him, as he'd been behind her when they fucked and she hadn't been able to turn her head. God, he was powerful, and so beautifully muscled. He bent down and, with a quick move, undid the clasp on the collar.

It dropped free and her neck felt bare, exposed. Vulnerable. What a strange thought. She flicked it away and summoned the energy to stand. "That was amazing. I need to go to my room and catch a little sleep. I have an early meeting, and it'll last all day. But I'll be at the hotel tomorrow night. How about you?"

He turned his back and started to dress. "I think not."

"You don't think you'll be here?"

He didn't answer.

"Neville?"

After a long minute, he faced her. He was fully dressed, his expression impersonal. "We won't see each other again."

"But . . ." Her eyes widened. "Are you saying you didn't like the sex?" No man had ever complained about her performance as a lover.

"For a while. But in the end, you didn't please me, Cassandra."

"What?" She fisted her hands at her hips and glared at him. "I did everything you told me to. I even wore a fucking dog collar, Neville! And you climaxed. What the hell do you mean, I didn't please you?"

His expression softened with what looked like regret. "*I hoped you would learn, but you still deny your true nature.*"

"*I called you master. I let you paddle me. I played your game.*" *She'd given him more—far more—than she'd ever given another man.*

He shook his head. "*But it's not a game. It's our true nature. Our sexual being. I'm a dominant and you're a submissive. When you deny that, you cheat both of us.*"

She hugged her arms across her breasts. "*All right, so a little pain adds an edge that turns me on and makes the orgasms stronger. I admit that.*" *It was kind of freaky, but she could live with it.*

He gathered his paraphernalia: leash; collar, paddle. "*There's so much more to being a submissive. That's why I made you wear the collar and leash. To see how you reacted.*"

"*I don't understand.*"

"*If you were truly my pet, I would own you. These*"*—he held up the collar and leash—*"*symbolize that.*"

"*Own me?*" *She huffed.* "*What century do you live in? People don't own people these days. And if they try to, they'll be thrown in jail.*"

"*Not if the pet chooses it.*" *He tucked everything back into his bag and zipped it.*

"*At first when you called me 'pet,' I thought it was an endearment. Now that I know how you mean it, it's offensive.*"

"*It shouldn't be.*" *He came toward her and stood a couple of feet away, not touching her.* "*It expresses the relationship. An owner cares for his pet in all ways. It is a dom's duty and pleasure to look after his sub's well-being and pleasure. It is her duty and pleasure to trust him utterly, to serve his pleasure, and to trust that he will care for her and provide what she needs.*"

"*Like a good paddling?*" *she taunted.* "*I'm sure every good doggy loves that.*"

His jade eyes stared intently into hers. "*You did.*"

"As a sex game! That's all." Ooh! She wasn't some sex slave out of the dark ages. Infuriated, she whirled and stalked to the bathroom to dress. No, she'd certainly never be seeing that male chauvinist pig again!

That was where the chapter ended. Lily closed her Kindle and went upstairs to check on Sophia. The baby was sleeping peacefully, looking so sweet and innocent, such a contrast to *Bound by Desire*. Lily leaned over the crib to press a kiss to her niece's forehead, then headed down to the kitchen, where she made a cup of Earl Grey tea and took a couple of raisin oatmeal cookies from a package on the counter. Snack in hand, she returned to the living room and turned to the next chapter.

Six months later . . .

More nervous than she'd ever been, Cassandra listened as the phone rang. Once . . . Was Neville in his room? She'd located him via the Internet and phoned his assistant on a business pretext, finding out where he was. And she'd come. Now she sat, bundled in a hotel robe after a long shower and grooming session, in the chair by the desk in her room.

Two . . . Her crossed leg bounced uncontrollably. He had to be there. He had to be alone. He had to want to see her. In six months, no man had compared to Neville. No sex had satisfied her. When she'd climaxed, it was a hiccup, not an explosion.

Three . . . Damn it, she needed him. She, who'd never needed a man in her life, who'd never imagined being subordinate to one, had come crawling back. Well, no, that wasn't exactly correct. She—

"Neville Winter."

That deep, rich voice sent ripples of desire throughout her, combining with the flutters of anxiety. Trying to steady her voice, she said, "Neville, this is Cassandra Knightley." *Would he even remember her?*

"Cassandra. Hello, pet. It's been six months. You're more stubborn than I thought you'd be."

He'd expected her to come back? Not knowing what to think of that, she said, "We only spent a couple of hours together, but I can't forget them."

"You want more. You need more."

Oh yes! More of that push-the-bounds sex, for sure. What she hadn't yet figured out was exactly what she was willing to do—what he'd try to make her do—in order to get it. "I'm staying at the same hotel. Let's—" *She was about to say,* "Let's get together," *then realized he would want it phrased differently.* "May I come see you, master?"

"You may, pet. First, take off everything but your panties and shoes. High-heeled shoes, of course. Then put on your coat and come to my room."

Parade through this elegant hotel all but naked under her coat? This was a test. One that made her wet. "Yes, master."

He gave her his room number and hung up.

She pulled on her sexiest black lace thong and highest-heeled black sandals, and checked her hair and makeup. Because it was summer, the only coat she'd brought on this trip was a lightweight trench coat that barely came to mid thigh. She buttoned and belted it.

Stepping through the hallway and riding the elevator, she was utterly aware of her near-nakedness. The light abrasion of the coat's poplin pricked her nipples to attention. Air brushed her butt cheeks. With every stride, the coat split at the bottom, baring her naked legs almost to the top of her thighs. By the time she reached Neville's door, her whole body was sexually sensitized.

She tapped her knuckles against the door, catching her breath in anticipation.

The door opened and there he stood, in slim-fitting black pants and a crisp white dress shirt. But he was more than a handsome man in expensive clothes; Neville had an air of confidence, of command, that called out to something deeply female inside her. Oh yes, he was exactly as she remembered.

"Pet." He flashed one of the charming smiles he'd bestowed on her when they first met.

"Hello, master."

"Take off your coat."

When she made to walk through the door, he put up an arm to bar it. "Do you remember the rules? You obey."

She frowned, not understanding. "I was going to come in and take off my coat."

"I did not tell you to come in."

"You want me to . . ." Shocked, titillated, she glanced around. The hallway was empty, but someone might emerge from a room or elevator. "I'm sorry, master. I misunderstood." Fingers trembling with excitement, she undid the belt and buttons, took another quick glance, then stripped off her coat.

With his free hand, he took it, but he kept the door barred so she couldn't enter.

Now her entire body trembled—with arousal and with fear of discovery. How long would he keep her standing here?

He scanned her from head to toe. "Very good." He moved back from the door. "Come in, Cassandra, and tell me what brings you here."

She hurried into the sitting room of his suite. He'd called her Cassandra. Did that mean she could now call him Neville? Or was this another test? He hadn't told her to sit, so she didn't. She stood in front of him, still a few inches shorter despite her five-inch heels. "I will be honest with you, master. The things we did together, the pleasure I felt with you . . . it's made me wonder." She forced the words, taboo words she hardly dared think, out of her mouth. "You may be right about my sexual nature."

She gazed up at him, letting him see her confusion and her need. "Master, I need to find out. I know that's not what you want. You want someone who knows she's submissive. But I won't lie to you, I won't pretend. I'm asking you to be my teacher, to help me discover who I truly am." And then she bowed her head, awaiting his verdict.

He kept her waiting. She didn't move, didn't speak again.

Then he said, "Go into the bedroom, pet. In my black bag, you will find padded cuffs for your ankles and wrists, and a blindfold. Put them on the bed and wait for me."

She'd expected the leash and collar. In fact, her neck felt naked without the collar. If he cuffed her wrists and ankles, she'd be completely in his power, unable to free herself unless she spoke her safe word. Her pussy clenched and the juices of arousal moistened her labia and inner thighs. "Master, may I speak?"

"You will not question me. You must trust me."

"I do." To give her pain, screaming orgasms, and enlightenment. "I only wanted to say that my safe word is—"

"Orchid."

"You remember?"

"Did I not tell you of a dominant's responsibility to look after his submissive's well-being? Be assured that if you say 'orchid,' I will cease whatever I'm doing."

Cease? No pain, no pleasure? She'd lose Neville's attention, his single-minded focus on her. And she knew, without him having to say it, that he would be displeased.

The idea of Neville ceasing was far less bearable than the idea of being handcuffed and blindfolded, entirely at his mercy.

An ultimatum. Lily rested her head against the back of the couch and reflected on that. Her first reaction was, *How obnoxious.* And yet, in every relationship, each partner had the ultimate power to walk away. Wasn't that the dilemma she and Dax were dealing with: deciding what each of them needed out of their marriage in order to stay? For her, it was love, trust, more time together, and children. A family.

She glanced around the beautifully decorated living room, where a stack of medical journals, *Canadian Lawyer* magazine, a child-rearing book, and a couple of stuffed animals attested to the family that lived here.

This. This was what she wanted. Could she have it? She saw many parallels between herself and Regina, but Dax was a very different man from Anthony. It was his difference, in part, that had first attracted her—and, to be honest, still did. His edge, his raw masculinity, his tough-guy independence. But as part of that package, came his need for freedom, his craving for the wilderness.

Would those qualities make it impossible to have a future together?

Two things, real quick," Jennifer, the receptionist, said as she caught Lily leaving one examining room and heading to the next. It was Friday morning, December thirtieth. "Hope it's okay, but I told Melinda Yee she could bring Jimmy in. He's got an infection and high fever."

"That makes four emergency squeeze-ins. But of course she can bring Jimmy." So much for the notion of closing at noon and doing some paperwork. Patients came first. "Second thing?"

"Your husband called and wants you to call him back. He figured you wouldn't be checking your smartphone."

Lily glanced at her watch. "Would you tell Eustace Grant that I'm running a little late? He's in room—"

"I know. Go, call your husband."

Lily hurried back to the large office the doctors shared and called Dax. "Things are crazy here, so I don't have much time."

"I'll make it quick. I'm picking you up at twelve."

"Thanks, but I'm going to stay for the afternoon."

"You said you were closing at noon."

"We've been squeezing in emergency patients, and when we do close I need to do some paperwork."

Dr. Vijaya Murthy hurried into the office, did a finger wave to Lily, pulled a medical tome from the bookshelf, and rushed out again.

"Let the other doctors handle the patients. I'll be there at twelve."

She huffed. The story of their relationship these days: steps forward, then steps back. Why couldn't he respect her needs? "Dax, I don't have time to argue."

"Then don't argue." A pause, then, "It was supposed to be a surprise. We're going up to Whistler for the weekend."

"What?"

"I've booked a place."

"Dax! Are you insane?" She shook her head vigorously, her short hair flying out as if she'd been hit by a static charge. He'd made secret plans without consulting her? "What were you thinking?"

"That you need some time off work. That we might both enjoy it. That it'd be good to get away."

All good points, she had to admit. "All right, I can see that." She lowered her voice as Dr. Harry Chew came in, opened a storage cupboard, and scanned the shelves. "If you'd discussed it with me a few days ago, I might have agreed, and prepared for it." Harry pulled out a prescription pad and hurried off. That was another thing the clinic needed: a better system of organizing and ordering office supplies. And maybe an office with more privacy for the doctors.

"I did ask you when the clinic would be closed. And what the hell's wrong with the occasional surprise?"

He had asked, at dinner on Monday. They'd been reminiscing about that wonderful Christmas in Moose Jaw. Had that given him the idea? "I don't do so well with surprises," she admitted, picking up the Zen garden's miniature rake and drawing patterns in the sand.

"You were more flexible when you were younger."

"I had fewer responsibilities."

"You need a break from all those responsibilities." He paused. "Noon. I'll be in the parking lot behind the clinic." Then he hung up.

Should she call him back?

"Dr. Nyland?" It was Jennifer again, poking her head through the office door. "Is everything okay?" Her gaze dropped to the rake in Lily's fingers.

Lily put it down and stood. "My husband announced that he's picking me up at noon and taking me up to Whistler for New Year's."

"Oh my gosh! How romantic!"

Romantic? Well, yes, she supposed it was. For a woman who liked surprises. "I'm a little stunned."

"You'll have a fabulous time. And you sure need—I mean, deserve—the break, Dr. Nyland."

Another person who thought she needed time off. Lily glanced at the Zen garden, wondering if it had come from Jennifer. "What about the emergency squeeze-ins?"

She waved a hand. "I'll work it out. Mr. Grant's waiting for you."

Leave it to a receptionist to manage the patient load? That went against the grain, but Dax had given her no choice. "Thanks, Jennifer."

Dax had given her no choice. The thought gave her pause. Was this a dom game? Or just Dax being a take-charge guy, like he used to be? Either way, a thrill of excitement rippled through her.

Anxiety followed quickly. A long weekend at Whistler, just the two of them. That was very different from spending a few hours together in the evening. Their feelings for each other . . . surely they'd become clear over the weekend. What if they found out they really no longer loved each other?

She took a deep breath. Well, then they'd know. That was what she wanted, wasn't it? A resolution. Divorce would be horrible, but if she truly no longer loved her husband, she'd be able to move on.

A thought struck her. What if she did love him, but his love for her had died? Her heart clutched with pain. But no, she shouldn't be pessimistic. Surely Dax wouldn't have planned this getaway if he wasn't hopeful that they'd renew their love and bring fresh commitment and energy to their marriage—and to building a family.

Sixteen

Dax pulled the Lexus into the parking lot behind the medical building on Broadway. The weather was on his side, offering up a crisp day and clear skies. Now if only Lily was as cooperative. At least she hadn't phoned or texted to say no.

He'd taken a risk. But if he'd asked her, she'd have found reasons not to go. She'd been brought up to overanalyze and plan things to death. It had always been a challenge to get her to loosen up. But when she did, it was worth it.

If this weekend worked out, it'd prove they could still have a great time together. Hopefully, they'd relax, have fun, recapture the love they felt before doubts crept in. Then they could restore their marriage to how it used to be. Now that his soul had healed after Afghanistan, he'd be happy to come back to Vancouver more often, perhaps intersperse remote jobs with local ones—if Lily decided that she wanted to make space for him in her life the way she used to.

This was his new strategy. Complaining that she worked too hard and suggesting she handle her clinic differently only got her back up. Instead, he intended to show her the benefits of taking time off to be with him.

The building door opened, letting out a woman with a cane, a young guy carrying a baby, and then Lily. She glanced around, saw the car, and headed over.

Inside the car, she said, "Whistler? We're really doing this?" Her tone said she hadn't decided if it was a good or a bad idea.

"Yup. I rented a cabin." He pulled out of the parking spot.

Her eyebrows lifted. "A cabin? Not a hotel room?"

He'd called contacts at Whistler, mostly other pilots, and located a cabin owned by Vancouver people who used it for weekends and holidays. This Christmas they had a brand-new baby and were staying in Vancouver. Occasionally, they rented out the place, and mutual friends had vouched for Dax. "We needed a cabin."

"Oh we did, did we? Why's that?"

He stopped at the parking attendant's booth and paid, then drove out onto the street. "It'll be like that Christmas in Moose Jaw." Snuggling by the fire while the snow came down. Making love. "It's a log cabin with a real wood fireplace. We can drink rum toddies by the fire. It's an easy walk to Whistler Village and they have clothing stores, so if I didn't pack the right stuff for you—"

"Wait a minute. You packed for me?"

"Yeah, so we wouldn't waste time. For meals, we can pick up groceries and cook, or get takeout, or eat at nice restaurants. Whatever you want."

"Oh Dax." She sighed. "You should have talked to me first."

"And have you run through a whole list of reasons why it couldn't work?" He glanced at her. "You have admin stuff to work on. You need to look for a locum. What if a patient has an emergency? Am I hitting the main points?"

"Some of them." She gazed out the windshield then, quietly, added to his list. "What if we don't get along? What if it's a disaster?"

He swallowed. Yeah, of course the possibility had occurred to him. "Then we'll know, Lily. And that's not such a bad thing, is it?" He eased the Lexus to a stop at a red light, behind several other cars.

Lily turned to him. "It's better than carrying on the way things have been." She swallowed. "But you wouldn't have planned this trip if you thought we had no hope."

He reached over to squeeze her pant-clad leg. "You got that right." And she wouldn't be sitting beside him if she didn't think so too.

She rested her hand on top of his.

Regretfully, he had to free his hand when the light changed.

She reached into her purse and pulled out her phone. "Haven't had a chance to check messages today." A moment later, she said, "Kim wants us to break the one-third rule."

"She's hooked and wants to finish the book?"

"No, just the scene. Apparently there's one in a BDSM club?"

"There sure is."

"Kim says that, purely for the sake of our discussion, it makes sense to finish the scene."

"Purely for the sake of discussion."

She tapped the screen. "And Marielle's response is, no surprise, let's for once throw out the rules and finish the book." More taps. "George agrees. She wants to get it over with."

"You gonna vote for breaking the rule?"

"What do you think?" Her fingers tapped busily away.

"I think your curiosity's aroused. Right?"

"Right."

"Curiosity's a good thing to have aroused, but there are even better th—"

"Dax?" she interrupted. "Where are you going?"

Finished with her phone, she'd looked up and realized that he'd turned off Smithe Street onto Burrard, and crossed West Georgia, which wasn't the route to Whistler.

When he didn't answer, she said, "Are we going somewhere before we drive up to Whistler?"

He tossed her a cocky grin, his spirits rising with each block they traveled.

"Wait a minute. You're wearing your flight jacket. We're flying up?"

"Why would I drive when I could fly?"

"Oh my gosh, you're flying me to Whistler!" Her voice rose with excitement. "Dax, you haven't taken me flying in forever."

He shrugged. "We've both been busy." He glanced over. "You didn't say you wanted to go."

"You didn't invite me." She made a snort-like sound. "And isn't that typical of how things went wrong with us?" She turned toward him. "Thank you for doing this."

"Thanks for agreeing." Teasingly, he added, "Finally."

"Give me long enough to get my head around it," she responded in the same light tone, "and I can be spontaneous."

They both chuckled. Light turned to darkness as the road took them under Canada Place. When they came out into the sunshine again, Lily said, "You were always good for me that way. You helped me be more spontaneous. More confident and—"

"Confident? Lily, you've always been one of the smartest, strongest, most goal-directed people I'd ever met." He'd always liked how different she was from his ditzy mom.

"I was going to say, more confident about trusting my instincts. My heart. My passions." Her tone was solemn.

He pulled into the Vancouver Harbour Heliport parking lot, turned off the engine, and released his seat belt so he could face her. "You mean about the two of us?"

Her eyes, the shade of the pale blue winter sky, were clear and candid. "Yes, and about my career."

"When I met you, you already knew what you wanted to do."

"And that my parents would disapprove. I hadn't told them I wanted to be a plain old family practitioner. You supported me, which gave me the courage to follow my heart." She made a face. "Even though it meant they'd give me flack about it for the rest of my life."

He bit back a disparaging comment about her parents, not wanting to get her back up. "Maybe you're not curing cancer patients like Anthony, but you make a difference every day in your patients' lives. That seems pretty damned important to me."

Her eyes softened and went misty. "You always believed in me."

"And you believed in me." He touched the gold helicopter pinned to the collar of his flight jacket. Battered now from all the places it had traveled, and from more than a couple of close calls, it was his lucky charm, his symbol of his wife's belief in him. "You gave *me* the confidence to go after what I wanted." Including her, which seemed kind of ironic now.

Her gaze rested on the pin then lifted to his face. She touched his cheek. "How did we lose all of that?"

Her hand was so warm, so gentle. Caring, he hoped. He took it between his and shook his head. "Not being together enough?"

"Each of us being so independent?"

"Could be." He lifted her hand to his mouth, pressed a kiss into her palm, and folded her fingers around it.

When he'd returned to Vancouver last Saturday, he'd believed their marriage was only worth keeping if they could recapture their passion and love. On Sunday, they'd confessed that they weren't sure they still loved each other, or wanted to save their marriage. Now here they were: struggling through awkward conversations, experimenting with kinky sex, heading off for a weekend in snow country. He grinned at her. "Let's go fly, sweetheart." The endearment popped out, and he couldn't remember the last time he'd used it.

"Let's go fly."

Her endearment for him had been "my love." He refused to let the fact that she didn't use it discourage him. They both had hope, and that was more than they'd had in a long time.

He and Lily climbed out of the car and he opened the trunk. He handed her an overnight bag. "This has jeans, a sweater, and your sheepskin jacket. They'll be more comfy for the flight."

"Thanks."

He hefted his duffel, her suitcase, and a shopping bag with the lunch he'd brought, and they headed for the waiting room.

"Did you arrange this with the company you've been flying with this week?"

"Yes, SeaSky." Automatically, he made an assessing scan of the bright, half-full waiting room that served the companies that flew out of the public heliport. It was the usual mix of businesspeople, students, and tourists. He gave a second look to a slim brunette, twentyish, sitting alone; she looked feverish and was rubbing her head. Sure hoped she didn't have something contagious. Not that it was his concern today, as he had only one very special passenger.

"I need to do some paperwork and a pre-flight check," he told Lily, who was gazing out the large windows at the harbor view. "I'll come get you in fifteen minutes." He went behind the desk to greet a couple of SeaSky staff and fill out the necessary forms. They'd given him a Bell 206B Jet Ranger turbine engine with seating capacity for four passengers. A classic machine he always enjoyed flying. He carted their luggage out to the waiting helicopter and stowed it, put on his helmet and did his check, then went in to collect Lily.

The passengers stood in a cluster, their backs to him, voices high-pitched, watching something he couldn't see. People shifted, and between bodies he glimpsed Lily, down on the floor. Heart leaping with anxiety, he rushed forward.

No, thank God, she was okay. The brunette girl he'd noticed earlier lay on the floor, with Lily kneeling beside her. Clad in jeans and a cream cable-knit sweater, his wife looked young and beautiful—but her manner was pure medical authority. She directed rapid-fire questions to a panicky looking girl and boy the same age as her patient, then spoke into her phone. "She's had the flu. A lot of vomiting over the past week. No doubt dehydrated. Friends report she had a headache and seemed a little disoriented. She obviously wasn't monitoring her blood sugar."

Dax checked the girl's right wrist, saw the medical alert bracelet, and put two and two together. Diabetic coma. He had some paramedic training, but Lily clearly had this under control.

He spread his arms and urged the clustered passengers away. "Move back, folks. Let's give the doctor room to work."

As Lily gave the girl's vital signs, he heard an approaching siren and realized she was conveying information to the ambulance crew. "She needs IV fluids stat," she said, "and possibly insulin."

Over by the front door, Jorge, one of the SeaSky staff, stood waving his arms to direct the incoming ambulance. Dax ensured there was a clear path from the door, and seconds later the paramedics rushed in.

He watched proudly as Lily worked with them, and in no time the girl was hooked up to an IV bag and being loaded onto a stretcher.

When Lily stepped back, he went to her side. "Do you need to go with her?"

Her troubled gaze flicked to him, then back to the woman. Could she bring herself to trust the patient to someone else or, as usual, would her job come first?

Shit, he was a selfish bastard. "If you need to go, I understand."

Slowly, she turned her gaze back to him. "St. Paul's is only minutes away and the paramedics have it under control."

Relieved, he caught her hand and squeezed it. "She's damned lucky you were here. What was she thinking, not taking better care of herself?"

"Kids think they're invincible. Her friends said they'd had the trip planned and she really wanted to go. She'll pay more attention next time."

Thanks to Lily, there'd be a next time. He put his arm around her shoulders. "You did good, Doc."

She shrugged. "Simple stuff. If I hadn't been here, the paramedics would have saved her."

"You gave them a head start so they knew exactly what to do when they arrived." He pulled her tighter. "What you do is important." If he told her enough times, would she stop letting her parents disrespect her?

"Thanks."

"And now your chariot awaits."

She put on her jacket, he collected her overnight bag, and they walked outside and down the ramp to the helicopter. She gazed at the shiny blue and white machine. "This is exciting."

No, she was exciting. And impressive. And sexy. "Lily." He cupped her head between his hands.

"Dax?" Then, as he bent to kiss her, she smiled and rose to meet him.

Her lips were chilly in the cool air, but warmed quickly. He kept the kiss slow and tender, aware that the people in the waiting room could see them.

When their lips parted, her gaze was solemn. "I want this. Us. I want our love back. But it feels like such a big task, trying to fix all the things that have gone wrong. How are we going to do it?"

Like he had magic answers? She was the planner. "One step at a time, I guess. And here's the first." He ushered her into the helicopter then took his own seat and they buckled up. A flight was due in from Victoria, and he needed to get this bird in the air.

She touched the clear window beside her. "I remember the first time you took me up. How disconcerting it was, having almost nothing between us and the sky. With the huge windows, it's so much more immediate than being in a plane."

"Another reason I prefer helis."

Lily put on her sunglasses and the headset that would let them talk to each other, and kept quiet as the engine caught, the rotor blades spun, and he got clearance from the air traffic control tower to lift off.

The helicopter vibrated, power gathering. Dax never lost that tiny thrill of anticipation and the leap of his heart when the machine's skids broke contact with the ground. He took her up and set her on course, scanning the air space and water of Vancouver Harbour, then Coal Harbour, noting the HeliJet flight from Victoria, a seaplane landing, and another taking off. Visibility was great, the sky a clear, chilly blue. After they'd flown over Lions Gate Bridge, he spoke to Lily though their headsets. "Great day for flying."

"We couldn't have asked for better weather."

"There's a bag beside you. I bought a couple of sandwiches. Egg salad and ham and cheese. Take your pick."

"Mmm, nice. You remembered I like egg salad."

Not about to accuse her again of being predictable, he said, "Hoped you still did."

She opened the lunch bag, handed him the ham sandwich, and started eating the egg one. He'd also included a couple of fruit drinks.

In cruise flight, Dax kept his right hand on the cyclic, balanced the sandwich wrapper on his lap, and moved his left hand away from the collective periodically to take a bite.

When he flew tourists, he had to tell them about the scenery and answer questions, but his preference was to not talk when flying. Up in the sky on a day when the weather was stable, a sense of serenity came over him. Perhaps Lily shared that mood, because she spoke little, only an occasional comment about the world unfurling below them. The pristine whiteness of the snow capping the North Shore mountains; how the view from the gondolas at Grouse Mountain couldn't compare to the one from the helicopter; how nice it was to cruise above the traffic on the busy Sea to Sky Highway. Dax pointed out the controlled development at Furry Creek, a tug towing a huge log boom, a pair of bald eagles on a tall tree in Brackendale, the abandoned town of Garibaldi.

Too quickly, they arrived at Whistler, and he set the helicopter down at the heliport.

"Thank you," Lily said as he helped her out. "That was a lovely flight."

"My pleasure."

He retrieved their luggage and they went into the office, where he did paperwork, then they climbed into a taxi.

Whistler sparkled with the dazzle of sunshine on snow, a ski village designed to harmonize with the natural environment. The center of town, the tourist area, was too ritzy for Dax's taste, but he did love the majestic scenery, and most of the residential areas were understated and appealing. That was true of White Gold, where they were staying. Christmas lights and decorations were still displayed at many houses.

When the cab pulled up in front of the rental cabin, Lily said, "How cute. It looks like a gingerbread house." The peaked roof was covered with snow and icicles hung from the eaves. Shuttered windows looked like sleeping eyes waiting to open.

Dax lugged their stuff to the snow-covered porch. "I'll get the key." He found it, as the owners had promised, tucked behind a shutter on a side window. The front door led into a mudroom. On one side, a long rectangular box formed a bench seat, and on the other wall jackets hung on hooks above several pairs of boots. Three pairs of skis and two snowboards—one big, one small—were stacked in a corner.

"Don't take your jacket off," he warned. "It'll be cold inside. We can turn on the heat then walk into the Village and pick up groceries."

They did both take off their boots before stepping into a living room with log walls and a sizable fireplace made of rough stones, with a basket of logs and kindling beside it. The furniture was casual and suited the room: a couch and sofa done in blue and green upholstery, comfy looking chairs, wooden coffee tables, all a little the worse for wear. Bookcases on either side of the fireplace overflowed with books, DVDs, and games. Framed photographs covered the walls. He moved closer to take a look. "This must be the couple who owns it."

Lily stepped up beside him and they both studied a photo of a tanned man and woman a little older than them with a boy aged seven or eight. Posed with mountain bikes, they wore shorts and tees and held helmets. The woman had a baby bump.

The people who owned this house had the life he'd once dreamed of: a happy family with easy access to wilderness adventure.

"A nice-looking family," Lily said with a hint of something—wistfulness?—in her voice. Did she too feel a moment's regret for a youthful dream they'd both outgrown?

"I like this place," she said.

"I doubt your mom would think much of their interior decorator."

She laughed softly, but when she answered, her voice had that same wistful tone. "No, but this is a home." More of a home than the house she'd grown up in. She didn't have to say those words; they both knew the truth. As for him, he'd never really had a home, yet gut instinct recognized this as one.

Seventeen

Lily gazed at her husband, so handsome and rugged in his jeans and flight jacket. Dax fit this room with its big stone fireplace and comfy, if shabby, furniture. He fit here better than in the Vancouver condo.

The room had personality and character; it looked lived in. In her parents' home, she and Anthony had learned to leave no sign of their presence. An image came into her mind, of Anthony's and Regina's living room. Her brother had loosened up since he'd married, and again since they'd had Sophia. But Lily maintained the discipline she'd learned as a child and had trained Dax to tidy up after himself. No wonder he rarely came back to a place that didn't look like a home.

He reached for her hand and intertwined their fingers. "I'll turn on the heat then let's go buy food. Do you want to eat in or go out tonight?"

"Let's eat in. By the fire." Food, wine, and a crackling fire. Relaxation, if such a thing were possible when so many huge issues hung over their heads. Even if they did rekindle their love for each other and decided they wanted to make their marriage work—which was a huge *if*—could they ever find a lifestyle that worked for both of them? One that gave Dax the freedom and outdoors life he needed, yet included a real home and the children she yearned for?

"Sounds good," he said. "Before we go shopping, you should check your bag, see if there's anything I forgot."

He'd packed for her—which sort of annoyed her, yet she understood why he'd done it. The take-charge guy she'd fallen for had wanted to kidnap her and give her a romantic surprise. And he'd tried to be considerate: he'd given her egg salad and a spectacular flight, a real fireplace and her choice of dinner options. She wrapped her arms around his waist inside his unzipped jacket, tipped her head back, and gazed up at him. "Thank you, Dax. For all of this." She swallowed. "For not losing hope."

"You're welcome." He rested his hands on her shoulders and kissed her.

This kiss, like the one they'd shared before leaving Vancouver, started out gentle, but when Dax slipped his tongue between her lips, she met it eagerly. Mmm, if only the house wasn't icy cold, how lovely it would be to light a fire and make love in front of it.

Reluctantly, she pulled away. "To be continued."

"Count on it." He picked up their luggage. "I'll take these upstairs."

She followed him up a wooden staircase. The second floor had a large bedroom with an en suite, the little boy's room, a spare bedroom, and a bathroom. Dax placed her suitcase on the bed in the master bedroom and she checked the contents. He'd done surprisingly well, packing all the necessary toiletries, casual clothes, a dressy pantsuit, and one of her half dozen good dresses, this one tan and conservatively styled. Lingerie and high-heeled shoes but—she shook her head, amused—no panty hose. He had packed the lightweight, rose-colored sweater he'd once given her. Usually, she stuck with beiges and grays, but she got compliments when she wore this sweater.

Dax had also included the butterfly top Kim had given her, which she had yet to wear. It had been a birthday gift two months ago. A birthday Dax hadn't come home for. He offered, but she figured he didn't really want to and told him not to bother, she'd be working that day and then there'd be dinner with her parents. How typical of the way their relationship had gone.

Remembering something, she checked inside her cosmetics bag. Yes, her birth control pills were there. When, if ever, would she be able to toss them out?

"How did I do?" Dax's voice drew her attention.

She tried to banish the regret and focus on the hope. "Amazingly well. But if we go out for dinner and I wear that dress, I'll need panty hose."

"Oops." Then he gave a wicked grin. "Or we could do that thing where you wear a dress and no underwear, and I play with you under the tablecloth until you come."

"Dax!" They would never dare to do that. Would they? Had he omitted panty hose deliberately? "It's winter," she reminded him. "No woman would go out in public bare legged."

"Garter belt and stockings?"

She huffed. "Let's go shopping."

But the idea stayed with her, teasing at the corners of her mind as, clasping gloved hands, they strolled the snowy path from the White Gold neighborhood into Whistler Village. She commented on how pure and crisp the air was. Dax traced a hammering sound to a red-headed woodpecker, and named the flock of tiny, chittering birds in an evergreen tree as pine siskins. They chuckled over a toddler in a pink snowsuit forming sloppy snowballs and pelting her father.

Entering the Village, they wandered past upscale stores, restaurants, and coffee shops. The town bustled with people dressed in winter wear, some carrying skis or snowboards. Everything was still decorated for Christmas: twinkling lights, holly, wreaths with pinecones, Santa Clauses, and reindeer.

Most of the clothing-store windows featured ski and snow wear but some had party clothes. A dress caught Lily's eye. In a silky looking blue and gold fabric, it was sleeveless with a deep vee neckline and a belled skirt that ended above the knees. Not as dressy as an evening gown, but prettier and more feminine than her dresses.

"Want to go out for New Year's Eve dinner tomorrow?" Dax asked.

"That would be nice, but I doubt we'd get in anywhere at this late date."

"Don't know until we try. Whistler doesn't seem like a place where people do a lot of advance planning."

"Maybe not. That French place we passed looked nice."

"Let's go back and see if they can fit us in."

Lily glanced across the street, where she'd noticed a lingerie store. "Why don't you do that, and I'll buy my panty hose?" And perhaps something sexier.

"Sure. Meet you back here." He gave her a quick kiss then strode away.

She hurried across the street and into the boutique with its display of lacy lingerie. A smiling brunette in a low-cut red sweater greeted her. "Happy New Year. Can I help you find something?"

Lily gazed around. Normally, she bought basic underwear designed for comfort, and Dax had never complained. "I need a pretty, lacy bra in 36B, a garter belt, and stockings. And quickly, before my husband comes back."

"Come with me. You'll want a matching thong?"

Lily followed her. "Right." Of course she wouldn't go out in public without panties.

"Black? With your coloring, you must look fantastic in black. Or how about champagne, to match your skin? You'll look almost like you're naked."

Black wouldn't work with the tan dress Dax had brought. Nor the blue and gold one in the shop window . . . "Champagne."

The brunette held up a low-cut bra with lace-decorated cups. "This is my favorite. It's very flattering. Want to try it on?"

"I don't have time. It's a surprise."

She winked. "Lucky man. He's going to have a great New Year's."

"I hope so."

The woman picked out a matching thong and garter belt, added sheer stockings, and quickly wrapped them. Lily paid cash to speed things up, and scurried out of the store to find Dax mounting the steps toward it.

"Hope you're okay with nine o'clock," he said. "It was that or five thirty."

"Nine sounds great. We can have a late lunch."

"Get your panty hose?"

"I got what I needed." She couldn't wait to see his face when he saw her new lingerie. Lily gestured toward the clothing store. "What do you think of the blue and gold dress?"

He turned to look. "I like it. Try it on."

Arm in arm, they entered the store. Lily found the dress in her size and went into a changing room. When she put it on, her breath caught. She looked so feminine and, well, sexy.

"How is it?" the saleswoman called. "Is the size right?"

"Perfect. But I need shoes. Size seven."

"I'll be right back."

A couple of minutes later, Lily gazed at her feet in strappy gold sandals with four-inch heels. She'd never worn shoes like that, but the dress demanded them.

"Hey there." This time it was Dax's voice outside the door. "Do I get a look?"

She spun, lighthearted, loving how the dress belled out. "Not until tomorrow night."

"Tease," he said, humor in his voice.

Just wait until he found out about the garter belt and stockings. She wouldn't say anything until they were eating, then she'd tell him. Maybe she'd raise the hem of her skirt and give him a peek.

"Do you have the right jewelry?" The saleswoman was back.

"I'm all set." Her new pendant and matching earrings would suit the dress.

She slid off the shoes and unzipped the dress, reluctant to take off a garment that made her feel pretty. But even when she was back in her cable-knit sweater, jeans, and boots, she still felt attractive, with tousled hair, pink cheeks, and bright eyes. She felt healthy, happy, and hopeful. "Three very good H's," she murmured.

Back outside, she slipped her hand into Dax's. "This was a good idea, coming to Whistler. Now what? Groceries?"

"Sure. If we're eating by the fire tonight, how about a picnic?"

"Picnic?"

"Yeah. Whatever appeals to us. Fresh-baked French bread and blue cheese."

Like they used to do when they were young. "Yum. Greek olives, Brie, grapes."

"Salami."

She wrinkled her nose. "You can have the salami. I'll take, hmm, maybe rosemary ham."

"Barbecued chicken."

"I'm with you there. And wine, of course."

"White or red?"

She mused. "How about pink and bubbly?"

His eyebrows went up. "Since when do you drink pink bubbly?"

"We're not doing the usual things, are we?" With a smug grin, she thought of her new dress and lacy lingerie.

"Pink bubbly it is."

"I'm getting hungry. This is why people get fat over the holidays. Too much food and not enough exercise."

"I don't think that'll be a problem for you. You're really slim and toned. All that running?"

"I've been doing self-defense classes too."

"Self defense is a great idea." He winked. "Think you can take me?"

"If I caught you off guard." Cheerfully, she added, "I could gouge out your eyeballs too."

He winced. "Remind me not to get on your bad side."

Dusk fell early, making Whistler Village's holiday lights and decorations even more festive and magical. The temperature dropped sharply, and they speeded their pace, leaving the Village and turning onto the trail, which was lit with a ski resort version of streetlights. Their boots crunched and squeaked against the snowy path, loud in the still night, and the chill seeped through Lily's coat and sweater. "I'm so not a cold-weather girl."

"If you lived in a place like this, you'd have the clothes for it."

"Says you, who's never been cold in your life." At least she'd never heard him admit to it, and whenever she touched him he gave off heat.

As they approached their rented cabin, Lily saw that Dax had left the outside light on, and their gingerbread house looked welcoming. He opened the door and they dumped their bags on the bench in the mudroom while they shed shoes and coats. Then they stepped into the living room and yes, it was blissfully warm.

"I'll get a fire going," Dax said.

"I'll put away the groceries." She shivered, far from warmed up yet.

"I can do that. Go take a shower or bath."

"That sounds wonderful," she said gratefully. Toting her shopping bag, she headed upstairs.

In a couple of minutes, she was in the shower, hot water streaming over her and penetrating into chilled muscles. What a lovely afternoon it had been, like the early days when it was so easy and fun to be with Dax. Humming, she looked forward to their picnic—and hopefully the second act of the "to be continued" kiss they'd enjoyed earlier.

Warm and dry, she contemplated her clothing choices. Tonight, she wouldn't wear same-old, same-old. Deciding that the rose-colored sweater would be perfect for tomorrow morning, she fingered the delicate silk of Kim's butterfly blouse. It was almost gauzy, which made the blue- and green-shaded butterflies with their gold veining stand out beautifully. She'd have to wear something under it. Fortunately, Dax had packed the powder-blue tank George had given her, and her black yoga pants.

Once dressed, she added brown mascara and a whisper of blue eye makeup. Her mom might think she looked frivolous, but Lily didn't give a damn. Dax would approve.

On slippered feet, she hurried downstairs. Sounds met her: the crackle of burning wood, Savage Garden singing "I Knew I Loved You." She smelled a hint of wood smoke and a rich, spicy, alcoholic scent. Dax had turned the lights off, so the room was lit only by the blazing fire.

He crouched beside it, poking at the logs. He still wore jeans but had taken off the heavy sweater he'd worn earlier. A black tee with a stylized helicopter on the back stretched across his powerful shoulders.

"Savage Garden?" she asked. They'd listened to the Australian duo in their early years together.

"From the owners' stack of CDs." He rose and turned to her. "Wow, look at you. You're gorgeous, sweetheart." He glanced down at himself. "And I'm seriously underdressed."

She shook her head. "You look gorgeous too." Dax was so striking, he couldn't *not* look great, and the faded jeans and tee with "Born to Fly" across his chest suited him.

He took two mugs from the stone hearth and handed her one. "Hot rum toddies."

The scent was heavenly: rum, lemon, cinnamon, and a hint of something else, maybe nutmeg. She breathed it in then took a cautious sip. The bite of alcohol, the sweet-sour mix of lemon and honey, and the richness of spice. "Mmm, nice."

"How's it compare to your usual martini?"

"Suits the place, the day. See, I can be flexible." She took another swallow, feeling the heat and the alcohol slipping down the center of her body. Contentedly, she sank to the large braided rug. "Good job with the fire."

Dax joined her, his own mug in hand. "I like fires. When I'm not staying on-site, like at the mining camp, I always try to rent a place that has one."

"A real fire, not gas."

"Gas is easier, but it doesn't compare."

"It really doesn't." Sipping her toddy, she studied his profile as he gazed into the flames. "What do you do in the evenings when you're out in the bush?"

"Read, mostly. The days are demanding. It's good to sit back and do nothing for a couple of hours. Sometimes I get together with some of the other folks, play cards or watch a game on TV. Go to bed early, get up early." He stretched his shoulders. "When I have time off during daylight hours, I hike around and explore."

"You don't get tired of being out in the wilderness? I mean, I know you love it, but . . ." But couldn't he see any virtue to life in the city—a life with her and their children?

"There are things I miss. Like gourmet takeout." He studied her face, then took a long swallow of his drink and put his mug on the coffee table. "And you. Wilderness, a fire, and you with me—that'd be pretty much my idea of heaven."

She suppressed a sigh. As he knew, while she liked the outdoors, she felt at home in the city. Still, today was great: a blend of spectacular scenery and city amenities, not to mention the dancing fire and the unaccustomed hot rum drink. And Dax. "This," she said softly. "This, right now, is pretty much my idea of heaven."

His gray eyes crinkled at the corners as he smiled. "It's a fine start." He touched her hair, framed one side of her face with his hand, and leaned toward her. "My beautiful wife." His lips touched hers before she could reply.

It was just a quick brush of lips, and then he pulled away. "Finish your drink so we can do that some more."

She obliged, draining the last mouthful of lemony, spicy rum, and put her empty mug next to his. "More, please. I want more kissing."

This time, when his lips touched hers, there was no pulling away. She closed her eyes, giving herself over to the kiss. Their tongues met. He tasted of rum and spice, heady and seductive. She must as well. This time, she didn't want some sex game that pushed the bounds, she wanted only to join with her husband. Right here, in front of the fire.

He nibbled her lip; she nipped him back. Laughing, their mouths separated as they drew breath. He kissed the corner of her mouth then trailed kisses across her jaw and down her neck. She arched for him and slid her fingers through his thick hair. His lips and short beard brushed sensitive skin, sending arousal quivering through her.

She steered his head upward so she could kiss him again, and flicked her tongue into his mouth. So good, kissing Dax. She could do it forever, except that those kisses resonated through her whole body, pricking her nipples to tightness, making her sex clench and moisten. She moaned, low in her throat.

Eighteen

Lily's sexy moan sent a fresh surge of arousal through Dax's body. The afternoon had been great and now here she was, so feminine and sexy in that pretty shirt, letting him know she wanted him.

Still kissing her, he eased her back to lie on the rug, and leaned over her. He moved from her mouth down her neck, tonguing the rapid beat of her pulse in the hollow at the base of her throat.

Her fingers tangled in his hair and she pressed herself against his mouth.

He continued down her body, rolling the flimsy shirt above her breasts so he could suck the hard nubs of her nipples through her blue tank top. With lips and tongue, he teased the bare flesh between the bottom of the tank and the low waistband of her stretchy black pants. He circled her navel then eased the waistband down her flat belly, following it with his tongue, dragging her panties along for the ride. He tugged the clothes off her slim legs, legs toned from running and self-defense workouts.

So she thought she could take him if he was off guard, did she? That touch of physical cockiness from his refined wife was damned sexy. One day they'd have a mock battle and he'd let her take him down, just to see what she'd do then.

His cock thrust painfully inside his jeans, but he ignored its demand as he kissed his way up those long legs. Vaguely, he was aware of the music ending, but who needed it when he had the crackle of the fire and Lily's soft whimpers and moans?

He could tell so much about her without her speaking a word. Those little sounds telegraphed her growing arousal, as did the twist and thrust of her hips. He knew she'd applied body lotion after her shower from the subtle orange-almond scent of her skin. The fullness of her pussy lips and the glisten of moisture on them said she was hungry for his touch.

She stretched sinuously. "This feels so good, being naked in front of the fire."

"Looks mighty good too." The firelight cast ever-changing patterns of light and shadow over her pale, supple body.

His own body felt more than a little overheated, thanks to his arousal and the fire. He stripped off his clothes and breathed a sigh of relief when his cock sprang free.

Lily watched, hands stacked behind her head. "Now that's a nice picture."

"Not as nice as this one." With firm hands, he parted her legs so firelight illuminated the glistening pink folds of her sex. He eased down on the rug and teased her with his fingers, lips, and tongue, taking his time. Prolonging release—hers and his own—made for more intense orgasms.

He pumped two fingers in and out of her moist heat, finding a rhythm that set her hips to twisting, then easing back when her body tightened like she was ready to come. He flicked her clit with his tongue, circled it.

"Dax, wait."

When he lifted his head, she slid out from under him, then turned around and slid back the other way. Now, rather than facing up her body, his head pointed toward her toes. And his genitals were inches from her face.

She grasped his engorged cock and guided it between her lips, licking the crown and around the shaft, sucking him in. Heat, moisture, and pressure, licks and sucks that made his blood surge. Now she took his balls in her soft, persistent fingers.

"God, Lily, that feels good." He buried his face between her legs again, taking up where he'd left off, but with a new urgency. Her mouth on his cock and the gentle pressure of her fingers caressing his balls drove him to the edge. As wonderful as they felt, he didn't want to climax like this. He wanted to be inside Lily—but not until she came once for him.

His fingers pumped faster, brushing the sweet spot that made her quiver. He licked and sucked her clit more intently, not easing off now.

Her body tensed and she stopped sucking his cock, just held it in her mouth as she focused on the sensations gathering inside her.

Then he took her over the top and she clutched and spasmed around his fingers, pulsing against his mouth. He kept caressing her, slowly and more gently, prolonging her orgasm until the last ripples faded.

His cock was rigid and it took a lot of self-control not to pump inside her hot, wet mouth, but he managed it. When her tongue circled his shaft again, he eased away.

"Dax?" Lily gazed at him questioningly.

He came up on his knees. "I want to be inside you."

"I won't argue with that." She held up her arms.

He came down over her, enjoying the way she gathered him in and held him. She raised her knees, tilting her pelvis, and he reached between their bodies to open her lush folds and slide himself inside. Her internal muscles gripped him. They moved together in a slow, pulsing rhythm, each thrust taking him one beat closer to the edge. He rolled, taking her with him, so they lay on their sides facing each other. Her top leg hooked over his hip as she slid closer, taking him deeper.

Her eyes gleamed in the firelight, a darker blue than usual. He bumped his nose against hers, winning a soft laugh, then took her lips. As they kissed, as their bodies pumped together, he teased her nipple, rolling it between finger and thumb, feeling tiny shudders go through her.

Those shudders pulsed through him too, and the need to climax built irresistibly. He caressed the dip of her waist, the curve of her hip, then moved to her clit. Gently, he rolled it the way he'd done her nipple.

She broke away from his kiss to gasp, "Oh Dax! Oh God, that's nice."

His balls tightened and drew up as his body readied for climax. When Lily began to quake, he let himself go, plunging deep and hard. "God, Lily."

"Oh!" she gasped, then "oh yes!" on a rising cry as she came, shuddering and pulsing around him.

They held each other until the last tiny quiver faded. He kissed her. "There's something to be said for the old-fashioned way."

Her lips curved. "Sometimes classic is best."

When he separated his body from hers, she rolled onto her back and stretched, then sat up, wrapping her arms around her bent knees. "The fire could use wood."

"I was busy tending a different one." He pushed himself to his feet.

"Very efficiently, I must say."

He poked what remained of the fire until a few embers burst into flame, and added a couple more pieces of wood.

Meanwhile, Lily went to the downstairs bathroom. When she returned, she pulled on her clothes. "I'm hungry. Let's get that picnic organized."

"Good idea." He dressed too, and followed her to the small kitchen. She was opening cupboards, assembling plates, glasses, cutlery, so he put the snacks on a serving tray. When he took the loaf of French bread from its bag and reached for a cutting board, she turned to get something and bumped into him. "Oops, sorry," she said. "I'm used to being alone in the kitchen, since you're away so much."

Before thinking, he responded, "If there was a reason to be home, maybe I'd be there more."

Her eyes narrowed. "It's my fault you're not home? And, by the way, I didn't say that as an accusation, just a statement of fact. Your job keeps you away most of the time."

It sounded like an accusation, but he kept his voice even. "I thought you supported me doing bush flying."

She nodded slowly. "I remember when we first talked about it. You were getting out of the army and you were sick of war, chafing under the discipline of the military. You wanted to fly"—a smile flickered—"somewhere free and pure, you said. In our northern wilderness, not in a war-torn desert. And you wanted to be your own boss. I saw how excited you were about being a freelance bush pilot, Dax. I didn't realize how much you'd be away, but even if I had, how could I not support you? I was establishing my practice, you were setting up your own business, both of us doing work we loved. It seemed like we were on parallel courses."

He nodded, then said, "Parallel," and weighed the word. "Parallel paths don't touch."

She blinked. "You're right. That's what's happened to us, isn't it?" A worry line creased her forehead.

Parallel paths; two people who'd lost their trust in each other and maybe lost their love as well. No wonder she was frowning. But this was better than where they'd been a week ago. "But we're together now." He smoothed the line out with his thumb. "And there's lots to talk about, I guess." He turned away and took the bottle of pink champagne from the fridge. "Alcohol will probably help, right?"

She sighed. "Yes. And food. Just because today's been so nice, it doesn't mean we've solved all our problems. Or," she added under her breath, "any of them."

"I heard that. And you're right." This was why he liked nature; the problems were concrete and he dealt with them by action. Could talking resolve the mess they'd made of their marriage? He could arrange his jobs to have more time back in Vancouver, but would Lily ever slow down at work so they could spend that time together? And then there was the elephant in the room, the thing they'd avoided talking about since Christmas Day: whether they still loved each other. None of the talking would count for much if they couldn't recapture the love.

The woman she'd been this afternoon . . . He could so easily love that Lily. Yet she was also the driven doctor who rarely had time for him. How could he give his heart to that woman?

Lily shook her head briskly. "No, I won't be negative."

And that was a good attitude. He stroked her smooth forearm. "Me either."

She put her hand over his. "Here's an idea, Dax. Rather than starting at the end—with the issues that are stressful to even think about, that are red flags for us—what if we go back to the beginning?"

Yeah, the red-flag subjects only led to arguments. Intrigued, he cocked his head. "How d'you mean?"

"Let's talk about when we first got together. Who we were, what we wanted. How our relationship developed."

"That's not a bad idea." It'd give perspective, and a reminder of how they'd fallen in love. She used to find time for him, find joy in being with him. If she remembered how much fun that was, maybe she'd want to do it again.

They carried their meal into the cozy living room and spread it on the battered wooden coffee table. Lily hunted through the CDs while

Dax tended the fire. He always enjoyed poking logs, seeing sparks flare, inhaling the scent of burning wood. It was a cozy, homey thing, a real wood fire.

"Madonna?" she asked.

"Sure."

"I played this 'Ray of Light' album a million times in twelfth grade."

Lily had suggested they start at the beginning. "You're not saying you want to start with high school?" He eased the cork from the bottle of Pol Roger rosé. They'd splurged on French champagne.

"Back when you didn't even look at me?" she teased.

"I looked, but your nose was so high in the air you never noticed."

"I was *not* a snob, Dax Xavier!" She stuck her hands on her hips and gave him a mock glare.

"Hanging out with your ritzy friends, doing your intellectual stuff like chess club and debate club?"

"I'd been friends with those kids all through school, chess was challenging, and I hoped debate club would help me argue more effectively with my parents."

"Your parents don't engage in debates." He handed her a glass of peach-colored champagne, fizzing with tiny bubbles. "They steamroll over the opposition." Too late, he remembered that he'd decided to back off on the hot button issues like her parents, but luckily she didn't jump down his throat over it.

Instead, she said wryly, "That does pretty much describe it. Kim said the same about her parents, though they've proven to be more flexible than mine."

"Maybe she'll give you some tips."

"I think mine are more stubborn. Anyhow, forget about them." She raised her glass. "To us. To talking and . . . trying."

He clicked his glass against hers, and they both took a sip.

"See?" she said. "Pink bubbly is perfect for our fireside picnic."

"It's good. Makes me think of summer. Be nice to drink this on an outdoor picnic in the sun, with a touch of breeze."

"Consuming alcohol in a public place? Risky."

He winked. "Who said anything about a public place?" He lowered himself to the braided rug. "You're married to a pilot. I could have us in the middle of nowhere in less than an hour. Would milady prefer an alpine meadow full of lupine and poppies, or the shore of a little lake that doesn't even have a name?"

Her face lit. "That sounds incredible. Why have we never done that?" She pulled a few cushions off the couch, tossed them down, and joined him.

He bit back the obvious answer: *Because you're always so freaking busy.* Trying to be more diplomatic, he said, "Too busy, I guess. Other priorities?"

"I suppose. Our lives always have been busy. And separate. Those parallel courses."

"Yeah, since the end of that first summer." He and Lily were such different people, but that was okay, both of them having interests they were passionate about. In the beginning, it had worked. "We used to make time to get together though, and those times were great."

"They were."

"And we're together now, having fun. That's a good sign."

"Right." She flashed a smile, but he saw uncertainty in her eyes.

Was he crazy to think that one weekend getaway could rekindle their love? That the embers still burned, steady and true, ready to leap into flame again? Could this time together be enough to convince her that he—that their relationship—was worth taking time away from her career? Trying not to feel discouraged, he turned his attention to the food, cutting a slice of salami and tasting it.

Lily spread Brie on French bread, took a bite, then popped a grape into her mouth. When she swallowed, she said, "Mmm, a perfect combo."

No one would call him and Lily that. Not when they'd met, not on their wedding day, and not now. He'd never been a guy who gave a damn about perfect, yet here he was, married to a perfectionist.

"So, high school," she said reflectively. "I enjoyed it, but I was under my parents' thumb. I had to take the courses they approved, get top marks. I could only see friends they approved of"—she shot him a wry glance—"not that anyone else was asking me out anyhow. They didn't prohibit me from things like going to movies, but I got lectured about using my time more effectively." She sipped champagne. "Your mom and grandparents didn't exactly keep you on a tight rein."

"Nope."

She put down her glass. "Dax, any time I ask you about the time before we met, you won't talk about it. I've respected that, but we promised to be honest with each other so I'm telling you, it makes me feel like you're shutting me out."

Crap. He hadn't meant to make her feel bad. "It's not that. It was just a bad time."

"What? High school?"

He gritted his teeth. "Everything, before that summer at Camp Skookumchuck."

"Then all the more reason to talk about it."

"I'm a guy. We handle stuff, we don't whine about it. My childhood's long past. Talking isn't going to change it."

She leaned forward, her gaze intent on his face. "No, it won't change it. But it will help me, and I hope help us as a couple. Our pasts are part of who we are. Dax, how can I truly understand you if a huge part of your life is a big secret?"

Hmm. When she put it that way, it did kind of make sense. It was a very long time ago, so why was he making a big deal of it? Besides, it felt good, knowing that Lily cared enough to want to understand him. Tension eased from his shoulders. "Okay, fine. Twelfth grade. No, I wasn't on a tight rein. My grandparents tried to set rules, but it's hard to stop a rebellious kid so they gave up. They said I was just like my dad and I'd end up in jail too."

"Dax, that's so unfair."

Unfair? The story of his childhood. But sure, he could talk about it, if it meant so much to her. If it could be a step toward saving their marriage.

"What about your mother?" she asked.

He assembled a sandwich of French bread, salami, Brie, and sliced tomato. "She ran away with my high school dropout dad when she was eighteen. Mom and Dad, well, discipline wasn't in their vocabulary. They lived for the moment, for pleasure." He bit into the sandwich.

"Sounds like a child's dream, but it couldn't have made for the most stable childhood."

He snorted. "You can say that again."

"Go on. Tell me more."

He'd never told anyone this stuff, so he had to search for words to describe his childhood. After swallowing the last bite of his sandwich, he said, "My parents never grew up. Never took responsibility for anything. Didn't hold a job for long before they got bored, or decided to move somewhere else, or got fired. They drank too much, did drugs. Their relationship was, uh, volatile."

"Volatile?"

"They said they loved each other, but they fought a lot. And made up. Loudly, in both cases."

"Ick. That's no way for a kid to grow up."

Tell me about it. He drained his wineglass and refilled it, topping up Lily's glass too. "It taught me things."

"Such as?"

"To look after myself."

She gazed at him solemnly. "Because you couldn't count on any-one else to do it."

This actually felt kind of good, telling Lily and having her get it. "Couldn't trust my folks for anything. Not to put food on the table, buy me new shoes when I outgrew the old ones, show up at a parent-teacher conference."

"That's awful." She sounded outraged, thank God, rather than pitying.

"They actually weren't horrible people, just immature and self-absorbed. It was all about them having fun."

"They shouldn't have had a child."

"No." Nor should he. Thank God he hadn't knocked Lily up when they were kids, the way his dad did his mom. "There's a lot of things they shouldn't have done."

"And after you graduated from high school, you all went your own way. That's sad."

No, being with them had been sad; he'd been better off on his own. "Dad was a screwup. It wasn't healthy, being around him, even before he went to jail. Mom was an airhead. But I guess she loved him, since she took off to live closer to the jail so she could see him."

"When?"

"Spring of twelfth grade."

"She left you with her parents? How could she?"

He snagged a drumstick of barbecued chicken. "Dad was more important to her."

"I knew you had family issues, but I had no idea how bad it was. Dax, I wish you'd told me this the summer we met."

"I didn't want to think about it." He also hadn't wanted Lily, the princess from another world, to realize how fucked up he was. "Any-how, yeah, Mom left. A couple weeks later I turned eighteen. Then I got suspended for cheating. Which I didn't do. I wrote my history essay on the use of helicopters in the Vietnam War, and I guess it was pretty good. Which didn't match up with my marks and attitude the rest of the time."

"That's terrible."

"Can't really blame folks for not believing me. I kind of was an asshole back then."

The corner of her mouth tipped up. "A sexy bad boy."

"Whatever. Anyhow, for my grandparents, that was the final straw. They kicked me out."

"What?"

"Kicked me out of the house. Said they didn't need any more of my bullshit, though they said it in fancier words."

Her jaw dropped. "Before you finished high school? Dax, what did you do?"

"Thought about dropping out and working full time for the construction company. But the site manager said I should finish school. He was the only person I respected enough to take advice from. He let me stay in the trailer at the site until school ended, then the company sent me to the project at Camp Skookumchuck. And that catches you up to the point where we hooked up." He gestured toward the chicken. "Want the other drumstick?"

She shook her head absentmindedly. "All I knew was that you didn't get along with your family, and that you all lost contact. I feel horrible that you didn't feel you could share the rest with me."

"You'd have thought I was a total jerk, or that I was pathetic and felt sorry for me. Neither's the way I wanted you to see me."

Nineteen

ily stared at her husband. That first summer, it had felt like they'd gotten so close, so fast. They'd shared their hearts, if not all the details of their lives. Now she realized she'd barely known Dax at all. Of course, at the age of seventeen, with her sheltered upbringing, how could she have related to the childhood he'd just described?

"No," she told him. "I'd have thought you were tough and resourceful and been even more impressed than I was." She now had an idea how deeply rooted his self-sufficiency was. It was a quality she'd always admired in him, and tried to emulate.

He ran a hand across his bearded jaw. "Huh. Now you tell me." A grin flashed.

"Dax, it must have been horrible. Having self-absorbed, volatile parents who didn't look after your needs, then grandparents who kicked you out. I can't imagine how you felt."

He shrugged and took a handful of olives.

"Tell me."

"Tell you what?"

"How it felt. Was it lonely? Did you feel shut out? Did you act out to get attention?"

"Oh Jeez, Lily, it's all in the past. Let it go."

"But the past affects us."

"You sound like a shrink."

"And you sound annoyed. I'm sorry, I'm not trying to provoke you." She touched his arm. He'd given her a lot already, opening up as he'd never done before, but she wanted—no, needed—even more, if they were to have a future together. "I know you don't like talking about feelings, but how can we know and trust each other if we don't share?"

He closed his eyes for a long moment and she wondered what was going through his mind. When he opened them, he said, "Fine. It was like you said. I felt like I didn't matter, like no one cared. It sucked. So I figured, screw them, I'm gonna live my own life. Then I met you and things changed."

It was a bare-bones summary, but a step in the right direction. She decided not to push further. "Thanks for telling me. I wish you hadn't kept it secret."

He frowned. "Yeah, that's funny, coming from you."

"What are you— Oh, you mean the inheritance?" Yes, that was information she hadn't shared with him: the fact that she'd inherited three million from her grandmother when she was sixteen.

"You didn't tell me until after we got married. I can't believe you thought I was the kind of guy who'd be with a girl for her money." The bitter edge to his voice told her this was still a touchy subject.

Because it had been a bone of contention, she'd avoided talking about her inheritance. Just like she hadn't pushed him to talk about his past. When he wanted to be a bush pilot, she never said she'd rather he stayed in Vancouver. This past year, she'd avoided asking him if he was cheating on her, or how he felt about their marriage, or whether he still loved her. The list went on and on. Now it was time to stop avoiding and open up.

"I didn't think that, Dax. Or, to be totally honest, I didn't want to. I really wanted—needed—to believe that you loved me purely for myself."

"Like I said, you didn't trust me."

"Hear me out. My dad had grown up with rich parents and he and Mom lectured me a lot about wealth. They said it's hard to know who your true friends are, whether people like *you* or just your money. That's why I stuck with those 'ritzy' friends, as you called them. We'd been friends since we were toddlers, all kids whose parents were professionals, well-off, from the same neighborhood. To this day, I never tell anyone about the inheritance. The only people who know are my family and you."

"Not your book club? Your colleagues?"

She shook her head.

"Huh." After a moment, he said, "You know I'd have liked you better if you were poor, right?"

The comment lightened the mood and she did a mock huff. "Oh, thanks for that." It was probably true, though. Before he'd started making good money, he'd protested when she wanted to pay for dinner or for travel to visit him when they lived in different cities. Dax wasn't sexist but he did have a healthy male ego. The only thing he hadn't objected to was her using her inheritance to pay for med school, rather than racking up student loans.

"If you weren't one of the ritzy kids, we might've gotten together in high school," he teased.

"You'd have tossed me aside like your other girlfriends. The timing worked out the way it was supposed to for us."

"Guess it did at that." He studied the array of delicacies on the coffee table, choosing a wedge of Brie and some grapes.

"Anyhow, the main reason I kept the secret was so I could tell my parents you didn't know."

His jaw tightened. "Not that it made them like me any better."

"They could have liked you even less."

"Hard to believe. They did everything they could to break us up."

"Dax, I know they're rigid and heavy-handed, but they do love me. They think they know best and—" She broke off at his quick grin. "What? You think I'm the same?"

"Just a little."

She frowned. The book club members teased her about being a know-it-all, and she'd overheard a grumble or two at the clinic. "Am I that obnoxious?"

He reached for her hand. "No. You're smart, focused, and a quick thinker. You analyze and reach a conclusion before other people, and when you reach it, you're pretty convinced it's right."

"Not always." She hadn't effectively analyzed the problems with her marriage or her clinic, or come anywhere near reaching conclusions.

"No. But when you do, you can be a little, uh . . ."

"Rigid and heavy-handed?" She repeated the words slowly, enunciating each syllable.

"You're strong-minded. That's much better than being wimpy. I've always admired your strength."

Hmm. That sounded a bit better. Before she could thank him, he went on. "Except when you're up against your parents."

She pulled her hand away. "I married you. That wasn't wimpy."

"Shit, I didn't mean to get into this."

"Into what? And why not?"

"Because it pushes your buttons and you get your back up and stop listening."

"I do not!" She glared at him. "I'm listening. Go on."

He raised his brows. "Okay, then hear this. You did two things that defied your parents: marry me and go into family medicine. On everything else, you back down. With other people, you state your mind and stick to your guns, but not with your parents. With them, you're a wimp."

She would *not* be defensive. Raising her wineglass, she sipped as she reflected on what he'd said. Yes, she sometimes chose avoidance. With her parents, and with Dax too, as she'd been thinking mere minutes ago.

"Lily?"

"Yes, with my parents I avoid confrontation unless the issue is really important. As you said, they steamroll over opposition. It's exhausting, stressful, and unproductive to argue with a steamroller." Besides, on the rare occasions she did win their approval, it felt so good.

A thought struck her. Growing up with her parents, had avoidance become such a habit that she used it with her husband too, even though he was a pretty open-minded guy? Had she subconsciously been afraid that if she challenged Dax or disagreed with him, she'd lose his love? How ironic if her failure to be open and honest with him had put that love in jeopardy. "Sorry." She realized Dax had said something and she'd missed it while she was musing. "What did you say?"

"Just that I see Anthony and Regina do the same thing. But Lily, it's costing you."

"What do you mean?"

"Your parents disrespect you."

"That's not true."

"Oh, yeah? 'You need a haircut; that shade of gray doesn't suit you.' 'Your brother's doing a clinical trial; his wife's on the partnership track; they've produced a beautiful baby.'"

Yes, those barbs stung. Her self-esteem had also suffered when she'd thought her husband might be cheating on her and she hadn't had the guts to ask. "You have a point," she admitted. "I can be a wimp, if that's what you want to call it, and I suffer for it. As for Mom and Dad, I don't think they intend to be that way. It's how they were raised."

"Oh come on, people don't have to be like their parents."

"You're right," she admitted. Dax himself was the perfect example of that. "I don't want to be like my parents," she added quietly. If—when—she had kids, she'd be a loving, supportive, demonstrative parent. She'd try to be neither overbearing nor wimpy. She gazed at Dax, her heart sinking. Right now, the likelihood of them having children together seemed very low. "I can't understand why you've stayed with me if I have all these personality quirks that bother you."

"Oh, hey Lily." He took her hand again. "No, that's not what I'm saying. You have way more great qualities than, uh, quirks that bug me. And no one's perfect. Me, least of all."

She softened, letting him intertwine their fingers. "Thanks. And, for the record, when I first met you, I thought you were pretty perfect."

"Me too. Young love." He grinned. "Or lust. Glosses over the less-than-perfect stuff."

"Which is inevitably revealed with time. And then, I guess people have to do what we're doing now. Talk about it, deal with it. Why did it take us ten years of marriage to do this?"

"Dunno. Slow learners?"

"Maybe, but here's a thought. In ten years of marriage, if you add up the time we've actually spent together, I bet it totals less than a year or two."

"Huh." He cocked his head. "Well, if we stay together, we need to spend more time together."

Hope pulsed in her heart. "I agree."

His face brightened and they shared a smile. Then he said, "I'm sorry if I was too hard on you, about your parents. It just pisses me off, the way they treat you." He gave a wry grin. "Though it's sure better than the way they treat me."

"I'm sorry they've never accepted you like they did Regina." How that must sting, when his own parents had been too self-centered to care about him, and his grandparents had kicked him out.

"I wouldn't trade places with Regina. She's under more pressure than me."

"What do you mean?"

"They gave up on me long ago." He released her hand and tore a cluster of grapes from the stem. "But she's under a critical magnifying glass, trying to measure up."

"Do you think she feels that way?"

"Yeah. She told me at Christmas. As a lawyer, Regina has to use strategies and tactics in her work, but in her home life she'd rather be upfront rather than deceptive."

"Deceptive?"

"You all lie to your parents to avoid making waves. It sucks. You know how your parents have that not so subtle way of letting people know they're disappointed in you? Well, you have more reason to be disappointed in them."

"I never thought of it that way." Over the years, he'd bitched about her parents but the things he'd said today were insightful, and the first to really sink in. Food for thought . . .

Dax rose to tend the fire, topped up their glasses, then stretched out on his side, head propped up on his hand. "Tell me about your grandmother. Your family never talks about her."

"Gran's the family black sheep."

"Hey, I like her."

"You would have. Grandpa had family money and was a prominent cardiologist—and yes, it was expected that Dad would be a cardiologist too, and that's what he did. They had a fancy house in Shaughnessy and she ran it and the garden, with staff, of course. They entertained a lot. Grandpa was on the board of directors of his golf club and Gran volunteered at the art gallery."

"They sound a little like my mother's parents."

"They probably knew each other. Grandpa was definitely the head of the household and Gran was, well, repressed. When he died,

I was eight and she was only sixty. She . . . well, Mom described it as going wild. She sold the house and bought a townhouse downtown, she traveled, she even went on a singles cruise and came home with a younger man 'friend.'" Lily put air quotes around the last word. "She took courses in anthropology, astronomy, and Indian cooking."

He grinned. "Sounds like quite the woman."

"That's for sure. She painted, mostly nudes, and she was good enough to have an exhibit. She stayed at an artists' commune in Mexico and an ashram in India. She rented an apartment in Paris, on the Left Bank. She had a male 'friend' there too. My parents were embarrassed by her adventures."

"And you?"

"I was more like, 'You go, Gran!' I loved seeing her so happy and free. We had some great times together. She was so easy to talk to."

"She died when you were sixteen? I'm sorry you lost her so early."

"Thanks." She smiled at her long, lean husband in his "Born to Fly" tee. "She'd have liked you, Dax. She'd have wanted to go flying with you. And tried to persuade you to teach her how to fly."

"And I might've. So she left all her money to you because you were the one who cheered her on?"

"And because I was a girl. Her lawyer gave me a letter from her. She said she wanted me to be financially independent—of my parents, and of any man including my husband."

He gave a thoughtful nod. "She wanted you to live the life that she couldn't until her husband died."

"Well, to have options."

Dax shot her a mischievous grin. "Like to live in an ashram or visit Paris and take a young lover?"

"She wanted me to be happy."

"And are you, Lily?"

That question made her pause, press her lips together, and reflect. "Sometimes."

"Such as?"

"Today, with you. Having fun together and also really talking."
It wasn't always comfortable, but it was hopeful. "And of course
when I help a patient. Or examine a healthy new baby and see how
much the parents love their little one. When I hold Sophia." Though
that was a mixed blessing, reinforcing her own desire to have kids.
She shook her head. "No one's life is all happiness. Everyone has
worries, responsibilities. Unfulfilled dreams."

"Your gran wanted to reduce those for you. You haven't touched
the money in years, have you?"

"Not since I paid for my medical education." She'd been so grateful for her grandmother's money. It had meant she didn't have to
choose between the undesirable options of student loans or parental
support. "I set up that trust, with the interest going to children's
charities, but I haven't touched the principal."

"Why don't you put some of it into the clinic? Hire another couple of doctors, a manager. Lighten your load."

"A manager? Dax, I'm responsible. I can't pass that off on someone else. And I can't subsidize the Well Family Clinic. It needs to be
self-sufficient."

He paused then said quietly, "Why? Because you have to always
be in control, and you're trying to impress your parents?"

Her mouth fell open. "I can't believe you said that! You know
how important the clinic is to me."

Dax studied her for a long moment. "I do know that. And I told
myself I'd leave this subject alone because it's another hot button.
But Lily, it's stressing you out, taking over your life. Why are you
letting it do that?"

Because hiring a manager would be a confession that she couldn't
handle things herself. She was *responsible*, not a control freak. Besides,
she *could* handle this; she'd figure things out. The crucial thing was
that patient care wasn't suffering. "It's just a tough period right now."

"What's going to change?"

"I'll work it out."

He sighed. "What's the part you most enjoy? Dealing with patients, right?"

"Yes, of course."

"Hire a manager to do the other stuff."

The man who'd cut his family out of his life had given her advice on dealing with her parents, and now the guy who'd admitted to avoiding admin tasks was trying to tell her how to run a medical clinic. She swallowed a knot of anger. "I don't tell you how to run your business."

"Right." His eyes were gray steel. "Parallel courses, all the way."

She took a breath. If they carried on like this, those parallel courses would split wide apart and never touch again. Deliberately, she softened her tone. "Remember how I suggested that we start back at the beginning? Perhaps tackling our current issues is . . ."

"Beyond us at this point? Yeah, I guess it is."

"Fighting will only drive us apart." If they were going to recapture love and fix their marriage, she sensed it had to happen in slow, gentle steps.

Dax sighed. "Yeah." He rose and tended the fire, then went through the stack of CDs.

When the music started, she cocked her head. "Who is that?"

"Tony Bennett. I thought your gran might like him."

The gesture eased tension from her body. "I bet she danced to him more than once."

When Dax returned to the rug, Lily lifted her glass toward him. "To Gran."

He picked up his own glass and clicked it against hers. "To Gran."

They both had a drink then he said, "D'you think you're doing what she wanted you to with the money?"

Hoping he wasn't going to hassle her again, she said cautiously,

"I hope so. One day maybe I'll see a reason to use it." Perhaps she'd spend some on her children, though she didn't want to spoil them.

"Wouldn't hurt you to do something frivolous every now and then."

"Frivolous?" Now there was a word no one ever applied to her. "Frivolous?" It felt light and fluffy on her tongue, kind of fizzy and fun like the champagne they were drinking.

"You're grinning." His eyes were warm and affectionate.

"I am? I wouldn't know how to be frivolous."

"You'll figure it out. Those book club friends could help. After all, they got you to a rodeo."

"You're right, I bet they could." She studied his face, the strong angles and planes, the reflection of firelight dancing in his eyes. "How about you, Dax? Could you help?"

"Uh . . . Guess I'm not known for being all that frivolous myself."

"No, not now. But think back. Remember borrowing a canoe at midnight and following the path of the full moon? Stealing a bunch of Mrs. B's flowers to give me, knowing she'd blame the deer? Whittling me a loon out of a piece of driftwood?" She paused. "Okay, maybe more romantic than frivolous. But fun, lighthearted things."

"Guess I haven't felt all that lighthearted in a while."

The words settled between them and neither spoke for a moment. Then he went on. "The past couple of years we've both spent most of our time working. Not, you know . . ."

"Stopping to smell the roses?"

"Or to steal them from someone's garden."

"I admit, I miss your bad-boy side."

"What? I tried so hard to grow up and be responsible. That's the kind of man you deserved."

"And I respected you for that, and you grew into a strong, brave, amazing man. But I do miss that daredevil bad-boy edge." She admitted, "I guess that's something I liked about the, uh, sex games."

"I'm taking notes here," he joked. "Bad boys tie women up, slap their butts, melt ice cubes on their bodies. What else?"

Happy that the mood had lightened, she said, "I'll leave that to your imagination, Dax. I think you're up for the challenge."

When he rose to deal with the fire again, she said, "Finished eating? I should put this stuff back in the fridge."

"Yeah, I'm good, thanks."

Creaky after sitting for so long, Lily stretched and picked up the tray of leftovers. In the kitchen, she nudged an empty shopping bag aside to clear space for the tray. Under the bag, she found several envelopes addressed to her and Dax. "You picked up the mail?" she called.

"Yeah, I grabbed it as I was leaving."

She shuffled through. A property tax bill, a charity looking for donations, a card-shaped envelope addressed to her and Dax from a cousin in England who she barely knew. A slightly larger envelope addressed to Dax, from CanTimber, the logging company he worked for before taking the job at the mining camp.

When he came into the kitchen with the empty champagne bottle and glasses, she said, "You got mail from CanTimber."

"Oh?" He took it, opened it, and an envelope fell out.

She glanced over, to see that it was addressed to Dax Xavier c/o CanTimber, with "Please Forward" written on it. In the top left corner was written "Jillian Sams" and an address in Prince Rupert.

"Who's Jillian Sams?"

Twenty

Jillian Sams. The name rang a faint bell for Dax. "I'm not sure."

He opened the envelope and pulled out a family photo card showing a man, woman, three children ranging from perhaps ten to sixteen, and an Old English Sheepdog. They were all beaming, even the dog.

Recognizing them, the picture made him smile too. So did the message written inside.

Dear Mr. Xavier,

It's because of you that my family will have a Merry Christmas. We are eternally grateful for your bravery. If there's ever anything that any of us can do for you, you only need ask.

I'm all healed now, as good as new. I look at life with a fresh perspective, and treasure every moment. It's amazing how things can change in the space of a heartbeat. I will never again take my life and my family for granted. And we'll never do something so stupid again.

I will also do my best to follow your example, and to help others in need whenever I can. Though, I'm afraid, never with the same amount of courage you showed when you rescued me.

*I wish you and your loved ones all the best for the holiday season
and the new year.*

*Forever in your debt,
Jillian Sams*

Oh yeah, sometimes life was good.

"Who's it from?" Lily asked.

"A woman I helped this year."

"May I?" She held out her hand for the card.

"It's not a big deal." He wasn't sure why he was reluctant to pass it over.

"Then show it to me." She took it from him and read the message. "Wow. That's amazing."

"It's really not a big deal," Dax repeated, putting leftovers into the fridge.

"What happened?" She touched his arm, stopping him.

He turned to her. "They were on a wilderness hiking-camping trip. Inexperienced, hadn't checked the long-range forecast. It was sunny when they set out, and they assumed it would last. Anyhow, on the second day, a storm came up, quickly. Lightning and thunder. The dog spooked and ran away and the youngest boy ran after it. The parents told the other kids to stay in the tent, and went to look for the boy and dog. They didn't stop to grab jackets, water, or cell phones. The mom slipped in the mud and fell off the edge of a cliff into a small canyon between two sets of hills. She tumbled down quite a drop, broke an arm and a leg, knocked herself out. The dad couldn't get down to her, the storm was getting worse, he still had a lost kid and dog."

"My God. The poor guy must have been out of his mind with worry."

"He rushed back to their camp and found that the boy and dog had returned. Fortunately, they had marginal cell service, so he called nine-one-one. The dispatcher contacted the RCMP, search and rescue, everyone who might be able to help. It would've taken quite a while to reach her from the ground, especially with the storm. No way could a small plane get in and land, but it seemed possible a helicopter could. I had my name on a list of volunteers to do aerial search and rescue, and I was close by."

Her grip tightened on his forearm. "You flew in the middle of a storm?"

He shrugged. "She was out there unconscious; no one knew how badly she was hurt. The sat photos indicated the storm wouldn't let up for twenty-four hours or more. I've flown in worse conditions." He gave a terse grin. "At least no one was shooting at me."

"I wish you wouldn't take that kind of risk." Concern creased her forehead.

In the past, he hadn't shared these kinds of stories with her, so as not to worry her. But now he realized that sometimes he had to share with her, if those parallel courses were ever going to touch. Wanting her to understand, he took her hands. "Lily, she mightn't have made it. She had a life, a husband, kids. She didn't deserve to lose that."

She bit her lip.

"I'm not crazy." He flashed her a grin. "I just happen to be an excellent pilot."

"I know. That's the only reason I survived when you were deployed in Afghanistan." She squeezed his hands. "I understand why you did it. I'm proud of you."

She'd said those words only a few times before, like when he graduated from college, and they carried weight. "Thanks, sweetheart."

"When you first started bush flying, you said you were flying people and supplies back and forth, transferring logs and equipment, that kind of thing. Now I've learned you fly into accident sites. What else? I want to know what's involved in your work."

"Well, when there's a forest fire, I've dropped firefighters and evacuated people who were in danger. Picked fishermen up from a rough sea when their boat went down. Done helivac off the deck of a tanker."

"Helivac? But there are special helicopter services that are equipped for medevac work."

"But they're not always close enough to help."

"I'd like to hear more stories. Though I admit, you're scaring me a little."

"I'm careful."

"I almost believe you." Still, a worry wrinkle creased her forehead.

"If we spent more time together, we could share more stories. I'd like to hear about your work too. You used to talk about some of your patients, but you haven't in awhile."

"The kind of things normal people talk about at the end of each work day."

"I guess." Their lives had never been like that, but it sounded appealing. If only Lily loved the bush and would consider living somewhere out in the wilds. And that was just as likely as him wanting a desk job. But that didn't mean they couldn't have more time together, and make the most of it. He looped his arms around her neck and dropped his head so his forehead touched hers. "It's late. Time for bed."

"I won't say no."

"You go on up. I'll finish here and bring in wood for the morning."

When she'd gone, he put on his boots and jacket then headed out into the chill night. Before going to the woodpile, he stopped to stare up at the crystal-clear stars scattered across an indigo sky. No city lights; no haze of pollution. He breathed deeply, feeling peace sink into his soul.

His world. If only Lily wanted to share it . . .

He shook his head. Earlier, she'd said that everyone had unfulfilled dreams. He had to accept that fact, and let this dream go.

Twenty-one

In the unfamiliar bathroom, Lily swallowed the birth control pill that had come to symbolize so much: the future she longed for, and the problems that stood in the way.

Her heart was still bruised and wary—she wasn't ready to let herself fall in love with Dax all over again—but she felt closer to him than she had in years. The honest communication, even if sometimes painful, was essential if they had any hope of resolving their issues. Some great sex wouldn't hurt either.

After stripping, she put the butterfly top back on, her breasts clearly visible through the sheer fabric. When she climbed into bed, she piled pillows behind her back and pulled the covers to her waist, no higher. From downstairs, she heard doors open and close, thumps and thuds. Such a simple thing, lying in bed hearing Dax and knowing he'd soon join her, and very pleasant.

With her glasses perched on her nose, she resumed *Bound by Desire* where she'd left off. Neville and Cassandra had negotiated the terms of their arrangement and were going out together.

At the door to his luxury suite, Cassandra nervously clutched the front of her short trench coat, painfully aware that beneath it she wore only a red leather bra and panties, both with cutouts that left nothing to the imagination. "Where are we going?"

Neville had been about to open the door, but stopped and turned to her. He didn't say a word, but his raised eyebrows and cool expression spoke volumes.

She hated it when he looked at her with such displeasure. "I'm sorry, master."

He brushed his fingers over the collar that circled her neck. "I am your master. What does that mean?"

"I obey without question."

"And?"

"I must trust you to know what's best for me."

"More than that, pet. I own you. I own that lovely body. It is mine to do with as I please. Do you understand?"

Everything he'd done so far had pleased her. Even the things that initially scared her, or the ones that hurt, ultimately brought her a pleasure more intense than she'd ever imagined. "I understand, master."

"If I choose to display you to other men, I will do it."

A thrill rippled through her. He found her lovely; he wanted other men to be envious. Having strangers lust after her—yes, that turned her on. "Yes, master."

"If I choose to fuck you in front of them, I will."

"Oh yes, master!" It was unbearably erotic to think of being watched as they fucked.

"If I choose to stick a ball gag in your mouth, paddle you until your ass cheeks are on fire, then fuck your ass while they watch, I will do it."

Paddling hurt like hell but it also aroused her. Anal sex aroused her. But a ball gag? And doing all those things in front of other people? How could she speak her safe word while gagged? Still, she trusted him, and if these things pleased him, she'd do them. "Yes, master."

"If I choose to give you to other men, to have you suck their dicks, to let them beat you and fuck your cunt and your ass, I will do it."

The leash jerked again and she realized she'd been shaking her head. Yes, when they'd negotiated their arrangement, he'd given her a list of activities and she'd said she was fine with them. Now, hearing his implacable voice, she knew she wanted only Neville. She wanted him to want her, not to give her to other men.

"I own you, pet," he said again. "I know what you need, better than you know it yourself." His jade eyes cool and commanding, he went on. "You came to me because you wanted to find out your true nature. Tonight, it's time to stop being a coward and find the strength to accept the truth: you are a submissive."

Was she? Neville had done things to her that she'd have thought would appall her, yet they'd aroused her intensely. He did seem to know her sexuality better than she did.

"We are going to a club," he said. "Top and Bottom. It's a BDSM club. You will be under my total control. If you misbehave, you will embarrass me in front of other doms. If that happens, I will punish you. Severely."

Of course she didn't want to embarrass Neville. She wanted, more than anything, to make him happy. But if he asked her to take some strange man's cock in her mouth, or let some other dom fuck her ass, with an audience watching her humiliation . . .

"You can say your safe word now, Cassandra, and go back to your own room."

If she did that, she knew he'd give up on her. He'd given her a second chance, but there wouldn't be a third. Their relationship would be over. The incredible sex that walked the tightrope of pleasure and pain, weaving back and forth from side to side. The sense of being cherished and protected. Of having the security of rules. Of having Neville.

She gazed into his eyes. Perhaps he really did own her. Perhaps that was a good thing. She ducked her head in a submissive gesture and kept quiet.

"Very good, pet." He stroked her face, her neck. Traced the vee at the neck of her trench coat.

She pressed against him, trembling at the approving caress.

He reached inside her coat, located one of her aroused nipples as it poked out of the heart-shaped cutout of her red leather bra. "Mine." And he tweaked it. Hard.

She winced as pain lanced through her, but when he finally released his grip, tingly heat spread from the spot, a delicious wave of it, and moisture coated her inner thighs. "Yes, master. Yours."

Dax stepped through the bedroom doorway. "Look at you, Lily. Those prim and proper glasses and that see-through shirt. Talk about sexy."

She put her Kindle on the bedside table and enjoyed the view as he pulled his tee over his head. "Could you imagine giving me to another man to screw?"

"Jesus, no!" Then, warily, "You don't want that, do you?"

"God, no. What about making love in public?"

He paused in the act of unzipping his jeans and cocked his head. "How public?"

Intrigued that he hadn't given a flat-out no, she said, "You tell me."

"Well, not at some sex club like in the book." He shoved down his jeans and underwear, and stepped out of them. "But if we were someplace semiprivate and someone happened to see us, that could be a turn-on."

His naked body as he moved unself-consciously around the room was a turn-on. And an inspiration. A scenario popped into her mind. "Like if we were having that picnic in a remote alpine meadow, naked in the sunshine, making love in the grass."

"I like that picture."

"If a hiker came past and saw us, I guess that could be kind of titillating."

"Sounds sexy to me. Or," he sat on the edge of the bed, his eyes gleaming and his cock stirring, "if we didn't pull the blinds and someone had a telescope."

"Dax!" She remembered the blindfold and ice cubes Sunday night. "You don't think . . ."

He winked and ran a finger along the neckline of her blouse. "Probably not."

"I hope not," she said firmly. "That's our home. But, hmm, maybe a hotel room . . ." The idea, and the sight of his arousal, made her pussy throb.

"Oh, yeah. We'll strip each other in front of a big hotel window." His fingers drifted down the front of her blouse then he ran his thumb across her tightening nipple. "I'll hike you up in my arms and we'll go at it right there, never knowing if someone's watching."

"I'm not sure I'm brave enough for that," she admitted.

"Hey, you're supposed to do whatever your master commands," he teased.

"Yeah, right." Then she frowned. "Neville says he owns her. You don't think you own me, do you?"

"Jesus, no." He dropped his hand and stared at her. "And you don't own me. We're spouses, not owner and pet."

"Or slave. Ownership makes me think of slaves."

A gleam lit his eyes and he tweaked her nipple. "My very own sex slave? Hmm, maybe I was too hasty . . ."

"If you get a sex slave, so do I."

"Seems fair. Want first turn? I'm here to serve you"—he winked—"mistress."

What did she want from her sexy husband? Maybe she was too tired, or not very imaginative, but nothing particularly kinky came to mind. What she craved was the opposite of everything Neville had proposed. Sweet and gentle, not rough and painful. Well, she was the mistress, so why shouldn't she get it? "Turn out the light, climb into bed, and spoon me from behind. As if we were ready to fall asleep."

A few seconds later, the front of his hard body met the curve of her back and his arm reached around to hug her to him. The press of his thick, hot penis against her butt made her sex tighten and pulse in needy response.

"Slave," she said, "you've done a passable job of serving my needs today."

His body shook in a silent chuckle. "Thank you, mistress."

"So I'll take it easy on you. I require only one orgasm, but you must give it to me in this position and you must do it slowly and gently." She raised her arms to curl around the end of her pillow.

"Your wish is my command." He pressed a kiss to her shoulder then parted her legs and slipped his erection between them. He didn't attempt to enter her, just slid back and forth against her swelling labia.

Moisture slipped from her body, coating him as he moved. Arousal tightened inside her, urging her to press harder against him, to shift so he brushed her clit. Normally, she'd have done exactly that. But she'd made Dax responsible for her pleasure, and wanted to see what he'd do.

His big hand caressed the front of her body, starting at her shoulder, brushing over her breast, fanning out over her tummy with a couple of fingers brushing her neatly trimmed pubic hair. But he didn't linger there, nor go back to her nipple. He repeated the long, slow stroke from shoulder on down, and all the time his hips pumped just enough to keep his cock sliding back and forth.

Each inch that his hand touched pricked to awareness, craving more. The same thing happened between her legs. She was desperate to feel him inside her.

Perhaps he sensed it, because he separated their bodies beneath the covering of sheet and duvet, and reached between her legs. He caressed her slick folds and separated them. The head of his penis nudged her, then he entered her so very slowly.

They both adjusted their positions to improve the angle, increase the friction, but other than that, Lily tried to hold still.

The room was almost completely dark. Only a tiny amount of light from the starlit sky seeped around the edge of the curtains. In this near-black cocoon, nothing existed in the world except the two of them.

Dax pumped, in the same slow, small movements he'd used before. He ran a finger around her taut nipple, flicked it with his thumb, squeezed it gently, then harder. Harder again, in a touch that was not yet pain but getting close, creating darts of intense pleasure that wrung whimpers from her.

Because the movements of his fingers and his penis were so small and slow, they drew her focus. Nipple and pussy, it was like her body consisted of only those two things, both of them tingling with arousal, radiating erotic heat to spread through her body. The need to come grew, making her squeeze her thighs together and push back against his thrusts.

Dax kissed her hair then released her nipple and stroked down the front of her body. His fingers drifted through her pubic hair, then lower, and his thumb brushed her clit.

"Oh yes," she whispered. She didn't need clitoral stimulation to climax, but she sure did enjoy it, as Dax well knew.

He circled and flicked, squeezed gently. With her nipple, he'd kept up the relentless teasing, increasing the pressure, but this time his fingers drifted away before the exquisite tension could build too high and tip into climax.

She moaned in frustration. "More, please."

"Mistress?" His warm breath brushed her ear. "Permission to speak?"

"Yes, go ahead."

"You requested slowly and gently. I've been doing my best to obey."

"Fine, but now I want to come. Make me come, D—" She broke off before speaking his name. If he could keep up the game, so could she. "Slave, make me come now."

His thumb rubbed her clit, his strokes increasing in force and speed. Oh yes, she was close, so close, panting with need, squeezing around him. And then her body clutched—"Yes!"—and she climaxed in delicious spasms around him.

He slowed his strokes as her body pulsed with aftershocks. Then, when she expected him to pump again, to seek his own climax, he pulled out of her.

"What?" she cried. "What are you doing? You didn't come."

"You didn't give me permission to."

Now that was taking the game too far. "Then I give you permission now, slave. As your reward."

She expected him to slip back between her legs but instead he pushed himself up, thrusting the covers off their bodies. He caught her by the hip and rolled her onto her back. Her knees automatically came up, she spread her legs, and her inner thighs felt the brush of his legs when he kneeled between them. He reached under her to grasp her by the butt cheeks and lifted her lower body off the bed. She hooked her heels over his shoulders as he thrust deep inside her.

A cry of pleasure escaped her.

He held her almost immobile as he stroked into her in long, smooth, hard thrusts. There was something so primal and male about his actions. She couldn't touch him, couldn't pump her own hips. She was powerless to do anything but accept his thrusts. And respond. Fresh moisture slipped from her body, slicking his shaft, and she moaned as arousal mounted inside her again, and crested.

Dax gave a rough cry and his cock jerked, triggering her climax as hot gushes of come pulsed into her.

He held her hips in his steady grip as orgasms wracked both their bodies. After the final tremors died, he slipped out of her and eased her lower body down to the bed.

She stretched, wrung out with satisfaction. "Wow. And I only asked for one."

He settled beside her, pulling the covers up to cocoon them. "I'm an overachiever."

In the darkness, she turned toward him and kissed him. "Thank you for today, Dax." For the great sex, yes, but more than that. For not giving up on them. For being spontaneous and romantic, for revealing sides of himself he'd kept private before, even for sharing his concerns about her parents and her practice. For trying. With her kiss, she tried to tell him all of that.

Tomorrow was New Year's Eve. Tonight, she had hope that the coming year would bring her and Dax closer together, that they'd have a real marriage and she'd throw those birth control pills away.

Twenty-two

As Lily walked downstairs on New Year's Eve, stepping carefully in the four-inch heels, Dax said, "You look stunning."

"So do you." He wasn't much for formal clothes, but he looked classy and masculine in slim-fitting black pants and a black shirt.

He touched her cheek. "Got some sun today."

"On top of the world." After a lazy morning of sleeping in, sex, breakfast in front of the fire, and more sex, he'd taken her flying again. He had pointed out the various Olympic venues, telling her how Whistler had changed before and after the 2010 Games. But it wasn't the man-made structures that impressed her the most, it was the grand scale of the wilderness scenery: dense rain forest blanketed in snow, winding rivers and frozen lakes, and spectacular white-capped mountains. He had landed on Serratus Glacier and they'd hiked a ways in the snow, with a thermos of hot chocolate to supplement the winter sun's warmth. "Your world," she commented now.

"How d'you mean?"

"That's the world you love, isn't it? Nature as raw as you can get it. It's amazing and awe inspiring." And so was Dax. Seeing him in his element, she was powerfully drawn to him, yet it also emphasized how different they were. So did the stories they'd shared today about their work—careers they each loved that took them in opposite directions. This was all so confusing. She'd come to suspect that she'd never stopped loving her husband, only erected defenses to protect her heart. But given how different she and Dax were, maybe she needed to hang on to those defenses.

"Yeah, I do love it. I feel at home there." He studied her. "Could you ever imagine feeling that way?"

She shook her head, knowing she was disappointing him. "I admire it, but it's intimidating. It scares me. You have the skills to survive in the wilderness, but I've always been a city person."

"Sure, nature can be scary, but it's . . . I don't know how to explain it."

"Try, Dax."

"Often, when nature hurts people, it's their own fault. Like that Sams family, going out unprepared. Or like forest fires that start because someone's careless with a match or cigarette."

"But some fires do start because of lightning."

"Sure, and avalanches happen, and gale force winds blow up. But that's nature being nature. It's not personal; you can't get mad about it."

No, but you could get dead. All the same, she was starting to get it. "Unlike people. You want people to be decent, and when they're not it's maddening and hurtful."

"And harder to deal with. With nature, the challenge is . . . clean. With people it can be so complicated."

Understanding sank in, thanks to last night's conversation. "Like with your parents," she said softly, "who you couldn't trust to be there for you. And your grandparents kicking you out."

He nodded. "And like your parents."

"Yes, they're complicated. At least they can be trusted; they're predictable, even if we don't always like what they do and say." Talking about their parents, recognizing the distance between her world and Dax's . . . no, this wasn't how she wanted to feel as they headed off for New Year's dinner. *Change the subject; change the mood.* "On the subject of predictable, I bet you think I'm wearing panty hose." She flirted the silky full skirt around her knees, showing off her legs.

"Seem to recall you saying that women don't go bare-legged in the middle of winter."

Teasingly, she raised one side of the skirt to reveal a stocking top attached to a garter.

"Wow, a garter belt? You've never worn a garter belt before."

"Not so predictable, am I?"

"Hot. That's what you are." He was bending to kiss her when the doorbell rang. "There's our taxi."

Lily followed him into the mudroom where she put on her boots and coat and stowed her fancy shoes in the clothing store's pretty bag. Around her neck, she wrapped a new silk scarf they'd bought in Whistler, its blue and silver pattern more feminine than her normal scarves. Thank heavens they were taking a cab. In winter, Whistler was made for heavy layers, not evening wear.

Still, as she tucked her gloved hand through Dax's arm on the walk from the door to the waiting taxi, she enjoyed the snowy air, crisp against her cheeks, pure and fresh as she drew it deep into her lungs.

Dax opened the back door, but when she made to slide inside, he stopped her. Close to her ear, he murmured, "Tonight, I am Falcon, your master, and you will obey me."

Shocked, she gaped at him. Tonight? At a restaurant? He couldn't intend . . . What, exactly, did he intend? Excitement quivered through her, mixed with a hefty dose of anxiety. Behaving properly in public had been drummed into her from an early age. Dax knew that.

She could say no. But she loved his bad-boy side. Besides, if she got too uncomfortable, she could always say her safe word. "Yes, Falcon," she murmured demurely, and swung into the taxi.

Dax went around to sit on her right. He gave the driver their destination then settled back. Putting an arm around Lily, he drew her closer in the darkness of the backseat and whispered, "Unbutton your coat and let it fall open."

A shiver rippled through her as she obeyed. Another followed when he loosened her scarf, flicked the dangling hummingbird earring, and caressed her earlobe.

When they drove under a streetlight, or an oncoming car's headlights flashed, the play of light and shadow made the bold lines of his face even more striking. His fingers stroked her neck, ear, throat, collarbone, the lazy sensuality igniting a fire inside her.

"Cross your right leg over your left. Let your skirt ride up above your knees." When she obeyed, he gripped her stockinged knee, his big hand spread out to curl around it, holding her firmly. "I don't own you, but I command you. You trust me to look after you, and your pleasure."

His grip on her knee and the seductive caresses at her throat made her totally aware of him and yes, she did feel like she was in his power. It was a strange sensation, but not a bad one. "I do."

"You will look after my pleasure and give me everything I ask for."

Everything? What might that entail, in a public venue? "I will," she said doubtfully.

His hand slid a few inches higher on her leg, nudging the hem of her skirt to mid-thigh. "What are you wearing under your dress, Lily? A garter belt and stockings and . . . ?"

"A thong and a bra."

"Ah." His thumb found the top band of her stocking, toyed with the garter but didn't unfasten it. Then he stroked the bare skin of her inner thigh above her stocking, inches away from her sex. The steady, provocative stroke was titillating and she quivered with the desire to feel that touch against the crotch of her thong, which was rapidly growing damp.

The taxi drove through Whistler Village, all sparkly and magical, and pulled up outside the restaurant. Dax released Lily and reached for his wallet. The loss of his touch, combined with having no idea what he intended, made her feel vulnerable. She rebuttoned her coat and, when he opened the door, slid out and took his arm. A few people strolled the streets, and laughter and music mingled in the air.

Inside the entrance of the restaurant, Dax helped her out of her coat and handed it to the host along with his own, then steadied her while she took off her boots and put on her fancy shoes.

Lily glanced into the restaurant, so elegant and romantic with ivory-draped tables and diners in dressy clothes. Candlelight sparkled off silverware, wineglasses, and diamond jewelry. The Christmas tree hadn't been taken down yet. Decorated in white and gold, it stood tall and twinkling in a corner.

"We're setting up your table," the host told them. "It'll only be a moment."

Dax thanked him then whispered to Lily, "Go to the ladies' room and remove your thong."

She sucked in a breath. She'd toyed with the idea of going without panties, but hadn't had the nerve. Now he'd ordered her to. She dipped her head in acknowledgment and walked down the hall on trembling legs.

The restroom was elegant too, with creamy white marble, burning candles, and a pine wreath scenting the air. The three stalls were private little rooms with wooden walls that stretched from floor to ceiling. Lily went into one and reached under her skirt. She peeled the thong down her legs and stepped out of it, crumpled it into a ball, and stuffed it in her purse.

In the stall beside her, a toilet flushed and the door opened. When Lily stepped out of her stall, a plump, attractive brunette in black chiffon pants, a spangly silver top, and silver sandals was washing her hands. Their gazes met in the mirror. "Happy New Year," the woman said.

"Same to you."

When the woman left, Lily stared at her own reflection. She'd never gone without underwear; in fact, she rarely wore thongs, finding them too skimpy. It was amazing how naked she felt, though no one in the restaurant could possibly tell that she was panty-less. It was her and Dax's sexy little secret.

She sauntered out of the restroom, very aware of her body. High heels, garter belt and stockings, the swish of silk against her skin, the shock of air against her pussy. Feeling sexy and nervous, she wondered what Dax would make her do next.

Twenty-three

Dax watched Lily walk toward him, her hips swinging. God, she was lovely. Was her pussy bare under that pretty dress?

Tonight, he had no plan; he was winging it. He'd asked her to trust him to meet her needs and fulfill her desires. That meant he had to figure out what those needs and desires were. He could ask, but he was sure that she, like Cassandra, had secret desires she hadn't even admitted to herself. It was those desires, the ones that pushed the bounds and delved past her inhibitions, that he wanted to fulfill.

Besides, bad boys didn't consult; they took charge. "Give it to me," he said to her.

Her eyes flared. "Now? Here?"

He raised his brows.

She fumbled inside her purse and her hand emerged, fisted. Glancing around nervously, she transferred a still-warm scrap of fabric to his hand.

Yeah, her pussy was bare. Heat surged to his groin, thickened his cock. He thrust the thong in his pants pocket and left his hand there, fisting it and stretching the lightweight black wool to conceal his growing erection. "Our table's ready." He tucked his other hand behind her elbow and steered her toward the maître d'.

When he'd made the reservation, Dax had checked the restaurant's layout. The large room was divided by tall pillars inset with

gas fireplaces, giving the illusion of several smaller rooms. Most of
the tables were the regular kind, but those along the outside of the
room were semi-secluded booths. He had reserved a small booth in
a relatively private corner.

Now, as he and Lily followed the tuxedoed maître d' across the
packed restaurant, he confirmed that the crisp cream-colored tablecloths fell almost to the floor. Perfect cover for some fooling around.

Lily slid onto the leather seat and Dax sat to her right. Two white
candles in gold-and-glass holders burned on the table and the center-
piece had white orchids, sprigs of holly, and small branches of pine.

"Your waiter will be with you to take your drink order," the maître d' said. "Have a lovely evening."

"Thank you," Dax replied. "We will."

Earlier, they'd had rum toddies along with cheese, olives, and
crackers. A snack to tide them over, but not ruin dinner. Now, when
their thin, fair-haired waiter arrived, Dax ordered a martini with a
twist for Lily and a Black Tusk ale for himself.

"Dinner is a three course table d'hôte," the waiter said. "You have
three options." He handed them both menus, then departed.

Dax and Lily both studied the menus. She said, "I think I'll have—"

"Stop." He needed to remind her of the game. "I didn't give you
permission to speak. And I'll decide what you eat and drink."

A spark of challenge lit her eyes. "Yes, Falcon."

He figured he could meet that challenge just fine. One of the menus
featured a variety of seafood; another had rack of lamb as the main
course. The third included roast duck breast with cranberry-orange
confit. Lily loved duck, and that menu also had one of her favorite des-
serts, chocolate soufflé.

When their drinks arrived, Dax told the waiter, "The lady will
have the duck menu." He noted Lily's slight nod of approval as he
went on. "I'll have the rack of lamb. Could you suggest a red wine
that would suit both meals?"

From the waiter's recommendations, Dax chose an eighty dollar pinot noir. "Please open that now so it can breathe." Yeah, he'd picked up a trick or two from those fancy meals with her parents, such as knowing that good red wine benefitted from aeration.

After the waiter had gone, Dax turned to Lily and raised his beer glass. "Happy New Year."

She opened her mouth then paused. "May I speak?"

It would be a dull dinner if they ate it in silence. "You can talk as you normally would. But when I tell you to do something, you will obey without question. Understood?"

"Yes, Falcon." She lifted her martini glass. "Happy New Year. The restaurant is lovely. And thank you for choosing the duck for me."

"You always hate it when the man orders dinner for the woman." Neither her father nor Anthony ever did.

She nodded. "It's presumptuous. Like she doesn't have a mind of her own."

"Or like he knows her so well he doesn't have to ask."

"Hmm. I suppose it's sometimes a sign of intimacy." She glanced up as their waiter arrived with their first course and the opened bottle of red wine. "Thank you. This looks delicious."

They both had soup, cream of leek with herbs for him, wild mushroom for her. After they each tasted their own, he said in his dom voice, "Feed me some of yours."

Lily'd always said that eating off another person's fork or spoon in public looked tacky. Now she frowned slightly, but obediently scooped up a spoonful. Holding one hand under the spoon to catch drips, she held it toward him.

He leaned forward, took the spoon between his lips, and let the warm soup slide into his mouth. In his normal voice, he said, "That's good. Thanks. Help yourself, if you'd like to taste mine."

She eyed him warily, clearly not knowing what to expect next. "No, thanks. Leek doesn't appeal to me tonight."

He moved closer to her on the banquette so their hips and thighs touched, and rested his left hand on her leg. She gave a start. Twice he'd teased her with the scenario of reaching under her dress in a restaurant and making her come. Her little jump told him it was on her mind and the fact that she'd taken off her thong suggested she was open to it.

With his other hand, he resumed eating his soup. After a moment, Lily did the same.

After a couple of minutes of silence, she gestured toward a pretty brunette with flushed cheeks and a sparkly top, sitting with a distinguished-looking guy with silver-streaked hair. "She was in the ladies' room when I went in." His wife was making small talk. It was something she did to mask nervousness.

"Oh?" Dax rubbed his thumb over the bump of her garter under the fabric of her skirt. If Lily reached under the napkin on his lap, she'd discover he had things other than small talk in mind.

"It's a lovely restroom, by the way."

"Uh-huh?"

"Lots of marble, and the toilet stalls are separate little rooms with real walls."

His attention perked and his cock pulsed. Now *that* was interesting information. He glanced at Lily, who was sipping her martini. Was she really making idle chitchat, or did she have an ulterior motive? Sex in a public restroom? They'd never done that.

Was it a secret fantasy for her? Tonight, she was his sub. If he told her to do it, she'd either obey or say her safe word. How far could he push his wife past her inhibitions to hidden desires she might not even have acknowledged to herself? He adjusted the white napkin that concealed his bulging fly.

When he and Lily finished their soup and drinks, the waiter appeared. He poured a mouthful of wine for Dax to taste and approve, then filled their glasses and cleared the empty soup bowls.

After Lily tried the wine, Dax asked, "How do you like it?"

"Very nice. It'll go beautifully with the duck. And the shallot tart."

A moment later, the waiter slipped the appetizer in front of her, and gave Dax a grilled portobello mushroom. After the first couple of bites, Dax, who knew Lily liked portobello mushrooms, said, "Would you like a taste?"

"I would. Thanks."

She reached over with her fork but he stopped her. "No. I'll feed you." He cut a slice and held his fork toward her lips.

After a momentary pause, she took the bite delicately, her pink lips closing over it in a way that had him imagining them on his swollen cock. She cut a slice of shallot tart and offered it to him on her fork.

"Thank you. You learn quickly." He ate it off her fork.

When they both returned to eating their own food, he inched her skirt upward, brushing her stocking-clad leg with his fingers. "Slide forward on the seat. Use the edge of the tablecloth and your napkin to cover my hand."

Silently, she obeyed, hiking her skirt up so she wasn't sitting on the delicate fabric. The rise and fall of her breasts told him her breath had quickened.

His fingers reached the top of her stocking and tracked the line of the garter upward across warm skin, smoother and silkier than the stocking. "Don't let me stop you from eating," he told her, using the edge of his fork to cut another bite of his mushroom.

"Dax, you aren't really going to—"

"Stop." He pinched her thigh, eliciting a startled squeak. "I gave you permission to speak, not to question my actions."

Her throat rippled as she swallowed.

"Do you want to say your safe word?"

Slowly, she shook her head. "No, Falcon."

In silence, they both ate, taking occasional sips of wine. His thumb stroked back and forth, back and forth, moving a bit higher now and then. Finally, it brushed hot, damp flesh, the swollen lips of her pussy.

She gasped and her fingers, lifting her wineglass, trembled. She stared into the red liquid intently, but didn't take a drink. Color bloomed on her cheeks.

The waiter came to clear their appetizer plates, and brought crystal bowls holding grape-sized balls of pale yellow sorbet. "A palate cleanser." He appeared not to notice anything strange about the way they were sitting. "Champagne and lemongrass sorbet."

"Thanks," Dax managed, while Lily kept quiet.

He ate a couple of the balls. Light and tangy, the sorbet melted on his tongue. Too bad he couldn't pack the rest of the balls inside his pants to cool down his overheated cock. But that gave him an idea.

"Eat your sorbet," he ordered Lily.

Obediently, she spooned up a ball.

He drew his hand from between her legs, noting the surprised flare of her nostrils. After glancing around to make sure no one was watching, he dragged his fingers through the remaining sorbet in his bowl then lowered his hand again. The brush of his chilled fingers against her hot flesh made her gasp again, and when he thrust a finger inside her, she squeaked.

"Shh," he warned. "You don't want to cause a scene."

"I . . ." She stared at him, blue eyes huge, glittering with shock and arousal. "Oh God."

She didn't say "Skookumchuck," so he pumped his finger slowly back and forth, her steamy flesh clinging to him.

Lily sat motionless but for the rapid rise and fall of her breasts.

"Finish your sorbet." He eased another finger into her.

She let out the faintest moan, but wielded her spoon.

With his wrist cocked at an awkward angle, he circled both fingers as he pumped in and out, swirling round and round. His palm brushed her clit.

Lily gulped down her sorbet and put down her spoon. She leaned back so her head and shoulders rested against the back of the banquette and her ass and hips were almost at the edge, pressing into his hand. Breathy little pants told him how aroused she was.

The pressure behind his fly begged for release, and he was almost glad to see their waiter heading toward them. He withdrew his hand. "Waiter, incoming."

She straightened hurriedly, glancing down to make sure the napkin and tablecloth still covered her. She took a deep breath and he heard it sigh out.

When the waiter cleared the sorbet bowls, he said, "How was it?"

"Surprisingly delicious," Lily said, shooting a sideways glance at Dax. "But over too soon."

Dax stifled a chuckle as the waiter replied, "I hear that a lot. I'll be back with your entrees."

When the other man departed, Dax lifted the hand that had been inside Lily and raised it to his mouth. He inhaled her heady scent then licked his fingers to taste her tangy juices.

Watching him, she let out another of those tiny moans.

"Over too soon?" he said. "It was only an appetizer. The main course is yet to come."

"When? How?" Remembering, she added, "Falcon."

"Don't question me. Trust me to look after you."

Her eyes narrowed.

"Tell me you don't find this sexy," he challenged her.

"It is, but I'm all worked up and I don't know what we're going to do about it," she complained.

"We're going to eat dinner, and you're going to keep wondering exactly when and how I'm going to look after you."

A grin tugged at the edges of her lips. "Okay, I admit that's titillat—" She swallowed the last syllable as the waiter hurried over with their dinner plates.

Both meals looked delicious and Dax dug into his, glad to let the arousal level in his body drop a few degrees. The lamb was tender and succulent, flavored with rosemary, pepper, and garlic. The small roasted potatoes, baby asparagus, and golden beets were delicious too. "How's your duck?"

"Scrumptious." She cut a slice and offered it to him on her fork.

He tasted it, said, "That is good," then offered her a bite of lamb. When she took it into her mouth and closed her lips, he ran his thumb caressingly over her top lip, then her bottom one.

Studying his face, she chewed and swallowed. "Dax, I can't believe what you did. I can't believe I let you. This doesn't feel like me tonight."

"Are you complaining?"

"Not yet." Mischief gleamed in her eyes. "I'm waiting to see if the main course measures up to the appetizer."

"I told you, you need to trust me."

They ate in companionable silence for a few minutes. Dax always ate more quickly, and by the time he'd almost finished, she was only halfway through. With a few bites remaining on his plate, he dropped his left hand to her napkin-covered thigh. "Slide forward again."

"Now?"

He gave her his best dom stare. "You're questioning me?"

"I . . . guess not," she said uncertainly, and slipped forward to the front of the bench.

His hand found its way under the napkin and between her thighs, all the way to the top. Her arousal would have cooled, as had his own. So he teased her with slow, gentle strokes across her pussy, but didn't enter her yet. "Keep eating. I know you can multitask."

She gave a surprised chuckle. Color blooming on her cheeks, she picked up her knife and fork and cut into the duck breast.

He kept caressing her as he finished his own meal. When she was damp and swollen with need, he slid two fingers into her, pumping and circling the way he had before. Her body gripped him; her breath quickened. His own body tightened, his cock springing to attention again.

Much as he'd like to prolong this, each moment heightened the risk of discovery. He knew how to make Lily come quickly, and he used that knowledge. Gently, he tapped the sweet spot hidden deep inside her, and with his thumb he rubbed her clit. Two magic buttons. He alternated pressure from one to the other, all the time stroking his fingers in and out.

With fumbling fingers she put down her knife and fork and gripped the edge of the table with both hands, reclining back and closing her eyes. "Dax," she whispered. "Oh Dax."

"Shh, sweetheart." He glanced around the restaurant. The other diners were occupied with their own meals and conversations. Their waiter chatted with a group of ten or so at a table near the Christmas tree.

A tiny whimper escaped Lily's lips.

He increased speed and pressure—tapping clit, sweet spot, clit in a quick rhythm.

Her body tensed, froze, then she came apart against his hand. While she pulsed and shuddered around him, her upper body was rigid, braced by her hands against the table. Her cheeks were bright pink, shallow breaths rasped in and out of her open mouth, and her eyes squeezed shut as if that would somehow guarantee her privacy.

She was beautiful. So beautiful. And gutsy, to opt into this sex play.

He wanted her. Now. His body was ready to explode with it. He leaned close to her ear. "I want to fuck you."

Twenty-four

Lily's whole body jerked at her husband's blunt words, her vagina clenching around his fingers. Slowly, she opened her eyes and gazed at Dax. His gray eyes glittered silver in the candlelight and dusky color bloomed on his cheekbones.

She couldn't believe what they'd done, yet she wanted more. "Yes," she murmured. "But how?"

Slowly, he eased his fingers out of her and dried them on his napkin.

Her body felt empty without him. As reality sank in, she glanced nervously around the restaurant. Had anyone seen them? No one seemed to be paying attention.

Dax took a long swallow of wine. "You'll go—"

"The waiter," she warned, seeing the man heading across the room toward them.

He took Dax's empty plate and glanced at Lily.

"I'm finished too." Her voice came out husky. "It was wonderful, but I'm saving room for dessert." Much as she loved chocolate soufflé, the dessert she really craved was sex with Dax.

"Would you like me to bring that now?" the waiter asked. "And perhaps some coffee?"

"No," Dax said abruptly. Then he added, "Thanks, but we'll finish the wine first."

"Take your time." The waiter poured the last of the pinot noir into their glasses.

When he'd gone, Dax said, "You go to the ladies' room. I'll be in the hall outside. When it's empty, let me in."

Sex in the ladies' room? She'd always thought the idea was tacky, but . . . She pressed her hands to her flushed cheeks. "This is what I get for wanting a bad boy."

"It's what you get for being a dirty girl." He slid out of the booth and jammed a fist into one pocket.

Her gaze focused on his fly. Even the distended pocket couldn't entirely camouflage his erection.

Dax moved around the table and, as Lily came to her feet and collected her purse, he offered her his arm. Gratefully, she took it. She rarely wore high heels and her legs were wobbly after that orgasm.

He smiled and bent to drop a quick kiss on her lips.

She smiled back. "Here goes." Straightening her spine, she started across the restaurant.

Dax put a hand at her waist, walking slightly behind and to her side. Her fullish skirt would help conceal his aroused state.

Glancing at the other diners, she was relieved that they were having too good a time to pay attention to her and Dax. His hand burned through the silk of her dress. It branded her, compelled her. Aroused her. In charged silence, she and her husband headed down the hallway she'd walked on her own earlier. Lily opened the door to the ladies' room and went in. A young redhead in a black cocktail dress was touching up her lipstick at the sink. They exchanged greetings, and Lily opened her own purse and took out her comb.

When the redhead left, Lily quickly checked the three stalls and saw VACANT signs on each door. She opened the restroom door. "All clear."

Dax whipped through the door, glanced around, and then tugged her toward the stall farthest from the door. The cubicle was tiny, with a toilet and barely enough room for the two of them to stand, but it was clean and elegant. If they were going to do this, at least it was in a marble toilet stall.

She'd barely put her purse on top of the toilet paper container when Dax pulled her into his arms. Eagerly, she wrapped her arms around him and met his kiss. Oh yes, this was her favorite dessert. She rubbed her needy body shamelessly against the bulge behind his fly.

He groaned. "Christ, I want you." He broke the kiss to reach for his belt. Hands fumbling with urgency, he unbuckled, unbuttoned, struggled to force the zipper over his erection. He shoved his pants and underwear down, groaning when his rigid cock sprang free, the head beaded with pre-come.

Such a tantalizing sight. Her hands reached out to circle his shaft.

He jerked in her hand. "No, crap." He grabbed her hands, forced them away. "I'm going to fucking explode."

"We could do it that way," she offered. "With my hands. Or—"

"Inside you. I need to be inside you."

And that was exactly what she wanted. She dropped her hands to the sides of her skirt. "While I wear these?" She raised the hem, revealing the tops of her stockings, the garters, and then her own nakedness framed by the lacy champagne-colored garter belt.

"You are so damned hot." The words ground out of him.

Bracing his back against the stall door, he caught her by the waist and lifted her. When she looped her arms around his shoulders, he rotated so her back pressed against the locked door. She hooked her stocking-clad legs around his hips and he held her, one hand under her butt, one around her shoulders.

His cock brushed her thigh, she shifted a little, and now the crown nudged her damp pussy, desperately seeking entrance. "Fuck, I need to get in."

She gave another wriggle and he slid into her. "Yes," she breathed, close to his ear.

He thrust compulsively, and her body, still sensitive from orgasm, responded quickly. She guessed this would be quick and raw, which was fine by her. But she didn't want to get left behind, so she shifted to ensure he brushed her clit each time he plunged into her.

Oh yes, that angle was perfect. Arousal escalated, making her bury a whimper in his black hair.

A door opened. The door to the ladies' room. Two female voices were in mid-conversation about the merits of chocolate soufflé versus Grand Marnier crème brûlée.

Dax froze and so did Lily, clinging tight to him.

Heels clicked across the floor and, still talking, the women entered the two vacant stalls.

"Can't do this." Dax's voice was only the breath of a whisper. "Can't think of a damn technical spec."

Technical spec? Had she misheard?

"Fuck," he muttered. His hips jerked and he drove into her, hard and fast, back and forth.

The movement, so fierce and strong, almost made her cry out with pleasure. She was dimly aware of the two women peeing, still chatting with each other. She pressed down, grinding against Dax, increasing the delicious friction.

His climax poured into her in pulsing, irresistible waves that took her up, up, and over the top.

As she spasmed around him, a toilet flushed, maybe loud enough to cover his groan and the whimper of release she couldn't hold back. The second toilet flushed. Both stall doors opened and the women resumed their conversation, giving no sign they were aware of Lily and Dax.

Trembling, she clung to him as their bodies throbbed together with the aftershocks. Water ran, a purse clasp snapped open, something clattered against the counter.

Dax eased out of her and slowly let her down. She tried not to let her shoes click against the tile floor. Panting, she leaned her forehead against his chest and breathed a silent "Wow." Her parents would be shocked beyond belief, but the book club members would definitely approve.

Finally, the door opened and closed, and the room was silent.

"Oh, man," he said quietly.

"Definitely." She remembered something. "Did you say 'technical spec'?"

He nodded, humor in his eyes. "If I recite helicopter technical specifications in my head, it distracts me from needing to come. But I couldn't even remember a type of helicopter, much less its specs." He put himself back together.

So easy for a man. Lily wanted one of the soft towels on the counter. A warm, damp towel. And then her thong. She reached into Dax's pants pocket for it, and stuffed it in her purse.

He raised his eyebrows but said only, "Go check the hall. See if the coast is clear."

She scooted out of the stall and peeked out the door to the hallway. "Yes. Go now. I'll meet you back at the table."

"Okay." He strode across the restroom floor and paused at the door. "You're something, Lily Nyland."

"You too. Now go!"

When he was gone, she held a towel under the hot water tap then went back into the stall to clean up. Once she'd washed and put her thong back on, she returned to the sink to splash cold water on her burning cheeks, comb her hair, and apply fresh lip gloss. Even neatened up, to her mind she still looked like a woman who'd been well fucked.

The book club novel popped into her mind. Dax hadn't taken her to a BDSM club; they'd gone to an elegant restaurant. He hadn't given her to other men to fuck—or whatever it was that Neville intended to do with Cassandra—but he'd made Lily do things she'd never believed she would do.

Except, of course, he hadn't *made* her do anything, no more than Neville *made* Cassandra do things. Neville was helping Cassandra determine whether she was truly a submissive. And Dax was encouraging Lily to push her bounds. When he restrained her, he in fact liberated her, sexually. When he commanded her, he absolved her of responsibility so she could let loose.

Because of him she was learning things about herself. She wasn't just her parents' well-mannered, conventional daughter. She was brave enough to take risks, and she could go a little crazy. Especially if she had Dax to both incite and protect her.

Staring at her own reflection, Lily barely noticed the restroom door open and an older woman enter and go into a stall.

Dax . . . She'd once loved him so much. Over the past couple of years she had questioned whether that love still existed. She'd pushed her emotions away, buried them; she'd rationalized rather than letting herself feel. All because she was afraid. Afraid he no longer loved her, that he'd break her heart if she let him. She hadn't been honest with herself; she'd erected defenses; she'd lived in fear. No wonder she was so stressed, suffered from headaches, couldn't focus clearly and make decisions in any aspect of her life.

Now things had changed. Their lovemaking was fresh, challenging, exciting. They were exploring their bodies, their bounds, their sexual connection in new and very adult ways. Their conversations were different too, and more adult, going deeper and venturing into topics they used to avoid.

She was coming to know the old Dax and the new one, and the end result was . . . she found him compelling. He'd grown more handsome and sexy with age; he flew into storms to rescue people;

he did romantic things like fly her to Whistler; he was more willing to open up to her. He was amazing.

How could she not love this man?

"Excuse me, but are you all right?" a diffident voice asked.

Lily realized the older woman was at the sink beside her, gazing with concern at Lily.

"Yes, I was . . . thinking."

"It's a time for that, isn't it?" She gave an understanding smile. "The end of one year and the beginning of another. A time of resolutions and possibilities."

"Yes, I suppose it is." Lily smiled back. "Happy New Year. I hope it's a wonderful one for you."

"And for you." The woman moved to the door, opened it, and paused expectantly.

Dax was probably wondering if she was taking a full sponge bath in here. Lily stepped forward to join the woman and they walked down the hallway. The woman headed toward a corner table where a handsome bald-headed man stood, smiling, to greet her.

Lily straightened her back and walked across the restaurant toward her own handsome man. She'd figured out the truth about herself. She was brave and crazy enough to have sex in a restaurant, and brave and crazy enough to love her husband.

Dax slid out from the booth and strode toward her. So strong and agile; so sexy and breathtaking.

Her heart fluttered anxiously. How did he feel about her? A week ago they'd both admitted they didn't know if the love was still there. Today he'd been acting like a man who truly cared. If he too felt the rekindling of love, could they dream new dreams together, adult dreams they could turn into a reality? It was a time for resolutions and possibilities, the older woman had said. Lily gave Dax a nervous smile.

His hand caught her elbow. "Are you okay? You were in there a long time."

"I'm fine. I cleaned up and chatted with a nice older woman." *And realized I'd fallen in love with you all over again.* The thought was heady. Surely he must feel the same way.

"Ready for chocolate soufflé?" He guided her back to their table.

"A second dessert?" she teased as she slid onto the seat.

"The first one was calorie free."

Laughing, she reached for her wineglass and raised it. "To calorie-free dessert and new adventures."

With a wicked gleam in his eye, he said, "To my wife obeying me without question."

"Hah. Only if you promise it'll result in wonderful"—she was about to say "sex" when she realized their waiter was back. "Dessert," she finished.

"Right away," the waiter said, and turned away again.

"Well, how about that? I have two men just dying to give me dessert."

"Mine's better."

"I'll decide once I taste the soufflé." Should she tell Dax about her revelation? It was New Year's Eve, the perfect time for new beginnings. Was she brave enough to confess her love? Perhaps on the stroke of midnight . . .

The waiter placed the soufflé in front of her, dark and steaming, the rich smell of chocolate drifting up to her nostrils. "This is going to be tough competition," she told Dax.

They both said yes to the waiter's offer of coffee. Once he'd poured it into gold-rimmed cups, Lily dug eagerly into her dessert. The soufflé was perfect, moist, and extremely chocolaty.

Dax tasted his mixed-berry crisp, served with vanilla bean ice cream. "This is great. Dare I demand a taste of yours?"

"You might have to fight me for it." But, since he'd given her such a memorable evening—and she really did love him—she offered him a spoonful. When he reciprocated, she said, "No, thanks. The taste of chocolate and coffee together is perfect. I don't want to put anything else in my mouth."

"Not even . . ." He winked suggestively.

"Maybe later." Definitely later, if things went the way she hoped they did at the stroke of midnight.

Twenty-five

Dax settled back in his seat as their waiter cleared the empty dessert plates. He felt full and satisfied in a way that went far beyond having eaten a delicious meal. This was right, him and Lily together like this. It was like the good old days, but even better.

A different waiter appeared, bearing a tray of filled champagne flutes. "Happy New Year." He placed two glasses in front of them, and moved on to the next table.

Dax glanced at his watch. "Ten to twelve. This is the best New Year's Eve I've had in a very long time."

"Me too." Her blue eyes were soft and, he thought, loving as she gazed at him. "It's been quite the evening."

"And quite the trip. When I planned it, I was thinking about the special times we used to have, the special things we shared. I was confused about us, our marriage."

"Me too."

"I hoped this weekend would clarify things." Feeling like he was jumping out of a helicopter without a parachute, he went on. "For me it has. I still love you, Lily."

Her mouth opened and surprise—pleased surprise, thank God—lit her face.

"You're the only woman I've ever loved. I want to fight for our marriage. I don't want to let it go. Let's try to fix it. I think we can." He took a breath. "What do you say?"

Her eyes squeezed shut for a long moment. When she opened them, tears welled and one escaped to slide down her cheek. She sniffled, and her lips shaped a trembling smile. "I say yes, Dax. I do love you. I loved you all along, but I tried to deny it to myself because I was afraid you'd fallen out of love with me. I didn't want to let you hurt me."

"I'd never want to hurt you."

"I know that now, my love. I trust you with my heart. Yes, I want to fight for our marriage too."

How long had it been since she'd called him "my love"? The naked emotion on her face confirmed everything she'd said. Pure joy filled his heart. He caught that beautiful face between his hands and kissed her. Her lips quivered against his and tasted of salt as she kissed him back fervently.

When they broke apart, she said, "Oh, my. This is quite an evening indeed." She swiped her hands under her eyes.

He caught one of those hands, linking their fingers. "We can do this more often. You need to figure out your work situation so you can take time off, and I'll take more breaks, longer breaks. Maybe sometimes you could come up, see where I'm working, meet some of the people."

"Um . . ." She frowned slightly. "Yes, I'd like to have more getaways like this, and I'd like to meet your colleagues. But I'm not sure what you're saying. How do you see our marriage going?"

He was about to answer, when he heard loud voices calling, "Ten!" Quickly he lifted both champagne flutes and handed one to Lily. Talk about perfect timing. Glass held high, he joined the chant. A countdown to a new year and a fresh, wonderful marriage.

Oddly, Lily's face looked a little strained, but maybe he was imagining that.

"Three, two, one!" The restaurant patrons and staff bellowed, "Happy New Year!"

He clicked his glass to Lily's. "I love you."

"I love you too, Dax," she said softly. They both took a drink.

He kissed her again, gently, deeply, sharing his love and joy and hope for their future. She kissed him back, long and slow. He tasted salt again and, sure enough, when they finally separated her cheeks were damp with fresh tears.

She smoothed them away. Voice quivering, she said, "You were going to t-tell me how you envision our m-marriage."

"More like the first years," he said eagerly. "We got together as often as we could, and it was great. When we were apart, I still felt close to you. I thought of you all the time, remembered the things we'd done, looked forward to seeing you again."

"But . . ." That frown line appeared in her forehead. "Is that your vision of a perfect marriage? Both of us on our parallel courses, but getting together more often?"

"Perfect? Well, no, but my vision of perfect isn't going to happen."

"Tell me."

Was there any possibility she might share his dream? His heart skipped. "Us living in some beautiful wilderness spot. A small community. A place where I could fly and you could be a doctor, and most nights we'd be home together."

The way her eyebrows drew together confirmed that this was anything but her idea of paradise. Pragmatically, he went on. "But I know you like Vancouver, you've built your clinic there, you want to stay close to your family. That's why I said it wouldn't happen. And the next best thing would still be pretty good. Don't you think?" It occurred to him to ask, "What's your vision of the perfect marriage?"

Slowly, she shook her head. "One that . . . I guess won't happen either. Yes, being home together most nights. But in Vancouver, and I know you don't want to live there. Having a couple of kids and—"

"Kids? What?" Where had that come from? "You don't want to have kids, do you?"

She gaped at him. "Of course I do. I always have. You know that."

He shook his head. "A long time ago, you said you did, but we were spinning all sorts of crazy dreams. You haven't said anything about it in a long time."

"We weren't at that place in our lives. But I'm thirty-two, Dax. My biological clock's ticking pretty fast. Especially when I'm with Sophia. I'm two years older than Anthony and four years older than Regina."

"It's not a competition."

"That's not what I meant. This is just about me. Well, me and you."

Baffled, he said, "At Christmas, you implied to your parents and Regina that kids weren't in your plans."

"I was hardly going to say that I desperately wanted to have kids, but our marriage was in trouble so I didn't know if we'd ever have them, much less stay together." She sighed. "I think the two of us would make wonderful parents. But I don't want to raise children alone, with you away so much."

"No, that wouldn't be right. But, uh . . ."

Her eyes narrowed. "Wait a minute. You want to have kids, don't you?"

"I know we talked about it once." Back then he'd been dreamer enough to think he and Lily might have the kind of home and family he'd always secretly wanted when he was a child. "But I thought we'd both given up the idea."

"That doesn't answer my question. Do you want to have children?"

Slowly, he shook his head. He wasn't parent material; he'd come to terms with that long ago. "No, I don't." As for Lily, she had things to come to terms with too. "And be realistic. How could you have kids? Would you dump them with a nanny while you put in crazy hours at work? The clinic's become your baby; it takes all your time and energy. And when I suggested you hire a manager, you jumped down my throat."

"I'd figure it out."

"How, when you can't figure it out now? Kids deserve attention." They deserved *good* parents. "They deserve a hell of a lot more than our parents gave us."

"I know that!" She pressed trembling fingers to her cheeks. Her voice, though, was calm when she went on. "So, here's what you want: a childless marriage where we live separately and have fun little breaks together. Right?"

"It worked before." Dimly, he was aware of the noise level in the restaurant, so much higher than it had been before midnight. How fucking ironic that everyone else was drinking champagne toasts and chattering excitedly while he and Lily had this conversation. A conversation that was sounding increasingly like a death knell for their marriage.

"We're older now. I want more, Dax." Again, tears welled in her eyes. "And you can't give it to me."

He wasn't enough for her. That was what she was saying. "You knew who I was when you married me," he said bitterly. "Now, suddenly, I'm not good enough for you? Damn it, you should've listened to your parents all those years ago and never married me."

She shook her head vigorously. "That's not what I'm saying! Of course you're good enough. And we did have a good marriage in the early days. But now we want very different things."

"There's no compromise, no way to meet in the middle?"

Her blue eyes were glazed with tears, but she held her head up. "I want to be a mom."

"More than you want to be a wife, obviously," he shot back. "You want to be a doctor and a mom, and you don't give a damn about being a wife. Yeah, that figures. I've never come first with you. I never did with my parents, so why would I think—"

"That's not true," she protested heatedly. "You're the only man I've ever loved. But I don't want a . . . half life, with my husband away most of the time."

"You have a half life now. All you ever do is work. How're you going to slow down long enough to conceive a child, much less raise it?" And who would she conceive it with? Would she marry the kind of man her parents had always wanted for her? God, he hated the thought of Lily with another man.

"I guess," she said slowly, tears slipping down her cheeks, "that won't be any business of yours, will it? You can get back to the wilderness that you love more than you ever loved me."

The ache in his heart was a physical pain. Yes, he loved the wilderness but in the past years he'd never been entirely alone there. He'd had Lily in his heart. Even when their marriage was strained, she'd still been his wife. His anchor; his home.

Hell, his parents had taught him not to rely on other people. He didn't need Lily. He didn't need anyone. "Fuck. We should've just broken up the night I came back to town."

She blinked against more tears. "It would have been easier. This hurts more. Getting close again and then . . ." She sniffed. "So we're breaking up?"

"I . . ." What a hell of a way to start the new year. "Seems like it's the only thing that makes sense."

"Seems like it is." She took out a tissue from her purse and blew her nose.

He stared out at the tables where everyone else was celebrating, anticipating a bright new year. His and Lily's champagne flutes sat on the table, nearly full. The bubbles had lost most of their fizz. The ache in his heart wasn't a stabbing pain, but a dull, empty, lonely one. He had a feeling it wouldn't stop anytime soon. Glad that he'd paid the dinner bill while Lily was in the ladies' room, he said, "Let's go. We'll beat the crowd and snag a cab."

She nodded. "Dax, let's not be mean about . . . things. We love each other. We can work out the details in a, uh . . ."

"Civil fashion?" he asked coolly.

"I was going to say 'friendly,' but that didn't sound right."

"No, it doesn't. But yeah, we'll be civil." The time for passion, for emotion, was gone.

"The easiest thing is to split everything down the middle."

Easy. How could she call breaking up a marriage easy? But that was Lily, already businesslike. "Whatever."

"I'll sell the condo and give you half the—"

"Jesus, Lily, that's your home. Keep the fucking condo." He slid off the seat, unable to sit still a moment longer.

She climbed hurriedly off the other side. "But you paid at least half. That wouldn't be fair."

"Fair? How the fuck does *fair* come into this?" He strode across the restaurant, vaguely aware of a few shocked glances, and of the quick click-click of her heels as she hurried behind him.

On the first day of the new year, Dax unlocked the door to the condo and stepped back to let Lily enter. She hung up her coat but he carried straight through to the bedroom, and the walk-in closet.

They'd left Whistler early, after a night of him tossing and turning on the couch in front of an ashy fireplace and her likely doing the same upstairs in the big bed. When he'd booked the cabin, he'd arranged for cleaners to come in at the end of the weekend. This morning, he left a note telling them to take the leftovers home, including most of a bottle of rum and the two bottles of wine he and Lily hadn't drunk.

It had been snowing when they left, in big, soft flakes. Flying south, the flakes turned to a sullen gray rain. Dax had kept quiet, concentrating on flying and on his own gray mood. Lily, pale and drawn, had at first tried to discuss how to deal with their property, but when he'd said, "There's nothing I want; it's your place, your stuff," she'd shut up. The silence had continued until now.

He repacked his duffel with the few clothes he needed to take back to the mining camp. When he toted it out of the closet, Lily was standing by the window, facing him, hands clasped in front of her.

"I'll get a hotel room tonight," he said. Tomorrow, he'd have a busy day, flying returning workers and supplies back to the camp after the holiday.

She nodded. "I'll be in touch when I've seen a lawyer."

"You can pack up my clothes and the stuff in my desk. Stick it in the storage locker. I'll deal with it next time I'm back." He had no home base now. Perhaps he'd look for a cabin up north for when he was between jobs. He could live in the wilderness full time.

All by himself.

He strode to the front door and she trailed after him. Face wan and strained, she stared up at him. "I'm sorry about how things turned out." Her blue eyes were bloodshot and glittered with tears.

He nodded. "I'm sorry I can't be the man you want me to be, Lily."

His fingers ached to touch her one final time. To catch the tear that overflowed. To sift her silky blond hair through his fingers. To press his lips to her trembling ones. But he wasn't that strong a man. And so he just opened the door and stepped through it.

As he closed it again, he heard soft words. "Can't be or don't want to be?"

Twenty-six

Lily stared at the closed door, tears drying on her cheeks. She felt frozen, as if she'd never again be able to move. Dax was gone. Their marriage was over.

She should have realized they'd never make things work. Every intelligent woman knew you couldn't change a man's basic nature, and Dax had never been a guy who put down roots. What they should have done the moment he got home was ask each other, "Where would you like this marriage to go?" Then they wouldn't have wasted a week.

She wouldn't have lowered her defenses and let herself love him again. She wouldn't have let herself hope.

He didn't want to have kids—or at least, not with her. How could she not have known that? When did he change his mind and why didn't he say anything? His silence felt like a betrayal. How could he think that her clinic had taken the place of children in her life, her heart? Didn't he know her at all?

Exhausted and aching, she managed to turn away from the closed door and plod down the hall.

Fine, she'd been stupid, and now she knew better. It was what it was, as people were so fond of saying. Last night, shattered, she'd cried until she was drained, shivery, and nauseous. No more of that. She'd never been a person to weep and wail. It didn't change a damn thing except make her feel even more miserable—though at the moment, she wasn't sure that was possible.

But she had to get on with things. Keep busy. Be practical.

Dax had dropped her suitcase in the closet. She unpacked methodically. Her beautiful new dress—the dress she'd worn when her marriage ended—went into the dry-cleaning bag. She'd donate it to the thrift shop at Vancouver General Hospital.

Tonight and tomorrow—a statutory holiday, so the clinic would be closed—she'd pull together financial information to give the divorce lawyer. She also had to finish *Bound by Desire*. Usually, she relied on intellectual novels to distract her from her problems, but perhaps the current book club selection would do the same. After all, she'd left off when Neville was taking Cassandra to a BDSM club. That might not be to her taste, but it wasn't likely to be boring.

She went to the kitchen to make herself a martini. Who cared that it was only two thirty on a Sunday afternoon?

Where to settle and read? Every place in the apartment held a memory of Dax. She should sell the condo. Find a new home that would be hers alone. No, a new home where she could raise a child or two.

She needed to make a fresh start. Find a new man. Or go to a sperm bank. That was a smarter idea than getting into the whole messy, frustrating, painful confusion of another male-female relationship. Not that she'd likely ever find a man who attracted her anyhow.

Stop. She pressed her fingers to her temples. Yes, she needed a fresh start but this was not the time to plan it, with her heart shattered into dozens of tiny, aching pieces.

She curled into a corner of the living room couch, took a hearty slug of her martini, and began to read. Soon her mind was reeling.

Neville hadn't followed through on his threat to give Cassandra to other men, but he did make a public display of her at Top and Bottom, the BDSM club. In front of a group of avid voyeurs, he stuffed a butt plug into her, tormented her with nipple clamps, had her suck his penis, and stripped her naked. He told her she wasn't to climax or he'd walk away from her. Cassandra at first felt embarrassed and titillated, then powerfully aroused. Never did she want to say her safe word.

At the end of the chapter, Lily shook her head. Nope, not exactly her idea of fun. Not that she was going to let herself think about her idea of fun, because that would mean thinking about Dax. She turned the page.

With club members watching, Neville cuffed Cassandra's ankles to the ends of a spreader bar, and cuffed her wrists to the bar between them. Her body was bowed over, her sex exposed, and she could barely even wriggle. He flogged her until she screamed with the inextricably mingled sensations of pain and pleasure, then he took the butt plug out and substituted his swollen cock. Her arousal mounted unbearably and she whimpered, cried, and begged him to let her come. Finally, as he climaxed forcefully inside her, he told her she could come and she exploded in the fiercest orgasm of her life—filled too with an amazing sense of power and joy at being able to give this incredible man such pleasure. After, he praised her, uncuffed her, cradled her tenderly in his arms, and carried her away.

Mulling over what she'd read, Lily rose and made herself a second martini. To her surprise, she found something in common with Cassandra. She could relate to the woman's delight at being the sex partner who did something so wild and forbidden with an incredible man, and gave him such a powerful experience. As Lily had done with Dax in that marble bathroom stall.

Not going to think of Dax.

Martini in hand, she turned to the next chapter.

The night after their visit to the club, Cassandra woke in Neville's bed. He brought breakfast on a tray, feeding her strawberries and bits of flaky croissant from his fingers. A gift-wrapped box sat on the tray, but he didn't mention it so neither did she, despite her almost unbearable curiosity.

"Last night was the best night of your life," he said.

"Y-yes, master. Does that mean there's something wrong with me?"

"It means you're a beautiful, sensual submissive. My submissive."

A delicious sense of well-being flowed through her. Neville thought she was beautiful and sensual. Of all those amazingly sexy women at the club, she was the one he wanted.

"We're special, you and I." He stroked her cheek then held out another strawberry. "We're not normal, not average. We belong to an elite group like the others at Top and Bottom."

Elite. That sounded very good. No, of course there wasn't anything wrong with her, or with Neville or any of the people at that club. They were special.

"You came to me to find out who you truly are, Cassandra. You know now, don't you?"

She gazed up at this striking, confident man who'd taught her everything. Who'd made her see the truth. "Yes. I'm a submissive and I'm special. And I'm yours." That was all she wanted in the world, to be his. "I want to please you, master."

"You do, my pet. You please me very much."

Those words sent such joy through her, she trembled with it.

"It is my pleasure to take care of your needs," he went on. "I did that last night, yes?"

"Oh yes, master. It was incredible."

"I'm doing it now, bringing you breakfast."

"You are so good to me."

"You trust me now, to know what's best for you."

"I do, master." More than that, she realized. He'd come to mean everything to her. *"I trust you and I love you."*

His face lit. *"My pet, I love you too. You belong to me and I belong to you. You complete me. You are the first woman who has touched my heart."*

His words filled her with deep, pure joy. *"You're the first man to touch mine, master. You complete me too."* It was true. She'd never have become her true self without Neville.

"We were made for each other."

"I never thought it was possible to find this kind of love."

He took the jewelry box off the tray and handed it to her. *"This gift is a symbol of our love. If you wear it, you pledge yourself to me as I pledge myself to you."*

Breathless with excitement, she untied the ribbon, ripped off the foil wrapping paper, and opened the box. *"Oh!"* It was a gold choker necklace with a diamond-studded heart. The heart formed the clasp, and had a tiny lock. *"It's stunning, master."*

He reached in his pocket and held up a miniature key. *"I have the only key."*

If she allowed him to lock the collar around her neck, she was saying he did truly own her and she was his submissive. The choker was subtle enough that no one outside the BDSM scene would have a clue of the symbolism, but those in that elite world would understand. She couldn't wait to feel the cool gold around her neck. She bowed her head and held the necklace out to him. *"Please put it on me, master."*

He took it from her hands and deftly locked it in place, then put his fingers under her chin to raise her head. *"Let me see. Ah yes, so lovely."*

The heart settled in the hollow at the base of her throat, nestling against the vulnerable spot where her pulse throbbed. She smiled up at him. For the first time in her life, she belonged, she was loved.

"We'll have a beautiful life," he told her. "You know that I'm wealthy?"

"Wealthy enough to stay in the penthouse suite in a very expensive hotel."

He gave a rich, throaty chuckle. "You have no idea, Cassandra. If I wished, I could buy this hotel with a snap of my fingers. Now here's what we'll do. You'll give up your job and we'll travel. I'll show you my penthouse in Manhattan, the apartment in London, the villas in the south of France and in Italy, the yacht in the Caribbean. You'll have clothes and jewels from the finest designers. We'll dine at the best restaurants, go to the theater, and visit the exclusive clubs designed for people like us."

Dazed, she said, "Seriously? It's like a dream come true, master. Except I've never in my life had such an incredible dream." Since she was seventeen, she'd had to work for a living and she'd assumed she always would. She'd worked hard, achieved success, but it was so stressful always having to perform, so exhausting always traveling. So lonely all the time. He was saying she could give all that up, and live a life of luxury at the side of the man she loved?

"That dream will be your life now, my pet."

"Oh master, I love you so much."

And there it ended. Lily put down her Kindle with a clatter. "And they sailed off into the sunset together," she muttered bitterly. Was she in too cynical a mood to appreciate romance of any kind, or was this happily-ever-after ending particularly unbelievable? It would be interesting to see what the rest of the book club thought.

And now, in the opposite of a happily ever after, she had to start pulling together the paperwork to start the divorce. The sooner it was done, the more easily she'd be able to move on.

Or at least so she hoped.

Twenty-seven

Late the next afternoon, Monday, Dax walked into the minuscule room he'd left a week and a half ago.

The mining camp was well established, not a tent city like some but instead made of modular units. Sleeping rooms were strung in rows off hallways, with central facilities for dining, exercise, and relaxation. Each bedroom held a single bed and a desk with drawers for storing clothes and personal items. At some jobs, he'd had to share a tent, and Dax valued the privacy here. He didn't mind eating and using the gym with others, playing some poker, or watching a game on TV. But he was enough of a loner that, when weather or darkness kept him inside, he spent much of his time lying on his bed reading.

He hadn't done much to personalize the room. A few sketches of wildlife that one of the guys had done were taped to the wall. Helicopter magazines sat on the desk.

Also on the desk was a framed photo of him and Lily, taken one long-ago summer. They'd holidayed on Galiano Island, rented kayaks, and found a beach to picnic on. Another picnicker took their picture. Lily was in a blue bikini, Dax in board shorts. Her hair, longer then, was pulled back in a ponytail but the breeze had tugged strands free to dance around her face. His arm was around her shoulders, hers around his waist, and they both smiled widely, eyes squinting against the sun. It was no fancy portrait like the ones from their wedding, but they'd been young, in love, having fun, and it showed.

Dax sank down on the bed. When he'd left for Vancouver, he'd figured he and Lily might end their marriage. He'd thought he was resigned to it. That breaking up couldn't feel worse than being alone here and worrying whether she was cheating on him, whether they still loved each other.

Well, it did feel worse. Now he knew how Lily felt: she loved him, but not enough. And he knew that he loved her, but couldn't be what she wanted.

What had she meant when she said, "Can't be or don't want to be?" From across the tiny room, he stared at her smiling face. That young Lily had been happy with him just the way he was. What did the thirty-two-year-old Lily want? A husband who'd live with her and raise children with her. A home and family. Dax had told her he couldn't be that man. She'd implied that he didn't want to.

Once, he'd wanted that—or at least dreamed of it, of a real home and loving family, something he'd never experienced. Later, as he and Lily followed their parallel courses, he'd decided the dream was foolish. That he wasn't that kind of guy.

He stacked his hands behind his head and stared at the ceiling. Why had he given up on that dream? Yes, he loved the energy and peace of the wilderness. He loved flying: the challenge, the freedom, the way it offered serenity one moment, excitement the next. But he loved Lily too. Did loving one mean having to sacrifice the other?

He didn't like how Lily always put her clinic ahead of him. But hadn't he done the same thing, choosing work that kept him away from her for long stretches of time? Yeah, at the time he'd been messed up, after Afghanistan. He'd believed he needed the wilderness to heal his soul and make him fit company for his wife. Maybe so, but he'd shut her out, and kept doing it for the last four years.

As for children . . . Holding baby Sophia had made him feel warm and fuzzy—but the idea of being responsible for a kid terrified him. His parents had sure sucked at it. Lily's were no prize either—and his wife didn't seem to have a clue how she'd juggle work with these kids she supposedly wanted so badly.

He and Lily had handled going to school in different cities and they'd handled his deployment to Afghanistan. Things ought to be easier now, not more fucked up. The two of them weren't stupid, so—

Wait a minute. Maybe they were. On New Year's Eve, they'd admitted that they still loved each other. And then they'd broken up. From the perspective of a couple of days' distance, that seemed pretty damned stupid to him.

The timer on his watch beeped, and he rose. He had another supply run—a short, hour-long one to the closest town—before the workday was done. As he strode to the door, he cast a final glance at Lily's lovely smiling face. The next he heard from her, it would be with details of their divorce.

Twenty-eight

Lily felt like an automaton as she walked into the warm, welcoming ambiance of the Copper Chimney. George had chosen the Indian fusion restaurant and bar for the club's first meeting of the new year, and she and Marielle were sitting in a corner table at the back. Side by side on a bench seat—the way Lily and Dax had sat on New Year's Eve—in animated conversation, they didn't see Lily. No surprise; she felt like a shadow of her real self.

So far, she'd spent the statutory holiday summarizing her and Dax's finances, then had taken the relevant documents to the clinic to photocopy. From the Internet, she selected a divorce lawyer and e-mailed to request an appointment. The lawyer had been working—or at least checking e-mail—today, and now Lily had an appointment for late Wednesday afternoon.

Divorce. She and Dax were getting a divorce. She no longer felt shattered, as she had on New Year's Eve. Now she was numb and empty, but for persistent dull aches in head and heart. As a doctor, she understood shock, physical and emotional. It could take time for reality to sink in, for the most profound pain to make itself felt—and when it did, it could bring you to your knees. She had to keep that from happening, had to hold herself together. Not only did she still have issues at the clinic to deal with, but there'd be all the hassle involved with a divorce.

She'd have to tell her parents. They'd say, "You should have listened when we said you shouldn't marry him."

On leaden feet, she approached George and Marielle's table. At least she had this hour of distraction and she'd do her best to enjoy it.

"Hi, Lily," George said. "Happy New Year." Marielle echoed the greeting. They both looked happy and vibrant, George in a blue sweater that made her red hair even fierier, and dark-haired Marielle in a pink and orange striped top.

"You too." Lily took the chair across from Marielle and shrugged out of her coat. A new year, and everything felt overwhelming. Hopeless, almost. But she was strong; she'd always been strong. It was one of the qualities Dax said he admired in her.

"Are you all right?" George's amber eyes narrowed with concern. "You look, uh, tired."

"I am." So tired that she'd like to lay her head on the table and sleep. Except she wouldn't sleep. For the past two nights, she hadn't. What she needed was conversation, a stimulating analysis of the issues raised in *Bound by Desire*. A martini.

The waitress arrived at the same time that Kim hurried in and took the chair beside Lily. Today, the highlights in her spiky black hair were yellow and the design on her scarf looked like bird wings in yellow, orange, and black.

They ordered drinks and snacks then Kim pulled envelopes from her canary-yellow bag. "We're having an engagement party!"

Just what Lily needed. She ripped open the envelope and, despite her misery, Kim's artwork almost brought a smile. The artist who was fascinated by wings and was marrying a cowboy had incorporated a dragonfly and a horse in the design. A quick glance showed that Marielle's and George's cards had similar motifs, but each was unique.

Lily opened the card. The party was a week from now. "Monday? Instead of book club?"

"I figured you'd all be free, and we did finish the book a week early, right?"

"Right. I'm surprised you found a venue on such short notice."

George raised a hand. "Woody's and my condo. Luckily, he'll be in town and doesn't have a game."

"Marielle found a terrific caterer," Kim said. "A recent graduate who's setting up his own business. I swear, Marielle knows everyone."

"You tease me about how I keep changing jobs," Marielle said, "but I learn something at each one, and I make contacts. Whatever you need, I bet I can find it for you."

"That's a valuable asset," Lily said. "You should be a concierge."

"Or a personal shopper," Kim put in.

"Guess I should think about what I'm going to do next," Marielle said cheerfully. "The holiday's over." She turned to Kim. "Your parents going to hang around town for the party?"

"No, they went back to Hong Kong this morning. They hate leaving their company for too long. Ty's folks are coming, though, and some ranch staff and friends from the Fraser Valley. Lily, Dax is invited, of course. And Marielle, feel free to bring one of your various admirers."

"Dax has gone back to the mining camp," Lily said. No, she wasn't telling them about the divorce. Not until . . . She had no idea when she'd feel ready to talk about it.

"Too bad," George said. "It's hard having Woody go on road trips. I can't imagine what it's like to have Dax away for weeks."

Or forever. "Let's talk about the book," Lily said firmly.

The waitress served their drinks and she reached for her martini. Given how tired she was, she probably shouldn't drink alcohol, but she didn't give a damn. After she SkyTrained home, maybe she'd have another drink or two, take headache meds, and actually sleep.

George had her usual winter drink, a glass of red wine; Kim, her typical fancy beer. Marielle generally went with a fruity, girly drink, but this time her cocktail was pale brown and creamy. Lily hadn't paid attention when the others ordered, so now asked, "What is that, Marielle?"

"Chocolate Godiva martini. Pure bliss. Want to taste?"

"I do," Kim promptly said, and George said, "Me too." Marielle passed the glass, and the other women took sips from separate parts of the rim and made approving sounds. When Lily took her turn, rich, creamy, chocolaty sweetness hit her tongue. "Bliss indeed." It was as sinful and delicious as sex with Dax. Maybe rather than a second martini, she'd have one of these. But no, not if it reminded her of Dax. *Focus, Lily.* "Everyone finished the book?"

They all nodded, and Kim said, "It made me think about how everyone has different sexual needs. Cassandra didn't even know what she needed until Neville enlightened her." She gave a mischievous grin. "After all, that's what a good boyfriend's for."

"I didn't like Neville," Lily said, "but I get it that Cassandra needed certain things to, uh, break through her inhibitions."

"How do you mean?" Kim asked.

"The commands and restraints, they took responsibility away from her. She chose to put herself in Neville's hands, and then she was free to go wherever he took her." Lily thought of the different ways she and Dax had made love over the past week and a half, the things she'd learned about her own sexuality. Would she ever have sex again? She couldn't imagine being with anyone other than Dax. She took another sip of her martini.

"And he took her where she needed to go," Marielle said. "Where, if you'll pardon the expression"—she winked—"no man had gone before. Thanks to him, she found the kind of sexual satisfaction she'd never experienced."

"Like I said, a good boyfriend," Kim agreed.

"But Neville said he *owned* her," George said. "He made her say it."

"That's the kind of thing that made me not like him," Lily commented.

Kim nodded. "Yeah, that's going too far. But he also said they belonged to each other. That sense of belonging is powerful."

"Only if two people are equal," Lily said. "It's one thing to initiate her sexually and look after her pleasure, but he treated her like a pet that he owned."

Marielle leaned forward. "Speaking as a former dog walker, I gotta say, some people are as owned by their pets as vice versa. Those animals have them wrapped around their little paws."

"A cute sentiment, but the owner's in control," Lily said briskly. "If the owner doesn't feed the pet, the pet starves."

"Okay," Marielle said, "but with Neville and Cassandra it's a balance of control. Yeah, he's commanding her and doing stuff to her, but it's the stuff she wants done, the stuff that gives her the sexual intensity she's been craving. She needs that dom stuff, even the pain, to experience true pleasure. Besides, if he's no longer turning her crank, she can always say the safe word and he has to stop. So doesn't she have the ultimate control?"

"No," George said. "That safe word thing is a head game. Neville's a bully, a rich, sophisticated, skilled one, but still a bully, and he makes her dependent on him. It's, like, sexual blackmail. If she says her safe word, yes, he'll stop—but then she'll feel crappy for not pleasing him, not to mention she won't get her orgasm."

"I agree," Lily said. "That's not equality." Lily's relationship with Dax had always been one of equals, each in control of their own life. But they'd also never really shared their lives. Having taken the first steps to doing that at Whistler, she now understood how seductive the notions of belonging and sharing could be.

"Yeah, but he won't get his orgasm either," Marielle said. "He needs her for his sexual pleasure just as much as she needs him. And George, you said she'd feel crappy for not pleasing him, but I bet that goes both ways. Men have performance anxiety, right? Well, imagine how bad a dom must feel if he doesn't satisfy his woman. Besides—"

She broke off as the waitress returned, and deftly slid steaming plates onto the center of the table. "Crab cakes, a naan pizza, and samosas. Enjoy, ladies."

"Besides," Marielle took up where she left off. "If Cassandra's unhappy with him, she can always leave." She transferred a crab cake to her side plate.

"Oh sure," George said. "Like a battered wife can walk out and go to a shelter? It's not that easy, Marielle."

Lily guessed George was thinking of her fiancé's mother. Earlier this year the media had outed the true story of Woody's childhood. His father had abused him and his mom. His mother never left; she was only freed when her husband was killed in a bar fight.

"Women should be stronger than that," Marielle said. "My mom and granny sure are."

Hmm. Did the brunette's refusal to consider a capital "R" relationship have something to do with her father and grandfather?

"Sadly, some women are so powerless they don't see the possibility of escape," Lily told Marielle. "You've heard of battered-woman syndrome? Often, they're so dependent—due to their husband's actions, maybe childhood abuse, perhaps lack of education and skills, even cultural or religious values—they can't imagine making their own way in the world. They may love their husband and believe he loves them. Maybe in some weird way he does. But even so, he's in the position of power and he's abusing that power."

"I hear you," Marielle said. "But Cassandra's well-educated, inde-pendent, a successful businesswoman who's traveled all over the world and slept with a bunch of men. I don't see her suddenly turning into someone who's so dependent she doesn't see options."

"Good point," Lily said.

"Think about Stockholm Syndrome," George said. "Where hostages start to bond with their captor."

"Neville isn't holding her hostage, George," Kim, who'd been munching a slice of naan pizza, put in. "Or abusing her. He's giving her the sex that, as Marielle says, turns her crank like it's never been turned before, and offering her a lifestyle beyond her wildest dreams. He's her perfect guy. We may not be thrilled to bits with him, but she is. I don't think either one of them's in control, I think it's a balance of power."

George blew out a long breath. "Look, I'm sorry if this offends anyone, but I think Neville and Cassandra have psychological problems. Something's happened in their pasts, like abuse or neglect, that's made them this way. He needs to have this total, *dominant* control over her and inflict pain in order to get off. And she needs to submit to his control and feel pain in order to have great orgasms. It's just not natural."

They were all silent a moment, then Lily said, "Do you feel the same way about gays? That homosexuality isn't natural?"

"No!" George shook her head vigorously, wavy red hair tossing. "Of course not! I don't care what sex the partners in a relationship are."

"But some people do think homosexuals are sick and unnatural," Lily said.

"Oh," George said slowly. "I see what you're saying. Who am I to judge other people's sexuality as long as they're consenting adults."

"This stuff is complicated," Kim said.

"Human sexuality is incredibly complicated," Lily said. "I didn't even realize how complicated until we read this book."

"I guess that means it was a good choice, Marielle," George said. "But I sure didn't like it. Obviously, it pushed some hot buttons."

"Hot enough that you're not even eating this yummy food." The brunette gestured to the appetizer platters. "You either," she said to Lily. Though Marielle and Kim had nibbled steadily, George and Lily had barely touched the snacks.

George served herself portions of everything, and Lily did the same, knowing she had to put calories in her body.

George cut a piece of samosa then put her fork down. "I want to apologize for that rant." Her hazel eyes focused on Lily's face. "You put things in perspective with that comment about homosexuality. I like to think I'm not a prejudiced person, but my hot buttons really came into play here."

"That's what's good about book club," Kim said. "We read different things, share ideas, learn, grow as people. Hey, I was prejudiced against cowboys until Marielle chose *Ride Her, Cowboy* and suggested that rodeo field trip."

"And now you're engaged to one," Marielle said. "Yeah, read and learn, girls! Speaking of which, maybe none of us have discovered we're closeted subs, but has anyone made, you know, personal use of anything in the book?"

"No way," George said firmly, picking up her fork again.

"Seriously?" Kim studied the redhead. "Not even in fun?"

"Kim has, Kim has," Marielle chanted. "So you and Ty tried out some new stuff?"

Kim's dark eyes danced. "Let's just say there's more than one use for a lasso."

And a bungee cord. But no way was she going there. It struck Lily that, if she and Dax were still together, it would be fun to toss out the bungee cord comment. Now, though, she wished she could expunge the memory.

"And belts," Marielle said. "I don't get off on actual pain, but just a little sting across the butt can—"

Lily broke in, pleading, "Could we keep the discussion to the book?"

"Spoilsport," Marielle grumbled.

"I'm with Lily," George said. "And I want to know if the ending worked for people. That they say they love each other and they're going to have this amazing life together?"

"Yes, because they give each other what they need," Kim said. "They complement each other, and that's what a good relationship is about."

Marielle shook her head. "It didn't work for me. He'll get tired of her and go looking for a fresh, dewy-eyed, closeted submissive. The way I see Neville, part of the excitement is the, uh, initiation. Teaching her, showing her that he knows deep, dark secrets she hasn't acknowledged to herself."

"Which points out," George said, "that we don't know what's going on in his mind. We only see him through her eyes. Cassandra believes him when he says he loves her, but the author didn't include his thoughts, so we don't know for sure. The author gives the power to Neville, making him mysterious, so the reader isn't sure what motivates him."

"True." Lily put down the fork she'd been using to poke at a crab cake. "But that's like real life. We're never positive what's going on in someone else's head, or heart. It makes us vulnerable."

"Did you buy into the ending, Lily?" George asked.

At the moment, it was hard to believe that any relationship could survive for the long term. "I have my doubts. Cassandra and Neville are at the beginning of a relationship, with the typical lust, fascination, excitement, a huge sense of possibility."

As George and Kim nodded, Lily drained her martini and

gestured to the waitress for another. No, she wouldn't indulge in a rich, chocolaty drink that reminded her of Dax.

"But those things don't give a foundation for the future," she went on. "Remember *Ride Her, Cowboy?* Marty and Dirk had that spark of lust but over the course of the book they also developed respect, liking, trust. I saw Marty's discontent with her old way of life, and how Dirk's lifestyle grew on her. That author didn't have Dirk's point of view either, but his actions showed that he came to care for Marty. In a way we could all easily relate to, rather than"— she lowered her voice—"cuffing her to a spreader bar in a BDSM club, which is harder to get our heads around. So when they said they loved each other, I believed in it, and that they'd try to make it work." Whether they succeeded was another matter. Love and good intentions clearly weren't enough to guarantee a happily-ever-after ending.

George, who'd been nodding as Lily spoke, now said, "*Bound by Desire*'s all about the sex, right until the very end. They don't get to know each other as people. They don't talk about their jobs or families. Do they have friends? Hobbies? What are their core values? I don't even know if they like each other, so how can I believe they love each other?"

"That bothered me too," Marielle said. "This was the first BDSM book I'd read, so I bought another. In this one, the woman's the dom. They're lawyers and they met through work but she didn't know he was a submissive and he didn't know she was a dom. At a convention out of town, they both visit the same BDSM club and have wild dom-sub sex in public. Then they go on to build a relationship, sexual and otherwise. Very hot sex, by the way. It worked better for me than *Bound by Desire*."

"Woman on top," Kim teased.

"Ha ha." Marielle rolled her eyes. "Anyhow, the guy's this really successful lawyer, and it's such a turn-on for him to give over control in the bedroom. Besides, he's been lusting after this woman, and totally respects her, and when they hook up, he gets off on being able to give her this amazing sexual pleasure."

"There can be a lot of satisfaction in that," Lily said. "I even believed that with Cassandra. That she not only loved the orgasms Neville gave her, but she loved giving him so much pleasure."

"Anyhow," Marielle said, "in that lawyer book, I could see how their lives might look: home, work, sex."

"Whereas with *Bound by Desire*," Lily said, "suddenly Neville's supposedly in love with Cassandra, she's the woman who completes him—"

"Gag," Marielle interrupted. "I've always hated that line."

"Aw, I think it's sweet," Kim cooed.

"A woman should be complete on her own, and so should a man," Marielle said.

"Agreed." Lily reached for the second martini the waitress was delivering, and sipped it while the woman cleared the now-empty appetizer platters. Lily's plate held a half-eaten crab cake, a nibbled piece of naan pizza, and an untouched samosa. "Anyhow," she went on, "so Neville says he'll give Cassandra this fabulous, luxurious life. By happy coincidence, she's tired of all that lonely travel and job pressure, and delighted to give up her success and independence to become his treasured pet. And he, who's screwed God knows how many subs, is suddenly going to be content with just Cassandra. I don't buy it."

"But don't you think that's the appeal for a lot of readers?" Kim asked. "Okay, maybe this book didn't do a great job of making it believable, but I think it's about the fantasy anyway."

"Which fantasy?" Lily asked curiously.

"Um, a few, now that I think of it," Kim said. "Let's start with the basic premise. Plain old vanilla sex gets ho-hum and Cassandra wants something more stimulating, but where can she find it? Isn't that something a lot of women can relate to? Women who've dated a bunch of ho-hum guys, or women who've been married forever and things have gone stale. Sorry, Lily, that's not, like, meant to be personal."

Lily took a gulp from her new martini. She'd learned this past week that sex with Dax would never go stale. And that sex with any other man would pale in comparison. Not that she was likely to be having any sex with anyone, ever again. "Go on." She forced herself to eat a bite of samosa.

"Okay," Kim said. "So what do women do? Fantasize, right? Mostly it's non-PC stuff they'd never confess to. Like being with two men. Or a vampire or werewolf. Or the old pirate fantasy."

"The old pirate fantasy?" George asked. "You mean Johnny Depp in eye makeup?"

"Orlando Bloom, maybe," Kim said. "You know. The incredibly dashing, utterly masculine pirate captures the ship and takes the prim maiden captive—and ravages her, and she loves every moment of it, even as she's protesting the loss of her virtue."

"So that's your fantasy, is it, girlfriend?" Marielle teased.

"Actually, it was more vampires for me, until I met Ty and found out that live guys are way sexier. Well, I'd bet that Cassandra, even if she wouldn't acknowledge she was a sub, had some fantasies that involved being dominated by a sexy, powerful guy. Neville brings those fantasies to life, which is the only way she'll ever have true sexual satisfaction, and she knows she'll be safe."

"Safe?" George said. "I know they say safe, sane, and consensual, but he's hitting her, causing her pain."

"Yeah, but she needs pain to get intense orgasms," Marielle said, "and if it goes too far, she can stop him with one word." She turned to Kim. "I hear you. I can see lots of women buying into that fantasy."

"There's another one as well," Kim said. "I see this with some of the girls at art school."

"What's that?" Lily asked.

"The old-fashioned one of having a man cherish you, take total care of you, and look after your every need. He not only provides fantastic orgasms, but you don't have to work. You can travel, study, pursue a hobby, not have to worry about earning money. You can paint, cook, garden. Ride horses." Her dark eyes twinkled, the city girl who now lived on a ranch. "He'll buy you a fantastic oceanfront house, a villa in France, a Ferrari. A yacht, with a crew, a chef, a gardener. A pool boy. Every yacht needs a pool boy, right?"

They all laughed, and then George said, "That's like those old Harlequin romances my mom read as a girl. Where the poor little nurse or secretary met the rich, powerful, handsome brain surgeon or CEO, and he rescued her from her mundane life. And all she had to do was be pretty and sweet and say yes to his every whim. Girls really still think that way?"

"Pool boy on your yacht," Marielle teased.

George chuckled. "All right, there's a certain appeal. But seriously, you'd never go for that. Right?"

"Nah," the brunette said. "None of us would, would we?" She lifted her cocktail glass in a mock toast. "We're a bunch of tough, independent broads." At the moment, she looked the opposite of tough, with her melted chocolate eyes, wavy dark hair, pink and orange top, and creamy girly drink. Yet Lily knew Marielle prided herself on not needing any man.

While the other three laughed, Lily forced a smile. Oh yes, she was independent and trying hard to be tough. What choice did she have?

"But, hmm," Marielle went on. "I haven't read those old books, George, but there's another interesting point in *Bound by Desire*, and it's way more obvious in the other BDSM book I read. It makes me think of that old movie *Pretty Woman*. You've all seen it? With Julia Roberts and Richard Gere, when they were young?"

"Love that movie," Kim said.

"I do too," George put in.

"Haven't seen it," Lily said. If she had spare time, it generally went to reading.

"Okay, long story short," Marielle said. "She's a hooker with a heart of gold. He's a rich businessman who does business takeovers, and has no heart at all. He says to her at the beginning that they both screw people for money."

"Oh, charming," Lily said.

"It is!" Kim protested. "You have to see it."

"He buys her services," Marielle went on, "and as they hang out together, they fall for each other. They break up, but he realizes how he really feels about her and comes to get her and—"

"In this big limo, and he even scales a fire escape to win her, when he's afraid of heights," Kim put in. "And it's like this girlish fantasy she told him about once, the white knight rescuing the princess in the tower."

"Let me guess," Lily said. "She doesn't have to be a 'working girl' anymore, and he'll buy her houses and yachts with pool boys."

"No," George said. "She'll go to school and get a good job, because him rescuing her isn't about giving her some ritzy life, it's about teaching her to value herself."

"Exactly," Marielle said. "He says, referring back to the fantasy, I think, 'What happens after he rescues her?' And she says, 'She rescues him right back.' And it's true. Because he'd never known love, and thanks to her he's discovered he has a heart."

"Exactly," Kim said. "He's this super-big catch—rich and successful and, hello, he looks like Richard Gere when he was young—and our heroine's the one woman in the world who wins his heart."

That was how Lily had felt when Dax, every girl's favorite sexy bad boy, had chosen her. "All right," she said slowly, "I'm starting to understand. Two flawed people meet and, through knowing and caring for each other, they both become stronger in the area in which they were weakest." And how interesting that Marielle, who steered clear of romantic relationships, would love a movie with that theme.

"Very analytical, Doc Lily," Marielle teased.

"But," Lily said, "I'm not convinced that's what happened in *Bound by Desire*."

"Maybe because it's an erotic novel," George said. "It's about Cassandra's sexual journey. I think that thing you just said, Lily, is more the theme of a romance."

Kim nodded. "It's what happened with me and Ty. We both helped each other find the strength to deal with our personal shit."

Lily'd thought she and Dax had been starting to do that too. "You both became stronger, but that's not what happened in the book. Cassandra discovered her sexual nature and found her perfect sex partner, but as a person she became weaker. She's giving up her job, her independence." She swallowed the last of martini number two. "A woman has to have a life of her own. Relationships end, so that's what she'll be left with." She stabbed at the barely tasted samosa on her plate.

No one spoke for a long moment. Then George said cautiously, "Not all relationships end."

"But they might." Lily frowned at her. "I know you and Kim are in love with your guys and you think it's going to last forever, but promise you won't give up your own lives."

George glanced at Kim. "Kim's launching UmbrellaWings and I've been talking to a couple of colleagues about starting our own marketing firm. We're not giving up our lives."

"Girls," Marielle said, "there's more to life than work."

"Sure," Kim said. "Family, hobbies, friends. Book club. Neither of us is giving up any of that." She turned to Lily. "We're okay. You don't have to play mother hen, all worried about your chicks."

Mother hen? Would Lily ever have the opportunity to mother her own children? And what was wrong with Dax—or with her—that he didn't want to do that with her?

"You really do live on a ranch, don't you?" Marielle teased Kim. "Who'd have thought the confirmed city girl would use chicken analogies?"

Lily reached for her glass and realized it was empty. That was so unfair. She needed another drink. A funny little sound escaped her throat.

Marielle's laughing brown eyes went solemn. "What's up, Doc? Are you okay?"

"Of course." Another sound escaped, like a hiccup. In horror, Lily realized it was a sob. Her eyes filled, and she pressed her hands to her cheeks in a vain attempt to hold back the tears.

Twenty-nine

Kim, sitting beside Lily, touched her shoulder tentatively. "Hey, don't cry."

"N-not crying," Lily choked out. She couldn't cry in public. That would be just too embarrassing.

"Okay," George said soothingly. "You're not crying. But something's wrong. Can we help?"

Lily shook her head.

"Sometimes just sharing the problem makes you feel better," Marielle said.

"Have to go." Lily dropped her hands from her face and fumbled for her coat. She didn't share problems; she handled them herself.

Kim's grip on her shoulder tightened and George said, "We can't let you go home on your own when you're so upset. Tell us what's wrong."

Lily shook her head and rested her hands on the table in front of her, trying to summon the strength to push herself upright and leave.

"Is it about Dax?" Kim asked quietly.

Lily shuddered and gave another hiccupy sob. If she could sink through the floor, she'd do it. If her parents were here, they'd be mortified. Thank heavens she was sitting with her back to the room.

Marielle reached across the table and took one of Lily's hands between hers. "What did the bastard do? I know people. If you want to take out a hit on him, I can connect you."

The comment was so out there, it actually stopped Lily's tears. "What?"

"I'm kidding. But seriously, what's going on? Talk to us, Lily. At least let us think we're helping."

George reached across to take Lily's other hand. "Please."

She felt surrounded, imprisoned. Kim's hand rubbed her shoulder while Marielle and George squeezed both her hands. She felt . . . anchored. Not as much by their hands as by their caring. How about that? These women she'd met less than a year ago had turned into friends who cared. "All right, I'll tell you." She sniffled. "But I need my hands back. Have to blow my nose."

Once released, she found a tissue in her purse and wiped her cheeks and blew her nose. "Dax and I have been having problems. We talked over the holiday and, well, we're getting a d-divorce."

"Oh, Lily." Petite Kim gave her a one-armed hug. "I'm so sorry."

"How horrible," George said, touching her hand again.

Marielle took her other hand and squeezed it firmly. "You don't know how to talk to girlfriends, do you? We need more than that."

The brunette was so blunt yet so warmhearted. Lily returned the squeeze. "I'll try." The last time she'd shared her deepest feelings with girlfriends was in high school. "That sense of belonging we were talking about? We don't belong together anymore."

"Why not?" Marielle asked.

"Marielle, maybe she doesn't want to share all the details," George said.

"Lance the infection and it heals quicker," Marielle retorted. "Right, Doc Lily?"

"Or you spread the infection. But all right, here's the bottom line. He loves the wilderness and his idea of the perfect marriage is for me to live there with him. Without kids. My life is here and I do want children. Badly."

"Ouch," Marielle said. "That's big stuff."

Lily nodded vigorously.

Kim said hesitantly, "Ty was, like, rooted at Ronan Ranch. And I was sure I belonged in Hong Kong. But we worked that out. I just wonder . . . do you totally hate the wilderness? Does he totally hate the city? Or could you maybe find an in-between place that worked for both of you?"

An in-between place. The idea teased at Lily's brain, but then she realized it didn't matter anyhow. "I don't know. We didn't talk about that. Because the kids thing is what really counts."

"Why doesn't he want children?" George asked.

"He's kind of a loner, wilderness sort of guy. And his parents and grandparents were pretty bad. My parents are"—she struggled for words, not wanting to be disloyal—"not the most supportive. In his book, the word *family* doesn't have positive connotations."

"But you and Dax could do better," Kim said. "Doesn't he see that?"

"He doesn't want to," she said bitterly.

"Doesn't he think you'd be a good mom?" Marielle asked.

"Hah. No, he thinks I'd work all the time." She pressed her fingers against the ache in her temples. "Which isn't true. Things are really busy right now, but if I had a child, I'd reorganize my work." How, she had no clear idea. "My baby would come first."

George nodded. "Good. My mom was always focused on the guy in her life."

"Dax's parents were focused on each other, not him." Her own parents had at least paid attention to her and Anthony, though she'd have preferred more support and fewer demands.

George's brow wrinkled. "Lily, didn't you two talk about whether you wanted children before you got married?"

"Yes, when we first got together, but after that, not really. We were both building careers. I always assumed we'd have children when the time was right. Turns out, he was deciding he didn't want to have any, and he assumed I felt the same way."

Marielle shook her head. "That's sad, but people do change. It's so much easier when you just have casual short-term relationships."

"Beg to differ," Kim said.

George nodded. "Me too. I want something deeper. I want a partner I trust to share the good and the bad, to plan and build a life with. Yes, Woody and I will both change but if we pay attention and talk, we can grow together rather than apart."

"You're smarter than I was," Lily said.

George's amber eyes softened with sympathy. "It's really too late? You're positive you and Dax can never agree on the important things?"

"Here's another question," Kim said quietly. "What about love? If two people love each other, they can find amazing solutions for their problems. If they don't, there's no point trying."

"We do love each other." She reflected on Kim's comment. Had she and Dax given up too easily? Had the years of not paying attention, not communicating, handicapped them? If they tried harder, was there any hope they could find an amazing solution?

"You need to compromise in a relationship," George said. "And be flexible, be willing to look at alternatives and—"

"Without becoming a doormat," Marielle broke in.

Kim nodded. "You both have to do it. It has to balance out."

"Right," George said. "Lily, you know I support you and care about you, so please don't be offended. But it seems to me maybe you and Dax are very alike in—"

"No, we're totally different."

"Let me finish. Alike in being strong-minded and independent. You're both used to running your own lives and not so used to sharing them. With my Woody having a job that takes him out of town,

I see how that can happen. We do our best to Skype or at least phone every day, so we keep connected. I wonder if you and Dax have forgotten how to share, compromise, make decisions together?"

Compromise, share. Be flexible, look at alternatives. "Perhaps we have," Lily said slowly.

"Then maybe there's hope," George said. "Maybe you can both learn."

Hope. A tiny word with such huge import. "Thanks, all of you. You've given me a lot to think about."

"Phone or text this week," George said. "Let us know how things are going and if there's anything we can do." Kim and Marielle both nodded vigorously.

They settled the bill, pulled on coats and scarves, and headed outside, where they scattered in different directions. Walking past a Thai restaurant, the delicious aroma drew Lily in. She had an appetite after all, and got takeout tom kha gai soup.

Once home, she opted for jasmine tea rather than another martini, and sat down with her meal. The spicy chicken, mushroom, and coconut milk soup heated her and somehow felt cleansing, like it was driving the numbness and sorrow out of her. The flowery fragrance of the tea soothed her. By the time she'd finished, her headache had gone and the ache in her heart wasn't so bitter.

She had to make changes in her life. For the past year, her strategy for dealing with pressures at the clinic had been to put in more of her own hours. Not only hadn't she solved the problems, but if she kept working horrendous hours and stressing out, it might have a negative impact on the thing she valued most: patient care.

Dax had suggested she hire a manager. Admit she needed help. Well, damn it, she did. She wasn't a superwoman. If her parents considered her a failure, so be it. When they disapproved, it hurt, but she was tired of twisting herself out of shape to win a pat on the head. Yes, Dax was right; they disappointed her too. She wished they were more like her book club friends, willing to comfort and support rather than judge.

She found a notepad in the kitchen drawer, choosing paper and pen over technology. On the pad, she wrote: *What do I want?*

Words flowed: *Children—and the time to spend with them. I want to be a good mother.* A loving, supportive one who encouraged her children rather than pressured them.

On the next line, she wrote: *To heal people.* Was there anything she wanted to add to that? She studied the three simple words. They were the reason she'd chosen family medicine. Yet now she was as much an administrator as a practitioner. As Dax had pointed out.

Without allowing herself second thoughts, she wrote on the third line: *Dax.*

Tapping the pen against the pad, she studied the three lines. At thirty-two years old, these were the things she wanted from her life. To date, she'd messed up on achieving any of them. Obviously, she was nowhere near as smart as she'd thought she was.

But tonight she'd come this far—and it wasn't because of her own brilliance, it was because she'd listened to someone other than her parents. She'd listened to Dax, even if she hadn't been ready to hear at the time. Then she'd listened to her friends, and she *had* let herself hear. They had no vested interest; they only wanted to help. When she opened herself to that, she'd discovered it wasn't so horrible to admit that she wasn't perfect, she was only human and she needed help.

An idea struck her and she examined it from all sides. It was scary, but it felt right.

She took her notebook computer from her bag, but rather than set up in her home office, she went into the living room and flicked on the gas fire. Though it was a pale imitation of the real wood fire Dax had tended in Whistler, the dancing flames gave a touch of coziness.

Notebook on her lap, feet up on the coffee table, she started an

e-mail to the distribution list that included everyone who worked at
the Well Family Clinic.

As you all know, the practice is expanding, Dr. Brown is moving
to half-time, and our resources are stretched. I want to cut back
my own hours, particularly when it comes to administration.
Others of you have asked about the possibility of flex time and
job sharing. It's time that I—

She backspaced over the "I" and carried on:

—we develop a different model for the clinic. Perhaps we need
an office manager or a management committee. Let's brainstorm.
I want to hear all your ideas as to how to make the Well Family
Clinic a place that not only provides top-notch service to our
patients but is a healthy, happy place to work.

Let's meet at 8:00 a.m. on Wednesday, for an hour. (Yes,
there will be muffins and Danishes!) All patient appointments
during that time period will need to be rescheduled. I'll gladly
come in earlier or later any day this week in order to
accommodate those patients.

She pondered how to finish then typed:

Together, we've built something to be proud of. I thank all of you
for your hard work, your enthusiasm, and your patience. We are a
team and if I've been slow to recognize that and to thank you for
it, I apologize. Well Family Clinic is not my practice, it's ours.
And from now on, that's how it will be run.

Lily read back over the message. It was a little stiff and clumsy,
but so was she when it came to reaching out to others. The message

wasn't perfect and neither was she. There was something amazingly liberating about admitting that she'd never be perfect enough to satisfy her parents.

From now on, it was about satisfying herself, about being the kind of person she wanted to be. About being a woman who might possibly find a way to rebuild her marriage with the man she loved.

She was tempted to e-mail Dax, but what would she say? *Today, I took a baby step?* No, she'd wait until her feet were firmly planted on a new course. Then she'd tell him she hoped that, rather than being on two parallel paths, they could find a way of making their paths join up.

Before shutting down her computer, she sent another e-mail—cancelling her appointment with the divorce lawyer.

Thirty

Friday, around noon on a drizzly day, Dax set down the Bell 212 on the landing pad at Vancouver Harbour Heliport. He assisted an engineer and an accountant in climbing out. As they walked away, Joe Sparrow, a fit, husky man from the Musqueam First Nation, strode to meet Dax, beaming. They shook hands firmly and exchanged back slaps.

"Thanks for doing this," Dax said.

"Hey man, my pleasure. Like I said, Marie and me have another little one coming and we can sure use the money. That's damn good pay, flying for a mining company."

"Tough on the two of you, though, being apart." He didn't want to be responsible for creating problems in Joe and Marie's marriage.

"I'm only signing on for three months to start, and I'll make it home a few days each month. You said there's Internet, so I can Skype with her and the kids every day."

Something Dax and Lily had never set up. No, they'd let their relationship drift apart until a gulf separated them. But they loved each other. Couldn't love build a bridge? This time, he wouldn't quit without giving it his best shot.

He and Joe loaded some supplies and assisted a couple of investors onboard, and then Dax stood back and watched his pilot friend lift the Bell into an overcast sky. A few minutes later, the duffel bag with all his possessions from the mining camp on his shoulder, he stepped aboard the SkyTrain.

From the Olympic Village stop, he walked to the condo. He hadn't told Lily he was coming, not wanting to risk having her say no. He'd needed to do this, though: to see her, talk to her, to be here. To show her how strong his love was, to prove he was a man who would be here for her.

Inside the apartment, he noticed small differences. The fridge had Thai and Indian takeout containers with leftovers. A bowl and coffee cup sat in the dish rack. In the living room, the coffee table was off-center and pulled closer to the couch, as if Lily'd had her feet up on it. The duvet on the bed was a little messy on her side. Tiny things, but the place looked more lived-in than usual—like he could put his own feet up on that coffee table.

How would Lily react when she came home and saw him?

At least he could stack the deck in his favor.

As afternoon turned to evening, Dax paced restlessly. He had no idea what time Lily would come home, or whether she'd have eaten. During his shopping trip to Granville Island Public Market, he'd bought picnic food.

The food was in the fridge, but he'd put place mats, plates, cutlery, and wineglasses on the coffee table. They could snack in front of the fireplace, even though the gas flames were pathetic. With any luck, she'd remember the good times at Whistler, not the horrible ending.

On the mantel and a side table rested vases filled with bouquets of colorful mixed flowers. There were more flowers in the kitchen and bedroom. Unlit candles were scattered here and there, and he'd hidden a box of designer chocolates in a kitchen cupboard. Flowers, candles, and chocolate. Could he be any more cliché? But he wanted to show her he cared enough to be romantic.

He was freshly showered and wore the hawk T-shirt she'd given him, over jeans. Maybe he should've chosen something more formal, but she'd always said she liked him in jeans.

The apartment was silent but for the faint hiss of the fire and the occasional squeak of the floor as he paced, barefooted. Flying in a blizzard was less nerve-wracking than waiting for Lily to come home.

Finally, just after seven, the front door lock clicked. The door opened then closed. This time, he didn't go to her. He waited. He heard the closet door. She'd have taken off her boots and she walked so quietly he had no idea what she was doing. From the kitchen, he heard a gasp. And then, "Dax?"

He stepped through to join her. She looked pretty and business-like in a pale gray pantsuit with a white shirt, accented by the blue and silver scarf they'd bought in Whistler. "Hi, Lily."

She gaped at him as if she couldn't believe her eyes. She glanced from him to the flowers on the kitchen table, then back to him, a smile forming. "Dax!" And she flung herself into his arms.

Hugely relieved, he caught her tight, never wanting to let go. Their mouths came together quickly, clumsily. She was half laughing, her lips forming words even as she pressed kisses against him. "I can't believe it. You're here. Oh my God."

"I said I wanted to fight for our marriage, and then I gave up. I'm an idiot. I love you, Lily."

Tears slipped down her cheeks, all the way to her smiling lips. "Me too. Oh Dax, there must be a way of working things out. There's an amazing solution if we work hard enough to find it."

"An amazing solution?" He sure hoped so.

"It's something Kim said."

He stepped back, a little pissed that she'd shared their personal shit. "You told your book club about us?" Then he gave himself a mental kick. She'd been alone, needed someone to talk to. "Sorry, of course you would. They're your friends."

"I didn't plan to, but I started to cry. In public, at a restaurant. It was so embarrassing."

His Lily, who prided herself on her self-control? "Aw, sweetheart, I'm sorry." Then, teasing gently, "More embarrassing than what we did in that restaurant in Whistler?"

Pink tinged her cheeks. "Kind of. There, we were discreet. But anyhow, I couldn't help it, Monday night. And I realized how wonderful it is to have girlfriends. They gave advice and support and, Dax, they care about me."

"How could they not? You're special, Lily." He peered into her light blue eyes. "I'm glad they're there for you, but I want to be, too. You always handle stuff on your own and you shouldn't have to. We should be partners."

"I know. But over the years, we grew more and more apart."

"Yeah, until there was a huge gulf. It was stupid." He thought of Joe Sparrow and his family, Skyping every day.

"We should have realized we couldn't span that gulf in a few days. It'll take lots of talk, and work. And compromise." She flicked tears away, beaming. "Oh Dax, I have exciting news."

He wanted to hear it. More than that, he wanted to take her to bed and make slow, sweet love. But common sense told him that all the great sex in the world wouldn't solve their problems. Right now, it was talk that counted. Or, maybe even more than that, listening. "I'd love to hear it. Want to tell me over dinner? Or have you eaten? I bought snacks because I wasn't sure."

She gestured to a brown bag on the counter. "I picked up Chinese on the way home."

"I saw the Thai and Indian containers. You're living on takeout?"

"Hey, it's better than what I was doing before: soup, crackers, and cheese, night after night. I'm making some changes."

"Let's put your Chinese and my snacks together and we'll picnic in front of the fire. Then you can tell me your news and I'll tell you mine."

"Perfect."

"A martini, or do you want to go straight to wine?"

"Wine, I think."

He poured two glasses from the bottle of Australian Shiraz that he'd already, optimistically, opened. They raised their glasses and she said, "To finding an amazing solution."

He clicked his glass against hers. "We'll do it, Lily."

After they both drank the toast, he asked, "Did you say anything to your parents?"

"No, only book club. And I made an appointment with a divorce lawyer, but I cancelled it."

His body, which had tensed as she spoke, relaxed again. She'd had hope, even before he returned. "Good." Eyeing her pantsuit, he said, "D'you want to change into something comfy? I'll get the food organized."

"Good idea. I'll be back in a minute." She hurried away.

He assembled the food on a big tray and took it into the living room where he lit the candles and turned out the light.

When Lily joined him, she said, "Oh, my, it's so romantic."

"That's what I was going for. I wanted to show you I still feel, you know, romantic about you." A poet, he'd never be.

"Thank you. I love it. And mmm, this looks delicious. A perfect Friday night feast." She sat on the couch and dished portions of this and that onto a plate.

She was the feast, in clingy black yoga pants, rose-colored sweater, and the Whistler scarf. He sat beside her and touched her thigh. "You look so pretty, sweetheart."

Savanna Fox

"And you look so handsome. That tee is perfect for you." She curled into the corner of the couch, her filled plate on her lap.

Dax helped himself to food. "Kim could make good money if she wanted to design clothes."

"I know. She plans to keep making them for friends, but she says so many people are in the clothing design business. She wanted that one unique thing that was hers, and found it with UmbrellaWings."

"Finding your unique thing is important." He took a bite of the Kung Pao chicken she'd brought.

"I kind of lost track of that. And that's part of my news. But before we get to that, tell me how you managed to be here. And how long you can stay."

"I'm here until we decide that I'll be somewhere else."

She cocked her head. "What do you mean? You didn't quit, did you? With no notice?"

He shook his head. "Found a guy to take my place. Good pilot. No burned bridges if I ever want to work for that company again. But I realized I didn't want to give up on us, and we sure weren't gonna solve anything if I was way the hell and gone in the bush."

Her eyes were warm as she smiled at him. "I planned to try, though, Dax."

"Yeah?" He wanted to believe her.

"I was going to get more organized, so you could see I really meant it."

"Uh, meant what?"

"That I'm making changes at the clinic." Her smile widened. "I'm so glad you're here. Maybe you'll have some suggestions."

This was a first: welcoming his opinion about the clinic. "I'm all ears."

"I called a brainstorming meeting with every single person who works at the Well Family Clinic. I told them I wanted it to be a team effort and I wanted their ideas for making it a better place to work, as well as providing great care to our patients."

"Seriously? You, the one who always needs to be in control?"

"Do you have any idea how liberating it is to give up being a control freak?"

He chuckled, but then reflected on her question. "I'm not sure. Guess I'm a bit of one myself. I mean, I do work for employers, but everything about the actual flying's in my hands."

"And maybe it needs to be. Ultimately, being a doctor is in my hands. But running a business doesn't have to be. I don't have a degree in business admin, so why should I think I can run a business?"

"You tell me. I'm not saying that flippantly. I want to know why you thought you had to do that."

She pressed her lips together. "I thought that if I single-handedly built one of the most successful practices in the city, my parents would be impressed. But they won't, so why not do what I want? And that's to practice family medicine."

"You always did, from long before I met you. Maybe I should've tried harder to make you see it, when you were bending yourself out of shape trying to impress your parents."

"I doubt I'd have listened. You know how they say, with addicts, that they may have to hit bottom before they see the light and want to change?"

He nodded, having known an addict or two, both in the Forces and out in the bush. Stressful situations preyed on people's weaknesses. "Are you saying you hit bottom?"

"I tried to tell myself I was resigned to a divorce and that I could do it and move on. But I felt so achy and empty and lonely. Then at book club we were talking about relationships, and trust, belonging, what it means to love."

"Belonging." He echoed the word slowly. Had he ever felt that way?

"Yes. And it really sank in, what I was losing. So there I was, having my little breakdown in a restaurant. Kim hung onto my shoulder and George and Marielle each had one of my hands. Like they were afraid I would, I don't know, fall apart if they didn't anchor me." Her eyes misted. "And maybe I would have. But they did anchor me. They've kept doing it all week, with phone calls, texts, e-mails."

"I'm glad they've been there for you, but I feel shitty. I should be your anchor."

She reached over to touch his hand. "I'd like it if we could do that for each other. You may be a big, tough guy, but I bet sometimes you need an anchor too."

He blinked. "Uh . . . Like I told you, I learned when I was a kid that the only person I could rely on was me. But yeah, when you and I were apart, I always carried the thought of you with me. Your photo, that helicopter pin. When I was in Afghanistan, knowing I had you . . . I guess it kept me sane. It was an anchor, a lifeline, whatever you want to call it."

"Oh Dax, I'm so glad. But in the last years . . ."

"That tie between us was, well, not broken, but . . ."

"Tenuous. Fraught with mistrust and fear."

The corner of his mouth kinked up. "You're better with words. Good description. So now we need to rebuild it." He sipped wine and reflected. "This guy who's filling in for me, he and his wife have kids and she's expecting another. He's taking the job for the money. I warned him it could be tough on their relationship but he says he'll Skype with his family every day."

"Like George and Woody, when he's out of town. Some people are smarter than we were. We got our priorities screwed up."

"Speaking of which, you were telling me about the clinic. How did that brainstorming meeting go?" He leaned forward to serve himself seconds of pasta salad and pepper ham, leaving the remaining Kung Pao chicken for Lily.

"It was wonderful, once they realized I truly did want to hear their ideas and make changes."

Dax munched food, sipped wine, and watched Lily do the same as she told him about the ideas the group had tossed around. Changing the hours of the clinic, taking shifts, job sharing. New processes for making decisions. Different ways of organizing every aspect of the work, from patient scheduling to dealing with supplies and files, even the layout of the office.

"It sounds great," he said. "Thinking about all the bosses I've seen over the years—in the army, the private sector, government—seems to me a good leader's the one who brings out the best in her people."

"Not the one who rules with an iron fist and thinks she knows best about everything?"

"Your words," he pointed out.

"Anyhow, we've got loads of work to do. And—feel free to say 'I told you so'—we agree that the clinic needs a trained, experienced manager."

"Makes sense to me."

"And, finally, to me." She frowned. "The only hitch is, Jennifer, a receptionist, is taking courses in health-care administration and would love to step up. I don't want to discourage her; she's great, but not ready to take on all the responsibilities."

"Hire a manager and make Jennifer her assistant. Maybe half-time reception, half-time assistant. She could keep taking courses and get on-the-job training and experience. And she can give the manager loads of information about the clinic, which will save you time."

Lily's face brightened. "That's a great idea."

"You've figured out the financing for all this?"

"Patient care and a happy, healthy staff take priority over my pride and my parents' opinion. If I need to dip into the trust fund, I think Gran would approve."

"I'd bet on it." He put down his empty plate and reached for Lily's hand, weaving their fingers together.

She gazed into his eyes. "This reminds me of that first summer, the way we shared things and helped each other. I talked about wanting to practice family medicine, and you encouraged me to stand up to my parents."

"And you suggested that I check out ROTP."

"You told me you wanted to go to college, but your marks sucked and you'd never get in, and you said your dream was to be a pilot. I did some research and found out that ROTP would pay for your education and the Forces would teach you to fly."

"Want to know a secret?" He gave her hand a gentle squeeze.

She squeezed back. "Always."

"You know why I wanted to go to college?"

"Uh, because everyone did?"

"And there, in a nutshell, was the difference between our worlds," he said ruefully. "In *yours*, everyone assumed they'd get at least one degree. But neither of my parents had postsecondary education or ever held a decent job. I worked construction, chased girls, and drank beer with guys like me. We talked about the Beavers' chances of winning the Stanley Cup, whether Coors was better than Molson Canadian beer, which waitress had the biggest tits."

"How evolved," she teased.

"Yeah, not. I figured that was my future. Best I could hope was that I'd stay out of jail. But then you came along and we got talking about dreams. I'd given up on dreams years back, but you got me dreaming again." And he'd dreamed big: being a pilot and having a real home with Lily. He'd achieved one dream so why had he let the other one slip through his fingers? He tightened his grip on her hand.

Blue eyes soft in the candlelight, she said, "You told me you'd always watched helicopters, planes, birds, and you wanted to be up in the sky. Where the world was spread out below and you could fly to wild, beautiful places. Where you could be free."

"Away from my shitty life, away from problems. Yeah." Lily remembered, all these years later. "I didn't need college for that. College was because of you. I wanted to be the kind of guy who deserved you, Lily."

"Dax! What were you thinking? You always deserved me. I'm nothing so special."

"You're special to me. And, honestly, I was kind of a loser. I'd have been a worse one if I hadn't met you." He shook his head. "Here we are, talking about the past again. We need to focus on the future."

Her hand tensed in his. "Yes, we do." She eased her hand free and got up. "Let's put the leftovers in the fridge." Then, "I'm not avoiding the discussion. I just don't want anything to interrupt."

"On that subject, you probably don't want to stay up too late, right? You go to the Downtown Eastside clinic pretty early on Saturdays." He rose and lifted the tray while she collected their glasses and the empty wine bottle.

"I do."

As they walked to the kitchen, he said, "There's no rush. I'm not going anywhere this time, Lily. We'll talk until we work things out." He stored leftovers while she rinsed plates and loaded the dishwasher.

She dried her hands on a towel. "Do you have any plans for tomorrow?"

He shook his head. "I could start hunting up some work here."

"How about leaving that until next week? I'm going to find someone to sub for me at the clinic. I want us to be able to talk—tonight, and then tomorrow—without distractions."

This really was a new Lily, willing to shift a responsibility to a colleague. He touched her cheek, which made him want to kiss her soft skin, so he leaned down and did exactly that. "I suppose sex counts as a distraction, right?"

She laughed softly. "Maybe an intermission? Talk, then make love, then more talk?"

"See, we can compromise."

"Let me go make a call."

When she turned to go, he caught her shoulder. "Thanks for doing that, sweetheart." For putting their marriage first on her priority list.

She rested a hand atop his. "Thanks for coming home, my love."

Thirty-one

Five minutes later, Lily, sitting at her desk chair, said into her phone, "Thanks, Vijaya. I owe you." A doctor at the Well Family Clinic, the other woman was single, childless, and not currently dating anyone. She spent much of her free time working out and visiting art galleries.

"No problem. It's not like I had anything better to do on a cold Saturday in January."

Normally, that would be Lily's situation as well. But tomorrow, she would have something better to do. She and Dax would apply their intelligence, creativity, and flexibility to finding an amazing solution.

They'd both have to compromise. Could she imagine giving up the Well Family Clinic and practicing in a little town in the middle of the wilderness? Maybe, if it meant that much to him. But what about the thing that meant so much to *her*? Having children. What if he stood firm, and she had to choose: Dax or kids?

"Lily?"

She turned to see her husband standing in the door of her office.

"Having problems finding someone?"

"No, it's fine." A surge of nervous energy pushed her to her feet. "Dax, we need to talk about children."

"Uh, yeah, I know." His words weren't exactly encouraging. "I made coffee."

Nerves plus caffeine? She'd be awake all night. But then, with her love for Dax and the whole rest of her life on the line, what hope did she have of sleeping anyway? "Coffee sounds good."

"I'll get it."

Lily went back to the living room, where she buried her nose in the vase of flowers on the mantel. Roses and freesia provided the heavenly scent, and other more exotic blooms and greenery made the bouquet distinctive. For some reason, the flowers made her remember how Dax used to give her bouquets of mixed blooms that he pinched from Mrs. B's garden at Camp Skookumchuck. When he came into the room, she said, "You didn't steal these from anyone's garden."

"Figured it wouldn't be so romantic if I got arrested." He put two mugs down and took a small box from under his arm. "Dessert."

She recognized the wrapping. "You went to ChocolaTas."

"Irish Coffee chocolates for me, Baileys and Grand Marnier for you."

Her two favorite flavors. She opened the box, took a Grand Marnier chocolate, and sat on the couch. "I'd almost think you were trying to woo me." Or soften her up.

"Only to show how much I appreciate you." He took a candy himself and sat beside her. "So, the kids thing. You really want them. I know you said that when you were a teenager, and I guess it's a pretty normal thing for a woman, but—"

"For anyone. Dax, it's one of the most primal biological urges. Mate, reproduce."

He closed his eyes briefly. "Fair enough. But beyond the biological stuff, can you tell me more about it?"

"How do you mean?" She studied him over the rim of her coffee mug, taking it as a good sign that he looked confused rather than dismissive.

"Why you want kids, how many you want, what life would look like with kids. You gotta understand, I don't really get what family life is supposed to be."

Poor Dax. With his upbringing, no wonder he couldn't relate to the idea of a happy family. "Very different from what you had. Different from my family too. I don't really care how many kids, but probably at least two. The important thing is that it be a loving, supportive family. Yes, kids should have rules, boundaries, goals, but also fun, play, encouragement."

He'd sipped coffee as she spoke and now put his mug down. "Do you want kids because you want to create, or make up for, what you didn't have yourself?"

It didn't sound like a challenge, only an honest question. She considered it seriously. "Maybe in part. But, more than that, it's just this feeling, deep inside me, that I really, really want to be a mom. I love children. I mothered Anthony to death until he got old enough to hate it. I adored my friends' kid brothers and sisters." Chocolate eased anxiety so she reached for a Bailey's candy. "And Sophia makes my heart melt. How about you? You looked pretty comfortable holding her."

One corner of his mouth kicked up. "She's a charmer." Then he ran his hand over his bearded jaw. "I like kids, I guess. I mean, what's not to like? But I don't know anything about raising them. I'd be crappy."

"No. You'd be responsible and protective, and you'd be there for them. You'd never make them think they didn't matter."

He twisted his fingers together. "Maybe."

"When we first got together, I talked about having kids and I thought you agreed with me. Was that true, but then you changed your mind and never told me?"

"I thought you'd changed your mind too." He rolled his shoulders like he was easing out tension. "That's what we get for not talking."

"So you were telling the truth?" she persisted. "You did want a home and children?"

"I guess. It was a crazy dream."

"It wasn't crazy. What happened to that dream?"

He frowned and she couldn't tell whether it was because his thoughts were confused, or there were things he was wary of saying to her.

"Dax, talk to me." She leaned toward him, but didn't touch him. "I need to understand. Do you no longer have that dream, or do you think it can't come true? Do you really think you'd make a bad father, or do you think I'd make a bad mom? I swear, I'd cut back on work and I wouldn't be controlling and demanding like my mom and dad. I'd—"

He'd been shaking his head and now held up a hand to stop her. "I believe you, Lily. Now, I believe you. Before, I thought the clinic was your baby and that it ruled your life. But now I see you making changes, and yeah, I do think you'd make more if you had kids." He took a deep breath and let it out slowly. "*You* need to understand? Hell, *I* don't understand. I thought I'd given up on the dream. I thought *we* had done that. And it made sense, because I never really believed I'd have . . ." He trailed off and bit his lip.

"That you'd have what you didn't as a child." She grabbed his hand. "Right? Well, I believe we can do it. We can create the kind of home and family we didn't have as kids. Why don't you think so?"

"I don't know." He said the words leadenly. "Lily, I wish I could tell you what you want to hear. But something's holding me back."

She let go of his hand. "You don't trust me? You don't trust us? To build a home together and be good parents?"

With a pained expression, he said, "I love you, sweetheart."

"Love and trust aren't the same thing."

"Maybe it's me I don't trust." He dragged his hands through his hair. "I don't know, Lily. I have to be honest with you and—"

"Yes, please, Dax." Even if the truth was hard to take.

"Okay. Until last week, I thought we'd decided against having kids, so I dismissed the whole idea. Now that I know it's so important to you, now that I have to think seriously about it, I . . . well, it's like what you said. You have this deep-rooted feeling that you should be a parent. I have this feeling that I shouldn't. That I can't. That it's not right."

Worry lines creased her forehead. "Maybe you're scared? It's some kind of defense system?"

He frowned, reflected for a moment. "I don't know where it comes from. But I promise, I'll try to figure this out, see if I can, uh, change my mind. Lily, I'm not saying no. I just can't say yes either. Is that okay for now?"

She bit her lip. "I admit it's not what I want to hear." He hadn't said a flat-out no, though. She picked up her coffee mug and rotated it in her hands. "But you know, even if we were both sure we wanted to have kids, we'd have a lot of other things to work out before I'd feel confident about doing it."

"If we have kids, we need to know they'll have a stable, happy home."

"Yes. And we won't do it until we're both absolutely sure." She caught and held his gaze. "But if you decide, absolutely decide, you don't want children, you have to tell me."

"I promise. Are you"—he cleared his throat—"are you saying you'd leave me if I don't want children?"

There it was: the question she'd posed for herself an hour ago, in the home office. He'd interrupted before she'd really considered it. A pang hit her heart. A deep physical ache. No children or no Dax. Now that she and her husband had rediscovered, or renewed, their love for each other, the idea of life without him was agonizing. But to never have children . . .

"Which would I give up, my left arm or my right?" she said softly. "My heart or my soul?" It was an impossible dilemma. "I don't honestly know." And she hoped never to have to make that choice.

He swallowed audibly, like he was forcing down a lump in his throat.

"I love you, Dax."

"I know. I love you too." He squeezed his eyes shut, gave his head a brief shake, opened his eyes again. His gray irises were soft and silvery.

Lily gazed into them, hoping and praying that he'd find the same dream that was so clear in her mind: the two of them cuddling a baby of their own.

Dax reached over to grip the bare feet she'd curled up on the couch. He cradled them easily in his big hand. "This isn't easy."

She sighed. "I don't think marriage is supposed to be. Talking to my patients, the staff, I hear stories about tough times. When people get married, they're full of optimism and dreams. But life happens, people get older and change, and after a while marriage is less about dreams than about getting through each stressful day. That's when a lot of people throw in the towel."

"Like we were going to." He gave a tired half smile. "But we found out it's not so easy to quit, not when you love each other. Nor is it easy to stay, and fight to make it work."

A thought struck her. "Do you love flying the most when it's easy, or when it's challenging?"

His smile widened and warmed. "You know the answer to that."

"Me too. Not that I wish illness on my patients, but I love solving the tough medical challenges."

"So we're fighters who thrive on challenge. This is a good thing." He released her feet and stood. "More coffee?"

"Just what I need." All the same, she held out her mug.

He took both mugs to the kitchen, then came back and returned hers full of dark, steaming brew. "So the other thing," he said as he resumed his seat beside her, "is my job. Those long stretches in the bush."

"Or my job," she said reluctantly. "I love the clinic, especially with the changes we're talking about, and I love living in Vancouver. But if it's really important to you to be out in the wilderness . . ."

"Something in me needs to connect with the wilderness regularly, but I don't have to live there. I've been thinking, I could get a job based here, like with the Coast Guard doing search and rescue. Or I could get my own helicopter and take freelance work, mostly day trips, occasionally for two or three days. Since we paid off the condo, I've salted away a fair bit."

Her heart flip-flopped. She touched his arm. "I'd love it if you were based here."

"But I'm not a condo guy, Lily. This place made sense with me being away so much. But if I'm home, I want a house and a big yard, the bigger the better, or maybe a park nearby. A wilderness park like Pacific Spirit."

If they had kids, she wanted a house and yard too. Especially if Dax was home to look after the heavy yard work and house maintenance. "That sounds good, but a house by Pacific Spirit Park would be really expensive. Like, three or four million, I'd guess." The moment she said that number, she realized something. Slowly, she said, "Gran's money . . ."

He shook his head. "No, that doesn't feel right. If we get a house, it should be one we can afford on our own. Here's another idea. We keep the condo but get a cottage in the country and go there for weekends. Long weekends, whenever we can both manage it."

An in-between place that worked for both of them, as Kim had suggested. "Like the people who own the cottage we stayed in at Whistler. Prices there are high but property values have dropped."

"Or a place closer to Vancouver, somewhere less developed, less touristy. Lions Bay, Britannia Beach, Squamish, Bowen Island. Hey, we could even live there and commute. It'd be less than an hour's drive."

"Which lots of people who work in Vancouver do every day, from Surrey, Langley, White Rock. I always feel smug, being a ten-minute walk from work. Not," she added quickly, "that I'm saying we can't do it. Only that it'd mean some adjustments. It's great to consider these options."

"It is." He stretched his arm along the back of the couch toward her. "Come here, sweetheart."

She fit herself into the curve of his arm. "I told everyone at the clinic that I not only want to focus my time on patient care, but also cut back my hours. We could coordinate our schedules and make sure we have most weekends free. Maybe even three-day weekends."

"We could work four long days. If we lived in the country, we could drive into Vancouver before rush-hour traffic and leave after it. We could afford to do that; we both make good money and we're not exactly extravagant about spending."

"So much to think about." She curled closer against the familiar, wonderful warmth of his muscular body. "We lost each other for a while, Dax. Maybe even lost ourselves. I feel like we're finding our way back. Or rather, ahead, together. It's wonderful." Particularly since he'd promised to seriously consider having children.

He kissed the top of her head. "I guess it's like with your clinic. There aren't magic answers, right off the top. It takes brainstorming, thought, time."

"Trust," she said.

He rose from the couch. "Sex."

Thirty-two

Lily stared up at him. "Sex?"

He'd clearly caught his wife off guard, which was fun. "I'm taking you to bed."

"Oh, you are, are y—"

Before the last word left her lips, he bent and scooped her into his arms.

To his relief, she grinned. "Taking me captive?"

"You got it."

Her blue eyes twinkled. "And if I protested, would you spank me?"

"Uh, d'you want me to spank you?"

She tilted her head, considering. "That little slap you gave me the first night was exciting. Coming out of the blue, not really hurting but tingling. Showing me your bad-boy side. But I'm not into pain."

"So I'll have to return those nipple clamps I bought?"

He was messing with her, and the quick flare of her eyes told him he'd almost got her, but she came back with, "No, we can use them on you."

"Ouch. Okay, no nipple clamps." Cradling her, he moved around the room blowing out the candles, and then carried her to the bedroom. For a bad-boy touch, he dropped her onto the bed so she bounced. He gazed down at her, so lovely and appealing. "I've wanted this since the moment you saw me and ran into my arms."

"I was so surprised when I saw the flowers, the wine on the counter. So happy when I saw you. I missed you this week, Dax."

"I missed you too." He sat on the bed beside her. "I don't want to spend any more time missing you. I know we still have lots to talk about. But right now, let's shut up and let our bodies do the communicating."

"What language are we talking tonight? He says, she says, or they say?"

"Whichever you want."

"Mmm, let me think. You did fly all the way here to claim me. And you did just take me captive."

"He says, it is. I'm Falcon and you will obey me." What kind of sex play should he initiate tonight, to arouse and satisfy her? "Off the bed," he growled.

"Yes, Falcon." Curiosity glinting in her eyes, she slipped off the bed.

"Take off your sweater and scarf."

She unlooped the scarf and pulled the sweater over her head, folded both, and walked over to place them on the dresser. When she turned back, her nipples were tightening against the thin fabric of her bra.

His cock swelled in response. "Now your bra."

She undid the back clasp then slid the straps down her shoulders and pulled the bra off, freeing her firm, rose-tipped breasts.

He rose, tugged the hawk tee over his head, tossed it on the dresser, and stood in front of her. "Take off my jeans and underwear."

Her warm fingers brushed his skin as she undid the button of his jeans and slid down the fly. By the time she tugged on the waistband, he was fully erect.

"Kneel."

She dropped to her knees on the carpet and peeled his jeans

and boxer briefs down his legs. He rested his hands on her shoulders, lifted one leg, waited until she tugged his clothing free, and then lifted the other leg. After she set the clothes aside, she glanced up.

Standing with his feet apart, he said, "Suck my cock."

Lily smiled and bent her head, swirling her tongue around the crown of his penis then drawing him into her mouth. Wet heat enveloped him, soft suction gripped and released.

He pumped slightly, not forcing himself too far into her mouth, only enough to increase the friction and remind her who was in control. What a turn-on: the sight of his swollen shaft sliding between her pink lips; the sounds she made; the stimulation of her tongue, lips, and teeth against his sensitive flesh.

He hadn't told her she could touch him with her hands, but neither had he prohibited it. Now she slid one arm around him to stroke and knead his ass, his hip. Her other hand caressed his inner thighs, brushed his sac, then cupped his balls.

Involuntarily, he jerked and tightened. This was too good. If she kept it up, he'd come, and that wasn't what he wanted. Not yet. "Stop."

She released him and lifted her head. So beautiful, with her flushed cheeks, her damp, shiny lips.

His cock rose straight up his belly, hard as a baton, craving release.

"Touch your breasts. Cup them, lift them, squeeze them together. Then take my cock between them."

She did it, and he thrust back and forth in her cleavage. Again, the sight and sensation of her soft curves hugging his slick, swollen flesh was almost enough to set him off. He forced himself to pull free.

Lily gazed up, waiting for his next order.

"Lie on the bed with your knees bent and your legs spread."

Her eyes gleamed. "Yes, Falcon."

She figured he planned to fuck her, but he had something else in mind first.

When she was in place, he admired her pussy, exposed to his view. Swollen and moist, she was clearly aroused. "Wet your fingers, Lily. Then touch your pussy. Stroke it, caress it."

Her eyes widened in shock and she didn't move. This was something they'd never done.

"I want to see you turn yourself on."

"I . . . It's too embarrassing." The feverish patches on her cheeks told him it was also arousing.

"You have a safe word," he reminded her. "You either say it or you obey me." Then he added, more softly, "Trust me, Lily. It'll be sexy for both of us."

After a long moment, she raised her hand to her lips. Her damp fingers went between her legs and she stroked herself tentatively.

"You can do better than that. Touch yourself the way you like to be touched. Tease your clit. But don't come. You're not allowed to come."

She squeezed her eyes shut and her fingers stroked more firmly, capturing her juices and spreading them across her labia. She flicked lightly across her clit, came back for a firmer press. Her breathing quickened and her back arched slightly.

Dax sat beside her, tempted to suck those tight, thrusting nipples. But he wanted her to do this all on her own. His cock ached, urging him to grab it and pump himself to climax right along with her. He had something better in mind, though, so he forced himself to take slow, deep breaths.

Helicopter technical specs . . .

Bell 206B Jet Ranger. Empty weight: 1,780 pounds.

Lily's head twisted on the pillow. Her breathing was fast and shallow, and it caught on a gasp. She pulled her hand away from her pussy and her body trembled.

"Keep going. His voice was hoarse from his own arousal. "But don't come." Did she have a technique to hold back climax? He guessed women didn't usually have to do that, not the way men did.

Useful load: 1,300 pounds. Maximum external load: 1,500.

Her fingers brushed between her legs. A few light strokes, a firm press, two fingers against her clit. Her middle finger hooked inside her channel, slid out, went in again. Her breathing rasped and her chest and cheeks were ruddy. Her whole body trembled with tension and her eyes were still firmly shut.

Service ceiling: 13,500 feet. Hover ceiling, IGE: 12,800. Hover ceiling, OGE: 8,800.

She was hovering on the edge, and so was he, damn it. "Look at me," he ordered.

"Oh God." Her lashes fluttered, then slowly her eyes opened and she turned her head toward him.

He took his cock in his hand. "See what you do to me?"

Her blue eyes were glassy. "Y-yes."

"Touch your clit. Bring yourself to the edge, Lily."

"I . . I already am. I can't go any further without coming."

"I didn't give you permission."

She moaned and lifted her hand away from her body. "I know." She was so taut, he was almost afraid she'd break.

He was rigid himself, his balls tight and hard; he could barely control himself. He grabbed his cock and squeezed firmly below the head, reducing the pressure. *Maximum speed, 122 knots. Maximum fuel range: 369 nautical miles. Endurance with no reserves: 3.5 hours.* Hell, he wished he had that kind of endurance. After fifteen or twenty seconds, the tension eased off a little.

"Lily?"

She stared at him. "Yes, Falcon."

"Come now."

She moaned again, slid her fingers across her slippery folds, pressed her clit, and exploded with a sharp cry, her whole body shuddering, her eyes unfocused and wild.

Fuel capacity: 76 gallons. Fuel capacity with auxiliary: 96 gallons.

When the tension started to ease from her body, he said, "Off the bed."

"What?"

"Get off the bed."

Looking dazed, she slowly clambered off.

"Stand three feet away, facing the bed. Spread your legs wide and lean forward, forearms and head on the bed."

Smiling now, she obeyed.

He stepped behind her, admiring the slender line of her back, the womanly curve of her ass, her slim, shapely legs. The folds of her sex exposed between her legs. "Up on your toes."

When she raised herself, he looped an arm around her waist, giving her added support. His chest curved around her back and his cock nudged the crease between her ass cheeks. His other arm went around her to reach between her legs and caress her. He adjusted his position so his erection slipped between her legs. Gently, his fingers parted her slick, heated folds and the blunt head of his cock nudged inside her.

He groaned as she enveloped him, hot and wet and clingy. "Shit you feel good, Lily." He pumped, the sweet friction demanding that he move faster, drive harder. Holding off climax was a bear and he damned well wasn't doing it any longer. He was the master here.

He fingered Lily's clit, gently because she'd be sensitive after orgasm.

She gasped and moaned, "Oh Dax." She'd stopped calling him Falcon, which was just fine by him.

"Sweetheart, I'm gonna come. Need you to come with me."

"Yes, oh yes." Her ass pushed back against him. "Now, Dax, come now."

Pressing her clit, he let himself go, thrusting long and hard and deep. She trembled and pulsed around him. And then, as his climax ripped through him and he let out a wrenching groan, she cried out again too.

He held both of them on their feet as shudders wracked their bodies, then faded to ripples and finally eased. Still keeping an arm around her, he slid out of her body. "Can you stand?"

"Nope," she muttered, her face half buried in the duvet. Without straightening, she crawled up on the bed. "Oh, my God."

"You can say that again." He pulled down the covers and flopped onto the bed. "Come on, Lily. Climb in."

"You say that like I have control over my muscles," she grumbled, but with a smile she found her way under the covers to lie beside him. She curled on her side and studied him. "I can't believe you made me do that."

"It was that or nipple clamps."

"Okay, that's my excuse."

"It was good, though. Right?"

"Very good."

"See what happens when you trust me?"

"Yes, Falcon," she said demurely. Then she yawned. "Even with all that caffeine, I'm beat."

"Sleep, sweetheart." He touched his lips to hers.

"Did I tell you how glad I am that you're here?"

"Me too." He kissed her again, felt her suppress a yawn, and chuckled. "Go to sleep."

"Mmm." She rolled onto her side. "Good night, my love."

He spooned his body around the familiar curve of hers and put his arm around her.

She caught his hand between hers, and it was mere seconds before her hands relaxed and her breathing slowed in sleep.

Oh yes, he was glad he was here. This felt so right.

Yet he had to wonder what Lily would do if he decided he truly never wanted to have children.

Thirty-three

Vancouver dumped rain as Lily and Dax drove to her parents' house Sunday evening. Lily was tired, but satisfied about how the weekend had gone so far. They'd talked, walked, shared meals, had sex, and talked some more. They'd brainstormed what the future might look like. Although they still hadn't found that "amazing solution" and Dax hadn't had a breakthrough on the subject of wanting kids, she was hopeful. In her mind was the fear he'd issue a "kids versus husband" ultimatum, but she tried her best to shove that thought to the far back.

He pulled the car into the cobblestone parking area. "Two family dinners in the space of two weeks," he said dryly. "This must really prove I love you."

She squeezed his arm. "Look at it this way. We did Christmas, this is the New Year's get-together, and then we're in the clear until Easter. No, wait, there's Regina's birthday at the end of February." That was how her parents did it: meals at their house or at fancy restaurants for the big events, interspersed with weekly phone calls. Neither Lily nor her brother ever initiated get-togethers with their parents.

Aldonza greeted them at the door and they wished each other a happy new year. When she took their coats, she said, "You look pretty, Miss Lily."

"Thanks. Everyone's in the sitting room?"

"Yes."

Dax turned to Lily. "You do look pretty, sweetheart."

Rather than wear the usual tailored dress or pant suit, she'd chosen black silk evening pants and the butterfly top worn over the blue tank. "You look great, too," she told Dax. He wore black dress pants and a shirt the color of coffee with cream.

He took her hand and they walked down the hall. Quiet voices came through the open door of the sitting room. A happy squeal that could only be Sophia quickened Lily's footsteps.

When they entered the room, formally decorated in shades of cream and charcoal, Lily's parents were in their usual chairs, with Anthony and Regina on a couch, an empty bassinet beside them. Regina held Sophia while Anthony tickled his daughter under the chin, eliciting another squeal.

"Happy new year," Lily said. As everyone echoed the greeting, she crossed over to Regina. "There's my gorgeous niece. Can Aunt Lily hold you?"

Regina said, "She'd like that," and Lily scooped the baby into her arms, warm and sweet-smelling in her footed sleeper dotted with butterflies. Delighted, Lily crooned, "Look at our clothes, precious. We're both butterfly girls."

Regina rose to tuck a burp cloth between Sophia's face and Lily's shoulder. "Let's protect that incredible top. Who's the designer? I'd love to get one, if you wouldn't mind."

"A friend. She doesn't do them commercially." She made a mental note to see if Kim might be prevailed on to make a top for Regina's birthday. "She does design umbrellas, though, and she's launching a new business. I'll give you her card."

"Your friend is an umbrella designer?" Lily's mother sounded disapproving.

Lily turned to her, the baby in her arms. "And very talented."

"Hmm. Well, come give me a kiss."

An imp made Lily pass Sophia, along with her burp cloth, to Dax. "Here, you look after your niece for a minute."

His big arms cradled the child a little awkwardly, but very securely. Sophia looked so tiny compared to him, yet she gazed up at him with a bright smile and a happy gurgle.

Lily went over to air-kiss her mother's carefully made-up cheek then touch her dad's shoulder. He wasn't much for kisses.

He got to his feet. "A martini, Lily? Dax, Scotch neat?"

They both agreed to her father's suggestions. Dax had told her the best things about her parents' house were Aldonza's cooking and her father's Glenfiddich single-malt Scotch.

"I was surprised," her father said, "when Lily told us you'd be coming today, Dax. I thought you'd gone back up north."

"Change of plans," he said.

Lily retrieved Sophia from his arms. "We're tired of being apart." She went to sit on a two-seater sofa.

"What work are you doing now then?" her father asked, handing a glass of Scotch to Dax and starting on Lily's martini.

"Don't know yet," he said laconically.

Lily suppressed a sigh. No, it wasn't in Dax's nature to make nice with her parents.

"You gave up a job without having another lined up?" her mother said. "That's hardly responsible."

All right, that was going too far. Lily jumped to his defense. "Dax is always responsible. And he has a number of options." And, really, why should they lay them out for her parents? None would win approval, because Dax would never be the medical specialist they wanted for a son-in-law. If her parents had been different people, she could have told them about the people he rescued, the lives he saved, and they'd have been proud and happy that she married such a fine man. She smiled at Dax as he collected her martini from her father and came to sit beside her.

Then she took a breath. Might as well get all the criticism over with at once. "Speaking of options, I'm making some changes at the Well Family Clinic."

"What changes?" Her father resumed his chair. "And why?"

"I want to work fewer hours and spend most of those hours with patients. I want to give the other doctors and the staff more options as well, and more voice. I'm hiring a manager and once that person's in place we'll do some brainstorming and analyze various models. I'll get Dax's input too. He has some great ideas."

As she spoke, Dax caught the slipping burp cloth on her shoulder and straightened it.

Sophia's tiny hand reached for his finger. When he let her capture it, she popped it into her mouth and sucked on it. Not the most sanitary practice, but of the various things a baby might stick in her mouth, Dax's finger had to be one of the least harmful.

"It's your clinic," Lily's father said disapprovingly. "You don't want other people telling you how to run it."

"It is her clinic," Dax said evenly. "She's the one to decide how she wants to run it." It was almost exactly what her dad had said, but phrased this way it pointed out that he was butting in.

"If you work fewer hours," her mother said, "you'd have time for research or a clinical trial."

The warm weight of Sophia in her arms helped Lily stay calm. "I'm not interested in doing that, though I'll probably continue to do volunteer work at the clinic in the Downtown Eastside. But mostly, I want a more balanced life and lots more time with my husband."

Glancing at Dax, she saw that Sophia's rosebud mouth had released his finger. The baby's head had tilted, curving into his big palm, and she appeared to be asleep. Holding his hand at that angle couldn't be comfortable, but Dax didn't move it. Did he see how wonderful this was? How could he not?

"With your brain and discipline, you could do so much more," her mother complained. "Family practice . . . Well, anyone can do that."

Lily sighed. She did believe her parents loved her, but their brand of love was tough to take.

"Can just anyone do it with Lily's degree of skill and commitment?" Dax said. "Besides, it's what she enjoys and she should be happy in her work." He leaned close to Lily and, with mischief sparking his gray eyes, murmured so only she could hear, "Probably not a wise move to mention your gran, right?"

She stifled a snort of laughter.

"It makes sense to me," Anthony said, surprising her with his support. "Lily was the kid who stuck bandages all over her dolls. She's a healer and a good one."

Regina nodded. "We trust her with Sophia's care. We wouldn't give our daughter's medical care to just *anyone*." Her crisp lawyer voice put a slight emphasis on the last word.

"You're thirty-two, Lily," her mother said. "This is the time to build a career, not cut back on it."

She'd disappointed her parents again and they'd disappointed her too. Same old, same old. "Mom, Dad, I'm a grown woman. Trust me to decide what's best for me. Practicing family medicine makes me happy, and so does spending time with Dax." The imp poked her again, and she added, "I know you love me, so I hope you'll be happy for me."

Dax's eyes twinkled as he gave her an approving smile. "And that would appear to close the subject," he said. "Those are our New Year's resolutions. Make some changes in our work, spend more time together, and be happier. How about the rest of you?"

"I think we'll adopt your resolutions," Regina said, reaching out to clasp Anthony's hand.

"Well," Lily's mother said, "if Dax lives in Vancouver and you reduce your work hours, Lily, then it's time for something else." She nodded pointedly to the baby in Lily's arms, dozing against Dax's big hand.

"And that would be Dax's and my business. Now, isn't it time for dinner?" Still, it might be the only time she'd ever agreed with her mom.

Thirty-four

So this is where Canada's Mr. Hockey lives." Dax studied the slate-toned lobby of the sleek Yaletown condo building. It wasn't to his taste, but each to his own.

"Yes, and George moved in a few months ago," Lily said.

"What's up with that nickname? She didn't look like a George to me."

"When I first met her, she was very tailored, downplaying her femininity." She gave a short laugh. "A lot like the way I dress, I guess."

"I like your professional look. But I also like it when you wear things like your new dress and that butterfly top."

"Which I'm rapidly wearing out." Inside the elevator, she pressed the button for the penthouse floor. "I'll ask Regina and my book club friends for suggestions on where to shop for more feminine clothes."

"On the subject of your friends, are they out for my blood?" A week ago, they'd comforted Lily when she cried over getting a divorce. This weekend she'd texted with an update, and said he'd be coming with her to Kim's engagement party.

He and Lily stepped out of the elevator on the penthouse floor, which had only four apartment doors.

"There'll be scrutiny," she said. "Maybe some grilling." She sounded way too cheerful about that. "Especially from Marielle. She's pretty blunt."

"Great," he said glumly. "I guess I deserve it."

"You do." She grinned up at him. "Look at it this way. At least no one's shooting at you."

Hearing his own words echoed back made him smile too. "Come here, you." He pulled her close for a kiss. But even as his lips touched her soft, sweet ones, even as he counted his blessings for how well things were going for the two of them, in the back of Dax's mind the issue of children hung there like a storm cloud. He knew it was in Lily's mind too. When he was flying, he avoided storm clouds. In his marriage, avoidance was no longer possible. And yet, though he'd mulled the subject over and over, he hadn't reached a resolution.

Though he tried to concentrate on nothing but his wife's sexy mouth, the delicate scent of her orange-almond body lotion got him thinking of the sweet, powdery smell of baby Sophia, her soft weight in his arms, the trusting way she'd fallen asleep with her head resting in his palm. She'd tugged at heartstrings he'd never known existed. But she also freaking terrified him. How could he be responsible for an innocent child, make a lifelong commitment to be *there* the way his parents never had?

Was he capable of giving the woman he loved the thing she most wanted in life?

The elevator dinged and a female voice said, "Oh man, you two need to get a room."

Lily broke away from his embrace. "Hi, Marielle."

Dax turned to greet his wife's friend, who was with a slim, tall-ish, fair-haired man. The brunette's brown eyes were assessing as she said, "So, Dax, we meet again."

Yeah, a few words could convey a lot. "We do." Then, because he knew it pissed Lily off when he was terse, he added, "It's good to see you again. And to be here."

Marielle gave a slight nod, and he knew he'd passed the first test. "Lily, Dax," she said, "meet Kent."

After murmuring "nice to meet you," they located the right apartment and Dax pressed the buzzer.

The door was opened by a tall, muscular guy dressed in a sandy-colored jersey top over black casual pants. Woody Hanrahan. Dax recognized him from watching hockey on TV.

Woody ushered them in and they went through another round of introductions as people put their coats in the hall closet. Dax, like Lily, wore Kim's clothing art and, he saw, so did Marielle. Her filmy tee had wing patterns in yellow and black with accents of blue and red, reminding him of a swallowtail butterfly. Kent wore a blue button-down shirt with black pants.

As Woody led the way through the apartment, where a couple dozen people of various ages mingled, Dax gazed around. It was spacious, with huge windows giving a view of the nighttime city. Dax liked the room; it looked like a lived-in blend of Woody's and George's personalities. The guy stuff featured black leather furniture, a large TV and sound system, and big paintings of winter lakes that really spoke to Dax. The female touch was evident in colorful cushions and throws, flowers, knickknacks, and a bookcase crammed full of books.

Woody took them to the kitchen. Dax recognized the other book club women. Redheaded George wore a slinky bronze top and a long chocolate-colored skirt. Petite Kim's spiky black hair was streaked with vivid blue and green, matching the peacock design of feathers and eyes on her top. She was cuddled up under the arm of a lean, muscular guy with sandy brown hair. He wore a Western-style shirt with rolled-up sleeves, black jeans, and a leather belt with a large, fancy buckle. Lily had said that Kim's fiancé, Ty Ronan, owned a ranch, was a horse trainer, and also rode in rodeos.

Kim handled the introductions and Dax endured assessing looks from George and Kim. Woody got drinks and Dax gratefully took a bottle of beer.

Marielle said, "I want to check out the food, since I recommended the caterer."

Dax, Lily, and Kent went along with her. The dining table at one end of the living room was covered with appetizers, presided over by a chunky young Asian man in chef's clothing. As Marielle greeted the caterer, the others loaded plates with snacks. Most of the food was cold: fancy-looking sushi, miniature taco cups, tiny meatballs with dip, skewers with prawns and red pepper in spicy sauce, raw vegetables and dips, and half a dozen other items. There was a cracker and cheese platter, and another platter of exotic fruits. Every item had a label with the name, principal ingredients, and any allergy warnings.

Lily and Dax moved along to where the chef tended two chafing dishes, one holding butternut squash ravioli with hazelnut oil, the other containing small chicken thighs in coconut-lemongrass curry.

"The food looks great," Dax told the chef, and Lily said, "The labels are brilliant. I've rarely seen things so clearly marked."

Marielle, who'd filled a plate of her own, said eagerly, "Let's go meet people."

Lily and Dax, along with Kent, followed her. Dax wasn't much for cocktail party chat. Still, it was interesting meeting art colleagues of Kim's, a few old friends of hers who dated back to elementary school, and friends of Ty's from the Fraser Valley. Ty's parents were there, an attractive middle-aged blonde in a yellow sweater and a silver-haired man in a white Western shirt and bolo tie, along with some people who worked at Ronan Ranch.

Dax looped his arm around Lily's shoulders. Knowing that his wife, who appeared so poised, was actually shy, he murmured, "Marielle makes it pretty painless."

"She does. But I wish it was just the book club and their guys," she said quietly. "I think you'd like the women if you got to know them, and I'd like to talk more to Ty and Woody. Cocktail parties are too much surface and very little depth."

"We could have them over for dinner," he suggested. "Or go out together."

"Really?" Her brows lifted. "You'd be okay with that?"

"Jeez, Lily, I know I'm a bit of a loner, but I like people. If we're spending more time here together, we should have a social life." He quickly qualified that. "Just not so much with your parents. Maybe your brother and Regina, though. Seems like you and Anthony are getting along better."

"Sophia is loosening him up."

"And you're not being so competitive." He squeezed her shoulder and teased, "Plus, you have to be nice to them if you want to see your niece."

"There is that," she admitted with a smile.

He went to get fresh drinks for them, and when he returned, Lily was talking to George, Woody, Marielle, and Kent. Kim and Ty came over too. "Thanks so much for coming to celebrate with us," Kim said. "Dax, that tee looks terrific on you."

"It's great. Thanks for making it."

"Hey Ty," Marielle said, "how come you're not wearing a Kim-designed shirt?"

"She wanted to show her friends I'm a real cowboy."

"See that buckle belt?" Kim boasted. "That's his World Rodeo Champion buckle for best all-around cowboy."

"Wow," Marielle said. "That's hot, Ty."

Ty rolled his eyes. "Women."

They talked about this and that for a while, the group shifting from time to time. At one point, Dax went to get more snacks, and found George at his elbow, reaching for a chicken thigh.

"I'm so happy for Kim and Ty," she said.

"Yeah, they seem good together. Congratulations on your engagement too."

"Thanks. You know, book club's been meeting for less than a

year and now two of us are engaged." Serious amber eyes studied his face. "It hasn't been easy for either of us, with our guys."

"Uh, it hasn't?" This seemed like a pretty personal subject for a cocktail party.

She shook her head. "Ty's very involved with Ronan Ranch, and Kim believed her future lay back in Hong Kong. They both thought their relationship couldn't work, but they found a way."

"That's good," he said warily. Was she winding up for a lecture?

"Woody didn't plan on settling down. I was a widow and believed my husband was my one soul mate. When we fell for each other, we had some big issues to work through."

Big issues to work through. "Right."

She gave an understanding smile. "It'd be nice if love was easy, wouldn't it?"

"That's for sure." Since she'd gone for a subtle approach rather than a lecture, he ventured, "Any tips on how to work out those issues?"

"Nothing profound, I'm afraid. Trust, communication, hard work. Examining your heart. Really examining it, with all your defenses down."

Something in his body clenched and his face must have reflected it, because she gave a rueful head shake. "That's a tough thing to do, isn't it? But when you love someone, when you're totally committed to them, you have to." Now a twinkle lit her eyes. "It's easy to be physically naked with the person you love. Emotionally naked is way harder."

"Did I hear the word 'naked'?" a male voice asked. Woody's arm came around his fiancée's shoulders. "You better not be thinking about getting naked with anyone other than me, Georgia." Dax had noticed that Woody, unlike everyone else, didn't use the nickname George.

She grinned at him. "No danger of that. I was just telling Dax that when a man loves a woman, he has to let himself be emotionally naked and vulnerable with her."

The wince on Woody's face—likely a twin to Dax's own expression a moment ago—had Dax hiding a smile.

"A guy has to commit," Woody said. "If you want something bad enough—whether it's a woman or the Stanley Cup—you commit and go after it. Period."

George put her arm around him and winked at Dax. "That too."

As Dax moved back to join Lily, he reflected on their advice. He and Lily had both said they loved each other and were committed to making their marriage work. She'd laid herself bare, emotionally, when she told him how badly she wanted children. He'd tried to examine his heart, the way George said, but what he saw there was no clearer than mud. If he loved Lily—and he did, deeply and truly—shouldn't he want to have children with her? Why the hell wasn't he sure? What defenses were so entrenched that he couldn't see deep into his own heart?

He'd won a Medal for Military Valour, but did he have the guts to strip away his defenses and examine his heart?

Thirty-five

The next Sunday morning, Lily enjoyed lazing in bed with Dax, dozing, making love, talking.

How luxurious to not be heading off to the clinic to do admin work. She, a couple of the other doctors, and Jennifer, the receptionist, had interviewed a candidate for office manager, and been blown away. The woman would come to work for them in two weeks. Jennifer had already taken on more administrative duties, bringing records up-to-date and creating reports using computer skills Lily'd never realized she possessed.

It had been a good week for Lily and Dax too, and she'd decided that rather than agonize over what she'd do if he decided he didn't want kids, she'd try to remain positive and hopeful.

The combination of sunshine outside the window and her growling stomach made her say, "Let's have breakfast and decide how to spend the day."

Lily donned her robe and Dax pulled on boxer briefs, then they went to the kitchen and put together a meal of fruit, yogurt, and toasted bagels with jam. She was ready to linger over a second cup of coffee and discuss plans, but Dax rose. "I'm going to take a quick shower then I have a couple of things to do. You relax; I'll be back soon." He dropped a kiss on the top of her head and strode from the kitchen.

She frowned after him. What *things* did he need to do, and why didn't he suggest she come along? In the past, this would have been normal behavior for both of them, but now she felt shut out. "Old habits," she muttered as she poured that second cup of coffee. "Hard to break." When he returned, he'd tell her what he'd been doing. If not, she'd ask. They'd agreed they wanted an open, communicative relationship.

Armed with coffee and her Kindle, she curled up in a chair by the living room window. Her current book—not a book club choice—had been a Giller Prize finalist. It was better written than *Bound by Desire*, but she had trouble concentrating. A few minutes later, Dax called, "I'm off. See you in a bit."

There was something—excitement? urgency?—in his voice. Or was that her imagination?

"Bye," she called, and then tried to refocus on her book. It was no use. She couldn't get into it.

She dealt with the breakfast clutter then had her own shower and dressed. Guessing they'd probably go for a walk on such a beautiful day, she chose jeans and one of the new lightweight sweaters she'd picked up this week at a store George had recommended. The crew-neck garment was the soft purple of lilacs and made her light blue eyes look even bluer.

Restless, she decided to look at the financial information her trust fund manager had sent her this week. In the small home office, her desk had the usual neat stacks of papers and magazines, while Dax's held only his open netbook.

As she walked past his desk, her hip brushed his desk chair, sending it spinning to catch the edge of his computer. Quickly she grabbed the netbook to steady it, in the process dislodging a large white envelope that had rested beneath it. She bent to retrieve the envelope and noted that it had a RE/MAX logo. A real estate company?

Was this what he'd done yesterday, while she worked at the Downtown Eastside medical clinic? When she'd discussed her volunteer work with Dax, saying that she'd made a commitment and wasn't comfortable bailing on it two weeks in a row, he'd been understanding. He'd said he'd keep himself occupied. Last night, when she asked how he'd spent the day, he said, "This and that. Nothing special." Had he started to hunt for properties that might interest them for a weekend cottage, or possibly a new home within commuting distance? Why hadn't he mentioned it, and shown her what he found? Probably he intended to tell her today.

She sat at her own desk and opened the trust-fund package. But now curiosity had set in. When would Dax be back? Surely he wouldn't mind her taking a look. They were in this together, after all.

She wandered over to his desk and fingered the envelope. It was unsealed. She eased the contents out an inch, to see a RE/MAX folder. A note was clipped to the top, handwritten on a female Realtor's stationery.

Get this back to me ASAP so I can make the offer. Think about how high you're willing to go if they counteroffer. But, as I said, they're in a hurry to sell and they might accept at this price.

Make an offer? What on earth? She pulled the folder out, flipped it open, and stared at a contract of purchase and sale. The purchaser names were Dwayne Arthur Xavier and Lily Elizabeth Nyland, and the price tag was hefty, higher than the value of the condo.

"Oh!" Her heart raced as she stared at the document in stunned disbelief. Dax had viewed properties, decided on one, and instructed a Realtor to draw up an offer? At a price that meant selling the condo, which meant this was no weekend cottage, but a new home. He'd done all this without even mentioning it to Lily? What was he thinking? An open, communicative relationship? "Hah!"

Steamed, she turned to the attached listing sheet and gazed at the photo. The reason for the price tag clearly wasn't the house. The photo showed a rustic cottage, fitting nicely into its natural surroundings. Rather charming, but quite run-down. The description told her it stood on a two-acre property on Bowen Island, not on the waterfront—which would have been prohibitively expensive— but on a hill with an ocean view.

Bowen was a location they'd discussed. It had a lovely natural setting plus the essential services, and was easily accessible from Vancouver by either water taxi or highway and ferry.

The house in the photo, with some repairs and paint, would be nice. But they were nowhere near being ready to make an offer. Not with the one huge unresolved issue hanging over them. "What on earth is he thinking?"

She scanned the details on the listing sheet. A thousand square feet? That was barely larger than the condo. One bedroom—"What?" This was a house for a couple, not a family.

Her knees gave out and she sank into his desk chair. No, this wasn't possible. Dax had promised that he'd seriously consider having children and he'd tell her when he decided.

Well, this damned offer was pretty clear evidence of his decision. Did he think she'd just go along? That she'd choose him over her long held, deeply rooted dream of having kids?

Would she?

She rested her head in her hands. She'd been sure they were heading in the right direction together. Discussing things, sharing, trusting each other. And now, just like her parents, he didn't give a damn about what she needed and wanted. He was trying to steamroll her into going along with what he wanted. With his vision of their future. A childless future.

No, she wasn't building *any* future with a man who shut her out this way.

Tears slid down her face and that horrible hollow ache was back in her heart. It was over. This time, their marriage really was over. And it hurt even more because she'd let herself hope.

In a daze, she shoved the folder back into the envelope and returned the envelope to its position underneath his netbook. She walked to the bathroom where she splashed cold water on her face. Her reflection stared back at her, eyes glittery with tears. She swallowed, trying to force the tears back. Dax wasn't worth crying over.

But . . . was that really true?

She pressed her hands against the counter of the vanity, the marble cold and slick under her palms. And she remembered . . . The summer when she'd fallen in love with him, and the dreams they'd shared then. The way he'd opened up to her recently, revealing painful things he'd never spoken of before. The many discussions they'd had over the past couple of weeks; the romantic gestures; the steps forward and back. After all that, would he really try to impose his vision of the future on her?

Her breath caught as a new idea struck her. Did he think she was trying to impose her vision on him? He'd asked her what she'd do if she had to choose between him and having children, and she'd told him she didn't know. It was the truth, a truth that had the potential of ripping her heart in half. But had he heard it as a threat?

Even if he had, what did this offer to buy a one-bedroom cottage mean?

He would tell her. She couldn't give up on him.

Steadier now, she washed her face again and applied a touch of eye makeup to conceal any signs of tears. She heard the front door open and went to greet Dax.

His cheeks were flushed, his eyes bright. "Okay, almost ready. I'm taking you for a ride."

"Oh? Where?"

"A surprise destination. I'll be back in a minute." He headed down the hall.

Let me guess, Bowen Island? She held back the words, collected her purse, and pulled on boots and her sheepskin jacket.

He returned and caught her hand. "Ready?"

"All set."

They rode the elevator down to the basement and climbed into the Lexus.

"You know I don't do that well with surprises," she warned.

"Yeah, but you're trying to be more flexible and spontaneous, right?"

She pressed her lips together. If she hadn't found the real-estate contract, how would she feel now? Pleasantly anticipatory that Dax was taking her on an adventure. "Right."

Dax drove out into the sunshine and they both put on sunglasses. Stuart McLean's Vinyl Café was just starting on CBC Radio. Telling herself to be patient, Lily tried to focus on one of McLean's stories about husband and wife Dave and Morley.

As McLean spun the story in his measured style, Dax drove down Broadway to Cambie, over the Cambie Street Bridge, through downtown, and over the Lions Gate Bridge. Yes, they were heading toward the Horseshoe Bay ferry terminal. Periodically, Dax laughed at something McLean said. The fingers of his left hand tapped the steering wheel as if he was full of nervous energy.

When he took the road to the terminal, rather than the Sea to Sky Highway that led to Lions Bay, Squamish, and Whistler, she said, "One of three options: Nanaimo, the Sunshine Coast, or Bowen Island. You know I'll find out when you pay the fare."

"Yeah. I thought of blindfolding you all the way, but that'd be hard to explain to the cashier." He pulled up to one of the booths and told the woman, "Bowen Island, please."

She took his credit card and directed him to a lane in the terminal.

Thinking of how she would normally act, Lily said, "We talked about looking for a place on Bowen. If we're going to scout out locations and places for sale, why's that such a big secret?"

"Relax and all will be revealed."

Relax. Hah.

The ferry was starting to load. Dax drove on and parked. "It's a twenty-minute trip. Want to stay in the car or go on deck?"

Despite the sunshine, it would be windy and cold on deck. "I'll stay and listen to Vinyl Café. You go on; I'm sure you'd like to get outside." And she could use the time apart. It was stressful, sitting next to her husband and worrying about the meaning of that real-estate offer.

"Sounds good." He swung out of the car, leaving the radio on for her.

Stuart McLean's style of presentation wasn't exactly dynamic, yet it was compelling. The appeal of the Dave and Morley stories was how relatable they were. The couple was a normal husband and wife with two children, going through a normal life with ups and downs, humor and sorrow. A shared life. The kind of life Lily and Dax had never had. And, quite possibly, never would. She blinked back tears.

It wasn't long until Dax was back and the ferry docked. When he drove off, he pulled over to the side of the road, letting the other ferry traffic pass by. Reaching into his jacket pocket, he pulled out the silk scarf she'd bought in Whistler. "Take off your sunglasses and blindfold yourself."

She didn't take the scarf. "You're not serious?"

"Call me Falcon and obey." His tone was mostly joking but held an undertone of seriousness.

No, this wasn't the time for sex games, and she wasn't in the mood for an unpleasant "surprise." Yet if she hadn't found the damn contract, she'd likely think this was fun. "Fine." She took the scarf and wound it around her head.

"You can't see anything?"

"I can't."

He pulled onto the road again.

It was disconcerting being blind in a moving vehicle, and she gripped the armrest on the door to steady herself. Even though Bowen was so close to Vancouver, this was the first time she'd been here and she had no way of getting her bearings. There wasn't much traffic, only the occasional sound of an oncoming car passing. The road got bumpier, and she sensed they were going uphill. Dax pulled the car to a stop and turned off the ignition, abruptly silencing Stuart McLean. Lily realized that, since the program was still on, it must be less than an hour since they'd left home.

He touched her arm. "Stay here and keep the blindfold on. I'll be back for you in five minutes."

"Fine." No, it wasn't fine at all. She could have asked him to put the key back in the ignition so she could hear the end of the story. But at this point, she didn't give a damn how Dave and Morley's story ended. Hers and Dax's was the only one she cared about.

"Promise me you'll keep the blindfold on."

She swallowed. "I promise."

"Thank you, sweetheart." There was tenderness in his voice along with the excitement. She blinked against the blindfold, forcing back tears.

Dax released her arm and got out. He opened the trunk then closed it again. Gravel crunched. Then all was silent and she was alone.

She could peek. She could remove the blindfold and opt out of his game. But she would keep her promise and try to cling to the remnants of trust and hope. It was possible she'd misinterpreted the situation, and Dax truly cared about her and her dream for the future.

Gravel crunched again, a warning before the passenger door opened. Dax's hand gripped her arm. "Climb out carefully. I've got you."

She stepped down and found her footing.

He put his arm around her and urged her forward, steering her along a gravel path that inclined slightly upward. "Steps," he said. "Going up. Four of them."

Side by side, they mounted the steps. He turned her to face the way they'd come. "Close your eyes." His fingers worked at the knot she'd tied in the blindfold, then the fabric fell away from her head. His arm came back around her shoulders. "Open your eyes, Lily."

She obeyed, blinking against the sudden glare of sunshine and then focusing on a stunning view. Roughly grassed land dropped gently away in front of them, down to a wooded area. If there were houses below, the woods hid them, and she looked straight out at the ocean, choppy today, with sun sparkling off white caps. "Wow."

"And look over there. See the stream?"

Her gaze followed his pointing finger to the right, where bare-branched trees meandered in a straggly line, and through them sunlight glinted off water.

"Imagine it in the spring," he said. "Dogwoods in bloom, the stream burbling, the fields scattered with wildflowers. Sailboats out on the ocean." He hugged her closer. "Total privacy, not a neighbor in sight."

It was a view to fall in love with, for sure. But she knew that she stood on the porch of a house built for a childless couple. Still, she gave him the truth. "It's a wonderful view. I imagine it's lovely in all seasons."

"Now come inside. You'll have to use your imagination."

Imagine a life without children? Could she do that? If he intended to steamroll her and issue an ultimatum—him or having children—then no, she couldn't. If he opened his heart to her, though, and told her why he couldn't envision having kids and begged her to let their love be enough to fill her heart . . . What on earth would she do?

She squared her shoulders. First, she needed to know the truth. Maybe then, her heart would give her the answer.

She turned and saw the wooden-shaked front of the cottage from the real-estate listing. When Dax shoved the door open, it groaned. *My sentiment exactly.* Biting her lip, she stepped through.

The door opened into a small living room. Hideous dark fake wood paneling lined the walls, grotty orange shag carpet covered the floor, and the room was empty of furniture. A small fire crackled in an attractive old-brick fireplace. In front of the fire Dax had spread the rug they kept in the trunk of the car, and beside it sat a cooler and a shopping bag with a loaf of French bread sticking out. So that was where he'd been this morning: buying picnic food to bring here.

The scene in front of her was a combination of hideous and charming.

Her mouth dry, Lily forced herself to say, "Another picnic in front of a fire? You brought me a long way for this." She faced Dax and gazed up at him. Now he had to tell her what was going on.

His gray eyes glowed silver with excitement. "I spent my spare time this week checking out properties."

"You didn't tell me." Yes, it sounded accusing, and that was how she felt.

"You were busy, interviewing the new office manager, working with your receptionist to figure out what kind of reports she could produce. Then you had your volunteer work yesterday. I didn't want to waste your time."

"Dax, we're supposed to be sharing things. Discussing things." Especially the one most critical decision: whether he wanted to have children.

His face fell. "I'm sorry. I just thought I'd narrow things down."

Narrow things down to a single property that he was ready to make an offer on. Right. Pretending innocence, she said, "So today we're touring the places on your short list?"

"Only this one. I saw it yesterday and it seemed perfect."

"Perfect," she echoed flatly. A one-bedroom cottage was perfect?

"It's an hour's commute to your clinic by ferry and car, with a ferry every hour. There's also a seasonal water taxi for commuters. The property's two acres, beautiful land. When I saw the land, the view, I was sold."

"Your own personal piece of wilderness." She could understand what that meant to him. Even believe that it might be great to live here. To raise children here. She could imagine a little girl and boy running through the wildflowers, floating sticks in the stream, going to the beach with their friends. Except Dax's vision didn't include those children.

"Our piece." He touched her cheek.

She closed her eyes for a moment, savoring the slight roughness of his calloused fingers against her skin, then broke away. "Show me the rest of it." Realizing she was warm, she took off her coat and hung it on a doorknob. "That fire throws a lot of heat."

He took off his jacket too, and tossed it on the floor. "The heat's been on for a while. I had the Realtor come in this morning to turn it and the water on, and to lay a fire so it'd be ready to light when we arrived."

Dax had thought of everything. Except the one thing that really mattered to Lily.

He moved across the room to a doorway. "Kitchen's here. Nothing special but it has the basics. Nice view from the windows."

She joined him and they stepped into a room that was empty of appliances and furniture. It had dingy green walls and tired beige-patterned linoleum. Two or three times the size of the condo's kitchen, there'd be space for a table and chairs by one window, possibly an island as well. The other window was above the sink. Both let in winter sunlight, making the room bright and almost cheerful. "With some polishing, it could be a pleasant room," she admitted.

"It's better than the bathroom," he said, taking her hand and tugging her along.

A short hall led from the living room, with what appeared to be a closet on one side and the bathroom on the other. She grimaced at the stained sink and toilet and the worn floor tile, shower tile, and wallpaper, all in different patterns. There was no bathtub.

"Not a room you'd want to linger in," she said. No lovely soaks in the tub with a good book.

"The bedroom's better."

It couldn't be worse.

They walked a few more steps down the hall and entered a room about twelve feet by fourteen, with a long closet at one end. Room for a queen-sized bed, bedside tables, and a dresser—which was all you really needed. A bedroom was for sleeping, reading in bed, and sex.

Again, there were windows, providing lovely views and, today, sunshine. She could imagine her and Dax using this bedroom, making it attractive. Perhaps installing a glass sliding door to replace one of the windows. But there was only one bedroom. No room for children. "Dax." She turned to him. Enough of wandering through this cottage, a little house that might, with some hard work and money, be comfortable for a childless couple. Time to resolve this, once and for all.

And, she realized, time to be honest. She was upset with Dax for not sharing the decisions he'd reached, much less his thought process. Instead of asking him, she'd pretended that she hadn't seen the offer, and nursed secret resentment. No wonder their relationship was so messed up. They had no idea how to be truly open and honest with each other.

A sense of calm seeped through her. "I can't go on like this. With neither of us being honest."

He frowned. "I didn't mean to be dishonest. It was supposed to be a nice surprise."

"Right." Which only showed how out of sync they truly were.

His frown deepened. "What do you mean about you not being honest?"

Standing about two feet away, she studied him. So dashing and handsome in a lightweight black sweater, jeans, and boots, with his over-long black hair and sexy beard. Her husband. The husband she'd never really known and possibly never would. "I saw the offer."

"Offer? What offer?"

"The one to buy this place."

"Oh, shit." He whacked his hand against his head. "So much for my surprise. Look, Lily, it's not like I meant to go ahead and buy it before you saw it and agreed. Both our names are on that offer, right? It's just, the place only came on the market this week. It's an amazing buy. It's an estate sale and the heirs need the money, so they're in a hurry to sell. The Realtor said the property market was slow over the holidays, but it picks up quickly in January. If we want it, we need to move quickly." Though he sounded a little apologetic, mostly his tone was still excited.

"And you want it? This"—she gestured, meaning not just the sunny bedroom but the whole run-down place, the cottage that had no room for children—"this is what you want?"

"We've done a lot of talking about different ways we might live, ways that would work for both of us. This is close enough to Vancouver that we could commute, work three or four long days then have the rest of the time off. If we sell the condo, we'd easily be able to handle the mortgage. The Realtor says it's a good investment too.

Not that I'm really thinking of it that way. I'm thinking it'd be our home."

"Our home," she said flatly.

He ran a hand through his hair, sighed. "Okay, I see you're not enthused. I hoped you'd see the potential."

"Potential? You mean, like fixing up the kitchen and ripping up that horrible orange shag?"

"Well, yeah, for a start, but . . ." He shook his head. "Wait a minute. I haven't told you what I'm thinking, have I?"

She planted her hands on her hips. "Dax, I haven't a clue what you're thinking."

"Okay. Well, even though it's kind of grotty, I figured it'd at least be livable. The kitchen and bedroom wouldn't take much work. The bathroom's a whole other story, but we could live with it for a while. We'd work out a new floor plan, expand the living room, put in a proper big bathroom with a tub."

"Oh." In her experience, you bought a place you liked then furnished it. "You see it as a fixer-upper?"

"The alternative is to tear it down and start fresh, but I think the cottage suits the land."

"Tear it down? Do major renovations? Dax, that would be incredibly expensive."

"Not so much. You remember what I was doing when we met, right?"

Light dawned. "Construction." It was so long ago and he'd changed so much, she'd almost forgotten.

"I can do most of the work myself and it'll save a lot of money, though it'll take some time. But in a couple of years, we could have a really nice house. We can come up with a design that lets us add whatever we need. Home office, more bedrooms, another bath, and—"

"More bedrooms?" she broke in. Her heart skipped a beat. Why would they need more bedrooms? Did he mean a guest room or . . .

"For"—he swallowed—"for kids, Lily. A couple, maybe three. I think this would be a great place to raise kids."

"You, you . . ." Her body trembled with nerves. Oh God, if she misunderstood again, let herself hope again, the disappointment would destroy her. "You've changed your mind about having children?"

He frowned in apparent puzzlement. "Lily, sweetheart, I'd never have had an offer drawn up if I wasn't thinking this place could be home for you and me and our children." He stepped forward and framed her face with his big hands.

"R-really?" Her heart was in her throat, making it hard to speak. Could she believe in this? "You do want to have children?"

"Yeah, I do."

If she was to believe that he'd gone from a flat-out no at New Year's to truly wanting children, she needed more. "Tell me why you changed your mind."

He swallowed. "I realized that, when you and I fell in love and got married, I . . ." Another swallow. "I held something back. The way things were with my parents, it made me wary of trusting that I really mattered to someone. That I deserved love. And you were so focused on your career . . ."

"I took you for granted and made you feel like you didn't matter to me? Oh Dax, of course my work's important to me, but I love you so much. I'm sorry I didn't show you just how much."

"Your parents weren't exactly a good example. They're more like partners than spouses. The opposite of my folks, who were so dependent on each other that it was unhealthy. Anyhow, I guess I never totally trusted in us. I figured those dreams we spun when we were teenagers were foolish, and the best we'd share would be some good times together. I convinced myself it was enough, that I didn't want more. I told myself I'd be a crappy dad, that I didn't want kids. Like I said before, I assumed you'd chosen your career over having kids."

"And now?" She knew her eyes must reveal all the hope in her heart.

"Now I'm tired of holding back. How can I achieve a dream if I don't totally commit to it, and throw myself into achieving it?"

"You can't." She blinked back tears of hope. "I can't. Are you saying you're really ready to commit to us, and to making a family together?"

"That's what this is about." He gestured to the sun-filled bedroom. "This place may not be the right one, but I wanted to act. To take steps forward to show you I'm committed."

Dax, the man of action. It made total sense. Tears spilled down her cheeks. "When I saw the property listing," she confessed softly, "I saw there was only one bedroom. I thought you'd decided you didn't want children and hadn't even told me."

"Shit, Lily." He stared into her eyes. "And yet you came with me?"

"I wanted to trust you. But I should have said something right away, not brooded."

"At least you trusted me enough to give me a chance. And I guess I should have told you as soon as I realized I did want to have kids with you. I promised to do that, but I didn't."

"We both still have some work to do." Reality was sinking in. "You really mean it?" Her voice rose with excitement. "You want children with me? You're not just saying it to make me happy?"

He clasped her hands. "To make me happy too." He tugged her closer and bent to touch his lips to hers in a tender, loving kiss.

She would have sunk deep into that kiss and stayed there forever, but he pulled away. "I need to check the fire. And I brought a picnic lunch. Let's go back to the front room." He sounded nervous, perhaps awaiting her verdict on this property.

When he headed for the other room, she followed. He added wood to the fire, taking chunks from a battered wooden box. They could sit in front of the fire on winter evenings. Picnic in front of the fire. Make love in front of the fire.

She gazed around the shabby room, imagining it with the paneling stripped off, hardwood floors, area rugs. Furniture. Not the formal furniture from the condo, but something more rustic and homey. "Dax, I think this place might work out."

He turned and gazed up at her. "Really? You like it? Do you think this could be part of our amazing solution?"

"I can see the potential. You're sure you want to do so much work?"

A smile split his face as he came to his feet. "Finest work in the world, building a home for our family. I'd much rather do that than move into a place that's all finished and perfect. This way, we can plan it out together, make it exactly the way we want it."

She'd never imagined doing anything like that. "Oh my, that sounds amazing." She let out a bubbly laugh. "Dax, I think we've found our amazing solution!"

"I think we have." He caught her by the waist, lifted her off her feet, and, as she gripped his shoulders in surprise, he swung her in a circle.

When he set her down, laughing, a wicked gleam lit his eyes. "When we furnish that bedroom, we'll need a four-poster bed."

"We will?"

"So we can take turns tying each other to it."

She chuckled. "Be still my heart."

He bent to remove his boots then sat down on the spread rug. "Come on down here."

She slipped out of her own boots and sat beside him. "I'm getting addicted to picnics."

He opened the cooler and took out two chilled flute glasses, then a bottle of Dom Pérignon.

"Oh my, Dax. To toast the cabin?" Had he been so sure she'd love it?

He shook his head, deftly opened the wine, and poured two glasses. "To toast us, and the future." He handed her a glass.

She raised it high. "I'll drink to that."

"Before you do"—he swallowed, again looking nervous—"there's something I want to ask you."

"I'm not sure I can survive any more surprises today."

"I hope this is a good one. Will you marry me, Lily?"

She gaped at him. A tentative smile tugged at her lips. "Didn't we already do that?"

"We did, as kids. Now we're grown up, we're stronger and smarter, and this feels to me like a fresh start. I want to say those vows to you again, Lily, with one hundred percent commitment. To love, honor, and cherish, from this day forward until death us do part. You, me, and the children we'll bring into this world."

Those crazy tears of joy were falling again as a deep sense of contentment and belonging filled her. "Oh yes, Dax. I'll say those vows happily, my love." How about that? First George, then Kim, and now her, engaged to marry wonderful men.

They clicked their glasses together, drank deeply. Then he took her glass and put both of them down. "We'll do it our way this time," he said. "Not a formal wedding to please your parents, but whatever the two of us want. Maybe here, when the spring flowers are up."

She nodded. "Yes." Then her imp made her add, "Whatever you say, Falcon."

"You're an impertinent woman, you know that?" he teased.

"Perhaps I deserve to be punished?"

"You certainly do."

"What do you have in mind, oh lord and master?" Sexy anticipation tingled through her body.

"Let's see. I think I'll start by having you strip, then you'll lie absolutely still while I drip champagne all over your body and lick it off. Very, very slowly. And if you disobey and move, I'll start all over again."

She quivered at the thought. "I just might be very, very bad." And then a thought struck her, and she started to laugh.

"What's so funny?"

Trying to speak between chuckles, she said, "Do you realize, we may well owe our marriage to *Bound by Desire?*"

His eyes widened, and then he started to laugh too. "If I hadn't read it and tried something different in bed . . ."

"I might not have loosened up. You and I might not have connected, talked."

"It broke down some barriers, in more ways than one."

She smirked. "Book club's supposed to be educational."

"Keep reading. I can't wait for the next book. But for now . . ." He held up her scarf.

"You're blindfolding me?"

He shook his head. "It's my turn. Blindfold me. But wait a minute." He stood and shucked off his clothes, then returned to sit beside her. "Now."

"You're going to do the champagne thing blindfolded?"

"That's the idea."

"I'm not complaining, but why?"

"So we're both giving up a little control."

Just like in a true marriage, where two equal partners shared, compromised, and trusted. Oh yes, she and Dax were learning to do all those things. "Bend your head." She wrapped the scarf around and around, firmly but not too tight. The feminine design made his tousled black hair, hawklike nose, and beard look even more masculine. "Can you see anything?"

"Nope."

"Is it comfortable?"

"The scarf is. Being unable to see is weird."

"Believe me, I know. But I'll look after you."

"And I'll look after you. Now, Lily, take off your clothes and lie down."

She complied quickly, glad of the fire's warmth. "Ready."

He reached out, patting the rug. "Point—uh, I mean direct—me toward the champagne bottle."

"You're not really going to waste expensive champagne on—"

"Waste?" A wicked grin flashed. "Believe me, licking champagne off your body will be far better than drinking it from a glass."

Smiling, she said, "If you insist. The bottle's a little more to your right."

Cautiously he stretched out his fingers, located the bottle, and grasped it firmly. Then he slid across the rug and reached out with his other hand to brush her bare thigh. "There you are." His fingers explored down her leg, then up. "All naked. And I don't need to see to know you're lovely. Warm enough, sweetheart?"

"Plenty warm." And getting warmer as his hand reached the top of her thigh.

He cupped her briefly between her legs, but before she could press against him and ask for more, he moved upward. He caressed her tummy, rib cage, breasts, chest, then framed the side of her face. With his other hand, he lifted the bottle and took a drink, then he put the bottle down carefully on the floor by her head.

Bending over her, he brought his lips to hers and kissed her slowly and deeply, parting her lips with his tongue and delving inside. Kissing him back, she tasted champagne and Dax, a heady combination that made her pulse race.

He eased away. "Now lie still, Lily. I can't see you, so I have to trust you."

"I won't move." She held still, watching as he retrieved the bottle.

Again he bent over her, running his free hand questingly across her shoulder, her chest, her right breast. As if he'd marked the spot, he tipped the bottle as he removed his hand. Chilly liquid dribbled over her breast and she gave an involuntary shiver of reaction and anticipation.

He put the bottle aside, lowered himself, and found her damp flesh with his tongue. He licked in long, firm swipes that made her nipple pucker and resonated all through her body. Then he carried on, surprisingly coordinated as he adjusted to being blind, dripping champagne across her belly and into her navel, following it with licks, sucks, the occasional nip.

Sensation built, her skin tingling with it, arousal growing inside her. Her voluntary immobility enhanced her awareness of every touch. Watching Dax and knowing he couldn't see her doing it, noting how his cock had swollen to rise up his belly, made her even more turned on. When, finally, he put an arm under her butt to lift her and sent a trickle of champagne between her legs, she tensed, desperate for the touch of his tongue.

And then he was there, where she most needed him, tasting her until she stifled a moan. But wait, he'd only told her to stay still, not to keep quiet. So she let the moan escape, followed by, "Oh God, that feels so good."

"Tastes damned good too. So good I want seconds."

More chilly liquid trickled across her heated flesh. His tongue followed it, relentlessly teasing her until she let out breathy whimpers. "Please, Dax, I need to come. And then I need you inside me."

"Sweetheart, your wish is my command." He slid two fingers inside her, pumped them gently, sucked her swollen clit into his mouth.

Sweet release flooded through her. "Yes, oh yes!"

He kept her at the peak, pumping slowly, pressing lightly on her clit, until finally she groaned. "Enough. I can't take any more."

He lowered her butt down on the rug and slid up her body to blanket her.

"I want to move now," she said. "Can I please move? And I want to take off your blindfold so we can see each other when you come into me."

"You can move, Lily. Move as much as you want. And yes, I want to see your beautiful face when we make love."

She reached behind his head and fumbled with the knot she'd tied earlier. The silk fell away.

He blinked a couple of times, then focused on her face and smiled. "I like playing sex games by the fire."

"Me too." A thought struck her. "We won't be able to do this when we have kids."

"Sure we can. I'll build us a new bedroom with our very own fireplace."

She grinned up at him. "I should have known you'd come up with an amazing solution."

"You motivate me. I love you, Lily."

"I love you too, Dax, my past, present, and future husband."

ABOUT THE AUTHOR

Savanna Fox is the new pen name for Susan Lyons, who also writes as Susan Fox. *Publishers Weekly* refers to her writing as "emotionally compelling, sexy contemporary romance."

Writing as Susan Lyons and Susan Fox, her books have won the Gayle Wilson Award of Excellence, the Book Buyers Best, the Booksellers Best, the Aspen Gold, the Golden Quill, the Write Touch, the More Than Magic, the Lories, the Beacon, and the Laurel Wreath, and she has been nominated for the RT Reviewers' Choice Award. Her book *Sex Drive* was a Cosmopolitan Red-Hot Read.

Savanna/Susan is a Pacific Northwesterner with homes in Vancouver and Victoria, British Columbia. She has degrees in law and psychology, and has had a variety of careers, including perennial student, computer consultant, and legal editor. Fiction writer is by far her favorite, giving her an outlet to demonstrate her belief in the power of love, friendship, and a sense of humor.

Visit her website at savannafox.com for excerpts, discussion guides, behind-the-scenes notes, recipes, giveaways, and more. She loves to hear from readers and can be contacted through her website.